ARUBA MAD GÜNTHER

T.L. YEAGER

Blue Zenith Press

ALSO BY T.L. YEAGER

THE PARAGON TRILOGY

Science-Based Thrillers
set in a
Post-Apocalyptic Pandemic
Caribbean

TLYeager.com

For my TEAM.
A story in every adventure.
I love you girls.

Published by Blue Zenith Press

PART I

INVADE

1

MARACAIBO, Venezuela

FAZUL LEAPT FROM THE VAN, his shoes landing on a bed of damp stone. He paused outside the door, blocking the rest of the team from exiting. With a deep breath, he focused his attention on the bolus of anxiety that had spun up beneath his sternum. He rode the air out of his chest with patience, praying for the tightness to follow. Then he turned to the rest of the six-man boarding party, each perched on the edge of their seat.

"Our time has arrived. Remember our motto... Actions louder than words."

Fazul's words were punctuated by a bellow of thunder that crackled in the distance. Above them, the tail end of a coastal storm was marked by wide contrails. Towering cumulus clouds in the distance danced with light from within and the smell of wet clay drifted between the dented buildings. It reminded Fazul of a pottery-making plant he had once visited.

He brushed the silk lapel of his custom suit—his fingers noting the slim line from the strap of the shoulder holster cradling the suppressed Makarov pistol beneath his left arm. "Let us go." He offered the path forward like a restaurant maître d'.

Seconds later, the team was around the corner and heading for the entrance. The van departed, splashing through puddles behind them. Even from a distance, Fazul could see sleep creeping over the rumpled hump of a guard manning the security post. A structure barely bigger than an outhouse, it was nothing more than thin sheet metal tacked together. It struggled to provide security from the wind.

Surveillance of the marina had been established for nearly three weeks. It was enough time to learn that the darkening sky and drone of the roof-mounted air conditioner always got to the guard.

He was startled awake as the team closed in. Fazul watched him struggle to focus, leaning forward to improve the sight picture. Most of his shifts passed quietly, and visitors were rare. Six men in suits took even longer to comprehend.

As the group drew within speaking range, the guard rose from his chair and slid the window open in preparation to greet them. Fazul studied his every move. The stacked silhouette of his fat folds were clearly defined by the fluorescent light above him. Any movement toward the phone and Fazul would have to act. The guard had no authority to make decisions. He always placed a call before admitting anyone. Venezuela had developed a reputation for armed piracy in recent years.

Fazul had fabricated a story to stall an attempt to place the call. As they approached, it was clear the guard was relaxed and the diversion would not be needed. His adrenaline surged. Fazul felt excitement bubbling at the prospect of ending the guard's slovenly life.

"Good evening," said Fazul, reaching inside his jacket. Of Middle Eastern descent, Fazul had learned enough Spanish to get him through this conversation.

He pulled the trigger and sent the lethal shot spiraling toward the guard's forehead before the man's jaw had time to fully drop open. A dark circle carved by the sub-sonic bullet was visible for an instant above his left eye. The impact sent him backwards, rumbling the sheet metal to life. Then he folded with a grunt and fell to the ground headfirst next to his chair.

"Gate. Ten seconds." Fazul pointed to the chain securing the wide gate that served as the only entrance to the boatyard.

The young Assad stepped up, producing the bolt cutters from his backpack. Two others held the chain taut and looked away as he bore down on a link with the pincers.

"Get the body out of sight." One of Fazul's men had to climb through the open window to unlock the door from inside. Another soldier joined him, and the two struggled to drag the enormous corpse from the shack.

Fazul activated his mic and spoke softly. "Guard down. We're inside and moving into position."

2

ASHTON, Maryland

MADELINE GÜNTHER FAT-FINGERED the landline twice before selecting the proper number for her husband. He answered even before the first ring ended.

"Ross... Tell me we didn't forget a passport for Charlotte." It came out more condescending than she intended.

Maddie walked to the window and stared across the front yard of her suburban Washington, D.C. home. The leafless skeletons of the Bradford pears lining their idyllic street swayed in a frozen February gale. There was a long pause on the phone as Ross Günther considered the question. Neither of them realized that it would live on in infamy.

"Shit, Maddie."

A pause.

"We created a freakin' spreadsheet for the baby formula, but we forgot the passport?" Maddie could hear him slap something. They had indeed calculated the amount of formula powder they'd need for a week away, and then added twenty percent.

"Don't make a scene. We'll figure it out," she said.

Madeline had set an alarm on her phone for Saturday morning to remind herself to check in for the flight from Baltimore-Washington International to Aruba. The flight departed in less than twenty-four hours.

Part of the check-in process included entering passport information for her husband and two kids. She entered the information for herself, Ross and their eldest daughter, Isabelle. Then she got to the lap child at the bottom of the list. Her stomach had twisted.

"I was going to wait for you to get home, but I felt like I needed to get on it," Madeline continued. Ross was on a train headed south from Manhattan. He'd been out of town on a business trip since Tuesday.

"Maddie, I'm so sorry. We're moving so fast lately."

"No apologies. We did this one together. Here's the deal, Ross. You take Isabelle and head down on schedule tomorrow."

"What? You're nuts. I'm not doing that. We go together, or we stay together." He couldn't help but manage the situation.

"Ross, you've been working nonstop for months. If you stay home, you'll be on the damn computer. It'll be good for you and Izzy to have some time together... she wants her dad back." Ross had started his own business just a year prior. He left an executive job at a hospital, along with its stable hours and salary, to strike out on his own.

"Ross, I need a break from princesses and glitter. Plus, Izzy needs some daddy time. She's been missing you, she's been sad when you leave on these trips. More than I've been letting on. Plus, it'll be relaxing – Daddy and his big girl together again."

"I don't agree."

"You don't have to agree. Will you go anyway? Give it a try and let me handle this mess. I've been digging around the last couple hours, and it looks like I can go to D.C. and get Charlotte a passport on Monday."

She could still see the first line on the agency website, *the best strategy for expedited service is not to need it at all.* That snarky statement just pissed her off.

The website included sections on acquiring a passport in life-or-death emergencies and expedited service by mail. Then, at the bottom, there was a section titled *Expedited Service at a Passport Agency*. The twenty-eight agencies around the country provided in-person service. The one at the top of the list was only thirty miles away, in the heart of D.C.

The second bullet point said you needed an appointment and proof of immediate travel. Maddie dialed the number and an automated message said the next available appointment was two days after they were scheduled to return.

Chin in hand, she'd looked back at her computer screen and spotted a hyperlink that said, *More*. She'd clicked it. There, hidden below the virtual fold, was the line of hope. *Will Call service is offered for life/death emergencies and immediate travel.* The passport agency had deliberately hidden the fine print.

Maddie searched, *passport will call*. She found a stream of posts that said she could go in person and request same day service in situations like theirs, where they had travel in less than two weeks.

That's some bullshit, she thought to herself. The agency hid the fact because they wanted people to rely on the longer process that required no face-to-face interaction. *Gotta love the government.* For Maddie, it meant she'd only be marooned in cold rain for two days.

"You're a crazy woman. You know that?"

"If they give me any flak, I'll call Chuckles over at the Pentagon and see if he can make a call and help a girl out." Chuckles was a lifer. He loved being a Marine and stayed on when Maddie decided not to re-up. "You and Izzy just have to remember to pick us up from the airport Tuesday morning."

"I can't imagine how you're going to take our baby to the heart of D.C. where, by the way, you always get lost despite GPS... And then the next day you want to fly five hours alone on a plane with her. You needed a mission, didn't ya?"

He was right, although she'd never admit it. For all of her experience navigating over land, she never failed to make a wrong turn or three in Washington, D.C.

"Maybe, but mostly I want you to have a chance to relax. We'll be alright. It's no big deal. Just have a cold one ready in the car when we get there." She imagined the Balashi in her mind, the famous Divi Divi tree on the label sweating in the heat. "Ain't the beer cold." It was a saying she remembered a baseball announcer using when she was a kid. Her dad loved to listen to the games.

"You won't need an airplane; you can fly in using your super-Mom cape."

Maddie laughed. "Why you have to go and make me sound like a dork?"

"Thanks, Maddie. I couldn't do this without you."

"Yeah... you could do it without me. No doubt about that. But either way, you're welcome. You've had my back for years, Ross. It's only fair I get yours now and then."

* * *

WINTER RAIN HAD BEEN FALLING for days. On Sunday morning, miniature balls of slush thwacked off the windshield as Maddie drove Ross and Izzy to the airport.

"What if it doesn't work out in D.C.?" Ross asked.

"Then Charlotte and I— we'll see if we can find one of those inflatable palm trees and get a load of sand delivered into the family room. Put on our bikinis, build some sandcastles, drink a pile of Coronas. Maybe throw a beach scene on the TV." Maddie turned and smiled.

Maddie found an opening along the departure curb. She cinched the straps tight on Izzy's backpack while Ross pulled bags from the back.

"You're my hero. Always will be," Ross said, hugging her. He laid a kiss on her cheek as he broke away.

"Mommy, will you go down the waterslide with me when you come?" Izzy's expression reminded Maddie of a sad puppy dog.

"You know I will. A *hundred* slides. Deal?" Maddie squatted down in front of her daughter, a hand on each shoulder.

"Deal, Mommy. But we have to save some time for the wazy river, too," the five-year-old pointed, bouncing her finger with youthful conviction.

"A hundred trips around the wazy river, baby. Promise." She pulled Izzy tight to her chest, the hint of tears welling in the corner of her eyes. With a kiss on the forehead and a pat on the backpack, they turned for the airport entrance, Izzy tripping over her own feet as she looked back, waving.

"You two be good! Ya hear? Don't have too much fun without us!"

As she climbed back into the car she looked in the mirror. "Just you and me, sweets." Maddie could see Charlotte through two mirrors. The rearview caught the reflection from the one hanging on the headrest in front of her. She was chewing on a set of plastic keys.

People called her Ross's clone. They pointed, peering back and forth. *Look at the cheeks, the nose, the lips... Their forehead is the same. Her smile is just like his.* Ross had trouble seeing how Charlotte's beauty bore any resemblance to his aging countenance. Her skin was the porcelain epitome of a baby. Maddie had taken a picture in a dress where she honest-to-god could have passed for one of those American Girl dolls that Izzy used to have.

Yeah, but it's the eyes more than anything. Those deep blue eyes, they would say.

Maddie saw it, especially in the eyes. Not just the color, but the shape and depth. It was amazing how you could see a person in their child. Ross was 6'3", two-hundred and twenty odd pounds with a red beard and shaved head. If he wore a flannel and a hat to cover the baldness, people thought he was Paul Bunyan's doppelgänger. And still, he was there in Charlotte's face. Every time.

Maddie put the car in drive and pulled away from the curb. She shook her head and smiled. They'd gotten two girls, and each one resembled just one of their parents. Isabelle was her mini-me, an exact replica of her mother. Straight black hair with flecks of red and features that were stamped from identical molds. They both caught a tan walking past a window. Charlotte and Ross, on the other hand, would get burnt just thinking about the beach without sunscreen.

On the way home, Maddie hit the Starbucks drive-thru for the caffeine she needed to prepare for her own, less exotic trip —a visit to the Washington Passport Agency on a Monday morning, with a baby.

Once they were home and Charlotte was down for the morning, Maddie assembled all the requisite forms on the table. Outside her dining room window the rain popped on the taut pool cover in the backyard. The news was forecasting the rain to freeze overnight. In the past, this meteorological tidbit would have been the proverbial straw on the camel's back—the extra push that sent the whole situation to red on the *FUBAR* meter. But these days, she knew better than to take things for granted. It was time with her girl. Time and a bullet she was inches away from never having.

Charlotte did her part, cooperating with a rare long

morning nap. By noon, Maddie had the DS-11 passport document assembled in triplicate. One blank copy, one partial and another complete form. Having three sets was insurance against being turned away from a bureaucratic window because you filled in one too many boxes. She'd worked for the government for fifteen years. She knew how the system worked.

After Charlotte's nap, Maddie drove them to the pharmacy for the last piece of the red tape puzzle.

"Take it again, please," Maddie said. "Just one more. I promise." She couldn't leave a single stone unturned; there'd only be one chance to get it right.

The pharmacy clerk pretended to not be bothered, but Maddie could tell she wanted to gouge her with the scissors. She didn't understand the importance of contingencies.

"I've heard they're not strict on baby pictures." The goth clerk was standing above her daughter with a point and shoot camera.

Maddie wasn't against piercings per se, but the clerk had at least four running up her ear. In the lobe was one of those round hoops – *gauges*? Maddie thought – that expand the opening over time. A piercing in the nose, and another in the tongue, were paired with full tattoo sleeves on each arm. She didn't strike Maddie as an expert in passport photography.

Two hours and one disgruntled pharmacy clerk later, her mission was complete. She dropped a pen in the plastic folder, stacked her keys neatly on top, and went into the kitchen.

An ice cube clinked into the tumbler. She pulled the cork from a bottle of eighteen-year-old Lagavulin single malt and poured herself four fingers.

"*Salud*," she said, lifting her glass. "Here's to vacation."

3

MARACAIBO, Venezuela

BACK AT THE STAGING WAREHOUSE, Anas Atwah was at his desk studying Google Earth satellite images. He jumped in his chair when the call from the boarding party cracked in his earpiece. A brief round of applause rolled from the far side of his door.

He checked his watch. They weren't expecting the text message for at least another fifteen minutes.

Anas gathered his things. A humid breeze drifted in through the panes of broken glass and swept down across the desk. The air from the Maracaibo harbor stunk of stagnate oil and decaying industry. Anas was looking forward to leaving this forsaken wasteland of a country. He'd been here too long.

So many events had transpired in the last nineteen months. Anas was on the precipice of taking his crimes to an entirely new level. He relished the infamy his recent successes had gained him, but now he looked forward to the limelight. A life in the shadows, filling the coffers with ransom money, was not his ultimate goal. He wanted to show the world his genius, not rest on his laurels as an anonymous technological pariah.

Despite the organization's name, the leadership of the New Jihad Front espoused financial success over religious fervor, and they paid very well. Anas received a commission off every dollar he brought in. That was the main reason he'd gotten involved. The attention they gave him was the Kool-Aid—he'd only taken sips initially, but once he became a cornerstone of their plan to modernize the war strategy, Anas was hooked.

The plan started with the shredding of old playbooks. Anas had arrived at the perfect time. They needed an innovator to take their ideas to the next level. The group envisioned events of escalating psychological terror that provided the platform to sway hearts and minds. Of course, they would also bring handsome returns that bloated the bottom-line.

Traditional terror attacks were aimed at convincing Westerners that they needed to stay out of the Middle East. In reality, these had the opposite effect—more troops from more nations, pouring in to continue the fight against terror. More vicious attacks brought greater solidarity and larger numbers of troops.

Besides, Westerners were immune to images of destroyed buildings and mass shootings. They'd seen countless victims emerge bloodied in a veil of dust. Bodies motionless on the ground no longer struck fear in the masses.

Violence was not achieving the ultimate goal.

The NJF realized the power of showmanship and money. The threat of murder was worth far more than murder itself. They aspired to devastation wrought by bloodless blows that turned to festering wounds. The term *weapons of mass destruction* was antiquated in the pantheons of the New Jihad Front's leadership.

The idea was that creating a highly visible threat of mass

destruction would win them the platform, and eventually, the infinite pile of currency they desired. The events would get into the heads of the enemy, a terror that changed opinions. Terror without mass killing would be the key to victory that had eluded so many other organizations.

Their prototype operation consisted of an event that brought an entire industry to its knees—not by stacking bodies, but by creating the threat of doing so. They'd hold the world hostage for days by giving them a show that unfolded at an excruciatingly slow speed. Still frames and panicked moments captured on cell phone video would be a thing of the past. Their events would yield hours of video to afflict the weak infidel minds.

They'd use the hyperactive media and internet as a spotlight to force unprecedented ransoms that bulged the coffers. The wake of the operations would cripple entire industry segments and send waves of disruption rippling across Western economies. In the wake of the onslaught, they'd offer another ransom: *Leave our countries and this can stop.*

Anas had conceived of the mission while sipping a Mai Tai from a chaise lounge owned by the resort they'd be in control of within twenty-four hours. There in the chair, his mind had mapped the exquisite details of the raid. He could see the men running from the dock in a tactical posture with Kalashnikovs at the ready. He could see the yacht and the Pelican cases filled with the technology required to bring the event to a global cyber audience. It had come to him as a stroke of creative inspiration.

His plan was the first such large-scale operation. Everything done to date had been cloaked from the eyes of the world. When he'd suggested it, the leadership had quickly embraced the idea. Their ties with Venezuela were already firmly established, but the relationship had yet to bear fruit. Anas's idea was novel, took advantage of the South American relationship, and far exceeded the criteria set by the leaders of the NJF.

Thus, NJF soldiers trickled into Venezuela over the course of a year. They came from different directions, spent time in various cities and joined with the group only after a quarantine period marked by maneuvers specially designed to identify if they were being tailed.

The staging warehouse was purchased, bribes were paid, and egress plans laid. A dance of logistical choreography brought explosives, drones, uniforms and weapons from the Russian backed dealer that supplied the organization.

The plan's only drawback was that it required Anas be directly involved. The leadership had been calling him "The Broker." Anas had exceeded all expectations. The ransom awards he accumulated grew exponentially as his skills improved. To date, he had taken over thirty million dollars from Western corporations. Thirty million dollars added to the war chest.

He stole money from the enemy. It was the ultimate irony—using your enemy to fund a war on themselves. But almost every time they paid. Early on, Anas occasionally struck out by locking a low-value server. Those intrusions wreaked havoc on the target organizations, but they would only pay if the server was of value. As his skills improved, he became better at evaluating the target before locking it down. After a while he could find the mothership quickly.

Anas had written a program called Cyberlock that encrypted the data on a server and demanded a ransom. If it wasn't paid, then the system was locked for eternity and the organization was wounded.

"Having you on the front lines is careless, Anas," a senior NJF commander had told him. Anas remembered how the man eyed him, expecting him to give in to the pressure. It was clear why the NJF wanted Anas to stay off the front lines. He had amassed a fortune for the organization.

"The best generals lead from the front. Now is my time." Anas never budged from his request. He knew they could not deny him. No one else had the skill to pull off the technological marvel he proposed. Indeed, many believed even Anas would struggle to deliver on all he had promised.

Once the approvals were obtained, the wheels were set in motion. Nothing could stop them now.

His earpiece cracked to life again. "The boarding party is in position. Awaiting the order to proceed," said Fazul. Anas had personally selected his brother to lead the tactical aspects of the operation.

Anas keyed his mic. "Stage copies. We'll communicate when message received."

He checked his watch. "Ten minutes," he said to the empty room. They were expecting a text message. The rest of his army waited in the warehouse below him. An audio feed was established so they could listen to the transmissions as the events unfolded.

Anas picked up his tablet and turned for the door. He opened the metal door and stepped out on the landing. A crowd of thirty soldiers huddled around a series of tables that had been pushed together. The speaker was in the middle, surrounded by weapons and cleaning supplies. This was their last opportunity to prepare for the battle in front of them.

The reverberation of Anas's steps angled around the vast facility. He leaned on the railing, the team looking up in anticipation.

Anas surveyed the warehouse, noting the contrast between old and new. In years past it had been a seafood sorting facility; now it was a terror staging base. The rusted hulks of machinery and jumbled heaps of equipment had been pushed to the sides with a skid steer. The space had been cleared so they could practice.

Mock rooms had been erected, and a rudimentary shooting range constructed. Pods of their gear stood idle along the far wall, ready to go. A line of getaway vehicles, two wide, would await their return. Men, material, psyche—everything was in order.

He had memorized a speech to deliver. Having developed an obsession for reading about great combat leaders, he had embraced the importance of words. But he was not a writer. Others before him had assembled words that would suit his team just fine.

Anas keyed his mic open so that the boarding team could hear. "Soldiers of the New Jihad Front." He paused to allow time for the moment to resonate.

"You are about to embark upon the Great Crusade, toward which we have striven these many months. The eyes of the world will be upon you. The hopes and prayers of Allah march with you. In company with our brave Allies and brothers-in-arms on other Fronts, you will bring about the destruction of the Atheists, the elimination of Western tyranny over oppressed peoples, and security for ourselves in Paradise. Your task will not be an easy one. Your enemy is well-trained, well-equipped and eager to suppress the work of Allah. He will fight back savagely."

"But the tide has turned, my brothers. We have seen the escalation of our war over the past years. Today we begin a new campaign. Today we begin the march toward absolute victory." He paused for a beat to catch his breath. "Good luck. Let us beseech the blessing of almighty Allah upon this great and noble undertaking."

Anas's heart thundered in his chest as he descended the stairs. He had delivered a flawless, albeit edited version of the message General Eisenhower sent to the expeditionary force on the eve of D-Day. Having amassed 4000 ships, over 1,200 aircraft and 150,000 soldiers, the Allies were ready to make war on German-occupied France. Likewise, Anas's small but high-impact team was prepared to mount an offensive. They would make their own less dramatic landing, with sophisticated weapons, numerous autonomous vehicles and enough computer hardware to spring an upstart internet company.

4

Surfside Resort, Aruba

Upper floor, lower floor. Ocean view, resort view. Those combinations constituted the four levels of timeshare offered. Maddie had argued for the cheapest option, on account that the family would be on the beach or at the pool most of the time. Ross had a theory that the best bargains existed just above the midpoint but below the highest cost option. He applied this logic to every decision. Upper floor, resort view.

"Our 'Ruba house, Papa. It's still here. Yeah…" Izzy pranced through the front door. Floors six through twelve were all considered upper floors, but the condos were mirror images of one another. To Izzy they all felt like their home in Aruba.

It was their seventh visit to the island but a long year had passed since the last. Maddie was very much pregnant with Charlotte the last time they visited. Most of her time was spent walking along the lazy river and resting in the shade while Ross kept Izzy occupied.

They'd only missed one trip since they bought in three

years ago; they'd sold their week in the fall when Charlotte was just three months old and still too young to travel. At least now she'd be able to sit in the sand, no doubt stuffing it in her mouth like most other things she encountered these days.

"Can I sleep in Papa's bed until Mommy and Charlotte get here?"

"Maybe," Ross countered.

"Why maybe?" Izzy's hands were on her hips now.

"Maybe... As long as you promise to snuggle and watch a show before bed." Isabelle's smile widened at the thought.

"Deal, Papa." She ran to him and hugged his leg. She let go and took off squealing through the apartment.

Ross had to lean on the balcony door to break the tight seal. Dry, tropical air swept across his skin. It was like opening the door to a giant pressurized oven. He worked his jaw to equalize his ears and let the warm, dusty smell of the island blow by him.

Cascading water caught his attention as he stepped up to the railing. Thirty feet of manmade rock lined the side of the large main pool to his left. It was tucked up inside the giant U-shape formed by the resort buildings. Children lined up at the top of the rocks. They took turns on the water slide that disappeared inside and then shot them out at the base through the downpour of water.

A narrow canal connected the main pool to the lazy river. Just below him, the "river" itself was mostly obscured by the tops of palm trees. In between the fronds, bodies perched on tubes drifted along the current. Three teenagers waded sideways against it. They dodged left and right, avoiding the oncoming tubes like avatars in the *Frogger* video game.

Ross rested his elbows on the railing and continued his scan out toward the turquoise blue of the Caribbean. Patrons sipped cocktails in the waist-deep water at the pool bar, and a water volleyball game was on in the sport pool. Small specks dotted the kiddie pool. Mothers lounged around the perimeter in wide-brimmed hats.

Further on, closest to the beach, tall hedges shielded the adult pool from view. During the girls' naps, Ross would stay in the apartment and give Maddie a couple hours alone with a book and the quiet of the adult pool.

They'd gotten lucky with Aruba and the Surfside. The first visit happened on a whim. His boss was selling his week and Ross happened to be the first person he told. They knew it'd be nice, but neither of them realized that the Surfside held a top spot on most lists when you searched for the best Caribbean resorts for families.

A loop of a lazy river that ran for a quarter of a mile was just one of five separate pools forming the core of the resort. Palm trees lined the walkways while desert shrubs and flowering plants provided ground cover for the resident iguanas. The island formed by the lazy river was accessible by bridge only, and hot tubs were hidden amidst its dense foliage. Beyond the expansive pool promenade, guests were treated to albino sand and a leeward oceanfront that looked like the blue zenith of kiddie pools. Waves that lapped the shore were usually from parasailing boats or wave-runners. The offshore trade winds pushed everything out and away, leaving a sheet of Caribbean glass for families to play in.

On their first trip, Madeline forced Ross to sit through the timeshare presentation to get the two-hundred-and-fifty dollar voucher. Madeline came out offended by the hard sell, but Ross was smitten.

"Think of all the memories we'll have with Izzy. And I know you want another. The two-bedroom would be perfect." Madeline's eye was twinkling for a second child at the time. For years to come their vacations would be about chicken nuggets, smoothies and maximizing time in the water to tire the kids out before their next nap. The Surfside delivered on all fronts.

"Plus it's a direct flight, Mad. You can't beat it. Come on, girl." Ultimately, she'd given in, even though it wasn't the best financial decision. Now she loved it; Maddie even got more excited than Ross. When they got back from a trip, she started a daily countdown on the dry erase board before they unpacked their bags. It had been a great choice.

Across the open space at the core of the resort, Ross watched a couple toast glasses of wine. The resort had started with just two buildings. As demand skyrocketed, the company invested in a third and fourth around the perimeter of the property. The structures were in place when they bought into the timeshare. A year later, they were complete. When construction was over, the resort had nearly doubled in size and the enormous *U* surrounding the man-made water features became a Caribbean fixture.

"I'm ready," Izzy called from inside.

Ross turned and looked. Something didn't look right. He cocked his head. "I think you're suit is on backwards, sweets."

Izzy pouted. "Will you help me?"

Ten minutes later Izzy's suit was facing forward and the suitcases were empty.

"How 'bout this, Papa? We go to the ocean... Then we go to the waterslide... Then the wazy river... Then we eat pizza. How 'bout dat, Papa?"

Ross loved that his daughter called him Papa. He'd never asked for it or even known he had a preference, but every time Izzy used it, Ross couldn't help but beam. "Sounds like a busy night. Salad first, then pizza. OK?"

"Gotta eat your salad so you grow big and strong." Izzy spoke in her sing-song daddy voice.

"You got it, girl."

5

MARACAIBO, **Venezuela**

THIRTY MILES from the staging warehouse, Fazul and the boarding party were hidden in the shadows of an open-sided marina building. Some prayed. Others waited impatiently. Those with eyes open could see the outline of the yacht *Contagious* framing its lit windows.

The vessel had been in port for two months. She'd been given a fresh coat of paint and had her electronics upgraded with the latest technology.

Their earpieces crackled open. "You're a go... Repeat. Message received. You are cleared to proceed." Fazul was surprised by his brother. The speech had been ridiculous, but for once, Anas sounded like a leader of men.

Fazul led the team forward. They climbed a plank and stepped aboard through an open gate at the rear of the yacht. His knock on the salon door was answered by the captain.

"Good evening, Captain. Dr. Mattos has commissioned my firm to perform an independent audit of this magnificent yacht.

It's to be completed before you depart for your shakeout cruise." Fazul proffered his hand.

The captain squinted with the conviction of a man who didn't appreciate surprises. "I wasn't made aware of this." He looked over Fazul's shoulder at the other men now stepping aboard. "Let me—"

Fazul cut him off. "May we come in, Captain? Let us sit and review the audit plan with you. Such a significant investment has been made and the doctor wants to exercise the utmost caution. I assure you this decision is late breaking and the delay to your schedule will be minimal."

Without waiting for an answer, Fazul stepped into the luxurious salon. The captain's confusion was enough that he retreated instinctively, their neatly pressed suits helping to dull his reservations.

"But I—" The captain hesitated. Fazul sensed that confusion was an emotion to which he was unaccustomed. It no longer mattered.

The yacht's crew took a collective step back as the other five men poured through the open door at the back of the main salon. They spread out into a semi-circle, un-slinging the Russian made Vityaz submachine guns hidden beneath their suit jackets.

The click of a pistol hammer at the front of the room turned the crew's heads. Their confusion grew as one of their own leveled a gun in commune with the intruders.

Fazul smiled at the sight of Ilan moving to action. Strategically planting him in the boat's crew had been Fazul's idea—a brilliant one. Ilan had been hired shortly after the *Contagious* was brought to dry dock for upgrades. The chef had mysteriously disappeared; Fazul killed him with a bullet to the temple, just a day after they made landfall. Ilan was overqualified for the job and the unending list of praise from fictitious references won him the replacement position easily.

"I am sorry, comrades, but we are taking control," said Ilan. "You are a party to terror, my friends."

The captain raised his arms without thinking. Two of the others did the same.

"This is an outrage," said the captain.

Fazul cleared his throat to regain the room. "Please, Captain. Not as much as a single word, or I will be forced to take your life. We have no time for disruption." The captain looked poised to counter but Fazul pointed the Makarov pistol at his forehead. He stepped forward and pressed the end of the steel silencer against the captain's skull.

"Which of the crew will be joining us, Ilan?" Fazul stared into the captain's eyes as he spoke.

"We only need the captain and the engineer." Ilan swung his micro-sized pistol in the direction of a gaunt man standing to Fazul's left.

Fazul looked up, scanning the room. "Very well. For now, take them all below and secure them in the forward quarters." The captain leaned back as if preparing to join his crew. The concentric rings of the pistol's barrel were imprinted on his forehead.

"You stay here," said Fazul, motioning with the pistol. Then he announced to the room, "If everyone cooperates, there will be no harm. Resist, and the response will be a bullet."

The yacht's steward stood up from a sofa in the center of the room where he had been sitting uncomfortably since the team entered. A man of the people, his life had no doubt been all about service. His natural reaction to conflict was to mediate the situation. He couldn't help himself.

"Excuse me."

The room was quiet. Fazul pivoted the Makarov. "Actions louder than words, my brothers." He pulled the trigger and the pistol huffed what sounded like a blow dart from the end of the thick suppressor. The hollow point round broke into nine different pieces of lead on the way through the steward's skull. The fragments spread out, each carving a hole ten times their diameter through his brain tissues before lodging in bone at the rear.

Brain function persisted long enough to initiate a step back, absorbing the energy transferred from the bullet. Then his neural circuitry failed. With his muscles no longer receiving signals from the brain he collapsed to the side, falling on the arm of a loveseat and rolling to the floor face up.

The sous chef screamed. Hassan pivoted the weapon once again.

"Scream again!" he yelled. She covered her mouth, her eyes bulging with fear. "Go now, before more examples are required." Hassan could feel vessels at his temples thumping with blood.

As the remaining crew members were led below, Hassan offered a seat to the captain. "Captain Timmin, you will be taking my crew to the island of Aruba. There is absolutely no room for error on your part. Ilan and the other members of our team are capable of taking control. *You* are expendable. Your execution will be stayed until you make a mistake. No mistake and you remain alive. Those alive at the end of this action will be released. I will now give you the opportunity to ask a single question." With hands on knees, Hassan leaned close, again casting a cold glare into the captain's eyes. "This is your opportunity, Captain."

The silence seemed to grip the captain by the neck. A tight vise of paralyzing fear that strangled any words he was considering.

"No questions?" Hassan grinned. "Smart man."

6

Ashton, Maryland

"Shoulda knocked off after the first scotch." The dull ache in Maddie's frontal lobe had greeted her in unison with the alarm claxon on her phone. Her eyes were slow to focus in the predawn. "Nothing like getting up at zero-dark-thirty on a vacation day."

As much as she enjoyed whiskey, she hated the hangover. All she had to do was drink some water and no hangover, but you get into the whiskey and forget. She lay there remembering how she developed a taste for it by accident. With the exception of Aruba's Balashi, Maddie wasn't big on carbonated beverages—no beer, no soda, no seltzer or tonic. It made her feel too full. She didn't mind the taste of wine, but Jarheads weren't big on vino. What they *were* big on was beer and whiskey – Jack Daniels and Jim Beam, to be exact. She hadn't tried good whiskey until after her last tour. Ross had seen pictures where she had a bottle of Beam in her hand. When she got back, he bought her a bottle of the good stuff.

"Only the best for a hero," he said. Maddie gave him a punch to the gut, then, after he recovered, they shared a glass that hooked them both.

Maddie rubbed her head then pushed herself up to an elbow. She got up and headed for the door. The scent of freshly brewed coffee was just making its way to the top of the stairs. *Why settle for bankers' hours when you can work government hours?* she thought.

Propelled by the promise of caffeine and loathing the prospects for the day, she made her way down the stairs. The passport agency was open from 8 until 3. Seven hours in the core of the day was convenient for no one, of course. And oh, by the way, you probably had to be in line around an hour early to give yourself the best shot of getting a passport same day. That's what the posts online indicated. Imagine having all your shit in order and still getting screwed because you thought it might be okay to arrive when the agency opened for business. *Sorry ma'am, you missed the un-posted cutoff for same-day service because you didn't stand outside in the cold with your baby before we opened. Please come back tomorrow.* She'd be the first mother to go postal with a baby in her arms.

She stirred the cream down into the bottom of her mug and reviewed the handwritten itinerary she'd made for the morning. 5am: Coffee. 5:20: shower done. 5:30-6: Charlotte up and bottle. 6am: departure. She felt like a psychopathic mother. *What the hell is wrong with me?* she thought. She usually shot from the hip, plans came together, they jelled, the day happened. She was never this meticulous since leaving the Corps. She woke at various times every morning, despising routine after years of regimentation. Apparently, bureaucracy brought out her hidden anal-retentive side.

Coffee in hand, she turned for the stairs to head back up. "Soldier on." The words emerged as a moaned. Her legs were still heavy with sleep as she climbed the stairs. "Soldier on, my ass."

Fourteen minutes later a gossamer layer of steam hung in the bathroom as she leaned in toward the mirror. She lifted her chin and dabbed at red mark on her neck. A zit, maybe. In her mind, she imagined an extraordinary snaking line in front of the passport agency. The scowling souls each sneaking a peek at Charlotte in her arms before looking away, feeling like they'd have to offer their place in line or some form of assistance if they engaged too long. People always felt more compelled to help when there was a baby involved.

The most insane line she'd ever experienced was at Disney. They spent a week in San Diego visiting Chuckles before he moved back east for his job at the Pentagon. They drove north to Anaheim one morning for a day at Disneyland. Izzy was into everything *Frozen*. You might have thought Anna and Elsa were permanent family fixtures.

Madeline read that you should get to the gates before they opened and run to the princess meet-and-greet line as quickly as possible. As she read it, Maddie had felt a phantom chest cold brewing. She despised the ridiculous complexity and competitiveness—all to secure a voucher for a meet-and-greet with a couple of teenage girls dressed in princess outfits. The whole concept was more than just a little fucked up, and yet everyone did it.

Once inside the Disney gates, she hurried ahead of Ross and the girls. She had to stop and ask for directions twice but still arrived nine minutes after the park gates opened. The term *line* was not fitting for the nose to tail humans she encountered. They all seemed to smirk as Maddie passed toward the back; relishing every parent they beat to their prized position. Any time she thought about a line since then, all she could see were the smug smirks of those damn parents.

Glints of light caught her eye in the mirror. Over her

shoulder the neighbor's house had three hundred and sixty degrees of accent lighting. They burned lights like they owned the electric company. The power button on the radio filled the room with a voice reading a school closing list. Maddie lifted her chin again and dabbed the cover-up a second time, the glints over her shoulder still winking at her like tinsel on a Christmas tree.

"Talbot County schools are two hours late. Washington County schools are closed. Wicomico County schools are opening two hours late. And that's it for now, but stay tuned this morning. The freezing rain has made a mess across the state and we expect the cancellations and delays will be piling up faster than the ice. We'll keep you up-to-date here on WKLA. Speaking of ice, let's go to Marty Drone to get the latest."

"Thanks, Jerry. Yeah, the overnight wreaked havoc across the state. Temperatures, humidity and the timing of the precipitation were just right for a classic mid-winter, mid-Atlantic freezing rain mess."

Maddie stared through her image in the mirror. She knew there was a chance of freezing rain, but the report she'd read said they weren't expecting it to be too bad.

"Remember that freezing rain is different than sleet," the weatherman continued. "Sleet is frozen precipitation. Freezing rain falls as liquid and freezes on contact. It coats everything in a layer of ice. We've got a tenth of an inch on average across the state. You'll be waking up to Mother Nature's idea of a bad joke." Marty Drone's laugh seemed somehow sinister, like it took effort to not be happy reporting shitty weather. "It's like an ice rink out there, so be careful."

A young female squeal followed as Marty finished. Maddie looked down at the radio.

"It tried to take me out this morning when I was scraping the windshield." Kate, the young intern on the radio show, bubbled with energy. Her cutesy voice could barely wait for Marty Drone to finish his thought.

Tanya, the show host, laughed. "You youngin's almost seem like you enjoy braving the bad weather. Did you scrape the whole windshield or just make one of those little peepholes in the ice?"

Kate laughed again. "The peephole."

"Uh-huh... Figured as much," said Tanya.

"But... After a couple of blocks, I pulled over and did more, including the side windows." Kate giggled again, excited about her admission.

Maddie raised her eyebrows and shook her head. That's the kind of shit she'd be contending with this morning.

"Yup. You have to love those folks that just scrape the little hole," Tanya said, laughing. "Good thing you got out and finished the job. Seriously, though, it's days like this that make me thankful for a garage. Thank goodness for simple pleasures."

Maddie gathered her wet hair and pulled it forward over her shoulder. She picked up the hairbrush, running to through on her way to the window.

The evergreen boughs of the mature cypress trees lining the driveway drooped from the weight of the ice. The asphalt was littered with small branches dropped from the River Birch. It was a weak tree that seemed to shed its unneeded twigs like a husky dropping fur in the spring. Every surface glistened—trashcan tops, the tops of the lights next to the garage, the blacktop itself, all shining, winking, challenging Maddie to come out.

"Why not?!" Maddie yelled. "Goddamn ice storm. Izzy's missing the real *Frozen*." She slapped the cold glass of the window. "Looks slipperier than PAM on linoleum," she said with a chuckle as she turned away from the window.

The comment sparked her memory of the infamous bathroom incident. There was nothing Maddie liked more than springing a practical joke. Ross gave her a tough time for playing tricks on Izzy, but one of her best mother-daughter jokes was freezing her morning cereal. She'd put the cheerios and milk in the bowl and stuck it in the freezer overnight, then snuck it out in the morning and set it down in front of Izzy. The poor girl would proceed to clank away with the spoon before looking up with a wry smile and saying, "Mommy!" It always set a fun tone for the day.

In the Corps, especially overseas, she was a notorious joker who rarely ever got caught and refused to admit responsibility even when she was at fault. She routinely used her software engineering education to up the prank ante. Hacking fellow Marine computers for fun was a favorite pastime. She'd load software that would lead them to believe they had emailed porn to the division general or a goodbye letter to their girl explaining how they were going AWOL for a seductive local peasant who lived in the mountains.

On her first tour to Iraq there was a three-day span where they lost four men. They were rolled back from the front and a depressive coma fell over the group—the perfect time for a practical joke, as far as Maddie was concerned.

She woke up before dawn and set a wi-fi webcam up in the men's bathroom, along with a Dewalt radio they had in the barracks. She tuned in WJAR, the Marine channel on the base radio network. She kept the volume low until she had it set. Then she turned the power off, cranked the volume to maximum and set it to come on at 4:50 A.M. using a Christmas light timer. 4:50 was also known as *AC/DC reveille*, thanks to a sadistic Marine show host who was addicted to waking up to the heavy metal lightning.

As Maddie made her way out of the bathroom, she coated the floor with cooking spray. A bottle in each hand, she backed out, ass first, then tip-toed to her private bunk room, one of the major benefits of being a woman in a combat unit. She slipped back under the covers and waited.

When the timer clicked on, the building shook with distorted bass. The screams and guitars from AC/DC reverberated down the hall. The men in the barracks were on their feet within seconds.

The man closest to the chaos was one Jerome Lee, also known as "Chuckles." A Texan with skin like midnight and a brawny composition that made people stare, Chuckles was a frequent target for Maddie. On this occasion, he wasn't specifically targeted, but Maddie had a hunch he might be the victim. His bunk was closest to the bathroom.

Chuckles was an all-star football player—a running back who walked away from a Baylor degree subsidized by his athletic prowess. He woke up one morning and decided he wanted to be a Marine, simple as that. He quit school and joined up. The majority of his free time was dedicated to lifting insane amounts of weight in the gym.

"What the fuck?" he yelled as he threw open the bathroom door. On the video, he cocked his head and stared at the radio with blithe aggression before he took the fateful step. No amount of hours in the gym could help a person look graceful eating shit on a floor covered in cooking lubricant. He fell three times on his way to the radio, which he proceeded to smash against the tile wall and scatter across the room. Then he flailed a fourth time in an ill-fated attempt to stop another fall to the floor. He crawled from the room, screaming.

"Guuuunt!! You're dead, Gunt! I'm going to fucking kill you, Gunt."

"What the hell's going on?' Maddie asked when Chuckles came in. She couldn't hold the smile that wanted out at the corner of her mouth.

"You're the hardest working son-of-a-bitch prankster." Chuckles looked down; reflections on his massive bare chest revealed the spots on his body that absorbed the impact of the falls. He shook his head. "The Mad Gunt strikes again... Only you could pull that shit off. You son-of-a-bitch." As he said it, he laid a punch on Maddie's shoulder that felt like a truckload of bricks.

The video went viral on base, originating automatically from an email handle that began with *Eatingshitbefore5am.* It hit everyone's email inbox at 5:01 that morning and the fog of death was lifted.

Maddie put on her robe and went to the baby's room. She noted the time on her watch as 5:28 before she lifted Charlotte from her crib.

"Two minutes ahead of schedule." It was barely a whisper as she pulled the baby close. Charlotte's head fell into the crook of her neck, fitting perfectly like the last piece in a puzzle. She bounced gently in the middle of the room, giving her time to wake up. As she bounced, Maddie gazed through the louvered blinds to the icy hell that awaited them. "Gonna have to suit you up with some crampons, Char-monster."

After her bottle, Maddie killed the lights and sent the upstairs back into darkness. The pair when downstairs and Maddie finished preparations to leave.

While Charlotte played in the pack-and-play, Maddie remote started the Grand Cherokee and went out to survey the situation. With the garage door open, she stuck her right foot out on the ice to confirm the reports.

"Only a tenth of an inch? You're right, Marty, you smug bastard, it's a fucking mess." Using a bucket filled with salt that Ross kept in the corner, she cast it in front of her and made her way out the tractor-trailer length driveway to the road.

County crews had pretreated surfaces before the rain fell and froze. *There's enough traction to give it a shot*, she thought.

With Charlotte secure in her five-point harness and a bevy of toys hanging above her, Maddie crept from the garage and out to the road. The rubber was making contact with the asphalt and by the time she made it to the edge of the neighborhood, her fear of having an accident waned.

The main roads were mostly clear. The new thing across the state was to spray them with a saltwater solution the day before the storm. It dried on the road and when the rain or snow fell it mixed with the salt and lowered the freezing point by ten degrees.

The cloud deck was solid. Highlighted by the lights of suburban sprawl, it added a margin of visibility to an otherwise black morning. Maddie opted to take the inter-county connector, a toll road that had lighter traffic and received better attention from road crews.

By the time she passed the toll booth, the GPS indicated that she was only thirty miles from the agency. With traffic, weather, the chaos of D.C. streets and the likelihood of getting lost, she figured it would take a solid hour and a half, not counting time needed to find a parking spot.

7

Maracaibo, Venezuela

Anas stood awestruck before the *Contagious.* "Absolutely majestic." He lifted his hands high above his head. "A privileged ride that we most certainly deserve." He was speaking to no one in particular, but several of the team heard him as they milled about. "Can you imagine owning something so bourgeois?" Only one man heard the third comment and he'd probably never heard the word before.

By dark of night, the NJF boarding party, with help from Captain Timmin, had moved the *Contagious* from the boatyard to a man-made armlet next to the defunct seafood sorting warehouse. Back when the warehouse was built, the shot of water was cut from the earth and walled with concrete before the bay was let in. It ran the length of the warehouse and was wide enough to accommodate two medium-sized fishing boats or one large yacht.

Years of rust and crumble had played on the facility since fishing boats pulled alongside to offload the day's catch. A roof jutted out from the warehouse. The front was partially collapsed, but most the structure was sound and high enough to accommodate the full height of the *Contagious*. The roof blocked prying eyes from above and to prevent it being spotted on the water, the team erected an aluminum curtain that they pulled into place across the opening.

Garaged in a cocoon of rusted sheet metal, the *Contagious* was a stark contrast of modern technological sculpture. Anyone who encountered her would have immediately recognized the planning and effort required to conceal the vessel.

Anas had slept on the yacht. Fazul had refused. Anas believed that leadership had its privileges. Fazul believed it was important to make a show of being a soldier's soldier. He bunked with the men and even if he'd had an inkling of desire to sleep on the yacht, it would have been washed away when Anas suggested the idea.

Before he settled beneath the goose down comforter in the Owners Suite, Anas had walked the corridors and decks. It was his only opportunity to enjoy it before the men filled it with the equipment and dirt of war. He ran his hand along the rich varnish of the mahogany cap rails. He pulled off his shoes and socks and felt the silky chill of the natural teak decks. The *Contagious* smelled of money. She exuded an aura of privilege and aristocracy.

Anas was inspecting a scratch in the lush flag blue hull of the yacht.

"Good morning, brother." Anas jumped at the sound of Fazul's voice.

He turned to face his brother. "Fazul..."

"It is a great day!" Fazul's eyes were charged, trembling at the edges with anticipation. "You're very jumpy. And your eyes... They look tired. Did you not sleep well?"

Anas didn't acknowledge the quip.

"I slept like a champion," said Fazul. He had a habit of

announcing the superior quality of his sleep to anyone who would listen.

"No doubt," said Anas. He took a sip of his coffee and squinted at the bitterness. They served better in prison.

"Next time we'll plan the operation somewhere with a Starbucks," Fazul said. He pointed to Anas's stainless steel mug imprinted with the company logo.

"Anything would be better than this."

"When you're done admiring the boat, we'll need you to move out of the way. It's time to start loading." Anas had noticed a significant uptick in the condescending comments in recent days. He'd attributed it to nerves, but it was still wearing him thin.

"You may proceed. I'll keep clear of the men. Thank you for framing it that way, though." Anas turned to leave. After a couple of steps, he stopped and turned back, intent on making peace. "Working together will be important, Fazul. Mutual respect is critical for this to happen."

Fazul said nothing. He kept his back to his brother and stepped aboard.

The truth was, Anas hadn't slept well. His mind was alight with thought. He'd read that a soldier must accept the inevitability of their death to realize their true potential in war. He wasn't there yet. The night had been long, his circling mind keeping sleep at arm's length.

Anas watched as the men set to work. Fazul busied himself orchestrating the logistical operation. Furniture was removed from the main salon and dining compartment to make room for men and material. The teak table and chairs on her foredeck were removed as well.

Once the removal step was complete, Fazul did a final inspection. He emerged onto the deck and proclaimed that they were ready. "Begin loading pod number seven!" He'd insisted on precise groupings that organized the equipment based on his deployment schedule.

"Remember, number seven goes in the galley!" Fazul yelled.

Pod seven consisted of the lowest priority materials. There were spare weapons, wooden boxes with additional rounds of ammunition, bags of tools, spare parts and equipment. Stacked on top were 38 gym bags with a change of clothes for each of the men.

Anas had enough of watching. He joined the soldiers as they hustled between the warehouse and the yacht. The galley could have served as the heart of a five-star restaurant. Now it was being consumed. Aisles were filled with crates, stainless steel tables stacked with boxes. Bags were stuffed close together on the counters around the perimeter of the galley. Pod number seven was aboard.

Pod number six went in next. Two gasoline-powered electric generators were wheel up to the doors of the galley. They would power the command post in the unfortunate event that the local authorities decided to shut down the electric to the resort. There were fuel cans and miles of extension cords still neatly wrapped.

Pod five was the oddity. It was Anas's baby—the one set of equipment that wouldn't have shown up on most terrorist prep lists. It included eight, military-grade, quad-propeller-driven drones, and all the communication equipment required to get the aerial surveillance net aloft and keep it there. The drones themselves were housed in eight separate hard cases the size of a horse trunk. Eight other cases, half the size of the mains, contained the flight batteries and served as charging units. Eight radio frequency transmitters, eight signal relay routers, cases of spare part kits and a specialized table used to maintain the systems, rounded out the lot. In total, the grouping consisted of over 40 hard-sided black cases.

Pod four consisted of heavy machine guns, plastic explosives, spools of detonation cord and wiring. The boxes and crates were aligned to the left in the main salon. They were stacked from front to back, moving ever closer to the aft door.

Pod three included cases of blockade bars they'd use to secure the exits. There were cases of zip ties, shotguns for breaching doors and boxes filled with empty sandbags.

By the time pod two was loaded, the elegant salon look more like the inside of a packed moving truck. They were out of room. Fazul ordered the men to stack things higher to free up space by the rear door.

Finally, pod number one was loaded into the reclaimed area. It was the assault pod, and included everything the team would need in the opening hours of the action. Pistols, submachine guns, knives, zip ties and enough ammunition to tag each man, woman and child several times.

They were ready before lunch. *Hurry up and wait*, Anas thought. He feared this part of the plan. They would now wait for sundown to come before leaving for the island. Anas had tried to convince Fazul that the loading would only take a couple of hours. He'd recommended they leave the same night the boat was captured. Even though no one was expecting to hear from the crew of the *Contagious* until after the landing, if anyone went looking, it would have been a very big problem. Fazul had argued that it would take hours. He felt they would need time to get things in order, that rushing would only lead to mistakes.

Anas stared at his brother, wanting to say *I told you so* with his eyes. Fazul kept his focus off Anas.

"I'm going to take a nap. Wake me if this plan falls apart and someone discovers the boat." Anas turned for the stairs. An instant of remorse struck him—he'd stooped to Fazul's level. After a beat, he continued up to the office, hoping the thin mattress on the floor would bring him the sleep he'd been robbed of the night before.

. . .

8 Washington, D.C.

Maddie made a left on 16th St. NW. Despite the darkness and blur of the rain, the *Welcome to Washington DC* sign was visible. She clicked the radio on as she crossed into the district.

"Carroll Country Day School is closed, Christian Hope School is closed, Charles County schools are closed..." Jerry's monotone droned on through the growing list.

The timing of the traffic lights along 16th street sucked. The programmer clearly had not considered parents with sleeping children. Tiny humans caught in the fog of sleep benefit from the hum of the open road, not stops and starts with intervals of only a block or two. Maddie hit red at every light. With each one, she checked the mirror, watching Charlotte squirm from the stillness, hoping the twilight nap would hold on long enough for green.

"The Federal Government is opening three hours late." Maddie felt a jolt and stared at the radio.

Come again. Did they say the government was three hours late? What did that mean? God dammit, she was almost there. She had everything ready. She had a dream about the cold Balashi. Was she screwed?

"Fuck!" Holding the phone against the top of the steering wheel she waited for a red light and tapped 'federal gov' into the browser. The main government website confirmed the bad news.

It could be four or five hours of waiting instead of one or two, she thought. Should she still wait in line? It was a damp, crusty cold that bore to the bone in seconds. Everything she'd read said that the pre-opening line ran along the front of the building. There was an overhang but nothing to block the wind and cold. Babies can't be outside in the damp and crusty fucking ice for four or five hours.

Besides that, she doubted there was any hope of getting the passport now. Could government workers arriving three hours late still be capable of producing something as significant as a passport same day?

But what was she going to do? Turn around and head home? Quit? She didn't have a choice.

"We're sticking to the plan Char-monster," Maddie whispered.

With eyes darting between the phone and the road, Maddie pecked out a message to Chuckles. 'Call me once u lazy ass out o—' A tone sounded from the dash and the Jeep's brakes applied automatically.

"Son of a bitch," she hissed as the phone bounced its way to the floor. Red glowed above her and what felt like fractions of an inch separated her bumper from the car in front.

At the top of a deep breath meant to calm her nerves, Maddie could feel a pile of anxiety in her chest. She laid her forehead on the steering wheel and counted in her mind. Then she reached down, retrieved the phone and finished the text. 'I'm in the district. Could use a hand.'

By quarter after seven she was circling a two-block section of real estate at the heart of the nation's capital. It housed the passport agency, headquarters for the international monetary fund, a café and a book store with dark windows.

There was no parking in front of the agency. It took three passes to recon the entrance. A few vagrants were curled under blankets in front of the book store. Twenty yards up, the lobby of the agency was lit. Glass, thirty or forty feet tall, gave it a stately look. Five huddled forms were lined up to the right of the door. Inside, two uniformed guards manned a desk in the lobby.

Maddie reached the end of the block and turned right. A high windowless wall protected the south side of the complex. The only break in the concrete led to an underground garage for employees only. A capital police officer stood in the freezing rain that was clicking at Maddie's windshield. The man was wearing a full-length parka and brimmed uniform hat with a plastic cover.

Now that's a shit job, Maddie thought. She wondered if the guard noticed this was her third time around.

Maddie pulled to a stop along a red section of curb short of the guard. With the Jeep set to park and the engine still running, she popped the door. Ice danced down the back of her neck as she got out. She drew up her shoulders, tucking her head as if to hide and was just about to close the door when she remembered Old Mr. Murphy and his law of chaos. There was no doubt he was out and about and hell bent on spoiling Maddie's party. She reached back inside and cracked the window. "Wait here Char-monster," she said as she closed the door.

The guard stared straight ahead as Maddie approached. Ice skittered off the plastic condom that protected the felt top of his hat.

"You gotta stand in this shit even when they call a three-hour delay?" Maddie asked.

The man's black skin was invisible in the morning light. Only the whites of his eyes told Maddie she was being inspected. "Yes ma'am. Twenty-four by three-sixty-five. Comes with the job."

"When you think this place will actually get going today? With the delay and all?"

The guard bounced on his toes. "They'll wait until they have enough people make it in to man the windows. Critical mass and all... It'll take a while. Eleven thirty maybe. Hard to say though."

"Is there anywhere I can get inside and wait it out?" Maddie asked.

The guard pointed. "The Café is usually open by now but

they're late this morning. There's a Marriott Courtyard around the corner. Underground garage."

"That'll work. Thanks," Maddie said. She was about to turn and leave. "Appreciate your service. Keep up the good work."

"Yes ma'am. Keep warm."

Charlotte was beginning to cry when Maddie got back in. The entrance to the hotel garage was only a block away. They descended out of the weather and into a forty-dollar parking fee. With a choice of spaces to pick from, it only took a few minutes to park and load up the stroller. A few more passed and they were riding the elevator bound for the lobby.

A couple of baristas were stirring behind the Starbucks counter in the lobby. One was filling the case with muffins. The front desk attendant barely noticed Maddie as she claimed a spot on a lobby sofa fronting a television running CNN.

She'd barely sat down when her phone rang. It was Chuckles.

"Why are you sending me cryptic messages all early in the morning on an ice day?" Chuckles asked when Maddie answered the phone.

"Good morning to you too Master Sargent," Maddie said.

"How you in the District? Ross posted pictures of the kids in the pool on Facebook last night."

"Ross and Izzy are in Aruba. Charlotte and I are at the freakin' passport agency."

The pause was long enough that Maddie had time to pull Charlotte from the stroller and sit her up on a knee. There was a laugh of realization.

"No... you didn't?"

"Yeah, sucks to be me."

"When'd they leave?"

"Yesterday morning. I didn't realize we'd forgot to get one for the baby until the day before. I've got all the passport paperwork ready to roll. Only thing in my way now is this fucking ice storm."

Chuckles let out a long, exaggerated laugh. "About time somebody got your ass back. Karma sister. Karma."

"Yeah, fuck you," Maddie said. "How about you help me get a passport? I read online you can get them same day but with the late opening..."

"Oh, that's true. Yeah, they're gonna be slow coming in. Give a gov'ie three hours off and they take four, maybe five," Chuckles said.

"You know anybody over here now that you're a D.C. insider snob?"

"I'll ask around but it's not ringing any bells for me Gunt. You might be on a solo mission. But listen, I'll come keep you company. Hold the baby for a bit if your arms are getting tired and what-not."

8

WASHINGTON, D.C.

MADDIE MADE A LEFT on 16th St. NW. Despite the darkness and blur of the rain, the *Welcome to Washington DC* sign was visible. She clicked the radio on as she crossed into the district.

"Carroll Country Day School is closed, Christian Hope School is closed, Charles County schools are closed..." Jerry's monotone droned on through the growing list.

The timing of the traffic lights along 16th street sucked. The programmer clearly had not considered parents with sleeping children. Tiny humans caught in the fog of sleep benefit from the hum of the open road, not stops and starts with intervals of only a block or two. Maddie hit red at every light. With each one, she checked the mirror, watching Charlotte squirm from the stillness, hoping the twilight nap would hold on long enough for green.

"The Federal Government is opening three hours late." Maddie felt a jolt and stared at the radio.

Come again. Did they say the government was three hours

late? What did that mean? God dammit, she was almost there. She had everything ready. She had a dream about the cold Balashi. Was she screwed?

"Fuck!" Holding the phone against the top of the steering wheel she waited for a red light and tapped 'federal gov' into the browser. The main government website confirmed the bad news.

It could be four or five hours of waiting instead of one or two, she thought. Should she still wait in line? It was a damp, crusty cold that bore to the bone in seconds. Everything she'd read said that the pre-opening line ran along the front of the building. There was an overhang but nothing to block the wind and cold. Babies can't be outside in the damp and crusty fucking ice for four or five hours.

Besides that, she doubted there was any hope of getting the passport now. Could government workers arriving three hours late still be capable of producing something as significant as a passport same day?

But what was she going to do? Turn around and head home? Quit? She didn't have a choice.

"We're sticking to the plan Char-monster," Maddie whispered.

With eyes darting between the phone and the road, Maddie pecked out a message to Chuckles. 'Call me once u lazy ass out o—' A tone sounded from the dash and the Jeep's brakes applied automatically.

"Son of a bitch," she hissed as the phone bounced its way to the floor. Red glowed above her and what felt like fractions of an inch separated her bumper from the car in front.

At the top of a deep breath meant to calm her nerves, Maddie could feel a pile of anxiety in her chest. She laid her forehead on the steering wheel and counted in her mind. Then she reached down, retrieved the phone and finished the text. 'I'm in the district. Could use a hand.'

By quarter after seven she was circling a two-block section of real estate at the heart of the nation's capital. It housed the passport agency, headquarters for the international monetary fund, a café and a book store with dark windows.

There was no parking in front of the agency. It took three passes to recon the entrance. A few vagrants were curled under blankets in front of the book store. Twenty yards up, the lobby of the agency was lit. Glass, thirty or forty feet tall, gave it a stately look. Five huddled forms were lined up to the right of the door. Inside, two uniformed guards manned a desk in the lobby.

Maddie reached the end of the block and turned right. A high windowless wall protected the south side of the complex. The only break in the concrete led to an underground garage for employees only. A capital police officer stood in the freezing rain that was clicking at Maddie's windshield. The man was wearing a full-length parka and brimmed uniform hat with a plastic cover.

Now that's a shit job, Maddie thought. She wondered if the guard noticed this was her third time around.

Maddie pulled to a stop along a red section of curb short of the guard. With the Jeep set to park and the engine still running, she popped the door. Ice danced down the back of her neck as she got out. She drew up her shoulders, tucking her head as if to hide and was just about to close the door when she remembered Old Mr. Murphy and his law of chaos. There was no doubt he was out and about and hell bent on spoiling Maddie's party. She reached back inside and cracked the window. "Wait here Char-monster," she said as she closed the door.

The guard stared straight ahead as Maddie approached. Ice skittered off the plastic condom that protected the felt top of his hat.

“You gotta stand in this shit even when they call a three-hour delay?” Maddie asked.

The man’s black skin was invisible in the morning light. Only the whites of his eyes told Maddie she was being inspected. “Yes ma’am. Twenty-four by three-sixty-five. Comes with the job.“

“When you think this place will actually get going today? With the delay and all?”

The guard bounced on his toes. “They’ll wait until they have enough people make it in to man the windows. Critical mass and all... It’ll take a while. Eleven thirty maybe. Hard to say though.”

“Is there anywhere I can get inside and wait it out?” Maddie asked.

The guard pointed. “The Café is usually open by now but they’re late this morning. There’s a Marriott Courtyard around the corner. Underground garage.”

“That’ll work. Thanks,” Maddie said. She was about to turn and leave. “Appreciate your service. Keep up the good work.”

“Yes ma’am. Keep warm.”

Charlotte was beginning to cry when Maddie got back in. The entrance to the hotel garage was only a block away. They descended out of the weather and into a forty-dollar parking fee. With a choice of spaces to pick from, it only took a few minutes to park and load up the stroller. A few more passed and they were riding the elevator bound for the lobby.

A couple of baristas were stirring behind the Starbucks counter in the lobby. One was filling the case with muffins. The front desk attendant barely noticed Maddie as she claimed a spot on a lobby sofa fronting a television running CNN.

She’d barely sat down when her phone rang. It was Chuckles.

“Why are you sending me cryptic messages all early in the

morning on an ice day?" Chuckles asked when Maddie answered the phone.

"Good morning to you too Master Sargent," Maddie said.

"How you in the District? Ross posted pictures of the kids in the pool on Facebook last night."

"Ross and Izzy are in Aruba. Charlotte and I are at the freakin' passport agency."

The pause was long enough that Maddie had time to pull Charlotte from the stroller and sit her up on a knee. There was a laugh of realization.

"No… you didn't?"

"Yeah, sucks to be me."

"When'd they leave?"

"Yesterday morning. I didn't realize we'd forgot to get one for the baby until the day before. I've got all the passport paperwork ready to roll. Only thing in my way now is this fucking ice storm."

Chuckles let out a long, exaggerated laugh. "About time somebody got your ass back. Karma sister. Karma."

"Yeah, fuck you," Maddie said. "How about you help me get a passport? I read online you can get them same day but with the late opening…"

"Oh, that's true. Yeah, they're gonna be slow coming in. Give a gov'ie three hours off and they take four, maybe five," Chuckles said.

"You know anybody over here now that you're a D.C. insider snob?"

"I'll ask around but it's not ringing any bells for me Gunt. You might be on a solo mission. But listen, I'll come keep you company. Hold the baby for a bit if your arms are getting tired and what-not."

9

Surfside Resort, Aruba

Ross felt like a helpless heel. Waves lapped at his ankles as he talked to his wife.

"Izzy wanted to get in the ocean first thing," he said. "Hang on a sec Maddie." He lowered the phone away from his mouth. "Don't go out too far sweets," he yelled.

Izzy waved in reply.

"She's got her lazy river tube out there and she's paddling around."

"Char-monster is chewing on my sleeve and watching some d-bag on CNN named Zain Axelrod. We're both having a ball, you and I."

Ross was happy to hear she was still capable of cracking a joke. It meant all the bad hadn't gotten her down.

"So, what's your plan?" he asked.

"Gonna wait here another hour or so. Eat a few muffins and down my third cup of coffee. Then go stand in the cold with your baby wrapped in so many layers you won't be able to see her. And then... I'm gonna pray."

Ross laughed. "You? Praying? A first time for everything I guess."

"Never had a need before."

"Izzy wants to go see Kavita and the kids for lunch," Ross said.

"She remembers them?"

"Yup. Didn't remember their names but she was like, you remember those girls whose mommy makes the smelly food? Can we go see them? I told her we could and she said, ok, but I only have to eat a cheese quesadilla right Daddy? Not the smelly stuff... and turned up her nose."

"That's too much. She's growing like a weed that one. Tell Kavita I've got my eyes on some spicy goat curry this time around."

Kavita and Geert Velden lived on the eastern part of Aruba in the town of San Nicolas. They operated Kavita's Café, an east Indian eatery that served unique dishes with unmatched hospitality. Maddie and Ross had come to meet the restaurateurs like so many other tourists—lost on their way to the remote but very popular *Baby Beach*.

Kavita's love for children was unrivaled. She had two of her own and a litter of unofficial adoptees. Izzy was just a baby when they met. Kavita was the first stranger that handled her without a tear. The Günther family was known to visit two and even three times a week when they were on the island. Maddie and Ross visited the Café in Aruba more than any restaurant back home.

When the Velden's were between restaurants, Kavita cooked up food at her house and served it in the backyard. Her landlord got greedy, so she walked out and constructed her own building on the other side of the intersection that made her famous. The couple and their children had become close friends that only added to Maddie and Ross's love for the island.

"I'll tell her. She'll get a kick out of the story," Ross said. "Hey listen Maddie. Thanks again. It is nice being here with Izzy but it's hard hearing what you're going through."

"Really baby? It doesn't sound all that hard to me."

"You know what I mean."

Maddie laughed. "No problem honey. A trashy novel by the adult pool and Cold Balashi. That's my motivation."

"And trips on the wazy river with your daughters?"

"No doubt."

"Just remember, this timeshare thing was your idea," Ross said. "You talked me into it."

"Uh huh. And it's suddenly more expensive than they told me. Lying bastards. You spend that kind of money, it ought to come with passports."

They both laughed.

"But seriously..." Ross said, hesitating. "Just don't forget the black bikini." As he said it, his mind drafted a picture of her stretched out on a lounge chair under one of the palapas. He loved the black bikini. Always had. The black bikini topped off with her sun hat and a cold Balashi in her hand.

"Oh, I forgot to tell you. I got one of those one piece mom suits with a skirt."

"Hell no!" he yelled back. "I don't want to hear it. I'm hanging up now. Love you Mad."

10

THE YACHT *CONTAGIOUS*

ISLAND LIGHTS WERE visible for nearly an hour before the word *searching* was replaced with bars on Fazul's phone. 'We have service. Proceed according to plan.' Fazul pecked at the keypad with his thumbs, punching each letter of the text message carefully. 'Estimate GO 40 minutes.'

Thirty-Two minutes later, the *Contagious* drifted gently into the dock. The tide was ebbing and lights along the walkway illuminated the glossy blue of her hull as she was tied up.

This was it. The time had come to take the fateful step. The time of bullets was upon them. The question now rested in whether the team had the resolve to become implements of war. Each of them were chess pieces on the table and all knew that some would be lost in the battle for ultimate victory.

Fazul stopped for a moment to watch his brother. Anas was looking back across the water from where they had come. A slice of moon drifted between wisps of Caribbean clouds. It danced in the distance on tranquil waters. Behind them, palms dotting the beach rustled in the breeze, shushing the resort as it slept. *No turning back now brother*, he thought.

The pier serviced the Surfside and the neighboring Holiday Inn. Snorkeling tours, scuba charters, parasailing boats and jet ski operators all used it to service vacationers along the albino sand strip. During the day, a look down the beach and a person could see that the docks repeated occasionally in the distance where other resorts lined Aruba's popular leeward coast.

Shaped like a T with two lines of dock at the top, most of the boats pulled alongside early to pick up passengers for their morning runs. Two tours boats tied up on the inside of the t-top, opposite the *Contagious,* were the only boats that remained overnight.

Forty yards of sand separated the men from their target. Fazul grabbed Anas by the shoulder. "Stand with me." They took up a position at the gate as the men gathered.

"Actions louder than words my brothers." It was a mantra Fazul had started. A rally cry.

With the men crowding up toward the gate, Anas was forced behind his brother. Fazul could feel him looking over his shoulder, watching him encourage the men with a pat as he repeated the mantra. "Actions louder than words."

Anas wanted to lead with words, but he hadn't the stomach for leadership in battle. He would get an education in true leadership from Fazul, as the operation unfolded.

The men poured from the port side gate like ants evacuating a compromised hill. In the dim light, they formed up into four single file lines along the edges of the dock. Four squads, each with eight men, took their positions as practiced. Squads one and two were on the left, three and four to the right.

Fazul jumped down behind the last man. Anas followed. Fazul strode up through the ranks. Anas slowed, watching from the back.

"Are there any final questions? This is our time brothers."

Fazul patted shoulders as he moved forward. "Remember, attention to detail is key." As he neared the front of the lines he turned and walked backwards slowly. "Any questions? Ask them now. Uncertainty is not good." As he passed the two men in front he stopped and stared at his army, the paw of silence palpable in the night.

"We meet in Paradise brothers." Fazul pulled the cell phone from his pocket and initiated the invasion. "GO!" It was 3:57 am.

The lines reached out like a caterpillar on the move, the front extending and then the back-half surging to catch-up. Stomping desert boots shook the dock to life as the men moved at double time, the noise falling to faintness as they hit the sand of Palm Beach.

Squads one and four drove hard left and right respectively. They were tasked with wrapping the complex in a sixteen-man phalanx. Their goal was to prevent anyone from coming in or out while the buildings themselves were secured. Squads two and three would sweep the center areas. They'd take control of the stairwells and secure the elevator shafts in each of the buildings as they made their way forward.

Fazul stood at the edge of the dock watching them go. His eyes followed squad one as they crossed the widest part of the beach. The man in the rear took up a position under a palapa half way up the sand. As the column rounded the building's edge, the next to last peeled-off at the corner. He leaned into the concrete pillar and swept his field of fire with the suppressed submachine gun.

Squad two fanned into a tactical V formation like a flight of Canada geese. They headed up the beach to the left of the center walkway that branched out and around the pool promenade. They'd sweep the adult pool first and then continue down the left side of the main pool.

Squads three and four bore right off the dock. Led by Ilan, squad three swarmed into the resort's beachside restaurant and bar. Squad four rounded the outside corner of the same building and made their way up the right-hand perimeter of the complex.

Squad Three

Ilan's point man was moving so quickly he nearly missed the young couple. They were making out in the dark of the open-air bar, the woman sitting on a stool with her shirt up and breasts exposed.

The point-man leveled his weapon at the couple. He side-stepped to his left, slowing to give Ilan time to move up and assess the situation.

"What the hell?" The man shot up straight, lifting his head from the woman's chest.

Ilan toggled the button on the side of his ear piece to activate the microphone. "Two in the beach bar. Intoxicated... Eliminating." The words rushed out. Ilan breathed deep, knowing he needed to slow down. He stilled his body as he exhaled and focused the reticule of his sight on the man's forehead. The diamond pattern of the weapons grip dimpled his palm. He drew in on his index finger, increasing the pressure on the thin strip of steel. The trigger fall felt heavier than he remembered.

P-ewww.

The silenced round knocked the man backwards, out of the woman's embrace. Ilan was unprepared for the shot and lifted his cheek off the weapon in surprise. The woman was frozen by confusion for an instant then whimpered in fear just loud enough to bring Ilan back to his senses. He shifted the sights down and squeezed off a second fatal round. The impact knocked the life out of her scream. She toppled forward, her face landing in the dead man's lap as the stool followed her to the ground in a clatter.

The first two deadly shots stung the ears of all thirty-eight men. The sounds erupted as deafening static. After the shots, Ilan's breath was heavy in their ears. Ilan looked down at the motionless couple. He coughed away the nausea building at the top of his stomach.

His point man reached out and tapped him on the shoulder. He pointed at his mouth. "Your mic is still open."

"Shit," said Ilan, broadcasting his frustration to the entire team.

As soon as the channel was clear, Fazul cut in. "Remember. Keep the button on your comms depressed when you talk. Don't double click it or the mic remains open."

Surfside Security Office

In the hotel's security office, Fahd Umari sat with the security shift supervisor in front of a bank of screens. Four monitors hung in front of them, each split into four rows showing images from the security cameras across the resort. They covered all the common areas and every floor in each of the four buildings.

As a hotel runner, Fahd had the wide access he needed. He worked the graveyard shift running shaving kits, extra towels and other assorted stuff up to the rooms of the resort. Fahd was one of two runners that worked on the skeleton night crew. He was responsible for buildings one and two but helped where ever he was needed. His counterpart was an older man who could frequently be caught napping in the maintenance shop at the bottom of Building Three.

In the beginning, Fahd supplemented part-time in the morning. After a few weeks, he started bringing in coffee and donuts to share. That, along with the occasional bottle of Anejo tequila for the night security supervisor, had bought him the political capital he needed to win his current post.

The nights were slower, it gave him time to investigate,

answer questions and prepare for the invasion. He fed Fazul endless details about the operation of the resort and formed alliances with the unsuspecting.

"Carlos. You have been a good friend to me." The security supervisor was sipping on the tequila he had poured himself just minutes before. He leaned back in his chair, his eyes scanning the security displays. Fahd often sat with him watching the displays, waiting for room serve carts to be pushed outside the doors so he could run up to collect them. "You are a good person. This will be my least favorite event of the night." A backpack rested on the floor between Fahd's legs. He had chambered a round and toggled off the safety before coming into the room.

The supervisor stared at Fahd, not understanding the comment. "Thank you Fahd, but..."

Out of the corner of his eye, Carlos noticed motion on the screens. Several of the small boxes showed the squads sweeping into the resort. Fahd lifted the pistol. He closed his eyes before he pulled the trigger. He opened them in time to see Carlos's head bounce off the desk. The motion sent his chair backwards. Fahd watched him fall to the floor, the life gone. It was the first life he had taken.

Carlos kept his radio on the desk in its charging station, right next to the photo of his family. Fahd pulled the picture from the tape and laid it flat on the desk. Then he lifted the radio and made a call.

"Security. Carlos asked me to request that you meet him outside the main lobby." It was designed to lure the other security guards toward the front of the complex and away from the advance of the main assault.

"Copy," said one voice.

"I copy as well," said a second through static.

Fahd then pulled a headset from his backpack. It had arrived along with a walkie-talkie and a set of instructions just days ago. He slipped the set over the top of his head and positioned the speaker over his left ear. He pressed the comms button. "This is the security post. Radio check."

"Welcome to the fight. We read you loud and clear," said Fazul over the radio.

Fahd held the radio in his hands and stared at it as he formulated his report. "The security post is secure. One guard is down. I've place a call to the others requesting them to the front entrance. One of them is in the parking lot by Building Four. He is headed toward the front now." Fahd was pointing to the man on one of the security camera displays. "The third guard was sent up a short time ago on a noise call. He is about to enter the main elevator in Building One."

Fahd stood and leaned into the security screens. "We've got a cleaner in the front lobby and two people in the back office. The night manager and a call operator." Sidestepping to avoid Carlos's body, he moved to a door left of the screens and pushed his way into the adjoining information technology suite. "Telephone service, internet and television will all be disabled momentarily."

"Very good. Continue as planned," called Fazul over the radio in reply.

11

Ashton, Maryland

Awooga. Awooga. The sinister 60's-era klaxon alarm startled Maddie from her sleep. She grabbed the phone from the nightstand and was about to place her thumb on the fingerprint reader when she ran out of cord. It fell from her grasp, bounced off the edge of the mattress and, *awooga-ed* its way to the floor.

"Dammit." Maddie stared at the ceiling for three more shrieks of the klaxon then swung her feet from the bed. It was 3:07. Preferring to rise on odd numbered minutes was just another quirk of character. Like calling a dress shirt a button-up, or emphasizing the second word of a sentence instead of the first. She was squirrely without trying.

"Enough already," she said, fishing the phone up by the cord.

One hand rubbed the sleep from her face while the other thumbed up the text message app. "Hi-ho the derry-o," she said as she waited for it to launch.

She was just a long workday away from getting to Aruba.

She'd taken possession of the freshly minted passport just after two the previous afternoon.

They had walked from the Marriott to the entrance of the passport agency. A line had indeed formed, but Maddie's experience was one-hundred-and-eighty-degrees from Disney. Despite the shitty weather, people were kind.

"No one should have to stand out here with a baby," the woman in line behind her had said. "Give me your number and go wait inside at the cafe. I'll call you once they open the doors."

Her excitement at reaching the window of a passport agent had been ruined by the nonchalance of the person working it.

"Come back in three hours and pick it up," she'd said.

"That's it?" Maddie asked, wanting a high-five or to do a dance. The woman said nothing, just nodded and clicked at the computer.

Maddie walked away from the window in disbelief. Something told her to go back and ask in clear words if this meant she was good, that she'd get the passport and be able to leave for Aruba in the morning. She resisted the temptation.

Her spirits were so high when she left that waiting in the hotel wasn't enough. After bundling Charlotte in the stroller, she navigated the icy sidewalks to the White House where she took a selfie with her daughter and sent it to Ross.

Maddie looked down, smiling at Ross's replies from the day before.

'Good luck with the flight tomorrow, Super Mom. Your beer is chilling in the fridge. Don't forget your cape—I feel like you'll need it... BTW, you're my hero if you didn't know... Repayment will be long and enjoyable. Thank you!'

Ross was an amazing husband and father—an even keel of support. He raised Izzy, sometimes alone for many months while Maddie was deployed, all while working a high-stress job. He looked like a lumberjack and cared for his family like a mother hen.

Maddie was convinced they were meant to be together. They dated two years in high school then Ross left for college. A long distance relationship wasn't in the cards, but they'd both accepted it with sad faces.

Seven years later, and four days after graduating from the Marine Corps Scout Sniper School, they stumbled into one another at a mall while she was home on leave.

"I like the short haircut," Ross said after hugging her. "What've you been up to?"

It took just one date to rekindle the flames, but a lot longer for Ross to accept that his high school prom date was now a Marine Scout Sniper.

"You were always a tomboy, but Jesus," he said, his mouth hanging open.

Maddie had struggled to find work after graduating from college. The economy was sagging and her computer science degree sat on the shelf collecting dust. In the space of two days, she read two articles about the military. The first was about women being placed in combat roles for the first time. The second was an article about how too many Marines were washing out of sniper school and how it was leading to a shortage of the specialists. Maddie's father was a veteran of the Marine Corps, a fact in which he had great pride. She was a country girl and always a better shot than the boys. With no job in sight and a flat love life, she joined up and helped shatter glass ceilings by becoming the first female Marine Scout Sniper and later, receiving a chest full of decorations.

Less than twelve months after their mall reunion, Maddie and Ross were married. A few months after that, Maddie left on her first deployment.

'I posted the pic of you and Char in front of the white house and the one of the two of you with the passport. A ton of likes! Sleep tight.'

Maddie stared at his words. Aruba didn't observe daylight savings time. It was an hour later but still four in the morning. Ross and Izzy liked to sleep in and wouldn't roll from bed for hours. But Ross always turned his ringer off at night so Maddie pecked her own reply out and hit send.

'Rising and shining here in the good ole MD. See you in 9 hours. Aruba or bust!'

12

Surfside Resort, Aruba

Back at the *Contagious,* Fazul paced back and forth along the dock, staring at the phone in his hand. He looked up at Anas who was leaning on a dock piling waiting his turn to engage in the fight. They made eye contact just as the phone chirped.

'Activating cell charges then headed to the entrance,' it read.

Fazul stared at the screen, knowing that his two other on-island operatives would be prompted to send their updates after seeing Jamal's. A second message popped up. 'In place at CJ.' Then a third in quick succession: 'In place at CC.'

Outside the resort, the three texting operatives had been triggered into action by Fazul's original message.

One quarter of a mile to the north and a mile to the south, two cellular substations serving the Noord district of Aruba were under siege. A series of thermite boring charges lit the fenced complexes as chemical reactions sent molten lead down through the delicate circuitry that made cellular service possible along Palm Beach. Minutes after the team laid boot prints in the pristine sand, hot slag was dripping from the transceivers and tens of thousands of tourists were stripped of reliable communication.

Jamal Hamadei had planted the charges on the cell towers between midnight and 2 A.M. As the invasion started, he was idling in a box truck along Lighthouse Road. He was to wait five minutes after Fazul's text message, which launched the operation, before he activated the charges. The grace period was built in so that any other pertinent information could be communicated before cell service in the Noord district was taken away.

Aruba was divided into six districts. The Noord district included almost all of the tourist-powered real estate. All of the high-rise buildings and most of their older, low-rise cousins to the south were dependent on the towers for cellular service.

At the five-minute mark, Jamal activated the reactions by placing two separate calls to cell phones rigged as detonators. They were the last calls routed by the towers.

After initiating the charges, he was to use the truck to block the entrance to the resort. Orange cones and heavy plastic barriers, stolen from a construction site, were used to make it look official.

To the southeast, Adnan Sali and Jaber al-Quso sat low in their seats in front of two separate houses. The Kia Picanto and Suzuki Swift they were driving were two of the most common vehicles on the island. They would not be seen as anomalies.

They were parked in front of the homes of two prominent island officials. The Chief Minister of Justice, aka CJ, and the Chief Police Commissioner, aka CC, would play essential roles in the official island response. They were known to be good friends, confidants who would be notified at once when local authorities realized the magnitude of the incident playing out along Palm Beach. Adnan and Jaber would assassinate them and effectively decapitate the marginal response the island's local police force was capable of mounting.

With its most savvy crisis managers dead and the Dutch marine contingent gone for training to Camp Lejeune North Carolina, the invading NJF force could operate from a position of considerable strength as they tightened thumbscrews on the world.

** Squad Two **

Hassan was Fazul's deputy in charge. He led squad two into the pool promenade. They swept through breaks in the tropical hedges enclosing the adult pool area. The water was lit a deep cerulean blue and perimeter lights made it obvious there was no one there. Hassan declared the checkpoint clear over the radio.

The five members on the left side of the V-formation emerged from the bushes. The three men on the right came down the walkway leading to the adult pool entrance. A spearhead bristling with eight submachine guns, the formation looked ominous as it pressed forward toward their first objective.

Buildings one and two ran down the left side of the complex as one approached from the water. They appeared to be connected from the outside but in actuality were two independent structures. Building One had a stairwell at both ends and just a single bank of elevators on the island side that brought guests down to the main pool promenade.

As the squad moved forward, the wide expanse of the main pool extended out and away on their right. It shimmered in a kaleidoscope of artificial color from the lights shone along its bottom.

To the left, the façade of Building One hid the parking level at its base and served as the second side of the chute the squad was tasked with sweeping and securing.

An unsuspecting resort guest emerged from the doors at the base of Building One as the team approached. Middle-aged, overweight and underdressed, the team rolled up on him before he had time to react.

His unbuttoned shirt was adorned with swordfish, leaving room for his Brillo pad of gray chest hair to bust out.

"Point men, take him to the holding room and lock down the building," Hassan yelled. Two soldiers at the front of the V-formation peeled off.

"Is this a drill or something?" Brillo chest asked. He bit his lip, sensing the answer to the question was written in the intensity of the armed men's eyes. "Goddamn insomnia," he mumbled.

Brillo chest took two steps back. The first soldier to reach him pushed his shoulder toward the door. "Go! Inside." The second soldier ran passed and opened the door to the elevator atrium.

"Wait here," Hassan ordered of the other five men in his squad.

He turned and followed his two point men as they pushed the prisoner inside. One paused by the elevator doors, leveling his weapon. He was to cover the elevators and the door to the stairs until his counterpart returned.

Hassan followed the other man into the windowless game room attached to the atrium. It flashed with light from the pinball machines and gaming stations that burned twenty-four hours a day. Fahd had indicated that it was an ideal holding area. Any guests coming down the stairs or elevators would be collected and placed in the room.

"Face the wall there." The soldier pointed. Brillo chest moved quickly to the open wall at the back of the room. A gorilla face was stenciled on the wall with the words "Game Time" written below it.

The soldier pulled a zip tie for his web belt. "Hands together, behind your back." He looped the plastic tie over the man's hands and around his wrists. The end was pre-fed into the square zipper. He pulled the tab, clicking it tightly.

Then he bent down and pulled a second tie out that was not pre-fed. "Feet together," he commanded. The second tie was looped around the prisoner's ankles, snugly tying them together.

The soldier stood and pushed Brillo chest hard to the side. "Stay here," he said as the man fell. Unable to compensate, the prisoner fell to the floor. His head clocked off the tile and he went limp.

Hassan activated his mic. "Squad two has taken our first prisoner. We're securing the elevator and stairwells on this end of Building One. Squad one, confirm you have the Oceanside stairwell covered."

** Squad One **

At the base of the ocean side stairwell, the second member of squad one to peel off had left his post by the pillar to secure the door. In his backpack were two door blockading bars. Using self-tapping masonry screws and a cordless driver, he affixed the blockade bars over the outward opening door. With one across the top half of the door and the other below center, the bars effectively prevented the doors from being opened. This mechanism would prevent prisoners from escaping. Bars would be added to every floor as the night wore on.

One of Fazul's worries was clearing out stairwells filled with people trying to escape through the blocked door. In an attempt to prevent the pile-up, he had laminated a sheet of paper that the soldier taped to the glass. It read, 'Anyone caught in this stairwell will be killed.' He hoped that this, coupled with the letters that would be delivered shortly, would be sufficient to discourage people from hiding out in the stairs.

"Building One oceanside stairwell is secure. Note in place. Returning to post."

** Squad Four **

Squad four was three quarters of the way up the right flank. Five of their eight men had taken up defensive positions when they encountered the security guard. He was walking toward the front as instructed by Fahd's diversionary radio call.

Squad four's leader spotted him first and took after him at a jog. Footsteps got his attention; he turned and was met with the barrel of a gun in the light of the parking lot.

"On the ground before I count to three! One! Two!" The guard dropped to his chest in a single fluid motion. "Hands behind your back."

Above them, the squad leader heard voices. He looked up and spotted silhouettes on a balcony, the red ember of a cigarette giving them away. He zip tied the guard's wrists behind his back and then helped him onto his feet, walking him under the cover of the parking garage at the base of Building Four.

"Squad four has made it to the front right corner. We've captured a guard and have a possible compromise. People on a balcony saw me tie him and walk him off."

"We copy squad four. All teams, move to protocol two. I repeat. Protocol two in effect," said Fazul.

Fazul had established three protocols of engagement. Protocol one called for taking prisoners alive whenever possible. Even this protocol allowed for a wide berth of interpretation as was evident in the execution of the couple in the beach bar. Protocol two stipulated that runners and any disobedient prisoners be shot. Protocol three instructed the team to shoot to kill any hostages not in their rooms or corralled in holding pens.

** Squad Three **

Once the restaurant and bar were clear, Ilan and squad three continued up the right side of the main pool. Ilan was watching squad two through the trees in the center of the lazy river. Hassan's team was ahead of them on the opposite side of the water.

Ilan's point man raised a hand and slowed again. He waved Ilan up, pointing to a fat shirtless man smoking a cigar on a lounge chair.

Ilan approached him from behind. He considered shooting him right away as he stepped out in front but he'd felt a pang of guilt over the couple. "Get up."

The man said nothing. He stared at him and took a drag of the cigar.

"Get up, now," said Ilan, enunciating each syllable.

The massive glowing ember on the end of the cigar again grew brighter.

"Fuck it," said Ilan. He lifted the barrel and shot the man in the temple at point blank range. His head lashed to the side from the impact of the bullet but the weight of his rotund body remained planted in the chair. The cigar dropped to his belly, the smell of burnt hair climbing instantaneously to Ilan's nose.

** Squad Two **

On the other side of the promenade, squad two continued forward, leading the charge toward the lobby where Anas could take control of the propaganda machine that would be the hallmark of the operation.

Two more men from the squad were dispatched to secure the ocean side atrium of Building Two. The remaining four pressed up the outdoor walkway. They passed the windows of the empty gym and entered doors next to the concierge desk at the back of the main lobby.

The last of the security guards emerged from the elevators as they came through the door. Hassan drew the butt of his weapon into his shoulder. He slowed, stepping toward the man in gray uniform. The guard tried to hide his confusion and then swallowed hard as Hassan drew closer. At ten yards, Hassan fired a shot through the man's heart. It ricocheted off bone in his back and thudded into the elevator, dark blood peppering the stainless-steel doors as they closed.

The men stopped, all four barrels tracking the body to the floor where they watched the final convulsions of life passing from the guard.

"Let's move," said Hassan.

A corridor linked the back lobby to the main. The men moved up it, the wall to the left concealed the hotel's business office. A blend of voices grew louder as they stalked. They were young voices, bright with energy, couples maybe returning from a night on the town or the casino next door.

"Police! Get on the ground! We're police!" Hassan moved aggressively toward them— two women, two men. "For your safety, please get on the ground!"

Seconds passed as the couples stared dumbstruck, unable to move. One of the women looked at the man to her right. He started for the floor and she dropped, beating him there. The man in back put his hand on the other woman's shoulder and looked poised to turn and run. She was already beginning to crouch as he reached and her shoulder dropped away from his hand. Frozen a moment longer the others, he came to his senses and made his way down to the floor.

Hassan ordered two of his men to secure them and the

other to follow him. He hustled past the group and into the openness of the main lobby.

His eyes were on the front doors as he entered the room but movement caught his attention to the left. A feather duster stirred, then beside it wide eyes—wide eyes that grew to an expression of pure fear as he turned his weapon.

"Police! Come out from behind the desk!" Hassan moved toward the figure. "Come out," he ordered.

She turned for the door to the business office. In three steps, she reached it and pushed it wide on the free-swinging hinge. Hassan pulled the trigger twice in quick succession. The first was short, piercing air where she had been half a second before and tearing into the wall. The second caught up, catching her in the shoulder. It spun her into the doorframe face first and then she dropped out of sight.

Hassan rounded the desk and was above her. The door was propped wide by the wounded woman. He lifted the barrel and scanned the room inside. Two blank sets of eyes stared back.

Hassan stepped inside, tripping slightly on the woman. "On the ground!" he screamed.

Minutes later, the two couples, the manager and the operator had ankles and wrists bound. They were seated along the wall at the edge of the office. Hassan helped the injured woman to her feet and walked her out through the lobby and down the corridor to the guard.

"Move closer," he said. The woman was staring at the guard's body framed by an ovoid of blood. Hassan finished her with a shot to the base of her skull. There was no time to treat the wounded and the bodies would be easier to collect later if they were together.

Hassan activated his mic. "Building Two secure. Six prisoners. One guard and a cleaning woman are down. The path is clear to the security room."

Jamal followed Hassan's transmission. "Entrance blocks in

place. I'll direct any traffic coming in to the garage below Building Three."

Squad one called next. "The left flank is secure, we've taken four hostages coming from the property next door."

Squad four followed in quick succession. "Right flank secure. We're in position."

There was a pause before Fazul's voice cracked over the radio. "Squad three. Status update?"

"All of my two-man teams are in place," Ilan reported. "Buildings three and four are secure."

"Excellent. Good work," said Fazul. "All teams hold your positions. We're moving up to establish the command post."

** The *Contagious* **

Fazul checked his watch. They were right on schedule. The rapid assault had established ground floor control and a solid perimeter in under twenty minutes. Cell phone service was severed by the thermite charges. Fahd had shut down the hotel's phone and internet service before the building was surrounded. As far as Fazul was concerned, his plan to disconnect the hostages from the rest of the world, had gone off without a hitch. Sure, there was the possibility of someone with a satellite phone, but that wouldn't matter. No one knew the magnitude of the force. Any probing police would be easily subdued.

He had ordered Fahd to track activity on the resort over the course of several weeks. The data plotted a circadian rhythm that showed 4 A.M. as the quietest time and ideal start for the raid. There was a clear uptick in activity around 5:30. Vacationers set out for the gym or scurried down to secure the best chairs around the pools by laying out their towels. With just over an hour remaining, the team would need every minute to establish the framework of control that would prevent a blood bath.

The next steps in the plan called for establishing a network of communication that would quell the hostages when they woke. The NJF team was outnumbered by more than 40 to 1. To keep hostages from monopolizing on this advantage, the plan called for fear-based communication that kept them in their rooms. The message... *Stay in your rooms and you will be spared. Venture out and you will be killed.*

Communicating the dire repercussions of trying to escape was no easy task. The announcement needed to reach 1,821 registered guests. Four hundred and eighty apartments, each with two entrances, meant that almost a thousand pieces of paper needed to be delivered. And it needed to get to them before they opened their doors and fled in a panic. But if the plan worked – or rather, *when* the plan worked – victory would be theirs. A resort full of vacationers would wake with the world into a day of infinite history.

PART II

OVERWHELM

13

Surfside Resort, Aruba: Room #1661

A full bladder and one of Izzy's feet pressing against his ribs woke Ross Günther. The room would have been pitch-black if not for the nightlight Maddie had packed. Being a water Nazi might keep your skin clear, but it also meant a trip or two to the toilet each night. He pulled his phone from the charging cord as he stood and then tiptoed around the bed and into the bathroom.

Maddie's message glowed on his lock screen, along with two Facebook update notifications and a junk email that had come in after he went to bed.

Snuggling with Izzy was great, even if it meant a foot to the ribs when she turned sideways in the night, but he missed Maddie. It seemed like the two of them had spent so much time apart. Less than a year separated them from her retirement from the Marine Corps and his starting his own business. The simple life he had imagined would come from her leaving the military, had been put on hold by him, of all people. He'd preached the importance of keeping the family close while the girls were young. *The cost of a thing is the amount of life you have to exchange for it.* That was his argument when Maddie second-guessed her decision to leave the Corps.

The hospital where he worked was one of the first in the country to implement a true population health strategy. He sold the management team on the concept and led it to profound success. His executive coach convinced him to join the speaking circuit, and in short order, requests for consulting engagements hit his inbox. Ross was a thought leader with street credibility. He suddenly found himself in high demand. One organization sent him a contract proposal and when Ross saw what they were willing to pay for his time, he and Maddie agreed it was an opportunity they couldn't turn down.

He enjoyed the success but a new fear preyed upon his mind each day. Would he miss out on his children's youth the way his father had? He had spent so much time with Izzy while Maddie was away. Things had changed, though. He hadn't made a dinner for his family in months. He hadn't spent much time with Charlotte. Each time he came home from a trip she had grown an inch and was doing something new. These breaks to Aruba were even more important now, key markers in the year. He couldn't wait to see Maddie and Charlotte.

Ross made his way back into the bedroom. Izzy was breathing heavy, both hands squished up under her cheek. Ross repositioned her on the mattress. He pulled the blanket up to her chin then walked to the window and looked out. Dawn hadn't broken yet.

A large yacht, docked at the pier caught his attention. If things kept up and the business kept growing, he might be able to buy one of those for his family someday. But that wasn't the simple life, either. Aruba was enough.

He turned away from the window and sat on the edge of the bed. The phone was still open so he typed out a message. 'Missing you. Can't wait til you get here. Keep us posted on your flight.'

14

SURFSIDE RESORT, Aruba

ANAS FOLLOWED Fazul through the Surfside's lavish pool promenade. A sense of dryness filled the wind blowing down between the buildings. *Smells like a desert*, he thought. Tropical vegetation rimming the oasis was thick but neatly trimmed. He hunched forward from the weight of the pack, the heavy machine gun banging at his knees with each step.

As they passed the edge of the main pool, the view opened enough that Anas noticed the bar on the far side. A square pavilion that was sunken to the level of the pool, three of the four sides were surrounded by water. Vacationers could drink and soak at the same time.

Anas had spent two weeks at the resort. He remembered sitting on the submerged stools sipping obnoxiously-colored frozen drinks. He'd analyzed them all, wondered which, if any, were wealthier than him. As women would pass, he'd eye them and assess from the arrogance of their stride if they'd leave their man for money and mystery. How could they resist a New

Age entrepreneur living life on the edge of the razor? A millionaire riding an escalator to stardom.

The thought was broken by the rustle of palms and bushes on the island at the heart of the lazy river. Anas looked down and forged ahead.

As they moved toward the front of the property, the force of the wind grew. Anas leaned farther forward, trudging into the tunnel of concentrated air slipping through the gap between the buildings. It formed up like the branches of two strong rivers and raced through the opening between buildings two and three.

Fazul was several paces ahead. He opened the door but didn't bother to hold it for his brother. Anas pulled the right-hand side of the double door. He only had one free hand and realized immediately that he'd picked the wrong side. The driving wind resisted the attempt and knocked him back a step. He steadied himself and jammed the butt of the rifle into the glass. The window gonged from the impact, sending a vibration resonating through the atrium. A soldier who had been following Anas grabbed the door and held it open for him.

Anas righted himself in the opening. A bead of sweat dropped from his brow. With his face drawn up in a grimace, the drop skipped off his cheek and landed at the corner of his mouth. The saltiness hit his taste buds as he looked up at his brother. Fazul had watched the struggle. He was shaking his head and smirking.

"What?" asked Anas. "Mind your business, and I'll mind mine."

Behind his brother, a soldier was standing in front of the elevators. Two bodies were splayed motionless on the floor near his feet, in what looked like a pool of dark wax.

Fazul turned and stared down at the death. Anas and the soldier that held the door drew up alongside. All three stared down, everyone silent for a moment.

"This is a bad spot for them," Fazul said. He motioned for Khalid to join them. He was walking toward them from the main lobby. "Drag these out and dump them in the pool." Fazul pointed at the bodies.

The men had pushed the corpse of the cleaning woman up against the guard. The smear of blood was nearly as long as her body and had darkened to a gothic shade of lipstick on the cold floor.

"Sir?" asked the soldier opposite.

"They're already starting to smell, and it's a mess. Put them in the pool for effect. When the resort wakes up there'll be no question if it's true."

Anas turned his head and glared up at his brother. "For effect?" he asked.

"Bodies in the pool at first light will remove any doubt of whether this is real or not," repeated Fazul. He motioned his head toward to main lobby. "Go on and do your thing, Anas. Leave me to the operational decisions." He turned his back to Anas and un-slung his weapon. "I'll watch the elevators while you move the bodies."

Anas stepped around his brother and started to slink up the hall toward the front. Why Fazul felt he had the authority to reprimand him like a child, he would never know. He cleared a crick in his neck that had formed from the pressure of the pack straps. Then he stretched his jaw, noting the telltale fatigue that came from clenching in your sleep due to stress.

Behind him, he heard Fazul say, "Take the woman first."

Anas stopped and turned. Khalid and the other soldier each took one of the cleaning woman's feet. They pulled her away from the guard and spun her in place before sliding her leaking body to the door.

They backed outside. The double doors were heavy on account of the wind. The inside edges pinched down on the small woman's frame and got hung up under her arms. Fazul went to the doors. He straddled the corpse and held them open. Following the shortest path to the pool, the men crossed through a small perimeter garden bed at the edge of the lazy river. They pulled the body up alongside and then dropped her legs. Khalid moved to her side and lifted her shoulders and hips. Her body disappeared from view with a splash.

As Anas walked, he saw the splash of the water arching up into the night—dark drops illuminated by the garden accent lights. *The bodies*, he thought. *How many bodies would it take*? *What would be their net per body*? It was the biggest unknown of the mission, but one thing was certain, his actions over the next thirty minutes would have a major impact on the answers. He shook the thought away and knocked on the door labeled Security.

15

BWI Airport, Maryland

Maddie stared ahead at the green 'E' on the pillar in front of her. Empty roads had cut the forty-minute drive to thirty. She wondered why she always left too early. Before leaving for the airport, there's always a sense of urgency so one builds in extra time. But when one arrives early, they get to sit around for an hour and a half telling themselves how they're going to leave later next time. Then next time comes, and we all do the same stupid shit.

Charlotte was a gem of a baby and had made things easy for her. She'd been as quiet and pliable as a rag doll. Maddie expected a protest from the early morning wake-up, but instead she got a catatonic Char-monster.

She was still asleep in the back and they had time to kill. Maddie fired up her phone. She checked the weather for Oranjestad. It was listed as a favorite in her weather app. Sunny. High of 88. Low of 79. The forecast repeated itself, varying only by a degree one way or the other for the full ten-day forecast.

She tapped her email app and scanned the messages she'd avoided reading yesterday. One thing she hated about civilian work was the damn emails. *Hordes of shit*, she thought. It was no wonder people hated coming back from vacation in the real world. The whole time you're gone, people shovel piles of shit on top of your virtual desk. When you get back, you sift through it by hand to find the nuggets of crap that actually matter.

The subject line, 'Don't forget your self eval,' stood out amongst the rest. *Real world self-evals, a time to document how great you are*. It would have to wait until she returned. She scanned the subject lines piling up.

'Architect request for DLP.'

'Avanti Quantum Contract Review: Endpoint protection platform.'

'Data Loss Prevention MVP ready for stakeholder review.'

'Security Analytics Enhancement Request.'

'Ransomware monthly update.'

'New phishing scheme foils tech giant's $14 million cyber defense.'

The job was good for the most part. It paid almost triple what she had made in the Corps and made her bachelor's degree in computer science suddenly worth the money her parents invested.

Summit Cyber Security provided network protection solutions for some of the biggest companies in the country. They were a boutique firm that added value to off-the-shelf products. They filled the twenty percent gap that the larger security providers couldn't address.

She came across an email with the subject, 'Char-monster Passport,' from Pich Tang. No one called her Char-monster except Maddie. It was her pet name for her easy child. But then again, PTang was like a third daughter.

'I see you make big mistake,' wrote PTang. 'One you never live down. Have fun on vacation,' she'd written.

Maddie snickered. Chuckles was right; karma was coming around to bite her in the ass.

Maddie had officially been hired by Summit through a government placement program that paired retiring service members with private sector jobs. That was true, but PTang was the real reason she got the job.

She'd met Pich during her stint with the United States Cyber Command. She was a civilian contractor and one of the most unique people Maddie had ever met.

A Cambodian immigrant, her parents were an odd couple. The father, a devout defender of the southeast Asian country, fell in love with an American missionary. The product of that courtship was one PTang—small in stature, immense in intelligence.

Her father took up arms in the Cambodian civil war around the time PTang was born. He was a leader with one of several freedom-fighting factions. After his execution, PTang's mother moved them in with his parents. She spent the first eight years of her life living at the edge of a rural Cambodian village in a two-room house with concreate walls and a thatch roof.

When she was eight, PTang's mother received a letter explaining that her father had been diagnosed with Lou Gehrig's disease. They returned to the states to care for a man PTang had never met and who her mother struggled to remember.

Her Cambodian accent never faded and the years it took to polish her English turned her into an outcast in school. She spent hours alone in her room with a pair of computers her dead grandfather left behind. At the age of thirteen, her mother remarried and questions about her real father emerged for the first time. Instead of asking, PTang tracked down all the answers she needed using her computer.

Maddie first worked with her on a Cyber Protection Team, defending priority DoD networks from attack. She was ninety pounds covered in mud, soft spoken and one of the most brilliant technical minds Maddie had ever met.

PTang never asked Maddie why she gave up being a sniper to join cyber command. By then, Madeline Günther was a name the news media had gotten ahold of. She was the first woman to complete the Marine Corps Scout Sniper School. She was the first woman deployed in combat in a sniper role. She had received decorations on par with the most successful snipers in US history. Madeline Günther was a legend.

Only one piece of information hadn't made it into the public eye following her retirement. Why she had left? Maddie believed PTang could read it in her eyes.

Her spotter, Will, was one of the best friends Maddie had ever known. She had a lot of brothers in the Corps—men that respected her for who she was. Military experience creates bonds stronger than DNA. Enduring training cycles brings people together, surviving combat glues them for life.

Will and Maddie had worked as a team, on and off for years. The day he died, Maddie laid down her sniper rifle for the last time.

Her commanding officer was supportive. "You've been of great service to your country. No better person out there to leave the mark you've left. You should be proud," he said. "I'll put in the request for Cyber Command posthaste, with the highest recommendation."

PTang was her online handle. Maddie had been paired with her to learn the ropes.

"She's a little different," explained her new commanding officer. "Certainly a far stretch from what you've been dealing with down range. But she's special. Good at explaining things. Pick her brain. She'll help you understand what we do here. No sugar coating or BS."

In a way, PTang had padded the fall. Her uniqueness, ingenuity and super computer of a brain helped Maddie transition from one pole to the other. They'd become close enough friends that for a time, she was a regular for Sunday dinner at the Günther house. The fact that her contract wasn't renewed added muscle to Maddie's decision to leave Cyber Command and retire from the Corps.

In the months between PTang's departure and Maddie's retirement, she had waivered. The lure of adrenaline called from the back of her mind. Then a teammate from the Corps reached out to her. He had gone to work for a private security firm. He was on a seventeen-month contract. The firm treated him like special operations royalty. They outfitted him with suits and armed him with the most advanced weapons. He worked on a six-man team providing VIP security in Iraq. He was rotated home every other month for a couple of weeks and said it was a good gig. They were looking to add a sniper, and the company was very interested in hiring Madeline Günther.

Maddie had considered it, but she couldn't bring herself to broach the subject with Ross. He was right about her needing to be home with Izzy. Truth be told, she wasn't convinced she could pick up another gun. A week later she realized her period was late and a pregnancy test announced the imminent arrival of the Char-monster.

Maddie looked up from the thoughts. She stared back at the green 'E' then lifted her phone and snapped a picture of it in case she forgot. A look in the mirror took the thought of the security job away. Charlotte's eyes were locked on her. When she connected with her gaze, Charlotte smiled and rubbed the morning from her eyes.

16

Surfside Resort, Aruba: Security Suite

Within five minutes of entering the suite, Anas was in the zone. He bounced in his chair, tapping a beat into the table beneath his computers. The music both calmed his nerves and helped distract his mind. It cut down on errors.

Fahd was in the front room monitoring the security cameras. Anas was set up in the tech suite to the rear. He turned his team radio down to avoid the distraction as he focused on establishing the critical networks that would be the heart and soul of the operation. Fahd would alert him to any relevant information coming from Fazul and the others.

All the wi-fi hotspots and ethernet connections across the resort were routed through the information technology suite where Anas was sitting. He would configure three separate computers from which he'd orchestrate technological control over the mission. One computer was connected to the resort's internal network. All attempts to connect to the internet would lead to this computer, and every request would be met with the same result. Users would be diverted to a static webpage. He modeled the program after software used in hotels and other public locations. It directed web browsers to a specific URL after a connection was established. Once a device was connected and a browser was opened, the user would be taken directly to the website Anas was running on his machine. The hotel's spiderweb of a network began and ended with Anas.

He required only ten minutes to establish this rudimentary network configuration. With the webpage up and running, Anas launch a connection tracking application that would log hits to the site. He programmed it to alert him when the number exceeded one hundred, two hundred and fifty, five hundred and one thousand. They were arbitrary numbers, but would provide a good indication of when the hotel guests were waking and logging into their digital lives. What they would find was a simple webpage that provided concise information on how and why they were now hostages.

Anas's second computer was connected to the internet and would be used to simulcast information to the world through a series of virtual private networks. These secure VPN's connected Anas to a complex of servers around the globe. These machines would disseminate information programmatically and serve as internet hosts to the insanely voyeuristic outside world.

He confirmed the internet connection by typing *Google* into the address bar and verifying that the search engine displayed. Anas double-clicked on an executable titled 'Automated VPN authentication.' He then entered a password into the prompt. The program that launched VPN clients loaded on his machine. It logged him in using an encrypted database of passwords and then ran validation scripts. It routed test messages to the servers, which in turn sent emails and posted test comments to public sites. The program verified the emails and accessed the sites to confirm the posts.

While the program was running, Anas pulled cables and a switch from his backpack. He stood and leaned over the computer, clicking a short cable into the back of the machine. The other end was connected to the switch which included eight additional ports. From the ports, Anas strung a series of cables to other computers in the room. The first was another black laptop that he extracted from his pack. This computer would control the aerial drone network that would be deployed as their eyes in the sky. Access to this computer would provide drone footage that could be captured or shared live with the world.

Next, he connected the hotel security computer to the switch. He'd add himself as a tenant on the network, which would provide access to the cameras around the resort. The last cable he strung was red. He connected one end to the switch and laid the other end next to the computer hosting the internal static webpage. This cable would allow him to download data to the website so the hostages hived above him in the resort buildings could see what was going on outside. He was a professional hacker and knew better than to keep the machines physically connected. He'd only connect it when he needed to move information.

Then, Anas pulled three small black bags from his pack. He unclipped three tripods secured to the outside and went through the door into the security room. Fahd looked up and nodded as Anas passed. Using his elbow to push down on the handle, Anas swung the door to the security suite open.

Khalid and four other team members were stacking sandbags in front of a desk just outside the lobby. They had positioned it a few of feet from the plate glass and where surrounding it with burlap sacks of sand.

Anas nodded to Khalid and held out the equipment.

Khalid dropped the sandbag he was holding on top of the

stack and came inside to Anas. He gathered the equipment into his arms.

"You remember where to set them up?" Anas asked.

Khalid nodded. "One overlooking the patio out by the pool. One on the roof of Building Three, looking down on the pool. And the last one goes on top of Building Four."

"Don't forget, you'll need an extension cord and some sandbags for the top of Building Four," said Anas. "Call me on the radio when you get up there, and I'll help you get the right angle. I want to make sure we get the machine gun nest and the main road to Oranjestad in the picture. It's going to be one of our cover shots."

17

SURFSIDE RESORT, **Aruba: Building One Garage**

FAZUL HEADED for the beach to check on the offload. Having moved into phase two of the operation, his teams were spreading out across the resort. Sandbags were being filled on the beach and carted to defensive positions around the perimeter. They were to start with the ground-level positions and then turn their attention to the rooftops. Fahd had secured the keys to the resort's utility vehicle, which simplified the task.

Fazul stood under the corner of Building One and watched the team of six as they shuttled material from the *Contagious* to the parking area beneath the building. Marwan and Ziad struggled across the beach. The men leaned away from each other as they sifted their way through the soft sand. Between them was a heavy unmarked wooden crate that Anas knew contained two RPK-74 light machine guns. He had been excited to see that they'd received the 'M' variant. 'M' for *Modefitsyrovannyj*, which meant "improved" in Russian. They were the latest production model with black synthetic stocks. Optics had been purchased to mount on the side rails to help the men sight targets from the rooftops thirteen stories up.

"Good work, men," Fazul said when they hit the blacktop of the garage. They shuffled by on their way to a mechanical cage, where the most critical supplies were being loaded. If an altercation broke out that required the full attention of the team, the cage could be locked to secure the most valuable items.

Fazul walked across the lot toward Hani al-Hazmi, who was diligently manning the first security position under Building One. He swept his AKM in a steady deliberate motion, panning the assault rifle from the sandy beach on the left, through the picnic table and grill area to an opening in the concrete wall lining the perimeter. The defensive positions were better than Fazul had imagined. A waist-high wall ran around the outside to mask the lower half of the vehicles parked underneath. The wide concrete foundation made for effective cover and was improved with sandbags stacked nearly chest-high.

Hani's position was open; the parking spaces stopped three-quarters of the way up to make room for the mechanical cage behind him.

"Hani," Fazul called as he approached. Hani spun toward him, the rifle resting high on the sandbags. "All is well?"

"Yes, Fazul. Very quiet, but we are ready."

"Good to hear," Fazul said as he looked to the right. There was a blue car twenty yards away and then several more hoods before the next position. A soldier by the name of Nawaf manned the second post just beyond the path leading to the neighboring property. The two men were close enough to deliver interlocking fire along this stretch of the perimeter.

Fazul stepped up to Hani's left. He ran his hand across the top of the AKM and looked up at the neighboring building. The first three floors were visible. "Once we reach phase four, you'll be responsible for keeping the balconies clear there." He pointed to the rows of ordered cubbies some sixty yards away and rising out of sight.

"Yes, sir. It will be no problem," said Hani.

He turned to go but stopped in thought. "Remember, take any visitors silently until we reach phase four. We need the resort to remain sleeping for just a while longer."

"Absolutely, sir."

Fazul nodded and turned, walking toward the pools at the heart of the complex. His men were ready. A calm focus emanated from them as they worked. His confidence was bolstered by the ease with which the plan was coming together.

He turned his wrist and looked down. They had been on the ground for an hour. With 15 minutes left in phase two, it was time to assess their progress. He pulled the small playbook from his pocket and turned to the first page. He pressed the button on his earpiece and said, "Let me have your attention. We're 15 minutes from the scheduled start of phase three. I want a full status check. Let's begin with perimeter security."

"Building One perimeter ground. We are two men in position. Our fortifications are complete." The report in his headset was a millisecond behind Hani's actual voice, which played faintly in Fazul's open left ear.

"We're a go on Building Two perimeter ground," called another voice.

"Building Three perimeter ground is a go as well."

"Building Four here. The last sandbags are being stacked now. Just a few minutes more and then we're done."

Fazul placed check marks in the margin next to the assignments as they called in. "Very good, perimeter ground. Keep it silent until phase four." Fazul let his pencil drift down the page. "Fortification team. What's your status?"

A broken voice cracked in the headset, just a quick on and

off separated by a panting breath. "We are stacking the last bags here at perimeter ground—" The voice paused, drawing deeply in an attempt to catch his breath. "Finishing Building Four now," he said pausing a second time. "We'll need two more runs to the beach for sandbags going up the elevators."

Fazul built extra time into the schedule but he loathed using it this early. "We must pick up the pace without cutting corners."

Phase three was the most important of the mission. The earlier it commenced, the better. Delivering the letters would be key to preventing a stampede. Fazul was not opposed to violence but he knew that a mass killing early in the mission would demoralize his men.

"We need to keep on schedule. Stay on point. We are doing well, but we must push harder." Fazul studied his playbook again. "Hostage team. Provide status and counts."

The three holding areas reported in. Twenty-one hostages had been taken. Most had come in from the sides of the property and the others were taken from their cars after being directed beneath building three by Jamal. There had been no attempts to resist.

Command post defenses were complete along with Anas's IT tasks for phase two. All eight elevators had been anchored to the ground floor and the cases of additional door blockade bars were pre-positioned and ready for phase three.

On the beach, the two-man defense team was positioned at either end of the beach with instructions to capture or stop anyone crossing in front of the resort. The soldier on the north end had approached an early morning jogger entering his area of responsibility. Attempting to flee, the soldier was forced to cut the man down with his suppressed submachine gun.

Fifteen minutes later, Fazul announced the start of phase three. Six-man teams would ascend each of the four buildings.

They would slip sheets of paper under each door and block the stairwells on either end with the blockade bars as they went. By the time phase three was over, the Surfside Resort would be a prison filled with cowering hostages.

18

SURFSIDE RESORT, Aruba: Room #1661

ROSS'S EYES fluttered as he worked to reconcile the sound that had drawn him from Dreamland. Reaching for the phone, the tap and echo he'd heard repeated in his mind.

It was 5:37 A.M. The message he had sent to Maddie earlier in the night had failed to go through.

A sharp crack rang out, its echo rounding up and out of the U-shaped complex like high-pitched thunder.

Ross looked at the curtains covering the door.

Another crack. Another echo.

He cocked his head and squinted. He could almost feel the shrill crack as much as he could hear it.

Ross stood and threw open the curtains covering the slider to the balcony. He fumbled with the lock and shoved it open.

Crack! The wave of the echo dropped Ross to the ground. He hobbled forward on a knee curling his hands around the metal spindles of the balcony and pulling his face up to look down on the source.

Crack! This time a zipping sound sang into the distance as the echo carried itself up and away from the resort.

"Jesus Christ," Ross said. It was the first time he considered it might be a gunshot.

He pulled himself tighter to the bar, centering his focus down and to the left where there was an opening in the U-shape of the buildings.

A dark figure jogged along the path at the top of the pool by the artificial rocks and waterslide. The figure then walked up to something on the ground.

Is that a body? Ross thought.

The figure in the distance pulled up short of the smudge of darkness on the sidewalk.

Crack! A flash strobed the space from darkness.

With the echo still fading, Ross reopened his eyes and tracked two more figures running toward the first. They formed up close around the body on the ground, standing for a few seconds and then turned and sprinted back in the direction they had come.

Ross held a death grip on the railing. He stared at the still shadow on the sidewalk, then scanned the area to the right.

An object floated into view in the lazy river. Having come around the corner from the opposite side, it glided in the steady man-made current and bumped up against the edge of the pool.

It's a float. It has to be a float, he thought. But it wasn't, and there was no denying it.

Red fear gripped him. He didn't know what was happening but he wanted to run. Run away with Izzy.

"Papa, what was that noise? Why is the door open?" Izzy was sitting up in the bed with the blankets pulled up to her chin.

"It'll be okay, baby. I need you to get up for me. We're gonna put on our clothes. We need to leave."

Isabelle tracked her father to the dresser. "Daddy?'

"Izzy, I don't have time to explain. I'm not sure what's going on, honey. We just need to go and I need you to help me, baby." Ross pulled clothes from the drawers and pitched them behind him onto the bed. "Scooch down to the end of the bed."

Izzy dropped the blankets and complied with her father's request. She clawed her way to the foot of the bed and Ross shimmied the pajamas off her.

A quiet sob formed and then Izzy said, "Where are we going, Papa?" The snivel built into a cry as she drew in shuddered breaths.

Ross grabbed his daughter by the shoulders. He shook her in a way he had never done before.

"I need you to be brave for me, Izzy. We don't have time for crying." He slid his hands down to his daughter's wrists and pulled her from the bed. "We need to go!"

19

Surfside Resort, Aruba: Security Room

"Someone tell me what's happening!" Fazul yelled into his microphone, his irritation unmasked. "The entire resort is awake. Prepare for resistance. Protocol three in effect. Order everyone back into their rooms and shoot any who do not comply."

"This is Building Two perimeter ground. A hostage ran from the main lobby. He headed for the road. I ordered him to stop. I fired twice. Jamal cut him off and turned him back toward the center of the resort. I finished him there."

Fazul had watched the execution on the security screen. He was standing above Fahd monitoring his men as they worked their way up through the floors of the resort buildings. Sixteen of the men were armed with silenced weapons. They were only needed for the night invasion when maintaining quiet was critical. The small submachine guns were not as powerful or psychologically terrifying as the high-powered AKM assault rifle that had just woken the resort.

The problem was that Fazul had hoped to avoid firing any unsuppressed weapons until they reached phase four. By then all the pamphlets would have been delivered and the noise would have been reinforcement instead of a compromise.

How had the fool guard let one get out? Fazul pushed his way out of the security suite and into the main lobby.

Assad, the youngest team member, was standing by the door to the main office. The boy had clearly known Fazul would come for him.

"What's *your* excuse?" Fazul pulled his pistol from the holster beneath his arm and held it by his side.

"The bathroom. I'm... I'm so sorry, Fazul."

"The bathroom!" yelled Fazul. He raised his hand and stepped up, bringing it down against the side of Assad's face. The weight of the pistol sent the boy to the floor.

"Piss on the floor. Do not leave your post!"

20

SURFSIDE RESORT, **Aruba: Building One, Sixth Floor**

HASSAN and his team stopped in their tracks when the faint thumps of gunfire echoed their way into the stairwell. They moved up to the sixth floor as the communication with Fazul uncovered the source. Hassan was still calculating the implications as they opened the door.

An Indian man stood outside his room, just four doors up the hallway. Wearing a dark red robe, he looked on in amazement. His eyes widened as they darted between their masks and the weapons they were holding.

Halfway up the hall, a man and small child bolted from their room. The man locked eyes with Hassan and then turned and ran, dragging the child behind him.

Hassan activated his mic and spoke calmly. "We've only made it to the sixth floor in building one. We've got people in the halls. They're running away from us. Press them back to their rooms from the other side."

"We copy. We're entering the atrium now," came a voice in reply.

Stairwells bookending the buildings were each assigned two men. One provided cover, looking up the stairs for anyone descending. The other secured the door blockade bars. They held the bar in place with one hand and used the other to mark the six holes in the blocks with a Sharpie. Then he set it down and bored the holes using a powerful cordless driver equipped with a diamond tipped masonry bit. They had practiced it hundreds of times on the walls of the seafood sorting facility. Each hole took just seconds to open. The bar would be held back in place and the top two bolts screwed a few turns by hand. Then a second cordless driver slung over the shoulder would drive the bolts home.

The doors were designed to open into the stairwell so that panicked guests could just push them open in an emergency. With the blockade bars in place, there was no escaping. The heavy threads of the titanium bolts held fast to the concrete and prevented the doors from opening.

Hassan and two other soldiers stood inside the hall as the bar was secured behind the door at their backs. The men on his left and right wore bags filled with pamphlets. Hassan provided cover as they worked their way up the halls. They stood ready, waiting for a knock from behind before starting down the hall.

At the far end of Building One, the other two-man stairwell team was already in position on the sixth floor. The cover man protected the stairs while the other stepped inside burnishing his weapon. His job was to ward off hostages as Hassan's team worked their way down the hall toward him. Once they arrived, the soldier would step back inside and ready the holes while Hassan and his men covered from the inside. Once the holes were prepared, they'd move into the stairwell and wait until the bar was secure before moving up to the next floor.

Hassan and his men would work each hall moving between

the opposite stairwells and the pairs of men assigned to protect them. This systematic process was designed to lock down the floors, one at a time, from the bottom up. Any hostages who left their rooms were herded back inside as the men made their way to the top floor.

The teams working Buildings Two, Three and Four were nearing the top floors when the shots rang out. They had made short work of it and descended the stairwells after all the pamphlets were delivered and the final blockade bars were secured in place.

Hassan's team had been delayed because his men were tasked with sandbag fortification. The task had run overtime and was not complete when Fazul initiated phase three. Their late start would plague them now.

"Go!" The voice from behind the door was followed by a knock. It was indication that the blockade bar was in place and they could begin moving up the hall.

The Indian man retreated, the lock mechanism of the door echoing in the hall as he secured the deadbolt.

"Let's move," said Hassan.

21

SURFSIDE RESORT, **Aruba: Building One, Sixth Floor**

ROSS PULLED Isabelle back to her feet at least twice as he yanked her down the hallway. He was operating on pure instinct now, instinct that instructed him to run the other direction when he saw the masks and guns at the end of the hall. They looked like Halloween skeleton costumes. One was all black, but the other two had flags painted on the front. One had the Union Jack painted across its face. The other looked like the stripes of the Dutch flag. He didn't want Izzy to see them. Ross would beat them to the stairwell next to the elevators. His habit of checking exits in hotels and on airplanes might actually pay off.

As they approached the elevator atrium, a lone masked man stepped out into the hall and pointed his black rifle at Ross. His mask bore the stars and stripes of the United States.

"Back to your room!" he commanded.

Ross stopped, Izzy slamming into his back. Before Ross could turn, Izzy caught a glimpse of the man and released a penetrating scream. Ross hefted her up into a bear hug and turned for their room.

"Daddy, what is that?" The screams pierced Ross's eardrums.

Several doors opened. People poked their heads into the hall.

"Back in your rooms! All of you!" The orders came from both sides.

The three masked men at the other end of the hall were making their way toward Ross and Izzy now. The one in the middle seemed to be protecting the other two as they pulled papers from messenger bags and slid them under the doors.

Their room was too far. They would have beaten Ross to it even if he ran. He just wanted to get back inside—back behind the protection that he'd given up so easily.

He moved to a door that had closed a moment before, the occupant retreating at the sight of the masked men. Ross tried the handle but it was locked. He banged on it with his fists.

"Open. Please open the door and let us in!" he yelled.

"Back in your room. Now!" The man near the elevators was closer than the others. He took several steps then lifted the rifle to his shoulder as Ross watched.

Ross leaned on the door. "Please. My daughter!"

"Go to YOUR room," ordered the man. Izzy screamed again then panted sounds of fear into her father's shoulder. Out of options, Ross turned and made his way back toward their room.

The three men at that end were past his room now, though. He slowed and pointed the hand that had been across Izzy's back.

"My room is there. I'll go back if you'll let us pass."

"Put the girl down." The man in the middle with the British mask motioned toward the floor.

Ross hesitated, and then released the grip on his daughter.

Izzy clung more tightly as she began sliding down her father's body.

"No, Daddy! No! Don't put me down." She clung to her father like a feeding tick.

Ross lowered her to the floor. He bent forward and kissed her head.

"It's okay, honey. It's going to be okay. I'm still right here."

He straightened and focused on the only part of the man that felt human, his auburn eyes. He felt the rippling tremors of fear run down to the floor of his body as the masked man stepped up and reached out.

Ross took a step back. "Don't touch her!"

The men distributing the papers had stopped and raised their rifles. The one in the middle looked down and closed in quickly, grabbing Izzy by the shirt collar.

"Get your hands off my daughter." Ross instinctively reacted to the fear of death that coursed inside him. He stepped forward with all his 200+ pounds and pushed the man backwards.

From the either side, unseen hands flew to his chest, the lackeys on either side stepping up to defend their lieutenant.

"Calm down! Now," said the man in the middle as Ross's back hit the wall.

The underlings had pulled up close in front, and for an instant, Ross thought about going for one of their guns. But he was separated from Izzy, and that pushed the adrenaline in his body to hysterical levels. He turned and swam passed the two men, nearly falling to the floor in an attempt to thread the only open path to his daughter.

A pop of pain shocked his left temple. The carpeted floor rushed up and then disappeared, replaced by white tracers streaming across blackness. He felt the friction of carpet heating his cheek and caught the front end of another of Izzy's piercing screams.

22

12,500 Feet above the Southern Caribbean

Madeline's flight had been in a holding pattern for 15 minutes when the pilot announced that they were cleared to land. Sitting stock-still for the better part of five hours had stiffened her joints and made her insanely restless. The flight had gone better than she expected. Traveling with kids was like everything else kid-related; people made it out to be worse than it was.

The Char-monster had been downright pleasant for most of the trip. For the first hour and a half, she played with toy shakers and chomped on puffs. She'd slept through most of the second half. There was just one tiny piece there in the middle that had Maddie sweating.

A baby's fussiness always starts out as a hint. Whether you're looking and listening for it is the key.

Two women and one young man were working the flight. The fit steward kept coming by to check on Maddie. His tepid smile lingered on beyond professional courtesy. It had Maddie's mind running enough that she'd missed the signs. Was he checking her out?

The frustration blossomed in Charlotte and unfortunately for Maddie, she hadn't picked up on the early cues. She had broken into a full cry before Maddie realized it was time to change her diaper and feed her a bottle. Ross would have laid out the plan halfway through the first whimper. It was times like that when Maddie realized just how much their roles were reversed from the norm before she walked away from the Corps.

What sucked the most was changing a squirming baby on a foldout tray table in the closet of a bathroom. There's nothing quite like swapping a baby diaper in an airborne port-a-potty. Luckily for Maddie, the dry diaper helped. Charlotte had calmed down a few notches by the time they were done—enough that the scowls had turned to grins, mostly.

Maddie kept Charlotte in the Baby Bjorn for most of the flight. She hung from her chest like a kangaroo joey. She'd never gotten used to wearing the baby. Being hands-free had obvious benefits, but there was just something about it that never sat quite right.

Fuck what anyone else thinks. She repeated the mantra as she made her way back to her seat.

Maddie had brought a Tervis Tumbler and a thermos of hot water to heat the bottle. She'd mix up the formula in the bottle, fill the Tervis with hot water and then float the bottle to heat it. It was a technique she and Ross had used for years. Typically a two-person operation, she had to hold the Tervis between her feet and pour the steaming water from above.

After she floated the bottle someone said, "Semper fi, Mommy-o."

When Maddie stretched for the cup, her shirtsleeve rode up and exposed a portion of the small Eagle, Globe and Anchor tattooed on her right shoulder.

She hesitated to look back. She knew who it was. The smell of the stale cigarette smoke entrenched in the man's clothes had been nauseating since they took-off.

Maddie glanced back over her shoulder, eyeing the overweight hustler. He was leaning back, his feet in the isle and his face drawn up into a Robert De Niro expression. The woman next to him had overapplied her makeup. She was half his size but twice as weathered. The man had killed a half a case of potato chip bags and they both had been ordering miniatures of tequila to mix with their orange juice.

"Were you in the Corps?" the man asked.

Maddie nodded. "Yeah. You?"

"Nah. Not me. I got 'spect for the leathernecks, though. Specially a woman leatherneck."

Maddie stared ahead at the tray table. *Too bad you don't have any respect for yourself*, she thought. She considered several inappropriate responses but then remembered the bottle and checked it to see if it was warm.

Maddie unclipped the carrier and held Charlotte in her lap. She polished off the bottle.

After she was done, Maddie cradled her on her chest, Izzy's head again resting in the notch between her neck and shoulder. After she was limp, Maddie lowered her back down into the carrier and secured the clips.

Charlotte drifted in and out of sleep, opening her eyes a crack to look up at her mother. She would have been lost to the nap right away if it weren't for the crinkle of chip bags coming from behind.

Semper fi, Mommy-o. The words played on her mind. Her two extremes. The yin and the yang of her life. Overseas she wore a helmet and combat gear adorned with the tools of war. Now she was wearing her baby. Being a parent was sort of like war—a series of battles and skirmishes strung together into a fight for a common objective—remaining sane. Both activities required a great deal of maneuvering to accomplish the mission. Lots of gear. Lots of planning. Lots of stamina. But the parental battles required a higher degree of psychological acumen. Success wasn't linked to the number of rounds you'd sent down the target range. It was on-the-job training.

Maddie's military occupational specialty had been 0317, United States Marine Corps Scout Sniper. In the civilian world she'd lost the numeric designator and was a director of product management for a cyber security firm. In the life that mattered, her identifier was 02—mother. Second in command to 01, her husband. Maddie was getting back to being a mom, but Ross was still the natural caregiver of the family.

Maddie hadn't really gone looking for any of the jobs. Drifting from one phase of life to the next was more her style. Looking back, she never considered herself the motherly type. After she returned from her first overseas tour, Ross brought it up. At first she'd said no. How could a Marine get pregnant? But then, over the next couple weeks, some type of internal clock clicked and what started in her mind as a maybe had become a full court press. Men in the Marines had babies, probably more than they needed. If they could do it, so could she.

Like most aspects of her life, Maddie hadn't needed to weigh the pros and cons.

"I thought about it, and you're right. We should have a baby."

Ross had smiled. "When does practice start?"

Eleven months later, Isabelle Margaret Günther was born. It didn't take long for Maddie to realize that the fundamentals she learned in the Marine Corps were also the keys to being a good mother. Brilliance in the basics, master of routine, dedication to the craft, preparation, independence—that's what it took to prevail.

Now she was a mom with a tattoo that told a story of her past. It was designed to minimize the reservations she might feel in later life when she turned her shoulder to the mirror. Smaller than the ones the guys got, the stylized double sig rune was hidden inside the globe. It was missed by the frequent faint glance, which was the point, but if you looked closely, the 'SS' that resembled the insignia of Nazi Germany, was hidden with purpose.

Scout Sniper—'SS'. A symbol with a bad reputation, it denoted their close fraternity. Homage to the Reich it was not – merely a differentiator, a symbol like so many others that set them apart from the rest.

Becoming a scout sniper and donning the 'SS' was almost as accidental as becoming a mother. She'd never set her sights on being the first female sniper. Hell, she figured they'd probably keep her out of combat. But times were changing fast in the military for women.

There were plenty of men in her unit that graded out as rifle experts, but Maddie cleaned up table one with less effort than most. A charismatic shooter, her father had taught sound fundamentals. The lessons had stuck with Maddie.

The unit paid tribute to the top tier shooters. Scores were posted and the best highlighted to garner competition. It no doubt made the boys try harder, but each time she placed in the top three, taking the ribbon on several occasions. Being a shooter is what earned her the respect.

She volunteered to work the coach's course for her battalion. Being around the range lifted Maddie from above average to unbeatable. Her battalion held an annual screener event to weed out the best of the top scorers. Fifty-three started. Twelve remained after 24 hours. Nine made it to the end and six were offered bids. Maddie received top billing.

"LOOK AT THE SMOKE." Maddie was woken by one of the two young sisters sitting inside of her and Charlotte. The parents and a brother were sitting in the row directly behind them. Maddie leaned and half stood, cradling Charlotte in the carrier on her chest. She knew the approach to the airport well, usually sitting by the window excited for a first glance of turquoise.

Outside she could see the island spreading out beyond the left wing of the plane. In the distance, the arid center was brown and uninhabited. As her eyes walked toward the bottom of the window, the density of the buildings grew. In the foreground, she picked up the Taj Palace, an Indian-inspired resort with curved turrets and a profile that matched the Taj Mahal. It was three resorts up the beach from the Surfside.

A sliver of Caribbean blue framed the bottom of the window. The girls were still pointing as the plume of black smoke came into view. It took a handful of seconds for Maddie's mind to realize she was looking at the Surfside. She had been fixated on the black column that appeared as an opaque brushstroke. For an instant, the pools in the center sparkled when the angle of the sun and its reflection lined up with the plane.

The buildings surrounding the oasis looked like elongated shoeboxes from this altitude. Rectangles at right angles made the resort look like a block letter "U." The plane was over the water and the fire producing the tarry plume was obscured by the building at the bottom on the U. The smoke was curling up and over the edge of the building in front. The vertical column quickly flattened into a fading horizontal line where the wind caught and dispersed it, playing it out toward the beach. It looked like a car fire had broken out.

Maddie leaned farther forward, trying to eyeball the origin of the fire as the angle changed. The plane continued down the beach and the smoke rising above the resort retreated back and out of view.

The island locals would probably have it cleaned up by the

time they landed and drove up island to the resort. As long as it didn't burn the building down, it ought to be alright.

In those final few minutes, her mind was locked on Ross and Izzy—and the cold beer that'd be waiting for her. It had been a long strange trip, but she'd made it unscathed.

"Ladies and gentlemen, listen up, please." The captain keyed the mic after the airliner had completed its landing roll and was taxing back toward the terminal building. "We've received more information on why we were placed in the holding pattern. Airport officials are telling us that there is some type of emergency on the island. Deplaning passengers will be asked to remain in the terminal. We'll know more when we hit the gate."

23

Surfside Resort, Aruba: Building Three Rooftop

Smoke wafted above Ilan's head as he made his way from the roof access door. Two fractured craters in the asphalt marked the RPG rounds that had missed. The one in front had thrown the patrol car into a skidding stop. Behind it, another hole was evidence of a rushed aim and a wasted round. Center mass in the windshield, spiderwebbed fragments of glass surrounded a baseball-sized hole. The kill shot looked to have clipped the dashboard before detonating. Fire ensued. The glass was melting and the vehicle would soon be a blackened skeleton. Brackets that held the rotating light fixture were vague evidence that it had been operated by the island police.

To his right, down the main island road, Ilan could see evidence of a barricade. Whirling red and blue lights blocked the road. "Command post. Do you copy?"

"5 by 5. Go with your status and recommendation." Fazul was in the information technology suite with Anas, leading their response to the police's first attempt to investigate and secure the scene.

Ilan leaned into the wind with the binoculars. He let go with one hand and double-clicked his earpiece to open the comm. "Two more patrol cars are stopped on L.G. Smith. Maybe four or five hundred meters." The highway was named after the first oil company president that brought commerce to the island. "I see three men. Maybe a fourth in one of the cars." Ilan panned to the right, sweeping the Palm Beach Plaza Mall. "Rooftops in the mall look clear."

"What's your assessment of an airburst shot?" asked Fazul.

Ilan panned back to the patrol cars. "It might work."

The High Explosive RPG rounds they had been supplied had a slow burning fuse that was lit on launch. Operating on a time delay, the slow burning material required four to five seconds. When it reached the end, it would ignite the charge and catapult a hail of steel fragments forward with devastating effect.

"We'll give it a try." Ilan clicked off his mic this time.

Ilan stood to the left of the soldier and extended his arm along the length of the weapon. They took aim several inches above the vehicles. A pat on the man's shoulder was Ilan's way of authorizing the firing. He squatted down and covered his ears.

Enveloped by a flash of light, Ilan and the weapons operator closed their eyes as the compressed gas in the booster sent the round jetting from the launcher. A fraction of a second later, the piezoelectric fuse ignited the rocket motor and a trail of whitish blue-gray smoke marked the warheads path toward the target.

Ilan counted in his mind. *One elephant, two elephant.* Stunned by the force of the weapons launch, he started the count late. A charge of light met their eyes. It was folding into an expanding orb of smoke as the concussion reached their ears. A second later, a sound that reminded Ilan of microwave popcorn rolled past them. The explosion had erupted some distance in front of the cars but the fragments had clearly impacted the metal of the vehicle frames.

Ilan stood and lifted the binoculars to assess the results. A haze drifting in the sightline obscured the view but a smear of oxblood red stood out on the hood of the left vehicle. On the ground, a form crawled away, inching toward the back for cover.

"The round detonated short but the fragments landed," Ilan reported. "There's movement, but the message has been clearly sent."

24

Queen Beatrix International Airport, Aruba

"Everyone is to remain here in the gate area." The woman's voice sounded digitized by the megaphone in her hand. She repeated the statement in a humdrum voice with undertones of a Caribbean accent.

Maddie looked around the heads of the passengers in front of her, trying to get a read on the situation. The rounded top of the police cap with its blue sash and turned up brim was indication that the woman was law enforcement. She wore a baby blue button up, standard attire for the island police. The pips on her collar were barely visible. She was probably pulled from meter maid duty or working one of the busy intersections in Orjanestad. When the megaphone dropped from her face, Maddie read a seriousness that sent warning flags racing up the pole.

Standing beside her was a signpost of a man wearing a khaki suit. His smile was so contrived it looked like it hurt.

Perspiration glistened on his brown cheeks and he swiped at his forehead with the back of his hand.

Maddie wanted it to be procedural. It was a natural tendency to harp on the myriad obstacles while traveling—especially when you had been in transit for over eight hours. The elusive fucking Balashi shimmered in her mind, the sweat dripping down the bottle, the amber liquid egging her toward the figment of a finish line. But something was up.

The plume of black smoke and a quote one of the trainers had used during sniper training, continued to push her from frustration to uneasiness. *Coincidence is the word we use when we can't see the levers and pulleys.* Her inner voice suppressed the panic fighting toward the surface. Ross and Izzy were out there. Were they stuck at the hotel? Were they waiting in the car wondering where the hell she was?

"Once everyone has deplaned, we'll brief you on our situation," announced the policewoman.

Charlotte squirmed in the carrier. Maddie moved to the window, bouncing her in the chest sling. In the distance, across the tarmac and runway, the water of the sea was a mix of electric capri blue and a comforting azure where the clouds threw shadows down on the surface. Over and over her mind triangulated lines from the smoke to the airplane window to the airport where she now stood.

The Aruba triangle, she thought.

Turning back, she scanned the mezzanine above. This was where departing passengers checked their bags, navigated the security checkpoints and then descended stairs to the lower level and the gates. Two uniformed officials stood sentinel at the top of the steps looking down on the new arrivals. To her left, a fourth stood at parade rest by the entrance to the hallway leading out to immigration and baggage claim. They didn't want anyone leaving.

Only three of the gates were visible from where Maddie was

standing. They were all crowded with frowning faces. Televisions in the gate area were switched off. The whole scene put her senses on high alert.

She reached into her pocket and pulled out her phone. There were still no messages from Ross. The last Maddie had received was the one he had sent before bed. She dialed Ross's number and held the phone to her ear. Seconds of silence were broken by an "all circuits busy" message.

Military mode began to take over, two years of rust shaking to the ground like imaginary glitter.

FAMILIAR FACES from the back rows of the plane crowded in around Maddie. Her attention was on khaki suit, who had turned his back to the group and lifted a phone to his ear. Maddie watched him pace behind the policewoman.

She cut the crowd, her eyes locked on the officer.

"Excuse me, ma'am." Maddie turned sideways allowing Charlotte to eye the woman. "We've been traveling for eight hours. My husband is waiting out front. Is there any way we can be let go to meet him?"

The woman eyed the baby, smiling for the first time since Maddie entered the terminal.

"You have kids?" Maddie asked, turning further to give her a better view.

The woman flashed a wedding band.

"No, ma'am. Just married three months ago." She reached out and touched the lip of the carrier pulling it down for a better look at Charlotte. "One day. Soon," she said.

"Would it be okay? For us to go on through?"

The woman looked up at Maddie, who put on her best motherly smile.

Suddenly, the policewoman looked past Maddie toward the

gangway, the grin melting away as business returned to her face.

"No, ma'am. Please step back." She motioned with her hand.

Khaki suit stepped up from behind and tapped her on the shoulder. He leaned down and whispered in her ear. She nodded twice then lifted the megaphone. Khaki suit moved back, watching from the side, ready to analyze the words from his appointed mouthpiece.

"Ladies and gentlemen, we regret to inform you that we have... We have an emergency situation." She enunciated each syllable carefully. "Violence has been reported in the Palm Beach high-rise district. Until further notice no one is being allowed north of Oranjestad." She paused, lowered the megaphone and licked her lips. "I repeat, no one is being allowed north of Oranjestad at this time. The low-rise and high-rise areas will not be accessible until further notice." She stopped and looked back at khaki suit. He nodded.

The low and high-rise districts constituted almost all of the tourist real estate on the island. There were a few hotels in Oranjestad and some rentals across the island, but the districts deemed off-limits where the epicenter of tourism.

"If either of these districts was your destination, please move over here." She pointed to her left. A man waved from the corner at the end of the terminal. "If your destination is elsewhere, then stay in this area, please." Maddie remained still, reading the frightened eyes of the cop and khaki suit. The herd behind her parted and murmured.

Maddie turned to watch the majority migrate toward the corner. The loud tourist outfits were being corralled out of the way. Pushed to the side, they'd be dealt with later. Maddie felt the lie coming on. Suddenly she sensed the folded immigration form in her pocket. It listed the Surfside as their final destination. She needed to be a local. But how?

As far as she knew, there weren't any hotels or resorts along the southeast coast of the island. She had no workable excuses for not following the herd.

Maddie turned her back to the policewoman. The crowd had thinned to a dozen curious faces. Mostly shades of tan, the few white faces topped European outfits – the cultural hodgepodge that remained either lived on the island or had family they were visiting.

Neighborhoods close to tourist town housed the resort managers and the few wealthy locals who benefited from them. The rest commuted in from the city and shantytowns to the south and east.

Maddie moved to the back of the pack, her intuition landing on Kavita. It was worth a try. She typed 'Kavita's Café' into the browser on her phone. They didn't have a webpage, but the Trip Advisor entry would do. It was listed #1 out of 6 restaurants in San Nicolas.

"Kavita's Café. How may I help you?"

"Is this Kavita?" Maddie asked.

"Yes, ma'am. How may I help you?"

"Kavita, this is Madeline Günther."

There was a moment of silence. "Yes, Maddie. Ross and Isabelle were here yesterday. Have you arrived? We've just now started hearing about the violence."

"Charlotte and I just landed and they're telling us no one is allowed up into the tourist area. They're not giving us any information. I need your help. What's going on?"

"Geert has been watching the news here in the restaurant. No one seems to know exactly. Only images of smoke by your resort." The worry in her voice sharpened the edges of her words.

"Kavita?" Maddie hadn't formulated the complete question.

"Yes?"

"Kavita, would you or Geert be willing to come and pick me

up from the airport? I'll tell immigration I'm staying with you and your family."

A pause.

Maddie continued, "I'm concerned they'll keep me here. The baby and I. We'll be stuck. Would you come and get us?" she asked.

Behind her, the policewoman was talking again. Something about the group forming a line and following her. She turned and took up a position at the back of the line. On the phone, she could hear Kavita talking to Geert, their voices volleying back and forth.

"He's leaving now, Maddie. Look for his white work truck. Fifteen minutes."

25

Surfside Resort, Aruba: Security Room

Anas had literally jumped to his feet when the first RPG round exploded. He'd cringed at the second and third, scared they were under attack and he'd be captured. It wasn't until after Fahd told him they'd taken out a police car that Anas had started to settle down.

Since then, sporadic rifle reports had been thumping at the walls of the information technology suite. The RPG explosions sounded like fireworks going off right outside his door. The rifle shots were softer. His headphones could almost drown them out. Almost. He tried to ignore the ones he heard but he couldn't help thinking that they sounded like the pounding of fists begging for freedom. The pit of his stomach churned with each one. They picked at him like nagging taps on the shoulder. Each shot carried, not just the potential for another dead hostage, but also a psychosomatic hit of hormone-borne anxiety that increased the chance he'd make a mistake.

Through the door, Fazul's voice barked commands and

requested updates. Hostages on the lower floors had acted exactly as Fazul had expected. They tied blankets together and tried to climb down. Some simply jumped and one enterprising individual pushed out a mattress to soften the landing.

Anas had talked about this several times. In this situation Fazul was to order his men out into view to stop the escape attempts. Instead he'd kept them back undercover and had them pick off the escapees one at a time. Anas was happy to hear that the escape attempts were dwindling now. The crumpled bodies lining the perimeter served to dissuade the others.

Earlier in the morning, Anas had watched with Fahd from the security room. The cameras captured images of the bodies dropping awkwardly to the ground, the report of the AKM whomping through the room a fraction of a second later.

Seven billion people walk the earth, he remembered being told. *Where was the harm in five hundred or a thousand lost for the cause?*

Mega corporations kill millions each year, infecting them, condemning them to a gradual death at the hands of capitalism. Better to be transparent than to hide the truth. It didn't erase the foul taste in his mouth, though—a metallic funk reminiscent of the iron-like flavor of a papercut sucked clean. He wished he'd packed gum or mouthwash.

Anas leaned in toward his main computer. Automating the processes ahead of time had been the single most helpful point of preparation. He didn't have to think, which was good, because his mind felt clouded by a physical pressure that bore down from just inside his skull.

He watched the final steps in the propaganda distribution program stream by. Command subtitles embedded in the code flashed across the screen. The names of international news media outlets popped up followed by the same two words: 'email sent.' Twitter feeds were updated. Social media posts entered. Then the script slowed as it reached the final steps. 'Enable website hosts.' The words hung on the screen for two seconds then country names flew by with the suffix, 'website online.' Argentina, Romania, Ireland, Finland. The list continued. Information on the happenings at the Surfside Resort in Aruba was flying around the world at the speed of light. Every corner of the globe would be given an opportunity to partake in the horror of this real-world show. Each tick of the clock brought human civilization closer to a new, more gruesome reality. And it all started here in this compact room, cast to the world as long lines of ones and zeros.

A bell chimed. The computer on Anas's right was sending out an alert ping. Drone number three was picking up heat signatures.

Four drones were deployed at any given time. Each was programed to patrol one side of the resort. They'd been in operation for less than an hour.

The cameras hanging on the drones recorded both visible and infrared wavelengths simultaneously. Anas had coded a screen reading application that scanned the displays from the thermal imaging cameras. Reds, oranges and yellows indicated warmer temperatures—more heat and infrared radiation being emitted.

Blood-orange oblongs on the screen attracted Anas's attention. He toggled the display from infrared to image view. Anas paused the drone, stopping its movement along a preprogrammed course.

It was over the Palm Beach Plaza Mall. Skirting along the outside boundary of the open-air mall, it had detected a team of men dressed in black tactical gear. They were making their way along the edge of the interior wall closest to L.G. Smith Boulevard.

"Fazul! We have a problem," Anas yelled.

Fazul was through the door and above Anas in seconds.

Anas's finger pointed to the screen. He zoomed the camera, tightening down on the team of six.

"Where is this?" asked Fazul.

Anas panned out. "L.G. Smith is here." He ran his finger along the line and over the two damaged police cars still blocking the road. "This is the road running between us and the mall." Anas traced a line running perpendicular to the main road. "The movie theater is here." Anas pointed to the rounded dome that marked the entrance. "We are here. Off the screen."

"Attention." Fazul had activated his headset. "We have a tactical team assembling in the mall to our south. Building Four rooftop, focus your sights on the movie theater and walkways on either side. Reserve team one, form up at the base of building four, ocean side. Reserve team two, take the island side of building four. We may have a fight on our hands."

All that the local authorities knew at this point was that one of their patrol cars had been obliterated in front of the resort. Two others had taken damage from an RPG round fired from the top of the buildings. They had moved into action faster than Fazul had expected. Deploying their meager tactical team this early in the engagement was a contingency Fazul had considered, but had not deemed likely.

Fazul produced a laminated map and spread it out on the desk beside Anas. He ran his finger over it. "We can flank them here," he said. "The trees here will provide cover of their advance."

The area between the Surfside and the mall was cordoned into two separate spaces. On the island side, closest to L.G. Smith Boulevard, there was the concrete skeleton of an unfinished high-rise. As his finger moved toward the ocean, Anas could see the service access road that led from the mall down to the Surfside. On the opposite side of the road was a stand of trees masking a parking lot and a series of tennis courts for the neighboring Holiday Inn.

"We can run a team up along these trees and into the mall here." Fazul pointed to an open spot in the exterior row of stores that provided pedestrian access to the internal courtyard. "As they come around the corner here, they'll have a line of sight and the element of surprise. An element we lose if we wait for them to approach."

Anas wasn't comfortable with jumping into attack mode so quickly. "Fazul, the websites are operational. As we speak, the information is being read. It will not be long before the island officials are made aware of the repercussions of a tactical assault. They will call it off." As Anas spoke he was bringing up one of the many websites now active on the internet. "Look here." Anas pointed to the top of the screen. A description explained that the Surfside had been taken over. A bulleted list detailing the rules of engagement followed. Bullet number one read, "Any action on the part of island authorities or other nations to infiltrate and take back the resort will be repelled. Punishment for such actions will be the public execution of hostages. The number executed will be determined by the scale of the attempt."

Fazul slapped the back of Anas's head. "Why must you insist on being soft?" Anas looked up, anger etched in his face.

Fazul pounded his fist on the map. "And what is your plan when they make it to the construction site?" He leaned closer, repelling Anas's anger with his stare. "What then? What then... if they are not pulled back?" The question was rhetorical, the pause momentary. He pointed to the unfinished building on the map. "This is our weakness. This is their target. Occupying this building would be a victory for them." Fazul traced a line from the theater to the unfinished building. "Their eyes will be here. Our men will be here." His finger slid to the opening in the internal courtyard. "They will not see the attack coming."

Fazul activated his comm. “I’m on my way out to brief the reserve teams on our plan to eliminate this threat. Five minutes.”

“Look at me, Anas.” Fazul again leaned down, having regained his composure. “We cannot merely hope they are called off and watch them take the building. The fight must be taken to the enemy.”

26

US Consulate's Office, Curacao

Margaret Baker leaned on the mahogany desk. She tapped her pen on the Brazilian wood grains and stared at a painting of Franklin Delano Roosevelt that hung on the opposite wall. The Consulate General for the Caribbean Netherlands, it was a post she'd been appointed to only seven months prior. Her mission presided over diplomatic relations with Curacao, St. Maarten, Bonaire, Saba, Aruba and St. Eustatius.

Reports had started rolling in from Aruba an hour earlier. The first had come from a deputy police commissioner Margaret had worked with on a rape case. Irma Peterson had been the Head of Aruba's Criminal Investigation Unit for ten years. The woman who had been raped was a US citizen; the assailant, an Aruban national. Margaret was wise enough to keep personal tabs on the progress of the case. The perpetrator had been brought to justice quickly. Margaret and Irma became fast friends.

"We're going to need some help here," Irma had said when she called.

The two highest-ranking members of the Aruba police hierarchy had been murdered. Executed outside their homes, the Chief Minister of Justice and the Chief Police Commissioner were found with bullet wounds in their foreheads. Without its leaders, the Aruban police force was struggling to regain its balance. Each departmental silo approached the issue in Palm Beach from their own perspective.

Irma downloaded what she knew of the day's events. Shortly after four in the morning, a patrol car had spotted light coming from the base of a cellular tower. The fire department was summoned but the flames had run their course by the time they arrived. Those on the scene reported to have found wires and a partially melted cell phone stuck to the wall above the hole. Cellular service was offline in the Noord District.

Later that morning, vehicles began arriving at the Noord District Police Station. They reported having seen men clad in military uniforms with assault rifles. One had seen men with weapons on the roof of the Surfside resort.

A patrol car was dispatched to the scene. The officers placed a single panicked radio call before contact with them was lost. They screamed about explosions and then went offline. Their car was found ablaze. A loose perimeter was established by lieutenants nearing the end of their overnight shifts. Everyone waited for the leadership of the Chief Commissioners: leadership that would not come.

"I wanted to let you know. There'll be someone reaching out through channels soon, I would think. They're not real big on going it alone," said Irma. She was on the sidelines. Her role in criminal investigation meant she didn't command active units. That hadn't kept her from seeing how quickly the seams were separating within the department.

1.5 million tourists visited Aruba each year. 60% of them are Americans. The Surfside was owned by an American company. Sure, there was a cross-section of other nationalities, but the mess was quickly falling into the lap of the United States.

Margaret's phone rang. "Have you seen it?" She'd only met the Secretary of State in person on two occasions. Ray Ladenburg was an attractive man with well-coiffed hair that was silver above the ears. He'd skipped the Ambassador to the Netherlands, Margaret's boss, and had gone directly to the source.

"Good morning, Ray. I just finished reading it. Do we have any intel on this group? Hard to believe they're in it for the money."

The webpage was up on the computer monitor in front of her. The heading read, "Engagement Aruba." It was a simple single page that listed the rules of engagement in four bullet points. Across the bottom were two videos with the words 'Live Stream,' beneath them.

The one on the left showed a wall of sandbags and a nasty-looking assault rifle with a belt of ammunition running down the side to a can. The bottom of a chair was visible, along with a pair of legs covered in gray camouflaged printed pants and desert-style military boots. Buildings were visible in the distance, beyond the sandbags. It was bright and elevated like it was coming from a roof.

The video on the right was of the pool area. A waterfall cascaded over rocks above a pool in the background. In the foreground, four blindfolded hostages were sitting Indian-style on the ground with a masked guard standing sentry above them. Most of his uniform looked military—a solid gray top bore camouflage on the arms that matched the pattern on his pants. What was different was the mask.

He was wearing a skeleton mask that someone might wear on Halloween if they really wanted to scare the hell out of the kids coming to the door. It had bony cheeks and a void where the nose wasn't. The Stars and Stripes overlay it all. The flag of the United States was painted on the mask.

"They certainly wanted us to know it's our issue," said Margaret.

"Agreed." Ray seemed to be reading. Margaret heard the click of a mouse. "Money and the eyes of the world," Ray said. "Listen, the fuel is going to hit this fire quickly. Defense will want to preposition special ops and a negotiation team is being assembled as we speak. The intelligence machine is cranking so I expect we'll have more information shortly. I'll be coming directly to you on this, Margaret. You'll be leading the show on the ground for now. Let's keep our words to a minimum until we have a complete picture. The president is clearing his schedule, and I'm headed over to join him for briefings. We'll be in touch."

Margaret hung up the phone. She read through the rules of engagement again. Bullet number one read, "Any action on the part of island authorities or other nations to infiltrate and take back the resort will be repelled. Punishment for such actions will be the public execution of hostages. The number executed will be determined by the scale of the attempt."

Bullet number two: "Severing of electricity or internet service will be seen as an attack of the greatest magnitude. Many will die as a result."

Bullet number three: "The four buildings in this complex are rigged with plastic explosives set deep within the concrete pillars. In the unlikely event that our defenses are overwhelmed, the buildings will be brought down, and those that initiated the attack will suffer the consequences."

Bullet number four: "Expect ransom demands and a deadline to be posted shortly. Our goal is to kill and injure as few as possible. Convince your leaders and politicians to pay for its people to end this ordeal. Then implore them to remove your soldiers from our countries. Once that goal is reached, events like this can stop."

It ended with, "We make good on our threats. Let's work together for a more peaceful world."

27

Queen Beatrix International Airport, Aruba

Maddie could sense the string of lies, a series of bad decisions in front of her that weren't optional. Her gut was in charge and there was no doubt what it was telling her.

By the time they made it to the hallway, Charlotte was squirming her way out of the carrier. Maddie pulled her from it and held her under the butt. She sat high, her head level with Maddie's as she looked around taking in the scenery. They made their way through the snaking stanchions leading up to the immigration window. Locals from another flight were waiting when their line caught up.

Only one of the kiosks was open. A single immigration official worked the line. Beyond him, at the customs checkpoint, another lone official waved people by the free-standing scanner. He nodded the passengers along without so much as a word, disinterested in inspecting the bags of locals.

The airport resources had been spread out across the

terminal to contain the tourists. Maddie wondered if the air traffic control tower had tried to divert them while they were in the holding pattern. They would have been low on fuel, but Bonaire and Curacao were close by.

They'd been allowed to land and now airport and police authorities had a new problem on their hands. Long-term crowd control was a difficult predicament to solve. A horde of disgruntled vacationers bottled up in the terminal might rival the *violence* they were dealing with up-island.

Maddie eyeballed the man in front of her, scanning his well-pressed digs from head to toe. He was talking on his cell phone and wearing a suit. It felt sacrilegious to travel the Caribbean in a suit. The wife and four children felt like charlatan additions to the Italian pinstripes. With diaper bag slung over her shoulder and Charlotte testing her biceps, Maddie wondered where the family sat in the island pecking order.

Maybe a hotel or oil refinery executive, she thought.

The word, "Terrorism," caught Maddie's attention. It was framed as a question. She stepped up and turned her ear to the man's conversation.

"Let's hope not. If it's terror, it'll shut the island down for years."

A pause.

"Both of them?"

A pause.

"The police were a mess without having to deal with that." He had a European accent.

A pause.

"Yeah they're holding the tourists up here at the airport. Not letting them go. Going to have a riot on their hands if they're not careful."

A pause.

"Yeah, you're right. They won't have a choice."

A pause.

"Okay, Bill. See you in a bit." He hung up and slid the phone into the pocket of his suit jacket.

Ten anxious minutes of bouncing and entertaining Charlotte passed. Maddie kept hearing the question. *"Terrorism?"*

The family was called up and slowed for just a minute before the agent let them pass with a wave of recognition.

As they made their way to the desk, Maddie studied the immigration man. If he was ever going to be distracted, today was the day. He looked like he'd only been shaving a couple of years. Maddie decided on a chummy approach.

"Good morning. Tough day?" Maddie waited for a response but the agent remained blank. "Sorry, but there was so much commotion back there with this mess. Somehow, I lost my immigration form. Can I get another?" The spiteful look she was thrown felt premature.

The agent rolled to the side in his chair, checking to see how many were in line behind Maddie. When he saw there were none, he rolled his eyes and offered up a new form.

"Passports?" Maddie was just about to put pen to paper when the agent asked.

She extracted them from her purse and offered them up.

"That one there is hot off the presses." She flopped them on the counter and rubbed Charlotte on the head. She leaned into Maddie as she watched the man swipe them with one hand and click at the keyboard with the other.

Maddie scribbled her name, date of birth and country.

"I need those back to complete part of the form," Maddie said.

The man nodded without looking up. "Just finish the rest."

When she arrived at the 'Address in Aruba' section, Maddie tapped the pen on the counter and felt a sweat break out. She couldn't remember Kavita's last name and didn't know the address. The name was really Geert's last name. Kavita and Geert... It was a son-of-a-bitch Dutch name. She thought about checking on her phone but remembered the sign that said, 'No Cell Phone Use in This Area.'

She wrote, 'Kavita Café.'

Behind her, Maddie could feel more people queuing up in the waiting area. She didn't look back, just bore down on the form. Address and occupation. Number of visits—she checked '6-9.' Type of accommodation? Visiting friends & family. She handed the form down to the agent and ran her fingers through Charlotte's strawberry hair.

When you hit a golf ball in the sweet spot you can literally feel the stroke connect. The contact and spring from the club is so natural your spirit lifts off with the shot. This was not one of those times. Maddie had shanked it with 'Kavita Café'. The agent was studying the form way too closely. She shouldn't have waited and been last in line. She should have filled out a new form ahead of time. It would have given her time to look up the name. Every letter of the fucking form was being scrutinized.

"Friends and Family this time?" the agent asked. "That seems odd with a husband and daughter at the Surfside Resort?" He paused, pecking at the down arrow on his computer. "Six visits. Six stays at the Surfside. But not this time?" He established contact from the corner of his eye then squared up and straightened in his chair, zeroing in for Maddie's explanation.

Maddie laughed and nodded. "I can see how it looks strange," she said, the lie still taking shape. "Me and my husband had a falling out. Forgot the passport for the little one here." Maddie rumpled Charlotte's hair again. "It was my fault. Next thing you know we're arguing. I was going to stay home but then we got the passport and decided to come down. I called Kavita and explained about the argument. She offered up her spare room. Kavita's daughter looks after my kids when we're down here. They're like family."

"Like family? Close enough to know their last name?" asked the man. He looked back down, closed their passports and pushed them to the side. "Please wait over there. Under the immigration sign. A manager will need to speak with you further."

Fucker. Fucker. Fucker, Maddie thought. She sucked as a saleswoman.

Backed into a corner, there was no way out but to fess up. A return to honesty was the best policy when you're caught in a lie with an immigration official.

As she waited, debating her limited options, the Aruba Triangle returned to her mind. If Ross had made it to pick them up, he might be right around the corner. But if he was here waiting, he would have called or texted. It only took a hint of intuition to know that shit was hitting the fan and being chopped into more pieces than the island could handle. The immigration and customs agents weren't going to care that her husband and daughter were at the resort with the black smoke. At best, she'd be sent back with the other tourist and kept here or forced to fly back home. At worst, they would lock her up for lying.

She was told to wait under a sign that was just outside of the immigration agent's peripheral vision. The customs scanner with the disinterested operator was right around the corner. The family, led by Pinstripe Suit, had pulled off to the side while a pair of the Vineyard Vines kids took a potty break.

After immigration, everyone not caught lying turned hard left into baggage claim. Once you retrieved your bags you walked by the scanner and found out if customs was in the mood to question you or scan your gear. Maddie hadn't checked anything. Ross had brought it all, leaving her with just the diaper bag.

The customs agent manning the scanner was biting at a hangnail when Pinstripe Suit emerged from baggage claim. He was towing a pair of burgundy suitcases.

Maddie watched him pass in front and form up with his family. He offered the handle of one of the bags to his oldest son just as the two on potty break reappeared from the restrooms.

As they gathered their belongings, the idea hit Maddie.

What the fuck are you thinking? You can't just walk out. They have your passports. They catch you walking out and you're libel to end up in a prison where the heat melts years off your life.

Watching the family approach, she knew the train had left the station. Her better judgment had lost out to gut instinct.

As they passed, she fell in with them. She crossed to the right so she'd be opposite the customs agent. She pulled up uncomfortably tight with the family, practically tip-toeing to avoid their attention. The scanner passed to the left and Maddie looked up to check on the agent. He was busy with the hangnail.

Once they emerged into the main hallway, Maddie peeled off quickly. Still balancing Charlotte on one arm, she hustled out the door.

A surge of wind-driven Aruban heat blasted them. Maddie scanned left, then right, looking for a waving husband or a white pickup. She saw neither.

Not sure what to do next, she turned right and started walking. She wanted to get away from the main doors and following the path vehicles took on their way into the terminal seemed reasonable.

Her phone vibrated in her pocket. Maddie pulled it out. Chuckles was calling. She silenced it.

As she cleared the end of the terminal building, they crossed into sunlight. A layer of dampness that had formed in the shade now broke into a full body sweat. Twenty seconds after, she ran out of sidewalk to follow as Geert's white pickup careened through the circle and into the airport entrance.

28

HOLIDAY INN, Aruba

"HELLO, ladies and gentlemen. This is Kyle King reporting from the Holiday Inn on the island of Aruba." He spoke quietly in a hushed tone. "The footage is a bit grainy because all I have is a webcam, but this is breaking news. I believe those figures on your screen to be six terrorists. They're making their way along a copse of trees across the parking lot from where I'm reporting." On the video, six blurry figures moved from left to right. Cone-shaped pine trees behind them made their silhouettes easy to see.

Kyle had contacted his producer after the explosions earlier in the day. He'd made it to L.G. Smith Boulevard and taken cell phone videos of the burning car. He'd been the first to report that a rocket of some kind had been fired from the rooftop of the Surfside Resort. The white streak of the RPG had been almost directly above him. He'd glanced up an instant before the explosion knocked him to the ground. What followed was the most terrifying three minutes of his life. He sprinted for the edge of the mall. The cars in the second video were clearly police. His courage lasted 48 seconds. With the footage secured on his phone, he retreated to his hotel room. He used the phone in the hotel room to call his producer at the Minneapolis news channel where he was a reporter.

His girlfriend would later report that they were on a week-long vacation and that she was in bed, scared by the explosions, when Kyle returned. Kyle hadn't explained how dangerous the situation was. "Could be the best thing that'll ever happen to my career," he told her.

"Just to reiterate our situation here. Our day started early with two attacks that were directed at the Aruban police. I've reported seeing at least four armed men patrolling the roof tops of the Surfside resort. I am coming to you via Skype from the Holiday Inn on Aruba. We're directly next door to the Surfside Resort, which we've just learned has been taken over by the New Jihad Front. I was out here on the balcony trying to capture a wi-fi signal from the Surfside when I spotted the team of men you're watching now. This is a live shot, ladies and gentlemen." At the time, Kyle had no way of knowing that his broadcast had gone international. The live feed was picked up by all the major networks.

"To my right, we've got an open-air mall. This is one of the primary shopping areas on the island. The cell phone video from earlier was taken just on the other side of the mall from where I am now." After a short pause, Kyle says, "What else do we know?" He'd scratched keywords on a Holiday Inn note pad. "I failed to mention that we've got drone activity above us. They're very hard to make out in the bright sky here but occasionally when the wind dies down, I can hear them. On several occasions, I've picked up their movement and was able to track them a short distance. I can hear one now. I can't see it but there's a buzz out there over what we're watching. Twice this morning I've seen the drones coming and going from the center of the Surfside Resort. This would lead you to believe that they're being operated by the terrorists. But of course, we have no confirmation of that."

In the video, the string of fuzzy gray soldiers bunched up into one distorted blob. Kyle cleared his throat. "They appear to be preparing to cross the road into the mall."

"Oh no. We've got some spectators who've come out looking. There were police warding people off earlier, but they've been gone for some time."

"There they go. They're crossing the road now." Kyle hadn't realized that holding the camera was giving viewers motion sickness and preventing it from focusing completely. Once he set it down on the railing, the lines cleared and hundreds of millions of live viewers watched as the terrorists crossed the road.

The five curious onlookers Kyle had mentioned were visible to those watching. As the assault team reached the middle of the road, they raised their weapons. The onlookers dropped, one at a time, in rapid succession.

"Jesus Christ. They just executed them," Kyle whispered. "This is unbelievable."

With the picture now crisp, Kyle and the rest of the world watched as the team formed a line along a storefront. An ice cream parlor sign hung above them.

"The opening you're seeing there to the right of the men leads to the interior courtyard of the mall – several popular restaurants, more shops, a fountain where a nightly light show is performed."

"There they go, folks." Seconds of silence followed after the team disappeared from view.

Feeling the need to fill the dead space, Kyle continued to talk from behind the camera. "Again, this is a live shot from Aruba. We've just witnessed six armed men moving toward the interior of the mall in an assault formation. They appeared to be stalking prey we're not seeing. Again, we've got several drones in the sky here above the Holiday Inn. If they're controlled by the terrorists, then they have a birds eye..."

Kyle went silent as pops of distant gunfire broke out. "I've lost sight..." were Kyle's last words.

Analysis of the video would later reveal the moment when the sniper round cracked above the camera and laptop mounted microphone. The supersonic round entered just below Kyle's left ear. It ruptured his windpipe and severed one of his carotid arteries before exiting out the lower right side of his neck.

Four seconds passed before there was any recognition by his girlfriend of what had happened. Kyle's suffering came through as a gurgled choking on the video. Then there was a shriek. "He's bleeding. Oh my God. Blood! Blood!" the girlfriend yelled.

With Kyle's dying breaths as background, viewers watched as three of the six terrorists emerged. They exited the corridor they had entered less than a minute before. The third limped across the road, making it to the center before collapsing. He struggled back to his feet but was left behind by the two other survivors of the failed assault. The men sprinted away, exiting the screen to the viewers left.

The wounded man made it off the road. His limp was more pronounced after the fall. Slowly, he made his way across the screen and was about to exit left on the wide angle shot when the Aruban SWAT team fanned from the corridor. Their weapons were shouldered and they fired immediately, their rifles popping faintly in the video.

One of the first rounds landed. The wounded man pitched forward. He hit the ground and barrel-rolled down a small hill to his left. Using his legs, he spun around to face his enemy. Able to lift his head off the turf only slightly, puffs of white smoke marked the fire he returned from his lap.

An eruption of popping sound on the video was followed by a white haze around the SWAT team. Machine gun fire from the rooftop of the Surfside resort had been directed down by the terrorists. It chipped at the concrete sidewalks and store front facades, forcing the SWAT team to retreat.

29

Queen Beatrix International Airport, Aruba

Maddie, Charlotte and the diaper bag were inside the pickup before Geert had come to a complete stop.

"Holy Dutch fucker, am I glad to see you. Let's get the hell out of here," Maddie said.

Geert hesitated, reaching across to rub Charlotte's head as Maddie plopped her on the bench seat between them.

"No carseat?"

"Ross has it, and I just ran out on Immigration. I need to get the hell out of here."

Geert shifted the truck into gear. He checked his mirror then pulled away from the curb.

"Ran out?"

"Yeah they're holding up tourists. Not letting them leave." Regret and fear had replaced the certainty in her gut. Charmonster was now an illegal alien.

"I told them we were headed to Kavita's Café. They've closed the tourist area. What the hell's going on up there?" The question hadn't left her lips when an agent ran from the automatic doors in front of the airport.

"Shit," Maddie yelled. She slumped on top of Charlotte.

Geert laughed. "You really just left?" He didn't wait for an answer. "Don't worry. He didn't see you."

"Oh shit," Maddie said, "What have I done?" She checked over her shoulder as Geert reentered the circle fronting the airport.

Geert looked over. "You some kind of lunatic?"

Maddie didn't respond.

Geert turned back to the road. "Here in the last few minutes they've been talking on the radio about a website the terrorists put up. Sounds like they've taken over your resort and are looking for ransom."

"So it *is* terrorists?" Maddie asked. "At the Surfside?" Everything was happening so fast.

"*Nu kmot de aap uit de mouw*," replied Geert.

Maddie looked over at him, confused.

"Now the monkey comes out of the sleeve."

"What the hell are you saying?" Maddie asked.

"It comes to the surface now. The monkey was hiding but now he is out of the sleeve. We see that terror has come to Aruba."

Maddie said nothing.

"When have you last spoken with your husband?" Geert asked.

"A text message in the middle of the night. Nothing since."

"Reports are that they took out the cell phone towers so that the people could not call out. Our two highest-ranking police officials have been killed. They have planned this in advance. The Dutch Marines, usually stationed not far from my house, are gone for annual training in North Carolina. They chose their timing wisely."

Charlotte was looking up at Geert with uncertainty. Her life of daily routine had been shattered the last few days. Maddie leaned down and kissed her on the cheek. She rubbed her head.

"Everything's going to be okay, Char-monster," she whispered to her.

Maddie looked up at Geert. "Thanks for coming to get us, Geert. Sorry you had to be a getaway driver. We won't stay at your place for much time. They'll be coming to look for us."

Everything about the man was long. Geert's elbows nearly touched his legs before the angle of the arm rose back to the wheel. Beneath it, his knees were peaks, like he'd been crammed in.

"We don't mind helping," Geert replied. "Your family was the first thing we thought of when they said this was happening at the Surfside." Geert's Dutch accent rode with his words. D's were sometimes T's and he turned ending S's to F's in a way that closed a word like the back half of a dog's bark.

Remembering the call from Chuckles, Maddie pulled the phone from her pocket. Her friend had left a voicemail. Before she checked it, Maddie opened her text messages again. There was nothing new, but she re-read the last one Ross had sent. What she would give for a few words from him now. Maddie's replies with updates on their progress had gone unanswered. She typed another anyway.

'Are you okay? We're here in Aruba. Worried about you two.'

The voicemail from Chuckles was short. "What's your situation, Mad? I checked the flight tracker and it looks like you landed after this shit broke loose. I'm here for you, sister. Give me a call."

Thirteen minutes later they pulled into the congested parking lot of Kavita's Cafe. Schools and businesses had been ordered closed for the day, but Kavita's Café was more than a business. It was a gathering spot, and the men and women of San Nicolas had filled it to capacity.

Maddie remembered Kavita telling them how she had three parts to her day. The locals filtered in early on the way to their jobs. The tourist wave ran from ten in the morning to four in the afternoon. Supper time was again limited to locals, the tourists having left for the 40-minute trek back to their resorts at the opposite end of the island.

In truth, Kavita's might never have succeeded without Baby Beach. Its address along the confusing route to get there played a part in making the restaurant the legend it had become. The out-of-the-way beach was a tropical paradise with silky smooth sand and a naturally protected bay. The circuitous route required to get there took nervous tourists through neighborhoods that appeared run down by American standards. Kavita's Café was a beacon, an oasis amidst the uncertainty.

Maddie followed the lanky Dutchman into the restaurant. His jeans were frayed along the bottom and his once blue *License to Chill* t-shirt was faded to a misty gray.

Inside the door, Geert curled fingers into his mouth and sent out a whistle that shook Maddie's eardrums. He turned to her and Charlotte and lifted his leathery brown hand above their heads.

"Listen up. This woman's husband and other daughter are at the Surfside. The police wanted to send her back *thuis*," He occasionally substituted Dutch words. "They may come looking for her. You never saw this woman. This woman and her daughter were not here. Do you understand?" The room full of patrons shook their heads in affirmation. They leaned into one another talking as they watched Maddie and Charlotte follow Geert across the room.

Kavita came running from a door that led back to the kitchen. Her braided hair was as black as her dress, broken at the top by pink and white flowers. Gold hoop earrings and jingling bangles caught the light, making her coffee-colored skin seem even darker.

She wiped tears from her eyes, grabbed Charlotte and puckered to Maddie who leaned forward, accepting the kiss on his cheek.

"Lotte! Esmie! Come, girls," Kavita called toward the kitchen. Her daughters emerged, hurrying to their mother with smiles of recognition that helped calm Maddie's nerves. Kavita lifted Charlotte and sniffed her butt. "Where are the diapers?"

Maddie un-slung the bag over her shoulder and handed it to Kavita's eldest, Lotte.

"A fresh diaper and some food... Mash an avocado for her." She turned to Maddie. "Is this okay?"

She nodded. "Thank you, Kavita. Thank you, girls." Then she reached out and touched Geert's shoulder. "Thank you, all. I'd be lost without you."

"This is no problem." Geert reached out and placed his hand on Maddie's shoulder. Their arms were aligned. "We are here for you. Together we get through this." He nodded and turned. "Family first."

Geert dropped to a chair that a patron had vacated a moment before. As he sat, the man next to him rose.

"Sit." The stranger motioned Maddie into the chair.

Her fall to the chair was heavier than normal. It felt good to unload the weight. Pulses shot through her ankles and the acid in her legs drained from the thighs toward her hamstrings. There was a tone ringing in her ears. It seemed to pulse subtly with the beating of her heart. *Stress*, Maddie thought. The autopilot that had driven her body to the table had switched off. She stared transfixed at the TV, the gravity of the situation closing in on her.

In that moment, with the news streaming down from above, Maddie was unable to hear a word. She was hit with the realization that she was facing the worst possible trauma life had to offer. She thought she'd already crossed that bridge, but now her daughter and husband were prisoners.

Her innocent six-year-old and her perfect husband were caught up in a web of terror. Caught up, not while traveling the Hindu Cush or pressing their luck in Indonesia, but here in this gentrified paradise where safety had never been an issue. Terrorism and Aruba didn't mix. This place was about sapphire water. It was about restaurants where patrons sit with their feet, not just in the sand, but literally in the water, being lapped at by folds in the ocean's edge. Here in this paradise she faced a grotesque violation of the order of things—a nasty wrinkle in the fabric. A war that was often so hard to find overseas had found her family.

30

Surfside Resort, Aruba

Fazul strode up to the camera and held the sheet of paper in front of it.

'The Aruban Police have attempted an attack with heavily armed troops. Four hostages will pay the cost of this mistake.'

He let go of the paper and moved behind the row of four blindfolded hostages. There were three men and one woman, each chosen at random from the game room.

They'd been in the shade of a palm for most of the day, but now they were illuminated by the full strength of the equatorial sun. Their hair was damp and sweat rings soaked the collars of their shirts.

Fazul said nothing before he pulled the trigger the first time. He pointed the pistol at the base of the skull. It only took one shot if you hit the brain stem.

He had killed the second hostage before the third and fourth had time to start screaming. Two beats later, they both had been thrown face forward to their deaths like the others.

31

KAVITA'S CAFÉ, Aruba

KAVITA CAME out of the kitchen carrying two plates, each drafting steam around her arms as she walked.

"Geert!" she yelled. He was at the bar leaning in close, talking to a patron. Kavita motioned him to the table where Maddie was sitting.

"Spicy goat curry. House special for today." Kavita slid the plate in front of Maddie, stirring her stomach to life.

She'd gone with Kavita and her daughters up to their house. It was walking distance from the Café. Lotte had pulled pieces of a crib from the shed and they'd put it together in the living room. Charlotte had grown fussy and Kavita had made the plan.

"She needs quiet and rest." Charlotte had taken a bottle from Kavita and fallen asleep without finishing it.

"I can't thank you two enough," Maddie said. "I don't know where we'd be without you." She'd given up worrying about walking out of the airport. It was over, and she needed to turn her attention forward. Maddie had watched Geert talk to patrons who took turns by the door monitoring the parking lot. She was sure they were there as advanced warning so Maddie could be shuttled out the back if police pulled up.

"You were like family before. This just makes it official," said Kavita. "Now eat!"

It was no wonder that Kavita's Café felt so comfortable. It was the embodiment of her soul. She deserved everything she had built. Kavita had started the café in a building further up the hill on the other side of the intersection. She had an enormous sign erected in the front parking lot so that tourists knew which way to turn to get to *Baby Beach*. The right-hand turn was not obvious. Before the sign was erected, about half went the wrong way at the intersection. After it went up, there were no excuses and many bound for the beach stopped at the restaurant on their way in or out from Baby Beach.

The owner of the building where Kavita started became envious of her self-made success. His intentions had started out gracious enough. After sitting idle for many years, he agreed to let Kavita start her restaurant in the building free of charge for six months. It had been a restaurant before and didn't need a full restoration. Kavita scraped away the layers of dust and sand that had settled. Friends and family helped restore the cooking equipment.

Once they were open, she harnessed the internet to spread the word. She asked everyone that came in to write a review. If they wrote a review and showed her the next time they came, Kavita gave them half off their already reasonably-priced meal. Things were already humming when Geert put up the sign, but the business soared after.

Kavita's following blossomed. As it grew, so did her ability to help the local community. She became a staple of employment in town and contributed funds for improvement projects at the local school. There was nothing not to like.

But then, "Damien Salazar," a name Kavita was quick to advertise, decided it was time to triple the rent. He dropped the contract off without explaining his motives and returned the next day to a furious Kavita. She had posted a sign near the entrance that read, "We are closing at this location. Please come to our home for food until our next location is opened." Kavita handed Damien Salazar a check for the final rent she owed. She never came back.

Geert constructed a patio in front of his shop. He used the structure not for its aesthetic qualities, but because it provided a stable foundation for one side of the roof. It was in their side yard, next to the house and had enough room to accommodate 20 people around an L-shaped table. The family cooked in the house and brought the meals out to the patio to feed the dedicated flock of locals and tourists who wouldn't do without Kavita's food.

It took three months to purchase the property, a parcel to the right of the intersection this time. It took Geert and his friends 13 months to complete the building. Kavita tells everyone how she reopened the new restaurant one and a half years to the day after Damien Salazar had the nerve to triple her rent.

Mr. Salazar attempted to run the restaurant for a time after Kavita walked away. Salazar's Café was open for a month.

The new building was a cleaner, more inviting space. Tourists were more apt to stop for that reason alone, but its real value was firmly grounded in the fact that it was to the right of the intersection. The new sign told tourists to, "Turn this way for Baby Beach, Cold Beer, Bollywood music and the best food on the island!" Business doubled again.

Across from Maddie, Geert pulled out a chair and sat. His bald spot was ringed by a salt and pepper donut that was still thick and would be with him until the grave. The TV burned on above his head. There was little new information to report and the BBC was rehashing the original stories from different angles.

"What are you thinking?" Geert asked, with draculin flair.

Maddie was surprised by the question. She felt numb, unfeeling, not thinking about anything.

"I could see you thinking from across the room." Geert motioned to the bar. "We were talking about how you must be feeling. The man I was talking to has three children."

Maddie moved the curry around in the silver bowl. It sat in the middle of the plate flanked by a homemade tortilla on one side and brown rice on the other.

"You try and figure out how to fix it," Maddie said. "That's just what we do. Us parents."

"Yes, of course. But fixing not always possible. No?" Geert lifted a spoonful of curry to his mouth.

"Easy to say. Hard to accept," Maddie replied.

Geert asked her about the girls. Was Isabelle reading yet? How about Charlotte? Was she beginning to walk? The questions were genuine comfort conversation to go along with the island comfort food.

"I was in the military also," Geert said, the change in topic jarring Maddie up from her meal. "Front line *infanterie* for eighteen months and then training as an electrician."

Maddie thought for a moment. "You never told me that before."

"Kavita told me about you being in the service. I missed the conversation," Geert said.

Maddie nodded. "What was your specialty?"

"Rifleman. First and always. Electrician second. The second one ended up paying the bills, though." The two of them laughed.

"We feel your pain, Maddie," Geert said, turning serious again. "Kavita and I both." He pulled up his cheeks, creating a pentagon of empathy that ran from the sides of his nose, down around his mouth and flat along the chin. "We're here for you. You are welcome to stay as long as this takes, my friend."

"Thanks Geert." The words had just left her lips when breaking news flashed on the BBC channel. Someone whistled from a corner of the room and the crowd grew silent.

"Breaking news coming to you now." The silver-haired commentator adjusted himself in his chair. An earpiece that would have otherwise gone unseen, became evident when he touched it. "Okay, we're going to roll video now."

An image of the terrorist webpage was brought up on the screen.

"What you're seeing is the recently updated website. The update was pushed just moments ago, and was choreographed with the delivery of an email to our news agency. We assume others have received it as well. The group says they are looking to raise two hundred and fifty million dollars, in what they call capital."

The news anchor listened silently for a moment before continuing. "While two hundred and fifty million sounds like a lot of money, the website points out that it's only half the cost of a single B-2 Stealth Bomber and equivalent to the combined salary of just the top five or six players in Major League Baseball."

"I'm being told that the total is being spread across six countries and one organization. The United States, Germany, Great Britain, Italy, the Netherlands and Sweden. As well as Wincopia International, which owns the Surfside Resort. The amount each is being asked to pay appears to have been selected using different metrics."

A table was pulled from the website and displayed on the screen. It listed three columns— the names, a dollar amount and a column titled, 'Why?'. Beside the United States, the number read, $138 Million. The, 'Why?' column said, 'The cost of a single F-22 Stealth Fighter seemed reasonable.' Wincopia

International was listed second. $15 million. 'The cost to construct a mid-sized hotel.' Germany was being asked to pay $37 million. 'Germany represents 38% of the remaining countries' GDP. $97 million x .38 = $37 million.'

"We're still working out the math ourselves, but you can see the ask here," said the anchor.

After that, silence fell over the broadcast. The graphic was left in place for viewers to absorb. Twenty-one seconds of dead air was an eternity for television. It likely set some type of record for a major news organization.

The table disappeared and the anchor was put back on screen.

"Bear with us as our teams are working to gather information. It's coming to us in real time here."

Seven more seconds of dead air reigned. During it, the news anchor looked to the side of the camera, his hand to his ear, listening.

"What we're learning now is that a second page was also pushed to the web. We're going to roll some actual video here in a moment. Oh my..." The anchorman closed his eyes and shook his head. "I'm sorry, folks. What we've got is seven videos that have been posted. The group is identifying these as the hostages that will be executed if the ransoms aren't paid. They're setting the deadline at 72 hours. This is all per the website. Here's the first video."

"My—My name is Ross Günther."

Madeline shot to her feet and raced to the television.

"This is my daughter, Isabelle. We are from Maryland, in the United States. The bruise on my head happened from me trying to escape. Since..." Ross hesitated on the video. He looked left at his daughter seated beside him. "Since then, we have been treated well. They have provided water, blankets and food. Oh, and medicine. So, please give them what they want so Isabelle and I can come home safely to Maryland."

PART III

ROUT

32

SURFSIDE RESORT, Aruba

CONSCIOUSNESS HAD RETURNED before Ross was fully awake. Soft fingertips stroked his forehead.

"Shhhh, Daddy." Izzy repeated the words. She switched between rubbing Ross's forehead and adjusting the blanket pulled up beneath his chin.

Ross retraced the events that led him into the fog. Carpet on the face, masks, guns—the thoughts streamed by, out of order.

After several minutes, the stroking hand seemed to burn his skin. He swatted, the swing enough to rile his senses to the enormous headache hiding inside his head.

"Daddy! You're awake!" Izzy cried out with excitement.

"My head," Ross cried, reaching blindly for his daughter.

"Shhhh, Daddy. You have a boo-boo." Izzy leaned down and kissed his cheek. "Shhhh. Mommy'll fix it."

With his eyes still closed, Ross felt for his daughter's hand. He held it for a moment then let go and outlined the knot above his own ear. Half of it was inside the hairline. It was tender and warm to the touch.

He tried to open his eyes but the sliver of light that entered triggered a pain deep within. If movement had affected the perimeter of his gray matter, the light went straight to its core.

"Are you okay?" Ross asked with eyes closed.

"Shhhh, Daddy. I'm fine. You want water? The man gave me water."

The next 15 minutes had been an exercise in tedious, deliberate movement. Ross had always felt for migraine sufferers. He'd never had one himself, but he'd seen the devastating effects they reaped.

He shielded his eyes from the fluorescent lights. His world was blurry. The lack of focus seemed to drip through his vision.

Izzy was sitting with her back to a wall. Once Ross righted himself, she did the same. They were in an aisle. In front, Ross saw what looked like the panel of an office cube space. It opened to their left. There was a calendar with cats on it tacked to the fabric.

Izzy's calming shush was the only sound at first. Sobs and English accented whispers eventually filtered in.

"Who's talking?" Ross asked.

"People on the other side. They came in right before you woke up," Izzy explained.

Eventually a pair of legs arrived in Ross's field of view. He couldn't look up into the light. There were feet and the barrel of a gun and an offer of pain medicine, which Ross accepted.

The legs left for maybe an hour and returned, accompanied by the rattle of a pill bottle.

"How many?" the voice asked.

"What is it?"

"Ibuprofen. Two hundred milligrams," the voice explained.

"Six. Please," he replied.

The man handed them down. "Stay here on this side until someone comes for you. If you need anything, just yell."

After that, Ross and Izzy were left in the corridor. He talked his daughter carefully through the events that had occurred after he was knocked unconscious. What he deduced from the information was that the men had shown a modicum of compassion. Izzy told her father how she'd laid with him crying. How the men had left them in the hall. She explained in as much detail as a six-year-old is capable, how they returned with a luggage cart. The men talked "nicely" to her. The men lifted Daddy onto the cart. The men let Izzy hold Daddy's hand while they took them down the elevator to see the doctor. They'd walked outside, Izzy explained.

Ross gathered that they were now in the office near the main lobby. Izzy had traced the line by describing the pamphlet rack near the back door. She was routinely scolded for taking brochures and stuffing them in her purse. She also explained how she got to go behind "the big desk," which Ross knew must be the area where people checked in.

What Ross could not reason was why he was still alive. Izzy had been given a blanket and two bottles of water. She seemed to have recovered from the trauma of the situation. Only kind words could have manifested that. Children were resilient, but Izzy seemed to have aged years while Ross was out.

"Get up and follow me." It had come as a command. "Anas is ready for you."

"Who?" Ross asked.

"Never mind that. Follow me now."

In college, Ross had taken up psychology because engineering excited him less than rice cakes as a snack. While the geeks in his class relished the thought of a Rube Goldberg competition, for Ross it was evidence that his parents had pushed him into the wrong field. He felt deeply. Analyzing the faint sparks that precipitated an event was more his style. It was the conjecture that fed him—supposition over mechanics.

Even with his head still searing with pain, there was enough space between the throbbing bolts that he remembered his training. *Comply*, he thought.

The psychology of the situation told him that they were safe for now. If they were to be killed, it would have happened already. There were bigger plans.

Ross knew that kidnap and hostage victims actually had a higher chance of escape than most people believed. When the violence was not immediate, the kidnapper usually had a vested interest in keeping them alive. Self-defense protocol dictated that potential victims try and escape a kidnap attempt. Ross had tried that. But if you're detained, compliance offers the best chance of survival. That was, of course, as long as the request being made did not place you in jeopardy.

Ross didn't sense danger. He lifted himself from the floor by sliding up the wall. Izzy held his hand, raising it as if to take the weight of her father's arm to help him up.

They'd been led out through the lobby. On the way out, he glimpsed three young co-ed's sitting side by side on the floor. He and Izzy were quickly ushered to the back of the lobby, toward the pamphlet rack.

Light angled off the floor. The brightness of the sun's reflection again amplified the pain in Ross's head. Through the squint, he saw a pool of dark liquid and smear marks that led to the back door. Something had been run through the liquid. As they got closer, the red tinge brought the realization to life. Ross pulled Izzy in tight. Someone had been killed, their body dragged to the door.

The gore ended before the door. A heap of towels was piled against the wall. Someone had cleaned the floor to prevent others from slipping in the blood. It was a thought that sent chills racing down his neck rather than comforting him.

A second soldier pulled open the door as they approached. Hot air curled around the corner and washed over them. Heat and light blasted the goose bumps from his skin. Ross cringed at the light, again shading his eyes. Looking down, the trail of blood picked up again, running over the concreate toward the pool.

They were led straight out from the doors, following the dark streak to an area near the pool.

A camera sat atop a tripod. It was oriented toward the waterfall, still cascading some thirty yards distant at the end of the pool.

"Why is there a camera?" Izzy asked.

"I don't know, sweets." Ross pulled his daughter close.

It almost felt cliché. Terrorists take hostages. Terrorists film hostages. Terrorists request ransoms. But then what? He shuddered at the thought and shook his head to throw it clear. It was a bad idea. The headache drove its spikes deeper. Ross dropped to a knee, his arm around Izzy's shoulders.

"Can I have a play date with Harper today?" Harper was another six-year-old Izzy had met the day before in the kiddie pool.

"We'll see." Ross said, his words strained.

"When can we go swimming Daddy?" Izzy's question lit the memory of bodies rounding the corner in the lazy river. Ross could see up the long straight leg on this side of the circulating pool. The path was clear, but the water looked murky. He scanned left and glimpsed the top of what might have been a body resting in the water by the stairs on the far side. It looked to have made its way out of the current and become hung up on a railing leading into the pool.

"Not today, honey. Not until all of this is done. We need to listen and follow directions. Okay?"

Moments later, a man exited the doors where Ross and Izzy had emerged. For a moment, Ross thought their ordeal might be over. With khaki pants, a white button-down and loafers, his business casual appearance looked suitable for an evening out.

He slicked his long black hair back as he strode up to the camera. Ross's sensors recorded the vanity and noted the stare he was trying to hide behind the tortoise framed sunglasses.

"How are you?" he asked. The wind caught his hair.

"Are you Anas?"

He lifted his glasses, uncovering one green eye, the other squinting from the light. "How do you know my name?"

"The guard. It was a mistake."

"And you are?"

For a moment, Ross wondered if he should use fake names. The tongue-tied moment hung awkwardly. If he was caught in a lie there could be repercussions. "I'm Ross, and this is my daughter, Isabelle."

"Ross, you have a wonderful daughter. Very sweet. I want you to understand that we are here for a reason and mean to do you no harm. Violence is merely a means to an end in this case." Anas paused and centered the camera. "As I've told the others I've worked with today, please do your best to follow instructions so they aren't forced to be rough." He gestured over his shoulder to guards standing sentry behind him.

"So, you're the leader?" Ross asked.

Anas smiled. "One of them."

"Have you considered letting the children go?"

"We're not here to debate, Ross. You and Isabelle are in my charge now. We'll be working together." Anas had a computer under his arm. He set it on the table and leaned down to inspect the screen.

"Here are the basics of what you'll—" He straightened and stepped around the camera toward Ross and Izzy. Ross felt the urge to retreat for the second time that day.

"Let me see your head." Anas touched the side of Ross's

chin with his index finger, turning his head to the side. His skin felt as soft as Izzy's.

"I'm sorry," he said. "Let's pull the chairs up. Each of you can sit in one. Side by side, of course." He helped with the chair behind Izzy while Ross pulled up the second.

"Why are you filming us?" Ross asked.

Anas finished situating the chair then looked down at Ross.

"We have our reasons. Sit, please." Anas offered the chair and then stepped away.

Anas's personality felt reserved, almost introverted in tone, but the look he gave communicated control. He knew what he was doing. What he didn't know was that Ross was counter-interpreting his every gesture.

"Once I start the recording, please state your names. Ross, you will do the talking. Tell us where you call home. Can you turn a little please?" Anas gestured for him to turn so that his left side faced the camera.

"I need you to explain that the bruise on your head resulted from you trying to escape. Then go on and explain how you've been in good care since then. How Isabelle has been cared for. Mention the blankets, water and medicines provided, please. Explain how you've been told you'll be safe as long as you follow instructions and our requests are met. Say something like, 'Please give them what they want so Isabelle and I can come home safely.' But instead of home, tell us the state. Where are you're from?"

33

US Consulate's Office, Curacao

Margaret Baker initiated the second call of the day. "Ray, what's our next move?"

"We're establishing channels with the other countries and Wincopia. This just hit us at the same time as you, Margaret. We need time."

"Is the non-compliance policy going to be reconsidered?" Margaret asked. The US and UK both had strict noncompliance policies when it came to ransom demands. "We've had news crews landing all day. Every charterable jet in the northern Hemisphere is parked on the runway out here."

"We've got three days, Margaret. This is going to take time. The only thing you can do for now is state the policy, verbatim, and tell them it's not in your purview." The keel of Ray's tone remained level.

There was a long bit of silence as Margaret considered the implications. The Secretary of State was known to labor for long hours and move quickly between priority items.

"Margaret?"

"We're not seriously going to allow this to happen?" Most in the State Department agreed in theory with the no ransom policy. They also knew that kidnapped Americans were executed faster than citizens from any other countries. The terrorists knew they never paid. Corporations were known to pay if the captured employees were high ranking or a public relations disaster loomed, but not the United States.

"Killing the father and daughter will be bad enough, Ray. But watching those buildings come down with people... Germany, Sweden, Italy, the Dutch, they'll pay. You know that better than anyone. They'll pay to free their people. What then? Are we going to let the world watch the Germans, Swedes and Dutch walk out? They'll bring those buildings down, Ray."

"We've got people analyzing the videos to verify the explosives." His monotone only added fuel to the fire.

"Isn't plastic explosive easier to buy and smuggle than machine guns and RPG's? That was the least of their worries. Why would they bluff?"

"Margaret, I know you're stressed, but I need you to be a pillar here. Shift the heat to me when you have to. Everyone knows D.C. is making the calls, not you. The list of options is long right now. It's going to take time for us to sift through them. Our goal tonight will be to identify the strategies likely to result in positive outcomes."

"I appreciate the situation, Ray. And I'm not worried about the reporters. I can talk a party line with the best of them. I'm worried about the people in those buildings. I'm worried about Ross Günther and his daughter. I'm worried about the sweet old Swedish lady and the family of eight on holiday from England."

"I hear you, Margaret. And I agree with your sentiments. Right now, it's all about the mechanism. We've got assets all over gearing up to head your way. We're sending a security detachment to provide protection for your team and the Forward Operating Locations. We'll be in touch, Margaret. Hang in there."

Even as a career politician, she struggled with the lack of humanity the top brass was capable of justifying. The internet was awash in videos of Americans and Brits being executed at the hands of terrorists. They were mostly unlucky reporters and renounced intelligence operatives. This was different, though. She could feel the proverbial blow to the gut that this group had just landed. The impact was still spreading across the torso of the government. They'd backed the United States into a corner like it'd never been backed into before.

The continental European countries operated without stated ransom policies. They made decisions on a case by case basis. More often than not, they paid to free citizens. This multinational ransom would create enormous pressure. Even through the monotone, Margaret could sense the sweat on Ray Ladenburg's brow. Washington was on eggshells. Political futures hung in the balance. Give too much ground to the terrorists and your political enemies would castrate you. Let citizens die en masse and you'll be eternally convicted in the court of public opinion. *Fieri non potest ut vincas.* You cannot win.

The Caribbean posting was supposed to be an easy one. Turquoise water, plenty of friends and family from home interested in visiting, simple-minded dignitaries; it was the easy life. Margaret and her husband would literally cruise their way into retirement with the most relaxing post of her career. Now she was watching videos of hostages who, from her estimation, did not know they might be executed in three days. There was a Dutch couple from Amsterdam, a German politician whose family was at the resort but not in the video. A Swedish woman who looked like a high mountain grandmother who had come down from the Alps. There was no mention if she was alone, but she struck Margaret as the oddest addition to the spectacle. From the UK, a group of three coeds on break from University that had decided on a holiday in the Caribbean. They'd started as two couples but lost one of the boys when he tried to escape to get help.

A family of five with two young daughters and an older son were selected to represent Italy. Imagine not paying and letting them go to their deaths.

The Wincopia video included a resort manager who was covering the night shift for a colleague. She did the talking. Beside her sat a security guard who'd clearly sustained a blow to the face, a housekeeper and a woman from the laundry facility.

After watching the videos a second time, Margaret was convinced that the hostages in the them didn't know of the execution plans. Their voices lacked the fear that would most certainly be embedded if they knew they were to be killed over money. The statements, *please give them what they want*, were monotone. There was no pleading or crying. Several appeared stressed and each of them looked confused, but they were all managing the fear.

An eighth video was recorded beneath one of the buildings. The camera walked from one end to the other stopping at vertical concrete pillars. Each time the camera zoomed in on the wires running from cylinders of plastic explosive. "More than enough to bring this building to the ground," a voice in the background said after each zoom.

What tore at Margaret the most was the video of the American, Ross Günther and his daughter. Margaret was a mother of two herself. She'd had a lump in her belly while she watched all of the videos, but the emotion in Ross's eyes carried a supernatural quality through to the screen. The complete cocktail of emotions was only discernible by another parent. Anger, resolve, fear, determination—it was all there, swirling in his eyes and on display for the parents of the world to see.

34

KAVITA'S CAFÉ, Aruba

MADDIE FELL into a state of shock. Sound dissolved and time ceased. As videos of other hostages played, her stare lost clarity. She entered an inner headspace that was wholly new to her.

There was a hand on her back.

"Have a seat, Maddie." A chair was moved in from behind.

"I just need a—" Maddie looked down at the floor. She rubbed her hands over her face, pressing so hard it felt like the skin might tear. "A minute—I just need a minute—or two."

She turned and walked toward the door, semi-conscious of Geert's hand, which dropped away after a step or two.

A hush had fallen with the breaking news. It remained as the people in the café watched the other videos. Maddie kept her head down. One foot fell in front of the next. Her hands didn't leave her face until she hit the front porch and descended the stairs.

Shock and disbelief began to boil into a red froth of anger as she crossed the parking lot. At the end of the gravel lot, she stopped and stared at the road, her body throbbing with fury. Her heart thumped, propelling the anger to the surface, just below the skin where it wanted out.

There was a car coming up from Baby Beach. For a moment, Maddie considered stepping in front of it.

After the car passed, she stood there thinking, still staring down at the asphalt. The video of Ross and Izzy flickered with images of Will's ruptured skull. The pain would be magnified exponentially this time.

Please give them what they want, so Isabelle and I can come home safely to Maryland. Will! Jesus Christ, Will! You're gonna be okay! Get me a corpsman!

Maddie's mind bounced back and forth between the scenes with evil possession. Her hands found her hips and she looked up at the sky, drawing long breaths in and out. She needed to keep her energy focused. The negativity had nearly killed her the last time.

Sometimes she still caught the sound of Will's last breaths drifting like ghosts through her mind. Morning, night, middle of the day—it had taken years to break away the cocoon.

Will was one of the best friends Maddie had ever known—second only to Ross and the girls. They were like bar room buddies, beating the hell out of pool balls, but instead of a pool table, their playing field was Iraq. They worked as a team, Maddie behind the gun and Will spotting targets and shots. It never sat right that the kills were credited to the person pulling the trigger. Will deserved the credit just as much, if not more.

Maddie had come to live with owning Will's death. She'd never get over Ross and Izzy.

She hadn't fired fast enough, and Will died. This time it was a fucking passport.

A fraction of a second made all the difference for Will. The round tore him open in the instant Maddie fired. If she would have pulled the trigger a few milliseconds sooner, Will would still be around to look after his three boys and wife.

Paperwork sealed Ross and Izzy's fate. If she would've remembered a passport for Charlotte, she'd be in that resort with them. There wouldn't have *been* a fucking video.

Will's death rode around with her like a parasite medicine that couldn't kill. Losing Ross and Izzy would turn it into a tissue-eating monster. Everyone would tell her to be strong for Charlotte—they'd give the only advice there was to offer—but she'd die from the inside out.

Will was dead before the corpsman hit the roof. Ross and Izzy had 72 hours.

Maddie straightened and continued the deep breaths. All around her the day was slipping into night. When she closed her eyes, the video was there, repeating in an unending loop. Ross had a look in his eye that told her it was far from over. He was up for a fight.

Maddie opened her eyes to an orange and purple sky in the west. Nature was perfect, even on its worst days. It didn't care that the United States hadn't paid a public ransom in years. It didn't have an opinion or take sides.

The US government spent seven million dollars per minute. A twenty-minute shutdown would cover the ransom. So many dollars were wasted, lost in the mountain of money. Here was a tangible use that would see none thrown at it.

Pay the ransom and then attack the bastards with reckless abandon, that'd be Maddie's plan. No US citizen would think twice about that strategy, except the ones running the government. Such a titanic shift of policy would only happen if one of their own was on the line. Common citizens didn't garner that type of exception.

Standing there, staring at the sky, her gut provided the second certainty of the day. She wanted in on the fight. This time she'd pull the trigger first, before it was too late. Standing aside and waiting on the outcome wasn't an option. She'd be torn apart, one chunk at a time.

Voices from behind caught her attention. Maddie turned. Geert and Kavita were standing on the front porch watching her. Geert had his arm around his wife. Both had tears in their eyes.

"Geert. I'm gonna need your help," Maddie said, as she climbed the stairs.

Geert nodded. "Anything at all. You name it."

35

SURFSIDE RESORT, Aruba: Ground Floor

TWELVE HUNDRED MILLIGRAMS of Ibuprofen worked wonders. Ross was worried it might burn a hole in his stomach, but it was worth it. The video session was a good thing. They were bait and needed to be kept alive.

He and Izzy were walked back to the administrative office after the video session. Anas accompanied them.

"You will not be going back to your room," Anas explained as they reached the lobby door. "You'll be staying in the office. Mattresses will be brought for you." His demeanor was anything but menacing. In fact, he seemed polite, his tone cordial.

Anas was leading and he held the door open. "Understand that you will be under guard at all times and any attempt to escape will..." Anas looked down at Isabelle. "Don't leave the room. For her sake."

Ross's eyes followed the blood smear back out toward to main lobby where a soldier was hunched over a machine gun.

It was resting on a tripod on a desk that had been pulled from the concierge area adjacent to reception. If he fired, the first shots would be through the lobby windows, Ross reasoned.

As he looked on, Ross felt Izzy cringe at the sight. He pulled her face to his stomach to shield her eyes.

"Stop it! I can't see where I'm going, Daddy!"

After they were past it, he let go. At the same time, Ross noticed that the lights had been turned on in the souvenir shop and convenience store. They were glass-fronted spaces set to the side of the main entry within the resort lobby. The first sold t-shirts, trinkets and inner tubes for the lazy river. Separated by a wall lined by shelves on each side, the other offered snacks, medicine, magazines and over-priced alcohol. Ross spotted the three Brits he'd glimpsed on their way out of the office. They'd been moved and were seated along the convenience store checkout counter.

In the souvenir shop, a man sat alone in a chair in the middle of the room. The two made eye contact, their short gaze broken as Ross turned to round the reception desk into the office.

"Where is your wife?" Anas asked after the door to the lobby drifted closed. Ross was caught off guard by the question. He had noticed another red stain soaked into the carpet at the entrance to the office.

"She didn't make it down," Ross said. "We have a one-year-old, and she didn't have a passport."

Anas shook his head. "I'll be in here most of the time. Knock if you need anything." He motioned to a door along the wall of the office.

"I could use some ice. For my head," Ross said. "To help bring down the swelling."

"I'll see what I can do." Anas left through the door they had entered. On his way out, he paused. "Don't let the emergency exit get you into trouble. It's blocked and won't open. Besides that, there's an armed soldier on the other side. Just stay put and you'll be okay."

It had taken close to an hour but the ice arrived. Along with it came a case of water and a box with assorted potato chips. Fifteen minutes after that, two mattresses, sheets and pillows were delivered.

There was a cluster of six cubicles set off to one side, leaving an open area along the wall with the door Anas had pointed out. The door was in the center of the wall. It looked heavy and had a deadbolt above the knob.

Past the door were marketing pictures of the resort. Ridiculously vibrant families played in the water. Picture-perfect couples smiled in the sun.

The back wall included an emergency exit and two windowless offices. It was about the worst office you could imagine on an island. Not a single window out to paradise.

The clock on the wall read 6:49. He'd left his phone in the hotel room when they made their ill-fated run to escape. Without the clock, Ross wouldn't have had any idea what time it was. It was hard to believe an entire day had passed.

He made the beds and straightened their space. Izzy was drawing pictures in a cubicle where Ross had set her up. It felt good to have some order after a day of chaos.

Ross had already searched the offices and cubes for anything of value. He'd come away with two pocket-sized flashlights, a miniature Leatherman multi-tool and an iPad.

Only six of the eight desks had a computer, and all of them were password protected. If Maddie was there, she probably could have hacked in. Ross looked for the passwords on Post-it notes, but the crew manning the windowless office was good about hiding the codes.

He'd found the iPad in the boss's office. Karen Wooten was the 'Resort Manager,' according to the plaque squared front and center on her desk. Karen's iPad was not protected by a password, which was the first good luck of the day for Ross. It *was* connected to the internet. Score two for the good guys.

Ross was careful not to use it in the open, for fear they'd take it if they caught him. With the mattresses delivered, it seemed they were settled for the night. There'd been no sign of Anas and the gunshots they'd heard throughout the day, the ones he lied to Izzy about, had all but stopped.

With the door partially closed, Ross sat in Karen's chair and wheeled himself up to the desk. He tapped his way into the iPad and launched the browser, hoping for news of any kind. As the bar across the top hesitated, it occurred to him that this had to be a top international story. Terrorists take over Aruban resort. He could see the headlines on CNN and Fox News.

The bar moved to the right and a webpage appeared. A fraction of a second was all that was required to know that the terrorists had taken control of more than just the buildings.

'This webpage is designed for the Surfside Resort guests. You are hostages. Stay in your rooms! Our goal is to hurt as few of you as possible. We are here for money. We are asking your countries to pay ransom. Follow the rules below and you will be safe.'

The rules were simple.

'1) Stay in your room unless told to do otherwise.'

'2) Anyone attempting to escape, resist, or failing to follow orders, will be shot.'

'3) When we sound the fire alarm, check this webpage. The alarm is an indication that this webpage has been updated with new, pertinent information. Follow any instructions posted here closely.'

Seven videos were listed vertically under the heading 'Hostage Videos'. Theirs was in the middle and Ross clicked it first.

He looked like shit. The knot on his head was the size of half a baseball. It was a purple hump sticking out the side.

He felt tears wanting to well in his eyes when he watched Izzy on the video—so young and innocent. Izzy never looked up at the camera. Her feet were dangling above the ground. She bounced her legs back and forth, staring down at her sandals. Ross wondered if Maddie had seen the video yet. He could almost feel her rage.

After it finished, he scrolled the rest of the page and was struck by the lack of information. There was nothing about ransoms. No reasons given for the videos. Nothing being asked at all.

Ross typed, 'CNN,' into the browser and hit enter. The screen cleared and the bar ran left to right but hopes were dashed when the same page reappeared. He typed, 'Google' and got the same result.

"Dammit!" He wanted to slam the iPad down and break it.

"Daddy! Are you okay?" Izzy asked from the room outside.

"I'm fine, sweets. Just bumped my knee."

"I'm hungry, Daddy," Izzy whined.

Ross ignored it, and clicked on another video. The trio from England showed a great deal of fear. They had trouble maintaining contact with the camera which made it hard to understand what they were saying. Someone, probably Anas, had clapped in the background. After the clap, the man in the video had focused and explained how they had been four. One in their group had been killed trying to escape.

Ross recognized the German man from the souvenir shop. He made it clear he was a member of the Bundesrat of Germany. A government official.

Ross had enough of the videos. He walked out of Karen Wooten's office and into the second cube where Izzy sat with a stack of computer paper and markers. Looking over her shoulder, he saw that Izzy had drawn a picture of a house with a rainbow arching over the top. Four people, two tall and two short, stood beside the house. She was working on a car.

"I'm hungry too, honey. Have another bag of chips for now and I'll see if I can get us some food."

"You never usually let me eat chips," Izzy replied, looking up.

"It's okay for now. Until we can find some salad." Ross smiled and tickled his daughter under the arm.

"Gotta eat your salad so you grow big and strong," Izzy said, in her sing-song Daddy voice.

"Right, right," said Ross. "That's a beautiful picture, sweets."

He turned and stared at the door Anas had pointed out. Ross hadn't heard any noise come from in there since Anas left. Something told him to knock.

The tumbler in the deadbolt above the knob rolled. The door was pushed open toward Ross. Anas was leaning back in a chair, looking over his shoulder.

"What can I do?" he asked.

Ross hesitated, a mix of renewed fear and curiosity catching his tongue. Anas was surrounded by computer screens.

"Hey... Um... I appreciate the food you've brought us, but is it possible to get something besides potato chips?" Ross knew that they needed to stay as fed and hydrated as possible. Food and water were often kept from kidnapping victims. There was no telling if or when their situation would follow suit.

"Can we get something else to eat, mister?" Izzy hopped up from behind, wrapping herself around Ross's leg.

Anas leaned forward. He turned in his chair, anger congealing in his brow. Seeming ready to speak, he held the words as he scanned her.

The tightness in his eyes faded. "Perhaps," he said. "How old are you?"

"Six. And..." Izzy said, drawing it out. "I have to wait like a whole year before I'm seven."

Anas smiled. He rocked his head, his expression softening.

"I had a sister." His grin turned sad. Ross noted the past tense as he waited for more.

"She was seven, like you." Anas leaned closer, his lowering eyebrows bunching the skin around his eyes. "Her favorite color was purple. What's yours?"

"Pink is perfect." Izzy's voice was hushed with shyness.

"Very nice." Anas puckered and then drew in a breath as he straightened in his chair. His nose and eyes lifted to the ceiling and he cocked his head as if clearing a crick in his neck.

"You've got a lot of computers going in there," Ross said.

"Yes. Enough that it gets a bit warm." Anas pushed the door further open and rolled his chair toward the threshold to keep it from closing.

"She's was about your height," Anas said, again leaning forward and focusing his attention on Izzy. "A similar nose, but darker hair. You are lucky to have family."

"Thanks," Izzy whispered, hugging Ross's leg tighter.

Anas sat back in his chair again. He crossed his arms and shifted his gaze to Ross. "Do you understand the gravity of your situation?"

Ross considered the question before responding. "Not fully."

"You are hostages." Anas's attempt to bring strength to the words was awkward. "We've taken over this entire resort."

Ross sensed him searching for recognition in the eyes—some acknowledgment of the authority implied by the statement. He knitted his brow and nodded.

"Our goal is not to hurt you or the others," he continued, shaking his head side to side. "Our goal is money." Anas paused. "And the pulpit," he said, nodding this time.

"I understand," Ross said.

"It's important that you follow the rules. While our goal is not to hurt many, those who do not follow the rules must be dealt with." He broke eye contact. "The penalties are severe."

"I promise you. My interest is in protecting my daughter."

The mention of her name brought Anas's attention back down to Izzy. "Yes, of course it is. It's a mutual interest." He unlaced his arms, turning the palms down and resting them on his knees. "Here's what we can do. There's pre-wrapped sandwiches and fruit. I'll have some brought to you. And, we're going to see about finding someone to do some cooking tomorrow."

Cooking? Tomorrow? Ross thought. *How long was this going to last?*

"I like sandwiches and fruit," Izzy said. "Thank you."

"Such good manners for a mere six years. You are most welcome, Miss Isabelle." Anas reached out a clenched fist. "We will *work* together." Izzy reached out and bumped her fist to his. Anas rolled away his hand opening in an exaggerated explosion, complete with simulated noise. Izzy giggled and Anas let out a bayed laugh.

"All will be well," Anas said, recovering.

"Are you leading the whole thing from in here?" Ross asked.

Anas turned toward the computer screens. There were three laptops arrayed on the desk. The one on the left appeared to be showing the webpage Ross had read on the iPad. The one in the middle—Anas closed the top, folding it down before Ross could see what was on the screen.

The laptop on the right had a number of small boxes with pop-up windows overlaid.

"What's that?" Ross asked.

Anas looked to see where he was pointing. "You should go," he said without moving.

Ross widened his eyes and put his hands up. "Okay."

"But to answer your question... Those are drones. We have four of them flying at all times."

"You mean the toy helicopter things?" Ross asked.

Anas chuckled. "Yes, but much more sophisticated."

"But the picture looks strange. Is that night vision?"

"It's infrared," Anas replied. "See here." He pointed to the bottom, at one of the boxes on the screen. Ross stepped into the threshold, grasping the door frame as he leaned into the room.

"These colors are from our men on the roof over there." He pointed toward the wall to his right, elevating his hand toward the ceiling. "Their bodies give off heat and with an infrared camera we see those wavelengths show as color. I can switch it to regular light." Anas sat forward and took a mouse in his right hand. He clicked two popup windows closed and then drew down a menu from the top and selected something from the list. The picture changed from a black screen with reddish-orange dots, to a dark video image.

Ross cocked his head, focusing his gaze as he stepped closer still. He could tell the image was from high above, but he couldn't tell what he was looking at.

"That's pretty cool," he said. "So you can see if there are people around the resort?"

"Exactly. And if I see anything, I can take control and fly over to check it out. There's a reason the US military has invested so heavily in drones. Having an eye in the sky over our operation is a significant advantage." Ross could sense his excitement. It was almost as if he'd been waiting to show it off.

"That's smart." Ross said, pausing to give the compliment time to resonate.

"What's on that one?" Izzy asked from below. She was still attached to Ross's leg but her grip had slackened. She was pointing to the screen with the webpage where thumbnails of the hostage videos were listed. "Is that Netflix?"

Anas turned back to look at her. "No, Isabelle. This computer is where everyone in the hotel is directed when they log into the internet. It has instructions which you and your father already have been told." He looked up at Ross and continued. "You know how at a hotel they can force you to their webpage to get wi-fi access?"

"Yes."

"I've written a similar program so that all traffic is directed to this page when their browser makes a call to the internet."

"So the information on there is for what reason?" Ross asked rhetorically.

"To keep everyone calm. This is very difficult. We want to hurt as few people as possible, like I said. To do this, we must provide information. Rules. This was my idea." Anas sat up tall in his chair.

Ross could sense that he was making progress. Some type of bond was forming, but he needed to be careful. He needed to stick with obvious questions and keep him talking.

"So... What's the point? Is it really about the money?"

Anas folded his arms again. "The money is key. It fuels the cause and provides a good life for the leadership. Taking the money is a form of economic war. But beyond the money, our success here will provide the pulpit. Once our mission is complete, we'll have the influence of a sovereign state. We'll be able to affect change in foreign policy. This is something that violence alone has not accomplished."

Ross bit his lip, the concept and theory hard to reconcile. He wanted to relay something positive but the words wouldn't come.

"For me," Anas continued. "The money is important, this more so." He spread his arms wide.

"This? What do you mean?" Ross asked.

"Technology. Waging war this way will be my legacy."

"But the others. With the masks and the guns." It was more of a statement than a question. Ross waited to see how Anas interpreted the words.

He stood abruptly and turned to face Ross. "I've already

said too much." His tone remained soft, but Ross knew he had made an error.

"I'm sorry. It's interesting to me."

"In this case, death was unavoidable," said Anas. "There are too many of you. Some were bound to try and run. Plus, we had to make a production. It's the only way to get real attention." He paused to catch his breath. "Seven billion people... Seven billion. Kill just a few and the world watches. Humans feed off it. They watch non-stop. The attention is what keeps terrorism alive. Reality TV." The two of them stared at each other. Anas's face showed a clumsy seriousness.

"Well, thanks again for help—" The door to his right flew open and Ross turned away, shielding Izzy and nearly diving for cover.

"What the hell is he doing in here?" said a new voice. Ross turned back. Every muscle in the man's face bore rage.

"Get out, Fazul. This is my command." Anas put a hand up as if to ward him off.

The man projected his fury, back and forth between Ross and Anas. "I'll get out when I'm ready." Each word was enunciated deliberately. His lips moved but his jaw remained still, teeth clenched. "This is what I am talking about, Anas. You do not think. Why would you allow a hostage in here? This man could overwhelm you. He's twice your size." He looked like he might spit at Ross.

He pointed at the door. "Get the hell out of here."

36

Kavita's Café, Aruba

"You know what, Chuckles... I'm done with the condolence bullshit. I got a thousand messages and almost as many calls."

Kavita had set Maddie up on the sofa beside Charlotte's crib. Word had apparently spread that she was on the island but not at the resort. People knew she was cut off from Ross and Izzy. She'd fallen asleep responding to text messages and voicemails.

"Let's get down to brass tacks," Maddie said. "What intel do you have for me?"

"Alright, Mad. But listen. You gotta talk about it. You know that..." He went silent for a handful of seconds.

Maddie said nothing.

"There's a shit-storm of activity. Word is that Delta and DEVGRU *are* both on alert. I made a few calls and it sounds like JSOC already punched the button. They're deploying next door to Curacao. Completely off the chain to have both deploying as full elements."

Chuckles was referring to the Army's Delta Force and SEAL Team 6 from the Navy. Seal Team Six was referred to within government circles by the acronym DEVGRU, thanks to their official title, United States Navel Special Warfare Development Group.

Delta and SEAL Team 6 were elite fighting units. They operated under the auspices of the Joint Special Operations Command, JSOC, and specialized in counter-terrorism. They'd choreographed simultaneous missions in the past, but they'd never been directed to work together on a single target.

"Sounds like they're sending a sledgehammer, instead of a scalpel."

Chuckles didn't have time to respond.

"What about the ransom?" Maddie asked.

"Still working on that. Speculation is the politicians will have to reconsider."

"Or wait until the payers get their people out, and then pull the trigger."

"Yup," said Chuckles. "That's definitely an option."

"An option that gets Ross and Izzy killed." Maddie was surprised by her words. "What else you got?"

"We've got recon birds on station. With the bluebird weather down there, they've got eyes on practically twenty-four by seven. Activity in the open spaces of the resort is minimal. Couple bodies in the pool and quite a few around the building perimeter. Best guesses are they took it trying to escape in the early hours. Somehow, they've got the place locked up now. Not seeing very much activity at all. It's got people a little uptight. They've got over a thousand people in those buildings. Some up here are worried about mass murder. Like the ransom was a cover to give them time to kill everyone. Anyhow, I guess these guys have been sending emails with instructions on how to pay. Our people are able to respond and are asking for proof of life on the majority."

"Uh-huh. Keep going."

"Looks like they're armed with some light machine guns. Intel is saying RPKs and Kalashnikovs mostly. At least two sniper rifles on the roofs, plus RPGs. Three or four launchers and cases of rockets. Intel is also reporting a case on the roof that looks like a shoulder fired surface to air system." Chuckles paused. Maddie heard a page turn in the background.

"They weren't fucking around, were they?" she asked.

"Nope. Took all the trimmings to play defense down range."

"No one saw this monstrosity coming? This is a huge operation, Chuck."

"Nope again. Looks like they came out of Venezuela. Our spooks have major blind spots in Venezuela. Been high on the risk assessment for a while now. They kill off informants and agents so fast it's hard to turn people. Anyhow, the recon birds show a big yacht parked at the pier in front of the resort. It was last seen in Maracaibo. Fucking Venezuelan regime's been inviting the terrorists in for a while now. It's an open-door policy down there. You got enough money, then come on in."

"What's the estimate on numbers?" Maddie asked.

"Still working on it, but they think it's quite a few. Maybe thirty or more." Chuckles sighed into the phone. "Listen Mad, I'll keep feeding you information, but you need more support than I can give you, sister. Where you staying?"

"We've got some friends down here. Locals we've gotten to know over the years. Been real good to me and Charlotte. We're fine."

"You oughta reach out to the Consulate and get hooked up with them. There's all sorts of government headed your way. They'll be able to give you a hand."

Maddie thought about it. "I don't need a nanny quite yet, Chuck. Besides I'm on the lam. They tried to hold me up at the airport and I slipped out."

"What?"

"Yeah. They were holding up tourists headed to the resorts. They probably ended up flying them home. I wasn't sticking around to find out."

"How the hell did you get by them with the kid?"

"Come on... How hard is it? I got sent to the corner and told to wait for a newbie agent's daddy to come see me. When he looked the other way, we walked out. The shitty part is I left our fucking passports." Maddie was still pissed about losing Charlotte's passport. The damn passport had spun this shit-ass web in the first place.

"Jesus, Mad. You better call the Consulate and tell them what's up. They'll get your ass out of there before the locals come looking."

"I think the locals are busy enough. Which reminds me, what's their story? You got anything on the local response?"

"They've been told to back the fuck off and to give these guys room. My guess is they'll take that advice. Now that everyone knows what's up—they're focusing on evacuations. Then it's wait and see. What the fuck do they care. Only a handful of locals are tied up in there."

"I'll hit you later, Chuckles. Thanks."

After she hung up, Maddie walked back into the house and picked up Charlotte. She was sitting in the center of a circle of girls playing.

"I'll bring her back in a minute." Maddie said, picking her up. Island schools were closed and Kavita's kids had invited friends over to play with the baby.

They walked to the front window. She kissed her daughter on the cheek and looked out. Their reflections looked back.

"We had you so your sister wouldn't be alone," Maddie said. "You girls would always be a team. You'd have each other after Dad and I got too boring to hang out with." She turned from the reflection and looked into Charlotte's fierce blue eyes. Baby Ross started back, a half-grin on one side.

"You miss Daddy and Sissy?"

Charlotte reached out with a finger, smiling as she touched her mother's nose.

Setting Charlotte back in the circle, Maddie was struck by the contrasts. Like oil and water, the reality of their situation was divided distinctly between the unthinkable and the natural.

She pushed her way through the squeaky screen door and stepped out on the front patio. The door needed assistance to close, the salty air having compromised the hinges. She walked slowly through the dusty side yard to the covered patio where Kavita had served food between restaurants. Maddie spun one of the seldom-used chairs away from the table and sat.

Morning sun cast heat across her chest and legs. It had just climbed high enough that the roof offered shade above the shoulders.

She rehashed the information from Chuckles and replayed most of what she'd read the night before. In the *Art of War*, Sun Tzu said, "To subdue the enemy without fighting is the acme of skill." The NJF had used the cover of darkness and harnessed the force multiplier of surprise. They'd come prepared, wielding overwhelming firepower and used both to take their objective intact. Ultimately, they'd brought their enemy to the field of battle using their own terms. Meet our demands or face the public murder of your citizens. It was fucking brilliant.

They used the internet as a conduit and a noose, disseminating information and tightening the chokehold.

The internet, Maddie thought. She turned over the phone she'd been tossing in her hands and called up Pich Tang from her contacts.

37

SURFSIDE RESORT, Aruba

ANAS HAD ONLY SEEN Fazul one other time the previous night. He'd spent most of it combing the buildings with a video camera and tablet. They'd gone door-to-door, videotaping and cataloguing nationalities. The United States government had requested video evidence that showed proof of life for their citizens being held in the resort.

Anas and his security team had knocked on more doors than he could count.

"Open the door and show your face to the camera. Your country wants to see that you're alive." The team had completed every floor of Building One. By the time they were halfway through Building Two, Anas had grown so tired that he needed sleep.

In the early morning hours, he posted the videos to the internet and fell to his mattress. Earlier in the day, he had two of the men stuff it in between the desk and the wall. It didn't fit, the edges curled up on both sides, but there was room for one in the middle and it kept him with his computers.

As he settled, it occurred to him that he'd never gotten food for Isabelle. They were just a few feet away, separated by the wall, but he'd forgotten because of Fazul. The email from the United States had come in as the two of them were arguing about his brother's intrusion. Anas had gotten to work immediately, needing the task to calm his nerves.

He slept just a few hours before he was up, rummaging in the store cooler for the last of the sandwiches. Isabelle's face had brought back ghosts that had long ago faded from his mind.

Fazul hadn't been close to their sister before she was killed, but Anas remembered her like a twin. She was three years his junior, but as the youngest, she was mature beyond her years. So smart at math, she had helped Anas with his homework a few times, and was eager to read storybooks aloud whenever given the chance.

Before the operation, Anas knew there would be death, but most of it was not to involve him. Dealing with the videos, and the thought of executions, swirled his gut sour. There was little chance the United States would pay the ransom. That made Isabelle a dead child walking.

"Sorry about last night. Ah... My brother and I are very different." Anas spoke the words as he stepped into the office and closed the door. Ross was sitting in a wheeled chair reading a magazine. He was in the cubicle directly across from the door and looked up when it opened. Beside him, Isabelle was facing away, her head down toward the desk with a marker in her hand. She stopped drawing and looked back at him.

"Can I call you Mr. Anas?" she asked. "At my school we put Mr. and Ms. in front of everyone's name."

Anas chuckled. "Yes, Isabelle, you may. Here... I've brought sandwiches. Also, some books and a game of jacks... For you,

Isabelle." Anas handed the heavy plastic bag to Ross. "Some cans of soda, chips and candy bars as well."

Ross looked into the bag. "Wow, thanks. We appreciate it."

"Sorry. I was busy last night and forgot."

"It's no problem," Ross said. "Thanks again."

"There are crayons and coloring books in the game room. I noticed them yesterday. I'll bring some later this morning. For you, Isabelle."

Isabelle smiled then leaned for the bag, tugging on the edge to inspect its contents. "Do you want to eat with us?"

"No, thank you. I have work to complete."

"Doritos! These are my favorite!" She handed them to her father, who opened the bag and handed it back.

"That was your brother last night?" Ross asked, as he started to unpacked the bag. He set a sandwich in front of his daughter. "You can put the chips on it like you do at home."

Isabelle looked skeptically at the sandwich. "Is this like Sub-a-way?"

"Yes, baby. Same thing. You just don't get to pick what goes on it."

Isabelle curled her lip. "I like to pick, Papa."

"Next time. Promise. Just eat, sweets."

Ross pat her on the head and turned his attention back to Anas.

"Yes. My brother," said Anas. "Unfortunately, we do not always see eye to eye. We are very different people."

"How are you different?" Ross asked. He wheeled his chair to the edge of the cubicle. "Do you want to sit? There's an extra chair around the corner."

Anas hadn't planned to stay long; he did have work to complete. "My brother is a smart man, but he's driven by emotions. This has never made for a very encouraging relationship between us. We have our own ways."

"That must be difficult. Especially in a situation like this. Very high-stress. Very emotional."

The word *difficult* caught Anas's attention. In truth, the relationship between him and his brother had always been strained. Their father died when Anas was a toddler. Mother was pregnant with his sister at the time. Some years later, his mother had taken up with a man who was rough with all the kids when she was gone from home. She caught him hitting Fazul one day and sent him away. The next morning, she had a bruise on her face.

When Anas joined his brother in secondary school, Fazul ignored him in front of his friends. On the daily walk-in, Fazul would hurry so that Anas couldn't keep up.

"I've got a brother. I want to love the guy, but he's just not a lot of fun to be around. You know what I mean?" Ross's words pulled Anas back.

"I do know. Being different is difficult. He's not been himself. Always... He's been difficult to work with. But here... More so, I would say."

"Well that's probably not a big surprise. You all look like you know what you're doing but it's still gotta be stressful and that makes people act up."

Anas didn't have a response and Ross continued. "How'd you end up with this group?"

The question came out in a way that felt scripted. It made Anas wonder why Ross was so interested in talking to him. Anas turned away for a moment. Something told him he should go. He rubbed his face. Using his index finger he pulled moisture up from the inside of his eyes to the bridge of his nose.

"You want a Dorito, Mr. Anas?"

He turned back. Isabelle had her hand extended, the orange triangle there at the end. He reached for it. "Yes, thank you, Isabelle. So nice of you to share." He took a bite, the crack of the chip seeming to fill the room. As he crunched on it, he remembered his reunion with Fazul.

It was several years ago now. Anas had almost literally run into his brother. They were heading opposite directions on a street in Bangalore, India where they had grown up.

"I don't have a brother," Isabelle said, again interrupting his thought. "Just one sister. She can be a little hard. She cries sometimes. But girls are better than boys. That's what Mommy says." Her thought complete, Isabelle turned back to her paper, picked up a marker and continued to color.

"She seems to be a very unique girl."

"Thanks. She is pretty special. All heart, that one." Ross paused and pat his daughter on the back. "So where are you from?"

"India. That's where I grew up. I'm probably more American now than I am Indian, though."

"Why's that?" Ross asked.

"I spent many years in the US for education. Undergraduate and master's degrees in computer science and engineering. Both from MIT."

"Oh wow. That's a top-notch place. How the hell does a MIT grad end up here? Doing *this*?"

Anas eyeballed him. Ross had an air of congeniality, like a salesman you didn't know was selling. Still, the conversation was engaging, which was a refreshing change. Anas went on to explain how he'd paired up with an MIT alum before he finished his degrees. Clayton was a serial entrepreneur from California. He'd heard of Anas and wanted to be partners.

As he talked, Ross settled in, listening and nodding. He seemed to hang on each word, interested in the unfolding of the story.

"I built a network doming application. It sat like a bubble over a network. I integrated artificial intelligence to separate normal traffic from intrusion attempts. It won the engineering competition at MIT. We put it in place over a test network and let teams of students try and hack in. The dome caught them all." Those were the best days of his life. The high horse of innovation is a prideful and rewarding place to be. Clayton had turned it all to greed.

"You must have felt very proud of yourself." Anas felt around in Ross's tone. There was usually a condescending qualifier hanging in people's words—like technology was for geeks who didn't know how to experience pride. Ross leaned in for more.

Anas explained how Clayton was a born salesman. If a potential customer wasn't interested, he'd drop a hint to Anas. "A little intrusion might encourage them to sign," Clayton would say.

"That's illegal though, right?" Ross asked.

"It is... I'd hack their network and leave a harmless Easter egg. Anonymous, of course... Since Clayton had just been there, he'd be the first person they'd call. We landed every one of those accounts."

"Wow, that's pretty ruthless."

As Ross's comment fell, Anas was remembering the times it happened. Clayton did more than suggest it. *We've got to keep up the momentum*, he'd say. *But it's up to you. I don't want you to do anything you're uncomfortable with.* Anas hated that he'd been sold. In the end, Clayton was nothing more than a greasy salesman.

"Companies would back up trucks full of money. It was pure profit. We did it for a year. The day after my birthday, a friend called to congratulate me on selling the business." Anas felt the lump in his throat that always returned with the memory. "I couldn't reach Clayton for four days."

Ross leaned closer. It was as if he could read Anas's mind.

"The lawyer said it would be difficult to fight without paperwork. Clayton's name was on all the company records," Anas said.

Ross's face drooped in astonishment. "He gave you something... Didn't he?"

Anas looked down. It was embarrassing to admit his stupidity to a complete stranger. "Sold the business for almost four hundred million dollars. Kept it all and never even bothered to apologize."

38

Kavita's Café, Aruba

"What's happening, PTang?" Maddie asked. It was Pich Tang's handle. It bore more pomp and circumstance than her 90-pound Cambodian frame deserved.

"Mrs. Gunt, how you doing?" PTang asked.

"Mrs. Gunt, huh… I'm okay. Thanks for sending the text."

"You hear from husband and daughter? Everyone worried for you. We hear that you're not with them."

"Not yet, PTang. They came down before me. I didn't make it in before these guys took over." Maddie took a breath before switching gears. "Listen, I need your help." PTang was a brilliant human being but chit-chat was not in her wheelhouse. Maddie had learned early that despite her need for small talk, Pich responded more favorably when you focused on the point. "Tell me what you know about their tech."

"Okay." Her breathing quickened. "Mrs. Gunt, they're using two different web processes. One for people inside hotel and one for people out. Reporter from nearby hotel picked up the inside webpage. Inside they have just little bit information. Outside webpage has much more. Inside, they provide, how you say… need-to-know information for hostages. On the outside webpage they say much more. The outside webpage is being randomly rotated to different servers. Ummm… This make it hard to shut down. Also, they are using homegrown VPN tunnels. Very sophisticated from what I read. These are virtual private networks…"

"Give me some credit, PTang. I don't know much but I know what a VPN is."

"VPN protects data with encryption and makes source access very hard. The webpages themselves are very simple. Basic WordPress on both. Everyone explore outside but not much to work with. VPN feeding page and no one crack it yet."

Within the hacker community, PTang was a white hat goddess. Anytime a new web source became the focus of media attention, the hacking public took it upon themselves to see how deeply they could dive into the site. White hats would graciously communicate any security flaws they uncovered. They'd often be paid a fee for their service and take credit for their work after the fact. The fee promoted the white hat lifestyle and the credit raised their position on the ethereal hacker leader board.

Most black hats would sell any loopholes they found on the dark web. Otherwise, if they were Luddites, they'd get to work immediately corrupting files or installing software to track or defame the source.

The NJF webpages were no doubt the source of intense focus on the web. Governments and hobbyists alike were all working their keyboards in search of a vulnerability. If they found it, they'd wiggle through it like a rat and take up residence.

"I haven't played with it myself," PTang continued. "Just

scanning the threads to see what's being tried. Only found one thing. Interest you, maybe... *We make good on our threats.*"

The phone fell silent.

The words rung familiar to Maddie, but she couldn't place them. "Give me more, PTang."

"We make good on our threats. At the bottom of the outside webpage. *We make good on our threats.* We see this in many Cyberlock attacks."

"That's right," Maddie replied. "The calling card."

"Font is same as cryptos. Size... same also." PTang's already brisk pace had increased. "Only ransomware community notice something like this."

One of PTang's many specialties was testing the company's software that prevented unauthorized database encryption. Cyber ransom attacks had become a profitable black hat business. Cyberlock was the preeminent open source trojan preferred by the black hat community. They'd gain access to an organizations network, plant Cyberlock and encrypt company files. A ransom would be demanded. If the target company paid, the private key required to decrypt the files would be provided. If not, then the files remained locked for eternity.

Maddie was one of three product directors at Summit Cyber Security. Ransomware was one of her service lines. Everyday engineers coded the monitoring software. PTang tested it.

"Everyone say, why drop a fake tell?" PTang continued. "No correlation. They do it on purpose, I say. Not sure what it means but it's something. We see this before. Small world. I hear you say this before, Mrs. Gunt." PTang laughed.

"Yes. A very small world," Maddie agreed.

"Let me ask you a question, PTang. What about the inside web? Could you do something with that?"

"Humm. Umm... Ohh..." PTang made odd noises as she thought. Maddie could picture her staring at the floor, her supercomputer of a brain racing through countless variables. In her spare time, she served as a sparring partner for chess masters. One of the stipulations was that she not disclose the outcome of the contests. They asked her back time and again. If demand was any indicator, then PTang's chess game was as good as her hacking skills.

"Might be fun. No one else able to try. Probably a physical machine. No VPN. Maybe on a network with VPN source. Worth a try. How far you from the wi-fi?"

"About sixteen miles at the moment. But I can get you closer. They're evacuating the area around the resort."

"Get me close as you can. Line of sight, at least. Maybe send me satellite image of location where you can be relative to resort. Then we work on how to connect."

"It's going to be later today or tomorrow."

PTang drew in her breath. "You need my help… I not sleep. Your family, my family. Mi casa es su casa… how they say."

"You're the best, PTang."

PTang's legendary status at Summit Cyber Security was established on day one of the job. When she'd arrived, everyone waited to see what the strange skinny Asian had to offer. Maddie didn't come until later, but she'd heard the stories time and again.

On her first day, PTang reported to her manager's office. He was about to take her to see her new desk when she pulled a stapled document from her Hello Kitty backpack.

"What's this?" the manager asked.

"A list of network vulnerabilities," PTang replied.

"Where?"

"Here."

"Here, as in this company?" the manager asked.

"Yes. I get into webpage and intranet both. Could have gone much deeper. If we fight hackers, we need to be much better."

Ewing Patrick, the company's founder, was heralded for his

architectural prowess. He claimed, that given the opportunity to build a network from the ground up, he'd deliver an impenetrable fortress. Summit was not in the business of building networks, however. They were in the business of protecting existing ones. The only network he had the opportunity to build from scratch was for his own company.

The manager leafed through the document. It was a functional specification that outlined the attacks, suggesting strategies to close each of the gaps.

"Can you reproduce this live?" the manager asked.

PTang shook her head.

"Our company president architected the network. We'll need to tread lightly on his ego." By the time day one ended, PTang had already proven she was a tech rock star.

"I'll be here. Waiting, Maddie. Day. Night. Whatever you need." The comment was about as heartfelt as Maddie had experienced from PTang. There was an unspoken closeness between them. A woman in a girl's frame, she hadn't ever known family in the traditional sense. Maddie had taken to her from the start and sensed that she'd assumed some semblance of that station. The trust in her, matched with encouragement and support, were alien in her terrestrial existence. Online PTang was hailed for her skill, but in the physical world, she garnered stares. To Maddie, she was like family.

"It goes without saying, PTang. I knew you'd be willing to help. I'll be in touch. Now get back to work."

She laughed. "Yes, Mrs. Gunt."

39

Surfside Resort, Aruba

"My mommy works on computers, too." Isabelle didn't look up from her coloring this time. The comment came at a lull in the conversation between the men.

"Is that right?" Anas asked.

"She catches bad guys on the internet."

"No. Really?"

Isabelle turned in her chair now. "You're not a bad guy, are you, Mr. Anas?"

Anas eyes fell toward the floor. If she only knew how bad—how traitorous this conversation. How false and adulterous the food and candy.

"Come on, sweets. What kind of question is that? Mr. Anas brought us food and crayons. A bad guy doesn't do that."

Anas's gaze returned. He met eyes with Ross who wagged his head and glanced toward his daughter.

"Okay," Isabelle said, turning back to her work.

"Getting left with nothing for your work," Ross continued. "That must have sucked."

Ross was a big man. Big enough to make you worry if you were on the other side. Despite the fact, there was a kindness, a non-threatening aura.

"I went back home to India. Fazul and I were... reunited."

There was another lull in the conversation. Ross cocked his head and leaned closer still, waiting for him to continue.

"There's more to it than that, right?" Ross asked, hinting encouragement. "I mean I can see getting pissed off, but how did you end up here?"

"Daddy! You said a *bad* word. The one that starts with P."

Anas couldn't hide his laugh.

"Sorry, sweets," Ross said, covering his mouth with a fist. "You're right. I won't do it again."

Isabelle returned to her coloring and Anas continued. "Family pressures can be persuasive. I had an uncle, a cleric in a small town outside the city. Everyone knew his views, they knew he had radical ideas. Fazul was spending time with him. I was with Fazul. At first, we had tea and harmless conversation. Then this uncle told me stories. He talked of how the West manipulated opinions. How wealth was the new imperialism. They used the economy to oppress people. How we were puppets in their game to accumulate the wealth of the world."

Ross sat forward in his chair resting his chin in a hand.

"Your situation was proof. You'd seen firsthand what he was telling you. Like a tinder bundle ready to catch."

"Exactly." Anas felt like he'd been dragging invisible weights behind him. Talking eased the burden with each passing word. "I had come from the West. The hook of prosperity was already sunk into my mind. All that lost money. Some of it was my money and I wanted..."

"Revenge," Ross finished. "Justice."

"Yes. That and much more." Anas turned his attention away and relived the indoctrination that followed.

"That's crazy. Right place, right time. You were ready to hear how people were bad."

Anas checked his watch. "I should go." He rubbed his wet palms on the legs of his pants.

"Alright," Ross said, sitting back in his chair and crossing his arms. "But I get it. That's a good story. One people would understand. You could turn that into a book and sell a couple million copies."

As he said it, the swollen knot on his head caught Anas's attention. It had turned a darker shade of purple as they talked. And yet, here he was, understanding, justifying.

"All I did was use my Western education," Anas said, surprised at himself. "I used what I learned from the startup working with Clayton to take money from companies... In America, mostly. Some in the UK. My uncle was a lieutenant. When I told him about how I had hacked computers, we got to talking about whether we could do it for money. If I could make it work, a cut of the proceeds would be mine. The rest would go to fund the war. A war to accumulate money and persuade minds. A war of nonviolence."

Ross stayed back, arms crossed. He nodded along with the story.

"I wrote a program. It could take control of vital information. Documents and things. The company could get them back if they paid. Some of the small ransoms were in the news. Hospitals and universities, mostly, because they're public. The big money came from corporations. In some cases, millions at a time."

Ross drew down one eye in a skeptical gaze. "Okay, that all makes sense, Anas. What I don't get is how you got from there to here."

"There was talk of doing something big. Something public... but for money. There was talk about changing the rules. How success would allow us to influence the world stage. We are soldiers, Ross, not suicide bombers. Our men execute a mission and live to fight another day. The leadership made it known they were open to ideas. I was here on Aruba when I came up with the concept. All of this was my idea."

"Your idea?"

"Yes. The concept was mine."

"But this isn't your thing. You're a computer guy. A smart one, by all accounts."

He was right, of course. But a life filling the coffers with ransom money wasn't enough. Anas had achieved the ultimate hack. Already he would go down as one of the most successful of all time. But the hook was set, his time in America made him a slave—there was never enough money or infamy.

"The technology part was what got me excited. I knew I would need someone to help with the military aspect. Perhaps my biggest mistake was recommending Fazul."

A jolt of nausea hit his stomach. Ross could not know that his life, and that of his daughter, were on the line. It hadn't been part of his original plan. The execution deadlines were Fazul's idea. Now a child's life was tied to the concept—a child who reminded Anas of his own sister. A sister lost to violence herself.

Anas wanted the first deadline to be a *soft* one. Pay quickly and no one gets hurt. Refuse and we escalate the threat. Fazul spit at the floor when Anas used the word *soft*.

"So you said you were living here? Ross asked.

"I travelled around to different places—kept moving to avoid having the source of the online attacks identified. I also changed routes of approach online. This brought me to the Caribbean."

"Why the Caribbean?"

"Many people do not know, but there are cables that run under the sea." Anas used his hands to illustrate. "These are network cables filled with optical fibers. They link the continents. Without them, the internet is much slower. The cables shorten the distance data must travel. Three of the biggest intersect in the Virgin Islands. The places where they surface are called landing points. There are several in the Caribbean. One here at Baby Beach, in fact. The closer I am to where these cables land, the harder it is for my actual location to be pinpointed. Attacks can be routed through Africa or a South American country. If I am far from a landing point, the triangulation becomes easier."

"I had no idea. That's fascinating."

Anas nodded his head. He'd explained this only once before when he reasoned to his brother and uncle why he needed to leave India.

"Plus, it's a good place to live." Anas smiled. He was backing away from the conversation now.

"One day I was on the beach here and it occurred to me that these resorts are soft targets. On clear days, you can see the coast of Venezuela if you go down past the airport. It was all much easier than even I could have imagined."

"So you came from Venezuela?"

Anas nodded. "It took time to assemble the team and get them there. We imported our supplies with help from the people I met in Venezuela. We stole a yacht and came over to the dock." Anas pointed toward the front of the office in the direction of the beach. "We arrived in the middle of the night when everyone was sleeping. We've taken control, we've demanded a ransom, we've explained our intention is to limit the violence. Once the countries pay, we'll leave."

"But you can't just leave. They can watch you."

"We'll take a small number of hostages when we leave to go back to Venezuela. Once we get there, we'll break into smaller and smaller groups as we move. We've given money to many people who will help us disappear. There will be no pursuit. And we'll live to fight another day.

"I must go." Anas said. He was halfway across the room now. "Coloring supplies. I'll bring them later. For you, Isabelle."

40

Kavita's Café, Aruba

After she hung up with PTang, Madeline walked down to the café to find Geert and get some food.

"Have a seat. I'll get you some breakfast. Geert will be back any minute," Kavita said. She looked worried, but smiled, her cheeks rising to expose immaculate teeth.

Madeline nodded.

She pulled out her phone and opened the map app, switching it to satellite view and sliding it with her finger to find the Surfside resort. It took a minute to find it, but the lazy river in the center was a dead giveaway.

Kavita set something down on the table in front of her. Madeline didn't look up right away; she was analyzing the layout around the resort. When she did lift her eyes from the phone, she was greeted by one of the most beautiful sights she'd ever witnessed—a bottle of Balashi sweating profusely in the morning heat. Beads of condensation grew on the glass until their weight became heavy enough to slip down to the table. Maddie lifted the icy bottle and took a long pull. Cold worked its way toward her stomach, chilling her core and bringing the hint of a grin to her face. Over the top of the tilted bottle she saw Kavita fading toward the kitchen. She stopped at the door before entering and checked. She smiled when she saw that Maddie was drinking. Maddie nodded her thanks and Kavita disappeared with a wink.

Droning above her, the BBC channel circled the wagons on what was known. They analyzed the website, scrutinized the rules of engagement and provided commentary on how it was set up like a game. They zoomed in on the website videos and speculated on the purpose of the skeleton masks. They showed video of the executed hostages, stopping it just before the trigger was pulled. There were tables with the ransom amounts and lists of countries whose citizens regularly vacationed at the resort. It all ran unending as the world waited for the next move.

Maddie was surprised by the level of sophistication. Loops of Kyle King's shaky videos churned on above her. The scroll at the bottom of the screen quoted his words in the minutes before he was killed. *Drones, assaults, armed men on the roof*; it looked and sounded like a professional operation.

"How we doing this morning?" Geert asked from behind.

"Better." Maddie turned and tracked him to the table.

"It's a Balashi breakfast, I see."

"Yes, thanks to your wife. She's always looking out for me."

"Did you get any *slaap*?"

"I did, surprisingly," Maddie replied. "Hey Geert, I'm thinking I'd like to take a drive up that way. See how close we can get to the resort."

Geert hesitated. He tracked her eyes to the TV then nodded. "That would be okay. My guess is we'll hit roadblocks on the mains. Maybe have to stay off to get close."

"Does this whole mess ring as professional to you as it does to me?" Maddie asked. "I mean, they cut the balls off the police by killing their leaders and they hit while the Dutch Marines are away. Seems like everything is going right for these bastards."

Again he hesitated, seeming to smile at the way she put things.

"I agree. Of course, I'm not sure any of that made much difference. They seem to have tied hands on their own. Even if the Marines were here, there's little they'd be able to do."

"How many Marines are stationed here?"

"A company. Maybe one hundred and fifty men. Small but professional. You've driven by the entrance to their base in Savaneta." Geert waved in the direction of the town that you passed through on your way to San Nicolas. Maddie had noticed the base in the past.

"They go to Camp Lejeune once a *jaar*," Geert added. He struggled to pronounce the word Lejeune correctly. He gave it more French emphasis than it required. Maddie had attended basic at Camp Lejeune. She spent years stationed there with One Six Hard. She could almost see the Dutch soldiers running the training grounds.

"They leave behind just a handful. The date is not announced but word gets around. It's not hard to find out," Geert continued. "The post is a good one. They work with the police to stop drug runners from South America. They run a small fleet of boats around the island. Search and rescue... that sort of thing. Lots of time at the beach, of course." Geert smiled. "That's the real attraction. They also train an Aruban militia. Volunteers that get a stipend to provide security at the barracks."

"Confused police *and* a ragtag militia?" Maddie asked. "That's what we're working with?"

Ten minutes later, they were on the road. Geert headed toward the airport on the main highway. He pointed out the

Marine base in Savaneta and a few miles later turned north on Route 4 toward Santa Cruz.

"This will get us up island without having to content with Oranjestad," Geert said.

North of Santa Cruz the road hooked into a slow left turn until they were once again driving with the lean of the Divi trees. Maddie had been told that if you're ever lost on Aruba, just drive in the direction that the Divi tree leans. The steady trade winds that sweep the island bend the trees to the west, which is the side where the resorts are lined up along the beach.

A few minutes later, Geert turned again, this time onto a dirt road.

"You've got your own way of getting up here, huh?" Maddie asked.

"There's a police station where this road meets up with Route 3. Route 3 runs alongside L.G. Smith." Geert motioned with his hands. The momentary lack of focus was enough to catch the edge of a pothole and the pickup sunk through it, the rear bumper dragging the ground briefly.

They weaved their way through a maze of potholes that dotted the rough interior island roads. The third world compounds rolling by on either side, made the shanties near the coast look luxurious. How they stood up to the sun and wind, Maddie could not understand.

A cocoon of dust rose from the road behind them. It ran through the Divi tree branches, heading west for the coast. Eventually the dirt turned back to pavement.

"We're far enough north now that we should be past the major road blocks. They'll have more in close to the resort," Geert said.

Resort outlines were visible in the distance.

"There's the mall!" Maddie pointed to a gap in the buildings where the domed roof of the Plaza Mall was sticking up. “There’s the Surfside.”

From this distance, the buildings of the Surfside looked innocent. Geert veered hard left. Maddie registered a neighborhood of single-family homes and then saw a sign introducing ‘Regal Palms.’ It looked new, the terracotta roof shingles still vibrant in the sun. “This is a big neighborhood. It runs right up to the salina,” Geert said.

Most had garages. The doors were down and the driveways empty. As they rounded their way toward the Surfside, a police car came into view. The uniformed driver was leaning toward the passenger side talking to a man halfway up the yard. A woman and child behind him were loading bags into the trunk of a Mercedes.

Geert attempted to drive by with a wave, but the officer put his hand out the window. He signaled them to stop and gave them the universal sign to roll down the window.

“This neighborhood is being evacuated. No work in here today.” Geert was an electrician. The bed of his pickup truck was rimmed with utility boxes.

“We had some work up the road. I didn’t realize how close it was to all of this,” Geert said. “We’ll drive on around and out.”

“Turn around and follow me. The road is blocked at the other end.”

Geert nodded.

“Go just one or two more houses, Geert.” Maddie was whispering, her eyes locked on the top edge of the resort buildings. “You have binoculars?”

Geert looked over at her. “You truly are a lunatic. You trying to get us locked up?”

“It’s right there, Geert. I just need a minute.”

Geert stopped in the road, a metal on metal scrape of the brakes accompanying it.

“I have a little of everything in the back. Just a matter of finding it." Geert was not the most organized man. Maddie had been inside his shop on two occasions. Geert popped the door open and disappeared to the rear of the truck.

Ross and Izzy felt so close. Maddie wished she could let them know she was here. She estimated the distance at eight to nine hundred meters—about a half a mile. The open space between the houses and the hotel was a flood plain. A *salina*, as Geert had called it.

"Here." Geert handed Maddie the binoculars. He climbed back in and shifted into gear. "The police is moving down the road. We've got a few minutes." He crept ahead as Maddie scanned the roofline with the ancient binoculars.

One side was frosted with a light haze. Maddie tried to clean the lens with her shirt but the cloudiness remained. She closed her right eye and leaned forward, resting the end of the binocular on the dashboard. There was a speck on the top left corner that very well could be a man. Maybe the sandbags of the machine gun position they were showing on the website. She moved the monocular to the right and picked up a walker. There was a rifle slung over the man's shoulder.

Maddie was less than a mile from her husband and daughter. How far would she make it if she charged across the field now?

A buzzing sound interrupted the thought.

"What's that?" Geert asked.

Maddie rolled down her window and stuck her head out.

"A drone." She opened her door and got out. Shielding her eyes from the sun she picked up movement in the sky ahead and above them. She tracked the white speck for several seconds before the sound and sight dissolved to their left.

The Marine Corps had been working with drones for years by the time she got out. Her unit was trained on a platform called the Aero Ranger. It was a jarhead proof system that was operated by a tablet. It came with a backpack that could be carried down range. All you did was click the arms in place, press a button and back away. Prompts on the tablet did the rest. She remembered the instructor telling her it could operate in 50-mile-an-hour winds.

Maddie looked down from the sky and checked the road. The patrol car was gone. She jogged across the yard in front of her, pulling up at the front corner of the house. From there, she could see down through the back yard to the last row of houses between her and the resort.

The neighborhood provided the line of sight PTang mentioned, but the distance was too far to capture the wi-fi. She didn't see an easy way to get closer. The police had to have the area around the resort cordoned off and the flood plain was a wide-open field. This would have to do.

Before she turned back for the truck, Maddie lifted the clear side of the binocular to her eye again. She spotted the walker with the rifle. *A sniper*, Maddie thought. *Probably the one that killed Kyle King.*

Maddie walked away from her rifle the day Will was killed. She turned her back on it and moved on. A friend had to check it into inventory for her. In that moment, looking out at the resort, she'd have given anything to have it back.

41

Surfside Resort, Aruba

White noise from the waterfall cascading into the pool lulled Fazul in and out of sleep. He was catnapping on a chaise in the shade of a palm. The day had grown boring. The escape attempts had stopped and Anas hadn't picked up anything with the drones since the attack that killed four of his men.

The distant crack of semi-automatic weapons fire shocked him awake. Two shots in quick succession.

Another rung out seconds later. He was already moving quickly toward the security suite in the main lobby. He scanned the palms at the entrance where the main road connected to the resort. It was clear. The shots sounded like they had come from the far side of building three.

"We've got a full-scale riot on the first floor," Fahd said as Fazul came through the door to the security suite.

Fazul leaned down on Fahd's shoulder. "Which building?"

"Here." Fahd pointed. "Building Three."

Hostages were lined up in the hall below the camera. There

was a camera positioned just inside and above each of the emergency exit doors. Fazul couldn't see the door itself, but based on the fact that the crowd was still there, he assumed the door hadn't yet been compromised. A separate box, to the right on the screen, showed video from the camera at the other end of the hall. The gathering looked more like a blob in the display but the rectangular window in the door at the other end of the hall was visible. They hadn't broken through yet.

They'd tested the blockade bars back at the staging warehouse in Venezuela. They held up to a tremendous amount of pounding, but they could be broken free with enough effort.

"The shots came from outside," Fahd said. "Another hostage trying to climb down on bedsheets. Probably was hoping the group might serve as distraction."

Fazul was still focused on the assembly on the first floor. The group parted as a man with a chair moved forward. Fazul felt like they were making eye contact.

"They're going to take out the camera."

Fazul stood tall and keyed his mic. "I need reaction teams three and four headed to building three at once. We've got a riot in progress. First floor. They're trying to break through the blockade bar. They're gathered on the north side of the building, closest to the resort entrance. We must stop them." He paused to gather his breath. "Team three, take the north stairwell. I'll meet you there. Team four, take the south. Wear your masks. Safeties off before you enter the stairwells." There were no cameras in the stairwells. The only way to know if anyone was in there was to enter from below and work your way up.

As Fazul finished his transmission, the man with the chair climbed up. He produced a frying pan. The first swing shook the display but didn't take it offline. At the base of the chair, the crowd surged backwards. A group of large men, likely the battering rams, were huddled closely. Fazul could imagine their conversation. They wanted to play hero like the assholes on

United Flight 93 that crashed in Pennsylvania on 9/11. He could almost hear the lead man say, "Let's roll," as they turned their attention back to the door and disappeared from view.

The man on the stool swung again. This time the strike knocked the camera loose from its mount. It danced on its wires, the image shaking indiscernibly.

"At least we have something to do," Fazul said as he hurried around the security desk and pushed his way into the IT room. Anas was at his computer watching the screen. He looked up as Fazul shot in.

"Anything on the perimeters?" Fazul asked.

"All clear," Anas confirmed.

"Then come with me. And bring your weapon. We could use an additional gun. We'll let you do some real work." Fazul spoke quickly and was out the door before Anas had time to react.

"Now, Anas!" he yelled as the door drifted closed behind him.

The seconds it took for Anas to emerge felt long and wasted. "We must hurry!" he commanded as he moved through the front entrance. He sprinted down the front walkway, the koi ponds flanking the decked approach just a blur in his peripheral vision. At the corral for the luggage carts, he stopped and checked for Anas again. "Come on, dammit!"

They ran into the shade beneath building three and caught a glimpse of the last man of the reaction team entering the base of the northern stairwell.

Fazul keyed his mic. "Team three. I'm right behind you." A second later, he was through the door and taking the steps two at a time. He heard the door close and then open again as Anas struggled to keep up.

"Let them see your faces and weapons," Fazul said as he reached the four men on the first floor landing. "That should move them back."

He gave himself a second to catch his breath then keyed his mike again. "Team four. Back down the stairs to the turn. We don't want rounds coming through the door and hitting you."

The soldier in front of Fazul pounded his fist on the door and yelled, "Backup!" Fazul moved in behind him. The soldier took a step back and leveled his weapon at the thin vertical strip of a window in the door.

Fazul looked over his shoulder. "They're far enough. Pull the bar and let's breach. Go in firing. We'll make examples of them."

As the soldier in front popped the first lever on the blockade bar, Fazul made another transmission. "We're going in," he yelled.

"We go on my count," Fazul instructed to the men around him. The lead soldier had his hand resting on the second latch of the blockade bar.

Fazul shouldered his weapon. He wanted to be first through the door. "Actions louder than words!"

On three, the blockade bar was lifted from its mounts. The soldier pulled the handle of the door almost simultaneously. Fazul could see the fear in their eyes as the hostages coursed back. He pulled the trigger twice before he cleared the door jam. A muscled twentysomething in a tank top caught both of the rounds in his upper body. They impacted just inches apart, cratering his chest and throwing him back at the others.

Many broke and ran. Several hesitated, looking back at the noise. Fazul aimed and fired a third shot. It pierced the neck of the next closest man. A cry of pain rang out and as the mortally wounded man dropped, Fazul could see that the bullet had passed through and struck another behind him. *Two for one*, Fazul thought.

Two soldiers drew up alongside Fazul, the hall barely wide enough to accommodate their width. In the next eight seconds, a fusillade of bullets ripped down the passage. Shrieks of surprise and cries of horror mixed with the thunderous concussions belching the jacketed lead down the hall.

"Hold your fire!" Fazul cried. The casings of the final shots chimed off the wall. Writhing bodies littered the floor.

Those that had not been hit quickly disappeared into their rooms. Halfway up the hall a woman pulled herself up off the floor. Her leg hung at an odd angle below the knee. She hopped away on her good leg, wailing with each limp.

Fazul closed his left eye and sighted the back of her shoulder. He imagined her heart pumping and then being torn apart. The shot thrust her forward, spinning her face up before she bounced off the floor.

Fazul moved up the hall. He stood above the first lifeless body, the tank top now soaked with the man's blood. He spit on the corpse.

"You were warned!" he yelled at the top of his lungs. "Stay in your rooms!"

He turned, the soldiers parting to let him through. Anas was standing outside the door, his mouth agape. The rifle lay slack at the end of his fingers.

"Feel free to finish the wounded if you can't stomach seeing them suffer." He shoulder checked his brother and turned down the stairs.

42

Velden Residence, Aruba

Maddie called up the map app on her phone and switched it to hybrid mode—this provided the satellite image but kept the road names and resort designators. She focused on the salina, a low, flat saltpan that separated the resort from the neighborhood where Geert had taken them. The row of houses curved toward than away from the resort. From above, the formation looked like a caricature of a wave, hanging too far forward and about to crash into the saltpan. Maddie dropped a pin on a house at the tip of the wave, closest to the resort. It would be a great surveillance location, but the lines of ingress and egress were exposed and under watch by the drones. It would have to do, though – getting any closer would require moving through police lines. That would take time and add risk that she couldn't afford.

She snapped a screen cap of the map, and then zoomed out and snapped a second. A distance estimator bar in the lower right corner of the second picture was locked into a scale that showed five hundred feet and two hundred meters. The meters were longer and just about matched the width of Maddie's thumb. Starting at the house with the pin, she counted just shy of three thumb widths. Five to six hundred meters. A great distance for sniping, but too far for wi-fi.

She emailed the screen capture to PTang. 'I can get to the pin', she wrote. 'The area in between is open. Any way to make that distance work? Getting closer will be difficult.'

Eleven minutes later, still waiting for Geert to return, she received a reply from PTang. 'You'll need a computer. Preferably your Mac, if you brought it,' PTang wrote. She had indeed brought her Mac. It was in her backpack.

'You'll have to construct a receiver-transmitter. See attachment. We can steal our own Wi-Fi from one of the houses. I'll load programs to your computer before you go. I'll connect to your computer through the house internet and then we'll use the receiver-transmitter to amplify the Wi-Fi signals back and forth from the resort. I think this can work. Reply your thoughts.'

The attachment appeared to have been stripped from the web. A crude copy-and-paste that showed steps for converting a basic satellite TV dish into a Wi-Fi antenna. At the top of the page, a list of supplies included the dish, copper wire, a square of metal and specific connectors. It looked fairly simple, but Maddie was not the woman for the job. Geert was the electrician. Based on the MacGyver-esque electrical connections running along the lip of his outdoor pavilion, Maddie guessed Geert was perfect for the job.

Geert pulled up not long after.

"Two old *pistools* and a *jachtgeweer* without ammo," Geert yelled as he approached from his truck. He produced a snub-nosed revolver from his pocket. "I went with this one. Not in the best shape, but he had two boxes of ammunition."

Geert hadn't questioned the request for a gun. He'd called

Maddie a lunatic again but he saw where her mind was headed. Geert had explained that there were few guns on Aruba. They averaged less than ten murders a year. Most of those murders *did* involve a gun, but usually an unregistered one. Owning a gun wasn't an inalienable right like in the States. You could get a permit if you proved you had a need. That might include sport, protection of property or self-defense. Still, Geert guessed that almost all the guns on the island were unregistered.

"A friend of the guy brought it to him by boat a good long while ago," Geert said. "Hasn't been fired in years."

Maddie took the revolver in her hands. It was a Colt Cobra. Before she even manipulated the action, she could see it needed oil. She pulled the pin in the cylinder and spun it. All six chambers were clear.

Jack Ruby had used a snub-nosed Colt Cobra to kill Lee Harvey Oswald. This one was old enough to be the murder weapon. The veneer was long worn off the wooden grip. Maddie ran her thumb over the Colt emblem at the top of the revolver's handle, just shy of the black American steel that formed the business end of the weapon. She drew back on the hammer, turned away from Geert and pointed it at the horizon. With a light pull on the trigger, the pistol snapped. Dry firing an old centerfire revolver was not advised. It could damage the pin. But the action needed to be tested.

"This is great, Geert. Thanks." Maddie reached behind her back and stuffed the revolver into the waistband of her shorts. She'd clean and oil it later.

"It came with a shoulder holster," Geert said, turning back for the truck. "I'll get the ammo as well."

After he retrieved it, Maddie told him she had another project for him to take a look at.

"*Wat de hel*?" he asked, as he scrolled through the steps.

"A Wi-Fi antenna. If we can get into one of those houses, we can point it at the resort and connect in. I have a hacker who works for me."

Geert raised his eyebrows. "I hate computers. But I can build this. Give me a couple of hours. Enough satellite dishes on this island to sink a cargo ship. I've probably got one in the garage."

While Geert worked in the garage, Maddie set up her computer in the living room. Once it was up and running, she dialed PTang.

"My friend here is building the antenna,“ Maddie told her. "I've got my Mac up and running. It's connected to the internet."

"I emailed you some software to load," PTang said. "Two executables – run them one at a time. The first is a remote desktop. This allows me to control your Mac. The second is an automated Wi-Fi connector. Run it from house and it will find, hack and connect to the strongest link available." A keyboard clicked away in the background.

Maddie hadn't started her computer in two days. The mass dump of emails was just dropping to her inbox.

"I've got the email."

After loading the remote desktop software, she backed away from the screen and watched as PTang took control of her Mac. Screens opened and closed. Download bars inched left to right. She soared through configuration windows.

"All done," PTang said over the phone. "When time comes to aim the antenna, point the center of the antenna's dish at the middle of the closest building. It'll look strange, like the receiver is facing the ground. But this allows the dish to collect the best signal."

"I won't be able to call you from up there. They took out the cellular service. I'll send a text when we leave here so you can keep an eye out for an email once I get in and set up. Or I'll Skype you."

"Okay, Mrs. Gunt. I be here."

It took Geert closer to three hours to craft the antenna. He'd needed to run out to his electrical supplier for the connections required to hook it to the Mac. The finished product resembled the pictures in the instructions so closely, it was hard to tell the two apart.

Maddie had searched online as Geert worked. She'd never heard of people using a dish for Wi-Fi, but sure enough, there was plenty of information on the web. Amplify the signal, and you have more than enough strength to stream data over distances. People living in remote locations, where internet wasn't available, posted stories of mounting a homemade antenna to a pole and capturing signals that were miles away.

"Text Pich Tang," Maddie commanded Siri. The text app opened. "We're leaving now. Probably take us an hour or two to get into a house and setup. I'll hit you with an email once I'm connected." She hit send and the text message whooshed from her phone.

They traveled the same path as before. With the sun fading into the afternoon sky, Geert turned from the little used dirt road onto the two-lane strip that passed for a highway in Aruba. Using the good side of the binoculars, Maddie looked for the police car as they approached the neighborhood.

Plan A was the simplest. They'd drive up to a house, force their way into a garage and pray there wasn't an alarm. Geert said alarms were rare in Aruba—solid doors and bars on the windows were more their style. They'd open the garage, pull the truck in, put the door down to hide it, and then get to work.

Plan B was more nebulous. If there were people around, especially police, they'd have to park out of sight and set out on foot. They'd wait for night fall if they had to.

Orange cones blocked the entrance to Regal Palms, but there was no sign of activity. Geert drove over the sidewalk to avoid the cones. They worked together, navigating the sleepy streets and making their way to the edge of the neighborhood. As they moved closer, Maddie eyed the upper reaches of the resort.

Geert followed a curve, heading to their right and then turning left as they made their way around the bottom lip of the wave. A white terracotta roof set the objective house apart from the rest. Maddie noted that the curtains and blinds were all closed as they turned into the empty driveway.

There were two houses that looked equally distant from the resort. Both were positioned such that the house would prevent the terrorists from seeing them in the driveway or along the left side where you entered the garages. Both also had a cement apron fronting a side door that was visible on the satellite images. Only one had a fence around the backyard. Geert and Maddie eyed it simultaneously, turning to one another and smiling. It was a privacy fence.

The concrete driveway was just long enough to accommodate the truck. Maddie got out and met Geert at the back. Piles of tools and spools of electrical wire filled the bed. Geert rummaged to the bottom and produced a long crowbar.

"That ought to do it," Geert said.

Maddie stepped on a landmine of dried dogshit as she pushed the gate open and held it for Geert. Each of them tried the door handle leading into the garage but it was locked. It did shake in the frame, though. Enough that the tip of the crowbar would fit in the opening.

They worked together to seat the edge of the bar into the small gap between the door and the frame. Maddie pushed the three-foot-long steel rod toward the door, almost making contact before the screws in the strike plate chewed through the wood frame and the door sprung open. It slammed into a trash can hidden behind it.

The garage was empty, the owners having taken their vehicles with them. With the house being one of the closest private residences to the resort, it'd probably been one of the first emptied in the mandatory evacuation.

Geert activated the garage door and went to the truck. Maddie scraped the dogshit off the bottom of her sneaker using the edge of the stair leading up into the house.

The front bumper of the truck was nearly touching the wall before there was enough clearance to close the door. Maddie hit the button and watched as the light from outside disappeared.

A small mudroom led from the garage to a kitchen with white cabinets. Adjoining the kitchen was a family room where a flat screen TV was mounted to the wall. Beneath it, two black boxes sat on a turquoise side bar. The smaller box on top bore multiple lights, several strobing periodically.

Maddie pulled a pen light from her pocket. She lifted the box and read the back, confirming it was a combination modem and wireless router. The factory password was included on the label. Maddie hoped it would be that simple.

They worked their way to the front of the darkened house where stairs led up to the second floor.

"Anybody home?" Maddie yelled from the bottom.

After waiting just a second, she led them up. Both straps of her backpack were pulled tight against her shoulders. In her arms, she cradled the dish, its wires bundled tightly with zip ties. Geert followed, a bag of tools clinking with each step.

To the left there was a hall bath and two bedrooms. They had a guest room feel—neat and tidy with little in the way of personal effects.

"*Massief* bedroom," Geert said. He'd gone straight at the top of the stairs, opening the only closed door.

Maddie turned and followed him in. Afternoon sun was trying to burn through the blinds. The windows faced west, toward the resort and the sun, which was heating the back of the house.

The room was a cavern compared to the others. A king-sized bed covered in a grey comforter with orange starfish took up the center of the room. Its four large posters were level with Maddie's eyes. A remnant of floral perfume hung in the air.

Maddie rounded the room, scanning. A romance paperback on the first nightstand showed that the woman of the house slept on the left. For the man, a weathered espionage thriller titled *Jackdaws* by Ken Follett. A jewelry box on a low-slung dresser was open and filled with bracelets and earrings.

Maddie stopped and scanned the windows. Two sets of louvered blinds flanked either side of the bed. All four were down and turned toward the floor. Light shone in around the edges, between the slats and through the holes where the strings that controlled them ran straight on either side.

"Let's leave all the blinds down for now. No sense in making any changes or taking a chance on them seeing movement." As she said it, she walked to the set of windows to the right of the bed. Maddie lifted a slat just enough to peak out.

The backyard was a thin strip of grass that surrounded a plunge pool. Maybe thirty yards wide, the yard was fully enclosed by the privacy fence which ran straight along the back and disappeared on both sides. Two palms marked the rear corners of the fence and the land dropped away not far on the other side.

"Got a clear view of the resort from here," Maddie said.

Geert had already busied himself. He removed the lamp and Ken Follett novel from the nightstand.

"We can *zetten* the dish here." He pulled the nightstand away from the wall. "Unless it needs to be outside."

"Nah. Inside is fine." Maddie grabbed an edge of the nightstand and helped Geert move it into position in front of the windows.

"It'll ruin the nightstand." Geert set the dish apparatus on top of the waist-high side table.

"Too bad," Maddie replied. "They'll have something to talk about. They'll wonder what the hell was going on when they find this."

"Hold it *bestendig*."

"You're using a lot of words I don't know," Maddie said, taking control of the dish. Geert pulled four lag bolts, a hammer and a ratchet from his bag.

"Hold it. Keep it constant," Geert clarified.

He set the first bolt in one of the holes in the plate at the base of the dish's arm. Using the hammer, he tapped the point of the bolt into the wood top of the nightstand. Once it was sunken deep enough to stand on its own, Geert used the ratchet to screw it down tight.

After the first bolt was secure, the antenna stood on its own and Maddie was able to release her grip. She moved to the other side of the bed and stared at the floor.

It'd make a perfect shooting position, she thought.

If she pulled the mattress from the bed, it would give her enough height to position a rifle barrel just above the base of the window. She'd crack it, to open the firing lane, but not enough to make it visible from a distance.

The bedroom's only drawback was that it was too obvious. The house was a natural pick. A tailor-made sniping position with direct line of sight and the shortest shooting distance. Any soldier worth his salt would pinpoint it as soon as they started taking precision fire.

For now, the only shots being fired would be invisible. The snub-nosed .38 was just about worthless beyond twenty yards. She'd have to be content sniping the resort's Wi-Fi from behind closed blinds. Hopefully firing PTang, a technological mole, would do some damage. If nothing else, they stood to gain some intelligence that Maddie could pass on to Chuckles.

"It's *gereed*," Geert said. "Ready." A few more clicks of the ratchet and the last bolt was tight.

Maddie pulled her Mac from her backpack and booted it up. She found a plug for the cord and set it up on the nightstand beside the antenna. Geert loosened the bolt at the back of the dish that allowed the angle of elevation to be changed.

"Angle it down a nudge. Then square it up on the window," Maddie said.

A few seconds later her machine had settled from the boot. She clicked on the network connection list and counted five Wi-Fi signals. The strongest, a random set of letters and numbers, had to be the router in the family room. She clicked on it and was asked for a password.

"I'll be right back." She ran from the room.

Downstairs she pulled her phone from her pocket and snapped a picture of the silver sticker on the router. The EESID matched the jumble of letters and numbers she'd selected. The WPA2, a password was listed below it.

"Hot damn!" Maddie yelled when the wireless connection accepted the password. "Didn't even need PTang's software."

She called up her email and typed out a message. 'Antenna in place and connected to my machine. The Wi-Fi password was listed right on the router. Didn't even need your software. You're free to take it away. Let me know what else you need from me.'

She hit send.

43

Surfside Resort, Aruba

Anas had never remembered vomiting before. As he stood looking down the hall through the small window in the door, he fought back the rancid taste of bile stewing at the back of his throat. Seven billion people – why should he be concerned if only a few were killed? It had sounded reasonable over tea in India. Now he saw it for what it was—murder.

He turned down the stairs. As he descended, the sounds of suffering seeped through the door. They echoed in the concrete encasement like ghosts circling before an attack on some poor soul.

He made the same mistakes time and again. It was Anas who asked for Fazul to be included on this operation. His brother wouldn't have had the muster to make the request himself. It would have been stooping to ask instead of waiting for a bid.

Anas now saw it for the huge mistake that it was. Over the

years, he'd repeatedly gone in search of acceptance from his brother. Every time, he'd come away defeated.

Fazul had called him a coward as he descended the stairs. He mumbled it, but like so many times before, the volume and enunciation was enough that Anas got the message.

Even as he reeled him into the NJF, there had been tension Anas should have distanced himself from. Since their youth, Anas had always been the golden child. Fazul's resentment was like an eternal flame. When the Cyberlock revenue started flowing in, everyone had shone the light of praise on Anas. When he'd detailed the plan that became this operation, the leadership was apparently impressed by his ingenuity.

ANAS WAS outside of the stairwell and under the building now. Dry, whistling wind and swaying palms replaced the smell of cordite and the gory sight that filled the hallway above him.

He could see Fazul in the lobby. *I should have stayed in the office*, Anas thought. *I should have read through Fazul's words.* "We'll let you do some real work." Murder was easy. Turning this game into an enterprise was hard. Anas knew now that the longer they stayed, the more his plan would be undone by Fazul. He needed to end it as soon as possible.

They'd already received the fifteen million from Wincopia. The plan was to release the hostages immediately once the ransoms were confirmed. Here again, Fazul had changed the plan. Germany, Italy, the Netherlands and Sweden had all publicly stated that they planned to pay. They'd sent a joint request asking that their hostages be massed for release before the bitcoins were transmitted.

Fazul had decided to wait before replying. "Let them simmer and worry. Let them know we make the decisions. They'll pay if we bring them out or not."

Even with the United States and the UK not paying, they'd still net over eighty million. Once the countries that paid had their people freed, the plan was to go in a completely new direction. It called for a phalanx of American and British hostages to be connected together to encircle the resort. No one was dumb enough to think those two countries would allow the buildings to be brought down without flexing their military muscle. They lived for the opportunity.

The phalanx had been Anas's idea—another way of changing the game and minimizing casualties. Fazul, of course, was skeptical of the plan, but only because it was Anas's idea. Others saw the merit and Fazul was silenced into agreement.

They'd brought cases of the zip tie handcuffs. By connecting one person's wrists to the next, a literal human shield would be strung around the resort. They'd set a new deadline for the executions of the British and American hostages. Anas even suggested a decrease in the ransom amount in an appeal for public support of payment.

But regardless of that, his plan called for the threat of execution to be drawn out as long as possible. Anas wanted the weight of the decision to be on the US and British governments. Part of the reason for minimizing the casualties was to change public opinion of whether ransoms should be paid or not. Being ruthless made people more hard-lined against it. Showing compassion and following through on your promises changed minds.

Once they committed the executions, they were just like any other terrorist organization. It created hatred and anger and ratcheted up the potential for an attack.

His newest idea was to forgo the executions completely—threaten it again, lower the ransoms and try their best, but if push came to shove, they should take the British and American hostages and leave. Ross and Isabelle would come with them on the *Contagious*. The public knew their faces and would have difficulty accepting the justification of a strike aimed at the yacht. If they carried out the executions... Anas's stomach quivered. If they executed them, then the hostages they took when they left would be unknown and the public wouldn't suffer their deaths the same.

"Fazul! I need to speak with you." His brother was standing at the back of the lobby, telling the story of what had happened when Anas came in from outside. Anas continued into the security suite, passing Fahd without a word.

Fazul took his time. "Place the video of the shooting on both sites. Everyone, inside and out, needs to see the repercussions of trying to undermine our plans."

Anas stood and faced his brother. "*Our* plans?" He stepped closer until a mere foot separated them. "Our plans have been thrown out on more than one occasion. Our plan is being undermined by your emotions." Anas poked his finger into Fazul's chest.

"Get your cowardly finger off of me," Fazul snarled.

"These fingers have done more to further the cause than anything you are capable of. Your pulling of the trigger takes us backwards." His brother's eyes were alive with fury. Fazul bit at his lip, his jaw muscles clenched so tightly they stood as bumps along the sides of his face.

"We're going to get back to the plan, Fazul." Anas paused for a beat. "Do you hear me? I'm not taking the insults and insubordination anymore."

Fazul smiled and started shaking his head up and down. "Oh, yes sir. Your way. Always your way. Your way is best..." Anas could see that his brother had crossed over to a point of no return. "I say screw you." Fazul pushed Anas backwards into his chair. Anas buckled when he felt it at the back of his legs. He'd hoped it would catch him but the arm of the chair came first. His center of gravity was high. The force of the push carried him over the chair and down to the floor. The back of his head hit first. It sent stars dancing through his vision.

"You're lucky if I don't kill you, Anas. Just post the fucking videos and stay out of my way."

44

Mid-island, Aruba

MADELINE AND GEERT hadn't waited around. After PTang confirmed she had connected to the resort Wi-Fi, they prepared to leave. As they left the room, Maddie's Mac flickered with activity on the nightstand beside the dish. PTang needed time to work her black magic.

Before departing, they'd both heard shots fired. It had come from the direction of the resort but they couldn't see much activity. The base of the building that ran perpendicular to the road was obscured by palm trees and plants that separated the parking lot from the highway. The one lens binoculars couldn't see through.

Geert started the truck and waited in the garage. Maddie hung upstairs in the front bedroom scanning the neighborhood for movement. It was still.

She ran down and jumped in. "Let's go. I grabbed the garage door opener." Maddie held up the gray remote control.

After they were out and confirmed the door was heading

down, Geert sped from the neighborhood. He weaved through the back roads, their retreat from the hot zone marked by rising dust.

Maddie's phone chimed as they passed through the town of Paradera. They'd come far enough to hit a cell tower that was functional. The voice message was from Chuckles. "Give me a call. Got new intel." His tone was dark.

She dialed him back.

"Bad news, Mad. They're still holding on the ransom. There's no official word yet, but rumor has it they plan to wait it out until the eleventh hour. Germany, Sweden, Italy… They're all paying. Wincopia already transmitted their bitcoins." Bitcoins were the ideal medium of payment for criminals because as an electronic currency it was easy to launder and almost impossible to track.

"Son of a bitch," Maddie said. "They're going to give the American public exactly what they want."

"A show of force," Chuckles finished.

"A bloodbath," Maddie countered. "I just hope they bring the fucking buildings down, Chuck. I'll completely lose my shit if I have to see Ross and Izzy…" She didn't finish the sentence.

"I hear you, sister. I just… I got no words."

After a second of hesitation, Chuckles launched into the intel. "The working plan is to infil Delta on commercial flights from Curacao. Tomorrow night sometime. They're looking to hit it from all four sides. Delta is taking the three ground approaches and DEVGRU is being airlifted directly onto the beach by SOAR."

The United States Army 160th Special Operations Aviation Regiment was known by its nickname, The Night Stalkers, as much as by its acronym. The unit operated the bleeding edge in lethal helicopter technology and was stacked with the best pilots the Army had to offer.

"Overwhelming force." Chuckles said, stating the obvious.

"Chuck, they do fucking realize these guys have operatives on the island, right? Someone took out the cell towers and the heads of the police and shit. They're probably still prowling around. The goat-fuck police force doesn't have a clue. They don't even know where to start looking for bad guys."

"The head shed knows. They're counting on speed. The hostages are separated from the bad guys—Right? We got bad guys on the roof and around the ground perimeter. I think the plan is to hit 'em hard and fast. They're hoping that keeps the friendly casualties down. They want to be on 'em before they have time to act."

"It's bullshit, Chuck. Chances of a sledgehammer working are a hundred to one. You know that."

"Listen, you know I'm not calling the shots. Just the messenger. The bad guys have their HQ setup in the hotel lobby. There's a security room in there with cameras and shit. Most of the activity comes and goes from there. Delta's gonna hit it hard."

"Why can't they just pay? Sounds like a recipe to get a bunch of people killed. These terrorists gotta have eyes on the airport, Chuck. As soon as they see signs of military they'll start taking heads off."

45

US CONSULATE'S OFFICE, Curacao

THE OFFICE of the US Consulate General Curacao was once the main gathering room in the Roosevelt House. After it was gifted to the States for use as a foreign relations post, the space had been converted into an impressive office.

The desk stood along the far wall with a sitting area in the middle. Margaret Baker paced the perimeter of the Persian rug that framed the furniture. Every fourth turn, she caught a glimpse of herself in the massive mirror on the wall opposite her desk. She hadn't slept for forty48 hours and had indulged in half as many cups of coffee. Purple bruises underlining her eyes looked like sagging Nike logo swooshes.

Once a week she closed the day with back-to-back 30-minute meetings. The heads of immigration on the islands that fell within her mission, each met with her separately.

"Commercial flights ceased yesterday afternoon. We've had empty airplanes landing all day to take people off the island. The airport is still busy, but the situation is better. You couldn't move in there this morning." Caya Tatonka headed the Department of Immigration and Naturalization in Aruba. She was young, four-foot-eleven and prone to getting overwhelmed.

"You're doing an admirable job," Margaret said. "What else?"

"Our scanners picked up a man trying to smuggle out a suitcase of cocaine. Apparently, he thought all the commotion would be a distraction."

"An American?"

"Yes. He's been in and out a few times over the last year. He's gotten by us in the past. Got greedy this time," said Caya.

Corruption and drug transit through Aruba had decreased significantly since the nineties. At one time a mafia clan had owned over 60 percent of the island's businesses and all of its government officials.

Margaret waited to see if there was anything else. Her brain was tired; she was only half-listening.

"One other strange thing... We had an American woman walk out with her baby. The agent asked her to wait for a second interview. She claimed to be staying with nationals here on the island, but her husband and daughter arrived Sunday. They're at the Surfside... We checked the video – she just walked out. Got in a white pick-up truck owned by the people she said she was going to see. Left her passport and her daughter's. Little girl isn't even two yet." Caya's tone made the situation sound as sad as it was. "We haven't sent a car looking for her yet."

"She got there and was cut off from the rest of her family?" Margaret asked.

"Looks that way. Can you imagine?"

"No. Jesus." Margaret went to her desk. She picked up her pen and leaned down toward her portfolio. "What's the name?"

"Madeline Günther."

46

KAVITA'S CAFÉ, **Aruba**

MADDIE WAVED GEERT OUTSIDE. "Listen, you've done so much for me already. You have to be willing to check out if I take it too far. You understand what I'm saying?"

Geert laughed a laugh she hadn't heard before.

"This is the most excitement I've had in years. *Opwinding*! As long as my family isn't in danger, I'm here to help." Geert felt like a true friend. There's no quicker way to bring humans together than to give them a challenge to overcome.

"This next part just might change your mind."

Geert stopped walking and put his hands on his hips. "Let's hear it."

"What are the chances we can get on the Dutch Marine base?"

Geert squinted at her. "That house was too tempting for a sniper? That it?"

"The US isn't planning to pay, Geert. You heard my call. My

friend in the Pentagon says they have full-scale assault in mind."

Geert nodded.

"Izzy and Ross are at the front of the hitlist. As soon as these guys catch wind of it..."

"But what can you do alone?"

"I've got two options, Geert. I can sit on my hands and watch what happens. Based on what I know... That doesn't bode well for my family. Or... I can get out there and do something. Right yet I'm not exactly sure what that is, but one way or another I've got to get myself on the property. I'll make some noise. Find my family."

Geert wasn't convinced. "They'll kill you. And then your baby, Charlotte, will be left alone. You risk the two already in *gavaar,* or risk all four. Three dead and one parentless child. Not saying you shouldn't do it – just offering a different way of thinking."

Maddie looked down. Geert was right.

"I can't explain it, Geert. My gut says I need to do something more."

"*Intuitie,*" said Geert. "Very powerful." He paused and kicked at the dirt. "You'd have to get on the base and into the armory. You'd need keys and codes. The whole shebang."

"Yeah. True. What do you know about the place? You ever been in there?"

"I have been in there, plenty. We've worked projects in just about every building. I've even been in the armory. It was empty at the time. They had it remodeled and brought us in on contract for the electrical work."

Geert turned for the house. "Let's have a beer and think this over. I'll meet you on the patio."

Geert's outline strode like a stick figure across the yard, a Balashi in each hand. He alternated between looking down at the ground and up at the sky.

"I've a friend who's an *officier* in the militia," he said, as he came under the cover of the roof. "Do you have pictures of your family?" Geert pointed at the phone on the table.

"Yeah. Of course."

"He's a family guy. Six kids, grandchildren, helps the ones in need. I think we should speak with him off the record. We put him in your shoes."

* * *

Captain Cedrick Kimbar excused his wife Anna and the children after introductions were complete. He offered Geert and Maddie the armchairs and took up a spot on the loveseat adjacent.

"You're lucky to have found me at home. I've been going non-stop since this started. I came home for a bit of rest this morning. Woke up..." He checked his watch. "Just an hour ago."

"What do they have your men doing?" Geert asked.

"Protecting the base perimeter. Same as usual. We doubled the patrols, though. The murders have everyone on alert for another attack. The police are convinced that the ones who committed the murders folded in with the rest at the resort. There's no basis for it. We're keeping our guard up – at least until the Marines get back."

"When are they due back?" Geert asked.

"Sometime tomorrow. Returning a week and a half early."

Geert shook his head. "Cedrick, we need some help."

"Anything for you and Kavita. So many meals on the house." The captain looked at Maddie for the first time since they'd sat. "These folks are a pillar of the community."

She nodded in agreement.

"Madeline's daughter and husband are at the resort."

The captain's expression changed in an instant.

Geert reached up and put a hand on Maddie's shoulder.

"She came down two days after them. Landed before the flights were stopped but arrived after the resort was taken."

"I'm sorry for your loss," the captain said, reaching out to touch Maddie's other shoulder.

Maddie said nothing. She shook her head and looked down at the floor between her feet.

"They're still very much alive. We know that because... they are the Americans due to be killed if the US doesn't pay."

"The father and daughter?" the captain asked.

"Yes. This is the mother and daughter," Geert said.

"My god. I'm so sorry." Kimbar patted Maddie's shoulder. "I can only imagine."

Feeling that the time to pile on had arrived, Maddie pulled her phone from her pocket. The room was silent as she thumbed up a picture.

"There's my husband, and six-year-old Isabelle. They're the ones at the resort. This here is Charlotte. She's one. Charlotte and I are staying with Geert and Kavita—waiting and hoping for the best." The captain's face exuded physical pain.

"I've got five of my own. So innocent, these children. They deal with anger and violence very young these days. Of course, we never imagined it would come so close to home, here on the island... How can I help?"

Geert took his time explaining the situation. After laying it all out, he went into Madeline's background as a decorated Marine Corps sniper.

"First female sniper in the United States Marine Corps," Geert continued. "First female in the history of the United State Military to see combat as a sniper." He paused allowing the concept to cement and the suspense to build. "Came out of it one of the highest decorated snipers of all time. A very accomplished woman."

The captain stared on with a mix of confusion, as if he'd been dropped into a room with an Imperial lordess.

"Where were you deployed?" the captain asked.

"Two tours in Iraq. One in Afghanistan."

His eyes doubled in size now, as the man conceptualized the fact. Maddie had seen it before. Men, even other soldiers, had a difficult time adjusting once they knew her background. It left them uncomfortable and at a loss.

"The ultimate force multiplier," the captain said, having taken on a look of reverence.

"It certainly can be," Maddie said, going with it. "Here's the thing, Captain – they'll kill my husband and daughter as soon as the raid starts."

The captain moved to the edge of his seat, the mix of expressions now converging to one of resolve. "Tell me how I can help."

"I could really use a weapon," Maddie said. "Something with long-range capability."

For a second, the captain's resolute expression remained unchanged. Then he cocked his head and spoke. "You're going to take this into your own hands? You could jeopardize lives beyond those of your family. They've been clear on how they'll handle attacks."

The captain had more to say but Maddie cut him off.

"They've talked about the repercussions of an attack by a nation, or the police. I'm going to let them know it's just one person. I'm going to challenge them. Tell them that executions are a waste of time. I want to provoke them into a fight."

"I see," said the captain. His face was a chameleon of expression. It morphed into a quizzical look, angled at the edges. He looked away and scratched the back of his neck. "Your situation is terrible, but I am not able to provide you with a weapon. Even though you were an American soldier, a sniper, they would lock me up."

"And I'm not asking you to do that," Maddie said. "I don't want blood on anyone's hands besides mine. I need to find a way to get a weapon without bringing harm to any of the good guys... Like you."

"The Dutch Marines do maintain a full complement of weapons here on the island. They issue us our pistols and assault rifles, but they keep everything else for themselves." Captain Kimbar looked down and rubbed his forehead. "They have sniper rifles. I've seen them up close on training missions. Whether they took them to Camp Lejeune or not, I have no idea."

There was silence for a handful of seconds then the captain continued. "There's one junior officer left behind with a squad of men. Only eight men in all. They run in two shifts. They patrol the interior of the base and we cover the perimeter. Our buildings are fenced separate from theirs. We're all in the same general complex, but fences separate the perimeter and the interior and we are expected to stay in our area." The segregation was clearly a sticking point for the captain. "The officer is the only person who would have access to the armory."

Cedrick stopped talking and another silence fell across the room. The faint voices of his family drifted down the stairs from the second floor.

"Koning is young. Promoted to Captain little more than a month ago. He has a baby back in Amsterdam." Captain Kimbar hesitated. "He operates by the book. I don't think—"

Bing-bong. The phone in Maddie's pocket chimed and audibly vibrated in her pocket.

"Excuse me," she said pulling it from her shorts. She stepped out onto the front porch and answered. "What's up, PTang?"

"I'm on the host machine. Not much to see so far. It's just a static PC that's not connected to the net. Very little activity. Looks like data is being downloaded to it from a different machine."

"Okay, so what do you recommend?"

"I can take control of it. I can update the webpage if you want. But this is not the machine controlling the VPNs and disseminating data to the web. They've kept it separate."

"Alright," Maddie said. She was trying to manage two thoughts at once.

"I'm going to keep an eye on it," PTang continued. "I wrote a piece of code that will tell me if a port connection is established. Then I can see about getting into the adjacent machine."

"Okay, sounds good. Let me ask you something else. Let's say I wanted to get on a military base. You've worked on Department of Defense networks. What would you need?"

There was a sigh on the other end of the call. "This very big job. You need an inside man. You need credentials and a machine that has access to the network."

Maddie's mind began to triangulate a route onto the base and into the Armory. It was a very low probability move, but if Geert could get them on the base and Maddie could get a hold of the officer Kimbar mentioned, she just might be able to get what she needed.

"Let me work on it. I'll keep you posted."

"I do the same."

Maddie slipped the phone back in her pocket and rejoined Geert and the captain.

"Captain Kimbar, what's Koning's first name?" Maddie asked.

"Ruben Koning. His wife's name is Anna. Same as my wife."

Maddie shook her head. "Good to know. Thank you, Captain Kimbar. Maybe once the Marines return, things will be different."

"Yes," Kimbar said, standing and proffering his hand. "I can tell the commanding officer your story. See if they might help."

"That'd be great. I can't thank you enough."

47

Surfside Resort, **Aruba**

Ross heard the commotion in Anas's office. The voices were muffled through the wall but not enough to mask that an argument had broken out. Something banged against the wall adjoining.

A door slammed and things went quiet.

The rest of the afternoon Ross had weighed his next move. He and Izzy had done their best to make the most of the situation. They'd taken turns trying to draw landscapes from memory. The beach, their backyard at home, the school playground. They played tic-tac-toe for close to an hour and then made a deck of math flashcards which was Izzy's spring break assignment for kindergarten.

They'd taken a break from the games. Ross was reading a young adult fantasy novel from the same bag where he'd found the iPad.

Anas came in quietly. Movement in the room caught Ross's

attention. He had a stack of coloring books and several boxes of crayons in his hands.

"For you, Isabelle." His demeanor was that of a caring uncle. Ross sensed that he'd not spent much time with children.

Izzy's eyes lit up. "Thank you." She said as she took them. After a jump of excitement she hopped back to the cubicle she'd claimed as her own.

"You doing okay?" Ross asked.

Anas shot a quick thumbs up from his waist. "How about you and Isabelle?"

"We're fine. Lots of games and things to bide our time." Ross pointed to the mattress. He'd pushed it up against the wall to get it out of the way. Sheets of paper marked with games of tic-tac-toe were strewn on top.

Ross looked him over. He'd come to talk. He'd fallen into their previous conversations but this time was different. The peace offering, the *how are you*. Ross sensed that he'd come seeking counsel. He needed to cease the opportunity.

"So what's up? Is the money coming in?" he asked.

"What's interesting to me is that when I work alone... my plans often play out as I imagine. But when I work with others..."

Ross nodded in agreement.

"Everyone says they're onboard with the plan. The problem is, when we arrive at that step in the process, they take it in a direction we hadn't discussed. Usually the opposite direction."

"When you say 'they,' who are you referring to? From our earlier conversation, it sounded like you and your brother were in charge." Ross's gut told him their infighting was not new. Indeed, most sibling relationships were built on rivalry.

"My brother," Anas said, shaking his head in resignation.

"It's always hard working with family," Ross added. He

wanted to laugh at the conversation. He was talking to a terrorist and it felt more like a counseling session for some small business owner whose operation was flagging due to family conflict.

"The thing you have to look at is whether the direction being taken... What you say is usually opposite of the plan... Is that a conscious choice? Is he going in that direction just because it's the opposite?" Ross was having trouble accepting the fact that this conversation was even happening. He watched Anas's face closely. He didn't want to go too far too fast.

Anas was quick to respond. He raised his eyebrows and said, "That's why I'm worried. It does seem premeditated. A sort of, *I'll show you* vendetta."

Ross shook his head and looked on, encouraging him to continue. Anas fell into thought. As he waited, Ross dug in his mind for the term. Stockholm Syndrome was when a hostage takes to their captors. For Ross, this was all acting.

"He's always been this way," Anas continued. "Since we were boys... this back and forth... it's been a part of our life. That's fine for boys. Expected. But in business you must put that aside." With that he stopped and looked Ross in the eyes.

Lima Syndrome, the thought popped in Ross's mind as they looked at one another. The name came from terrorists that took over an ambassador's residence in Lima, Peru. They ended up letting the hostages go after a time. They developed sympathy for their captives. But Anas didn't quite fit the mold. His was less sympathy and more loneliness, like he was jonesing for a friend to shoot the shit with. He was in over his head, and had no one to talk to about it.

"You're right," Ross said. "That behavior needs to end for cooperation to succeed." A counselor would have gone a different direction. They would have led Anas to see that sibling rivalry is deep-seated and that it takes time and effort to deconstruct the barriers. But patients often played to stops in counseling situations. They seek encouragement and Ross was happy to oblige.

Anas was clearly happy with the agreement. "So my problem then..." He patted the pinky side of one hand into the palm of the other. "My problem is... I laid out the strategy which we used to script the operation and the procedures, but Fazul heads the operation. In this configuration, I lose control of whether the tactical plan plays out in accordance with the strategy."

"And that's a significant problem. You're right."

"A big problem." Anas agreed. He was looking down at the floor now. "My problem."

Anas was about the speak again when a tone rang from his office. Without speaking he turned from the room and pulled the door to the office wide.

Ross rose and followed him. He stood back from the door frame where but could see all three of the screens. A red light flashed on the right-most laptop monitor.

"Is there a problem?" he asked.

"No, just a police car patrolling the far edge of the mall. See here." He pointed. "I'll replay it." Ross watched a red and orange blob move across the screen.

"The software picks up the heat signature and alerts me," Anas paused and reset the screen. "That patrol has been running by there once every hour or two."

Ross turned his attention to the left most screen. The one Anas had told him provided the webpage for the hostages inside the hotel.

"Have any of the ransoms been paid, Anas?"

"Two, in fact. We expect several more to clear this evening." As he spoke, Anas moved to the center computer and lifted the screen. On a webpage, Ross could see what looked like a video. The play button was centered on the image but behind it there looked to be bodies on the floor of a hallway.

"I'll need you to excuse me—"

"What's that?" Ross asked cutting him off. He pointed to the stilled video image.

"Fazul," Anas replied. "More disturbing video that should not be. A group tried to escape and several were killed as a result." Anas hesitated. "This is one of several examples where the strategy and the implementation have differed. Now, please excuse me, Ross."

Ross backed away from the door and watched it close.

48

San Nicholas, Aruba

Maddie was always amazed at how quickly PTang worked. The email she sent included an attachment with a complete dossier on Ruben Koning. Born in Utrecht, the religious heart of the Netherlands, the twenty-seven-year young captain had gone to university close to home and joined the People's Marine Corps thereafter.

Koning was eight months into an eleven-month deployment to Aruba. Anna, his wife of almost two years, remained at home with their six-month-old baby, Julia. PTang had collected most of the information from a family webpage. It included their history, along with email addresses and other personal information they'd have been wise not to share with the world.

If he was truly the only commissioned Marine on the island, than he was the acting commander of Marine Corps Base Savaneta. This meant he probably worked during the day shift and would be preparing for bed.

Maddie's phone rang.

"I send email that looks to be from his wife." PTang's voice was somehow reassuring to Maddie. Working with her made you feel like you had a team somewhere behind the curtain.

"You running the phishing expedition on him?" Maddie asked.

"Exactly. Except most phishing attempts fail because they lack personal touch. My email includes an attachment titled babyjulia.jpeg."

She went on to explain what would happen when Ruben Koning clicked on the image he believed to be a picture of his daughter. Unbeknownst to Ruben, a key stroke logger would be loaded on his machine. The screen would flicker and then a blue screen of death would follow. It would advise him that a reboot was necessary. Ruben would restart his machine and log back into the computer. He'd have to connect to the network as well. The key stroke logger would capture the credentials and secretly email them to PTang. When Ruben tried the attachment a second time, he'd get an error saying the picture was corrupted.

Even though Maddie worked in cyber security, it still never failed to amaze her how easily a network could be compromised. Humans are fallible and providing them with access to a secure network was the biggest risk any administrator could take.

PTang went suddenly silent.

"Everything okay?" Maddie asked.

"I've got it. The information is transmitting. The first packet just arrived. When do you plan to go?"

"First thing in the morning. Maybe around five," Maddie replied.

"So... Eight hours." PTang hummed for a moment. "Yes. It looks like two sets of usernames and passwords were entered. I may bring in some peers to help me compromise this network. I'll need a team working on it to gain full control."

As PTang continued to talk, Geert swung into the room. His face was filled with alarm.

"There's a government car out front."

"PTang. Do your thing. I gotta go. Keep me posted. If you can't get in, then we'll have to go with Plan B."

"The girls took Charlotte to our bedroom," Geert said. "Hurry!"

Geert and Kavita's bedroom was at the end of the hall in the back-left hand corner of the one-story house. Maddie slipped into the room and dropped to the floor. The daughters, Lotte and Esmie, sat opposite each other with Charlotte in the middle. A tub of building blocks was spilled on the floor among them.

"Stay quiet," Geert said, as he closed the door.

Lotte and Esmie had a patience that was not common in American children. They built small boxes and tracks with right angles, pausing constantly to demonstrate to Charlotte how it was done. For her part, Charlotte banged them together, smiling when long plastic connecters along the edges linked enough to hold them together.

"Good job!" One of the daughters would say, rubbing Charlotte's back.

Maddie heard voices in the background. She didn't think they'd break down the door and come looking but hearing their voices increased her worry.

She rose and went to the bedroom door, cupping an ear to listen. The voices were relatively clear through the hollow wood, but it still took a moment for Maddie to understand why their words made no sense.

Islanders often greeted one another in Aruba's official language, Papiamento. A blended language that evolved over time, it stole tidbits from about a dozen other languages. Portuguese, Spanish and Dutch formed the backbone with sprinklings of influence from Africa, France and the Americas.

It rang as a cobbled-together language when spoken. A jarring, awkward jumble of words that seemed pieced together by a language major to show off.

Maddie knew three sayings. *Bon bini! Con ta bai? Don, danki.* This meant, *welcome. How are you doing? Fine, thanks.*

The sounds making their way through the door materialized into words that Maddie recognized. With the greeting over, they had switched back to English. The unfamiliar voice asked about a white truck. His tone had grown more heavy.

"Yes, my truck is white," Geert's voice replied.

"Where is the American?"

A pause.

"The one you picked up from the airport yesterday," the man continued.

"Oranjestad... At least that's where I left them." Geert hadn't had time to formulate a story. Even from her side of the door, Maddie could sense the lie in Geert's answer. "I dropped them off there. She was going to get a hotel room."

More silence.

"Which hotel?"

"The Renaissance. That's where I dropped them off," Geert lied. "I don't know if that's where they stayed."

Kavita's voice came next. The sound arrived at Maddie's ear as a continual stream of words, none of which she could understand. Kavita switched back to Papiamento. Maddie could almost see her hands flailing about as she hammered the man with what could only be described as a mother's diatribe.

The onslaught ended abruptly. Then, after just a second or two of silence, there was another shot of words from Kavita that ended as a question. At least it sounded like a question. The end of the sentence was turned up on the ends.

The man's response was soft and hard to hear. Maddie could only make out every few words.

"Yes... Husband... Surfside." Then his volume increased

again. "I work for the United States. The Consulate General sent me. She understands the stress of the situation and wants to help. Madeline left her passport and her daughters as well. The authorities will come looking for them eventually, and the Consulate wants to help. Please pass this information along. If you see them..."

49

SURFSIDE RESORT, Aruba

ANAS HAD LOST track of time. Earlier in the evening he went to the lobby to confirm it was night. When he came back he turned off the bright fluorescent fixture leaving just the glow of the monitors to light his windowless office. He'd been stuck in the technology suite since they arrived. Somehow, he imagined it differently. He imagined the pool and the sand—the pale blue and green of the Caribbean Sea. The exotic backdrop for the operation seemed more appealing in the planning.

He should have known better than to forge expectations. Reality had always been far crueler than the fantasy he saw through the rose-colored glasses of his mind. But what made things all the worse was the incessant harping of the voice in his head. *You should have known better. How could you not see this coming? Will you ever learn?* It scolded him like a belligerent mother.

For the last hour, he'd been stewing in his own head. Anxiety built in his stomach as he imagined being marked by the killing—his brother's butchery. The world would not easily forgive a person who took part in the killing of innocence.

Haunting images of his sister had also returned. The gaping wound at her neck, deep enough that the cord of her spine was visible when Anas walked up. Her head was nearly severed in the attack.

His sister, Isabelle, was one of seven killed in the melee. A leftwing radical had walked into the school with just one objective. He'd taken the lives of six young children and one teacher who attempted to subdue him. Countless others suffered ruthless cuts from the machete he wielded. Shot and killed by police as he tried to escape, his motive remained unclear.

Anas attended the same primary school. In the chaos that followed, he snuck from his classroom and ran down the hall to check on his sister. He found her in the hallway with two of her friends, slipping in the blood as he reached in toward her open eyes.

Isabelle's class was on their way in from recess when the man encountered them. Her neck was laid wide by the blade; blood spanned the full width of the hall.

He stared at the door for several minutes waiting for the haunting to subside before he opened it. It was wrong in so many ways, but Ross and Isabelle were his only escape.

"Are you awake?" he whispered.

The business office where Ross and Isabelle were kept was mostly dark. A lamp burned in one of the three cubicles, its beam carried up to the ceiling in a square. Enough was cast back down that Anas could see Ross and Isabelle lying side by side on the thin sofa bed mattress.

Ross pushed himself up to his elbows. "Yeah," he replied quietly. He turned to his side and gently rolled from beneath the sheet.

"Is everything okay?" he asked as he stood.

"Yes. I'm sorry to disturb you. I just... I thought you might want to talk if you were awake."

"I don't see why not. Can we talk in there?" Ross was looking in toward the computers.

Anas turned and went in, standing on the edge of the mattress to make room for Ross.

"What's up?" Ross asked. He rubbed his eyes, although it seemed improvised. They weren't marked with sleep.

"I'm sorry for what we've put you through. I don't have children of my own, but I had a sister... long ago now. Her name was also Isabelle. She was killed by a madman when she was only seven."

Ross's eyes widened. He rubbed at the wrinkles on his forehead. "Isabelle?" he asked.

"Yes. Same as your daughter. In fact, your Izzy, as you call her, reminds me quite a lot of my sister. She was a good girl. A good friend." Anas stared at the floor, blurred images ghosting his mind.

"Oh shit," Ross said. He covered his mouth and turned his head, the beard moving across his palm like sandpaper. The pieces were falling into place. Anas had been kind for a reason, and now Ross was piecing it together. "That's terrible. I'm sorry for your loss, Anas."

Anas bobbed his head in thanks. "It was a different experience from yours, but having children of your own in harm's way must be a terrible thing. Before this all started, it was easy to ignore the fact that real people would be here when we arrived. Your daughter has given a face to all the people stuck in these buildings."

"I get it, man." Ross lifted his arm as if he was about to pat Anas on the shoulder. It stopped after just a twitch and feel back to his side. "This thing became very serious, very quickly. I get that. Just don't let it end that way. You have to own it from here on out. My only request is that you help us, Anas. You yourself have said your intentions were... are honorable. And I believe you. There's good inside of you." He pointed. "What scares me... is the others. I'm asking you, to please, do what you can to keep us safe."

The lie he held felt like lead. Ross and Isabelle were scheduled to die in less than twenty-four hours—a sentence for being in the wrong place at the wrong time.

"I'll do my best." Deep within, Anas knew this was true. He'd come too far to have a part in their sacrifice.

"Thank you. I know you will. You have a good heart, Anas. In fact, before you came in I was thinking about that. You've worked yourself into a tough spot. Your intentions were good. Things sound like they got out of control and went the wrong direction."

"This has been the case more than once," Anas added.

"Right. But only you can break the pattern. No one is going to come in and tell your brother to shape up. *You* have to do it. You can't let people fool you. Let them manipulate you. Let them take advantage of your compassion. You need to have some ruthlessness of your own. It was your vision. Your plan. Your innovation..."

Anas could feel his heart rate quicken at the encouragement. He bowed his head in agreement. Ross was right. He sat by and watched the plan fall apart. But for all the certainty he felt in Ross's words, he knew the opposition would be swift and strong. Any disagreement and his brother would take the opportunity to grind the ax further.

"I don't doubt your words. My worry is turning them into action. As I've considered the position I've created for myself, I realize I'll own this for the rest of my life. Every life turned into a body... I'll own each one. Even though my intentions were different."

Ross considered the words. He turned his attention to the computer screen briefly than back to Anas.

"You know your situation reminds me of the WikiLeaks guy... What's his name?"

"Julian Assange?" Anas answered.

"Yeah, him. Here's a guy that starts WikiLeaks for all the right reasons—sharing damaging information that's hidden behind a veil of secrecy. To some, he's a crusader. To others he's a terrorist. I think the vice president actually called him that. Some would see you as a crusader. Whether people agree or not... Some will, some won't, but you have a cause you're trying to forward. And you *wanted* to do it peacefully. That's the difference. But just like the Julian guy, the situation gets skewed and next thing you know you're in a corner. He bugged out and was granted asylum. I mean, he's stuck living in an embassy or something and can't leave for fear of being arrested, but he's still an international figure forwarding his cause."

Anas was stunned by the comparison. Assange was something of a hero within the hacker community. To be compared to him wasn't something he'd ever considered, but Ross's connection made sense.

"You could do the same, Anas. If you could get out of here and spare as many as possible. Then, instead of hiding the rest of your life, you could seek asylum. Tell your story. Further your cause. Remain an international figure."

Emotion swarmed Anas. He simply nodded in agreement. This stranger had renewed his courage.

"But *you,* have to get *your* men out of here before they kill more people. Then turn this around and be the crusader you're capable of being."

50

Dutch Marine Base, **Aruba**

Maddie hadn't slept. Her husband and daughter were scheduled to die today. She was running on waves of pure adrenaline.

Before they left for the base, Maddie checked online to get a status on the ransoms. All had paid, except the US and England. She'd put the plan in motion.

Charlotte was asleep in the crib in Geert and Kavita's living room. Maddie stood above her, watching her chest rise and fall, her face twitch with dreams. She was beautiful. She'd be alright.

She kissed her hand, planted it on Charlotte's cheek, and left.

Satellite images showed Camp Savaneta as a perfect square. Just five hundred yards by five hundred yards, it was far smaller than Maddie had imagined. The oceanfront box was divided roughly into four quadrants with just a smattering of buildings, maybe ten in all.

The inland east quadrant contained an obstacle course and

ground left open for training. Barracks for the enlisted soldiers, a parade grounds and a helicopter pad took up most of the inland west quadrant.

Along the shore of the oceanfront east quadrant stood the Commandant's residence. Beside it sat a single-story structure shaped like a Z where the rest of the officers were housed, according to Geert. Two other buildings set back from the water contained offices and were multiple stories high so the officers could maintain a view of the ocean.

The quadrant opposite contained the largest building as far as area under roof. De Grote Zaal was the hub of the base. Fronted by a circle and dual flag poles, the main hall contained the mess deck, the armory and an auditorium.

Getting through the gate had gone smoother then she'd expected. PTang had filed a work order for an electrical problem in the auditorium. When they pulled up, they were greeted by a militia soldier that Geert knew by name. Geert leaned out the window and yelled, asking how his mother was doing. A smile and a thumbs up were flashed in response.

Geert produced a sheet of paper with the work order number hand written on the front. The younger guard took it and handed it through the window to the more senior man. The senior man shot a glance at the paper then looked at Geert and flashed an index finger as if to say, it'll be just a minute.

It took less. Maybe thirty seconds on the computer were all that was needed. Geert rolled up so that they were level with the senior man.

"You've got a helper these days, Geert," the guard said, looking in to check out Madeline.

"Relative in for a time. Deciding if she wants to stay a while."

The guard nodded a hello to Madeline who returned the gesture.

"Appreciate it, Nelson," Geert said.

"Good to get it fixed before the Marines come back this morning. I'm sure they'll need the auditorium. They'd be upset if the lights weren't working." Nelson waved. "Let us know if you need anything."

Geert returned the wave and crept forward through the opening gate.

"This morning?" Maddie said, reiterating what the guard had said.

"Humm?" Geert hadn't picked it up.

"Your boy Nelson... He said the Marines were coming back this morning. We should've asked when they were due in." The thought was cut off by a text message chime from Maddie's phone.

'I've never seen you wear a hat', it was from PTang. Maddie reached up and adjusted the brim. Geert had given her the Velden Electric hat to make it official. She'd pulled her hair into a ponytail and run it through the opening in the back.

"Everything okay?" Geert asked, looking down at the phone in Maddie's hands. Through the night, he'd come to understand that this hacker, a concept Geert was unable to grasp, was key to the plan. Maddie had been texting PTang all night.

"Better than I thought," Maddie replied. She thumbed up an emoticon wearing a hat and shot it to PTang in reply. "Damn girl is watching us on the security cameras."

The official red, white and blue stripes of the Kingdom of the Netherlands snapped in the stiff westerly morning wind. It was set a full flag height above its predominantly blue Aruban sister flag.

Architects for De Grote Zaal hadn't taken much care to incorporate the turquoise-drenched view that stretched to the horizon. The main entrance, with the flags, was at a right angle to the shore. It faced the brick office building across the road. A single row of parking spaces lined each side of the building. The spaces were empty, almost eerily so.

They continued past the entrance and its flags to the far, ocean side of the building.

"Where are the cars?" Maddie asked as they turned right.

Geert explained that when the soldiers leave for training, they park their personal cars together at the parade grounds so that idle vehicles can't hide among the crowd.

Maddie studied the building, a crude map of its interior resting in her lap. Geert had drawn it in response to Maddie's fifty questions. It was a center hall structure with the mess deck, a mariner's term for cafeteria, and armory on the ocean side. The auditorium and magazine filled the other side.

As they drove, Maddie could see the tables and chairs of the cafeteria through the windows. They passed a door and then windowless siding where the armory was located.

Geert's picture showed that the kitchen shared what must certainly be a reinforced wall with the armory.

Geert turned right again at the back of the building. He pulled up passed the back door and stopped with the tailgate just a few feet from it. The plan called for Geert to kill the circuit breakers to the overhead lights in the auditorium. If someone came looking, the ruse would be their cover.

"You ready?" Maddie asked.

"Ready as ready can be," Geert replied. "Come get your hostage."

Maddie popped the door open and rolled from the seat. When she got to Geert's door she could sense the camera in her peripheral vision. She pulled the revolver from the back of her pants and made a show of flashing it in the clear. Then she opened Geert's door and motioned him out with the snub-nosed barrel.

Geert did as they'd rehearsed. Maddie followed him to the back of the truck. Geert stopped at the bed and extracted a bag of tools for himself and handed another to Maddie. With the bags slung over their shoulders, they went inside. Once they were out of the camera's view, Maddie tucked the revolver back into her waistband and fixed her shirt.

Another text message arrived. PTang was following them across the base. The message read, 'Picture perfect. Your friend is following orders at gunpoint according to the video.'

Signs over doors to the left and right read, *Magazine* and *Arsenaal,* respectively. A red light glowed from the key pads beside the doors. The locks were code and thumbprint enabled. PTang could tell from the audit logs in the application behind the security system.

The lights in the hall lit the path forward. As they passed the doors leading to the objectives, Maddie could see it was dark on the other side of the tempered glass windows.

She followed Geert down the double-wide corridor. Their footsteps angled away in both directions, breaking the silence. Apparently, the kitchen was closed when the troops were away. The few remaining had to fend for breakfast on their own. The quiet confirmed what PTang had told them. She'd been monitoring the security cameras all morning and hadn't seen anyone coming or going.

"Wait here," Geert said, as he pressed his way through a door on their left. As it drifted closed, the morning sun from the unshaded windows was enough for Maddie to see the curve of a stage. It had a single step of elevation above the floor. There was a podium in the middle and two white projection screens on the wall that were angled toward one another.

Maddie stayed in the hall. She turned forward and locked her eyes on the front entrance. A few seconds later she pulled out her phone and dialed up PTang.

"You all set?"

"Waiting patiently. Remember, there's another camera in the room with the guns. Two actually. They'll both be just overhead when you enter. You'll have to take a steps, and look and smile."

Geert whistled from the auditorium.

"Hang on, PTang." Maddie pushed the door open.

"Prop the door open with your bag," Geert instructed. He was removing the faceplate of the electrical panel at the back of the room.

"You actually going to fix something?" Maddie asked.

"Now you're smart, aren't you. No, this is just for looks." Geert pulled the last screw from the plate. He took the assembly from the wall and set it on the floor. After digging around in his bag, he pulled out a flashlight, turned it on and set it on the floor as well.

"You're awfully thorough. You sure you didn't used to be an actor?"

Geert laughed then started toward her. "I come and hang my *arse* and what do I get?"

"A hard time," Maddie finished.

They looked left down the hall toward the entrance to confirm it was still clear. Then they walked to the back door and looked out.

Maddie lifted the phone back to her ear. "You see anything on your end? Looks good from here."

Geert said that an officer would usually come and check in on him after arriving on base. They expected someone would be along eventually.

"Like I told you," PTang said. "They went light on the cameras. There are many blind spots. But the ones I can see are clear. No one seems to be headed your way."

"Then let me in," Maddie said.

She ended the call and dropped the phone in her pocket. The magnetic door to the armory buzzed as she reached up. She leaned forward and followed the door into the first chamber of the two-stage entrance.

Only armorers, gunsmiths and weapon technicians were allowed in the armory itself. At least, that's how it worked in the

US military. Most soldiers would only ever enter the first stage. The second stage was reserved for soldiers whose military occupational specialty, aka MOS, was affiliated with the armory.

Two steel plates in the wall opposite the doors marked the spot where the weapons where transitioned. Two more tempered glass windows sat above the metal plates. From the inside, the armorer could open the metal plate high enough to accommodate the weapon being passed from inventory to the field.

Maddie turned around and looked up. She smiled at the black dome on the ceiling. A moment later the second windowless steel door behind her buzzed with magnetic life.

Maddie's respect for PTang was growing by the minute. It was as much for her nonchalance of what other people thought as it was for her talent. She could almost see her in the gray beret and Star Wars t-shirt, working the keyboard. She wore it three days a week. Working with her the last two days had been a wholly new experience. Her ability to tickle the electrons of the internet into doing what they needed was a gamechanger. Significant enough that Maddie felt confident going forward with a plan that otherwise would have been ludicrous.

She turned and pressed down on the lever-style handle. The buzzing of the magnetized lock went silent.

The smell of gun oil was faint in the first chamber but the main room smelled like the machine of war. For all the technology the nations of the world had devised to kill one another, none of them had removed the requirement of a soldier and her gun. Achieving total defeat still required soldiers firing lethal lances of lead through the air to kill the enemy. The rooms that housed these weapons were marked by the dank, musty smell of the earth's most precious natural resource.

In the faint light coming from the window, Maddie could see a silver switch plate on the wall. She flicked at it and the room broke into light. Built like a locker room for a gun fanatic, the walls of the room were lined with cages where the weapons were stored.

Maddie had never actually been inside an armory. She'd only ever seen one through the windows of the receiving area. Even still, something about the place rushed her back in time.

Overall, the room was one contiguous rectangle. The entry area took up the corner at Maddie's back. In front of her, along the right-hand side, worktables lined the wall. Updating and repairing weapons was critical to any military organization. The small arms technicians that worked here were key to the unit's readiness. With spare parts and replacement weapons five thousand miles away, if they failed at their jobs, the unit would resemble a Stone Age horde instead of a modern fighting unit.

Maddie walked to her left. Five green racks filled the center of the room. Diamond-shaped holes perforated the sides and front to ensure the temperature and humidity controls built into the room also made their way to the weapons. The green armory cabinets were a standard for military and law enforcement organizations. A sort of locker system on wheels, the cabinets could be moved left and right using a three-pronged handle mounted on the side. The racks were pushed together to the left, toward the wall that adjoined the hallway. The ones in front were empty.

The rack on the end was wide open, its accordion doors folded to the sides and pushed back out of the way. The mounts were empty, a fact that was at once discouraging to Maddie. Had she placed herself in danger for nothing?

A separate set of racks lined the back wall of the room. Maddie counted ten chambers. Four were open and empty. Six were closed and appeared to have weapons.

Thick silver locks hung from a bar affixed inside the cabinet handles. Geert had brought a pair of bolt cutters that were half

Maddie's height. She'd need every ounce of the leverage they'd provide to fracture the hardened steel locks.

Maddie shot toward the cages. She hit the closest cage at a jog and laced her fingers through the holes. It was just over half full, the grips of what looked like Glock-17's facing her.

She dropped to a knee to inspect the bottom rack. It too was configured for pistols. A full rack of grips stared back at her. The third, fourth and fifth cabinets were more promising. Standard issue 5.56 assault rifles were resting ten abreast. They looked to be carbine models with a forward grip that was different than the ones used by the US military. Maddie knew she'd hit pay dirt, but she kept looking.

At first, the last cabinet appeared empty. The rack positions she could see were bare, but the lock was affixed. The empty cabinets had been left open.

Two long rifles materialized. She knew immediately that they were something different. Maddie had never been a weapons aficionado. Even as a sniper, her interests ended with the weapons on which she was trained. Still, she could feel her heart double at the realization. They were scoped weapons with black bags rubber banded over the optics. These rifles were designed for killing humans from far, far away.

The M40A5 she'd used in the Corps was as basic a rifle as there was. Many a farm boy had learned to hunt using the Remington 700 upon which it was based. Sure, they were modified by the Corps to increase their precision, but the variant she used in Iraq could have just as easily been at home on a white-tail deer hunt in the fall.

The rifles in front of Maddie were made by Accuracy International. She'd seen them before. They would have been at home in some futuristic video game. Somehow it felt beautiful and threatening all at once. Powerful but new. Using a weapon to which you were unacquainted was not as easy as people thought. Relationships between weapons systems and soldiers was built over time.

The stock appeared to be hinged. There was an adjustable cheekpiece, buttpad with spacers and an unorthodox pistol grip. Somewhere in their intimidating appearance Maddie could see potential, though. All the adjustable components would make it easier for her to fit the weapon to her body. She would need practice. It had been nearly four years since she held a rifle.

As she stared at the weapons, just inches away from the tips of her fingers, the reality of her plan seemed to culminate. Excitement, disbelief and abject fear assaulted her mind. Never before had she been forced to contend with such a cocktail of emotions.

Maddie turned and hurried for the door. She needed to move before she lost her nerve or started second-guessing the lunacy of her plan. Without another thought, she pushed her way through the steel doors into the first chamber of the armory lockout. She felt the phone in her pocket buzz as her hands hit the wide bar of the door leading out into the hall. As she spilled into it, she realized why it was buzzing.

51

US CONSULATE'S OFFICE, Curacao

MARGARET BAKER WAS through with it. She'd retire when this mess was over. The life of a civil servant had been good to her, but she was too old for this. The call to update her on the fluid plans had come just after four in the morning. It was an assistant to the Joint Chiefs of Staff.

The Dutch Marines had lifted off from Cherry Point North Carolina a full twelve hours ahead of schedule. Special Operations Command and the intelligence apparatus that had descended on Aruba in the last twenty-four hours were both forced into overdrive. Everything had been moved up, except the step-off time for the operation itself.

The landing of the Dutch Marines was to be used as cover to get Delta Force onto the island. There would be two planes. One with the Dutch Marines flying home early from training exercises at Camp Lejeune. And a second, full of US special operations soldiers that had assembled at the base on Bonaire.

The plan called for them to land within minutes of one another.

An email had been sent to the terrorists through established channels. They were told that the Dutch Marines were returning but that they had no intention of being used in an offensive manner. The Netherlands had paid their ransom and expected their citizens, along with the Italians, Germans and Swedes, to be released. The email explained that the Dutch Marines were returning to maintain order once the New Jihad Front departed. It further explained that the company of Dutch Marines would, immediately upon landing, be returning to their garrison in Savaneta.

The intent of the email was twofold. First, the Dutch had paid. They didn't want the landing of a military transport plane being interpreted as hostility. Officials in The Netherlands would have sent the email regardless of US involvement. In fact, the Dutch had initially been opposed to bringing US soldiers onto the island before their citizens were released. But US officials leaned on them. They had devised a plan to hide Delta Force until after the Dutch were released. Besides that, there were less than forty Dutch citizens being held. Ultimately, they'd caved to US pressure and accepted the risk to appease the Americans.

Second, the email and the whole operation, for that matter, was a ruse to hide the arrival of the attack force. After the two planes landed, both would taxi to the end of the runway where military facilities were located. The plane carrying the Dutch Marines would stop on the tarmac in plain view while the second aircraft was pushed into a hanger and out of sight.

The Dutch Prime Minster wasn't keen on the plan. His interest was in the safety of his citizens and controlling the damage being done in Aruba. He voiced his objection directly to the President of the United States. He'd made it clear to

POTUS that he intended to publicly voice his opposition to the operation if it sparked unintended consequences.

POTUS had argued that operational security was more important than scapegoating the US. He tried to convince him that his men would play a significant role. A show was to be made of the Dutch Marines. Even with the airport having been shut down for the better part of a day, the international media had stilled wormed their way onto the island. Many had hitched rides on the empty planes sent to fly stranded tourists out. Their rented vans could freely roam the open corridors. Some had even found their way within camera range of the resort, despite the cordoned-off bubble surrounding the epicenter.

The news crews would be the subterfuge. They'd film the arrival and tailgate the Marines to the Barracks in Savaneta. While the eyes of the world followed the Marines, an overwhelming force of Delta operators were to remain hidden in the hanger until after sunset.

It was being called a rescue mission, but Margaret was skeptical. There were too many variables. So many moving parts, in fact, that she considered voicing her own concern—but a lifelong bureaucrat knew better than to start a fight they had no hope of winning. Her ability to speak up had been neutered long ago, and her willingness to contest the fact was whisked away by the lost hours of sleep.

She hung up the phone and lay her head down on her desk.

52

Pescadero Marina and Boatyard, Aruba

Adnan Sali's contribution had consisted of shooting the Chief Minister of Justice in the forehead. Sure, he'd been sending emails on activity at the airport but that made him feel more like a birdwatcher than a soldier. Plus, activity at the airport had all but stopped late yesterday afternoon. His part in the action had been frustratingly short.

Tuesday morning had left him surrounded by a surreal aura—he was surprised by the adrenaline high that accompanied the killing. It had been easier than he'd expected. First light was just kissing the sky when the Minister opened his front door. Adnan walked right up to the man. He nearly touched his forehead with the barrel of the silenced pistol.

The man hadn't been thrown back the way he'd imagined. Instead, his knees sort of buckled and he crumpled to the ground. Adnan casually got back in his car. He remembered looking at himself in the review mirror as he pulled away. His face bore an expression he'd not seen before. With heart racing and a feeling of pride warming his body, Adnan drove to work.

He arrived earlier than usual that morning. He preferred to start early to beat the worst of the heat. Just twelve degrees above the equator with skies that were perpetually blue, Aruba was a hot place to work. The inside of a boat became an oven before noon.

Adnan was a mechanic for Pescadero Marina and Boatyard. Beginning at the age of six, he'd worked on boats, motors mostly. His father owned a small engine repair shop in Yemen —he had a knack for keeping ancient outboards running years beyond their useful life. He was like a medicine man to the local fishing fleet.

Finding a job on Aruba allowed Adnan to blend in. Working at a marina was natural. He had offered to work a few days for free. It had taken just one for him to prove his worth to the owner of Pescadero.

The ability to work flexible hours afforded him the opportunity to scout the Minister's routine. Ultimately, his role in the action was simple: murder the minister and then back up the team from outside the resort. Anas had suggested the marina by the airport. Once the operation was underway, Adnan would be able to watch over the airport without drawing attention. If all went as planned, he'd steal a boat from the marina and rendezvous with the *Contagious* when the team left for Venezuela.

Three weeks before the operation, he was given a set of GPS coordinates between Venezuela and Aruba. He'd met a fishing boat and been given several wooden crates. Inside were four silenced pistols, one for each of the on-island operatives. There were walkie-talkies and two AK-47 assault rifles. He and Jaber were to remain outside the resort once the action started. The assault rifles were to be used to defend themselves or to fight their way into the resort if necessary.

Adnan climbed the ladder to the top of the flybridge where he had a view across the airport. Queen Beatrix Airport was right on the water. Its western end, Runway Eleven, abutted the Caribbean and receive landing aircraft.

Pescadero was at the end of the road, literally. It was hemmed in on three sides with the airport fence as a barrier to the north and the sea to the west and south. The marina was tucked in next to the general aviation side of the airport. The main terminal was all the way across the tarmac on the other side of the complex.

THE FLY BRIDGES on the sport fishing boats served as Adnan's perch. He watched for planes and used binoculars to scan the airport. Anas had sent an email telling him to expect two military aircraft. He'd barely sat down when the first one came into view.

The first gray jet lumbered from the sky and onto the runway. Adnan watched it to the end where it exited and began to taxi toward the terminal. Jet number two appeared and followed suit. The first to land waited on the taxi way in front of the terminal. Once the second flight arrived, the two aircraft taxied back to the end of the runway where they had touched down. There was a single military hangar at that end of the runway in the far corner of the airport complex.

Adnan pecked an email, replying to let Anas know they had landed.

Jet number two parked in from of the hangar after the first jet was pushed in by an airport tractor. The hanger doors were closed.

Adnan watched buses drive into the airport and pull up alongside the hanger. Soldiers clad in desert camo deplaned the jet parked in front. They walked to the buses and boarded.

The amplification of the binoculars and the angle of his

perspective allowed Adnan to see between the buses and the hangar. Initially, he hadn't noticed. Then something clicked. It struck him as the last man streamed toward the bus from the jet parked in front. No one had come out of the hanger. He watched and waited. Maybe there was a problem with the stairs, or maybe they needed the ones from outside.

Another ten minutes passed before he decided to write. Once the mobile stairs were parked beside the hangar and the buses pulled away, he dictated an email into his phone and sent it to Anas.

53

DUTCH MARINE BASE, Aruba

THE STRAIGHT BARS on the epaulets of his desert camouflage uniform marked him as an officer. Captain Koning froze as Maddie spilled into the hallway. The professionalism of his boyish face transitioned rapidly from confusion to fear.

A small man, his head was even with Maddie's eyes, a fact she identified as an advantage from the start.

Koning stepped a foot back, instinctively moving into a firing stance. His arm twitched toward the Glock strapped to his leg.

Maddie leapt forward. She gripped his neck with her right and went for his gun with her left.

Within the width of a single breath, Maddie had Koning pinned against the wall. Her fingers found the snap on his sidearm and she was able to pull it free and send it skittering down the hall.

Then she took a step back and pulled the snub-nosed .38

out from behind her back. She gave herself a fell step worth of distance and squared up with both hands on the revolver.

"We mean no harm. We're not with the terrorists. We're here to stop them." Koning's eyes widened as the outcome of the engagement became reality.

Maddie stared deeply into the officer's eyes.

"Son of a bitch," she growled under her breath. "We just needed a few more minutes... How many men do you have left here?"

Koning tried to disguise his fear as anger. "Koning. Lieutenant Captain. 627—"

Maddie cut him off. "Listen, this isn't the time to pull the name, rank and serial number shit. We know who you are. We know you're protecting this place with a skeleton crew. I came here for one thing. Weapons." Maddie raised her jaw, signaling toward the armory with the back of her head.

"Fifteen more minutes and we would've been out of here. No harm, no foul..." She thought for a handful of seconds then look back at Konig to make it clear she was still on point.

"Listen, Captain. I already know I'm in a world of trouble. I've got nothing to lose. I also know you want to get back to your wife and that little girl of yours. You and I want the same thing. We need to work together. You understand me? You help me get what I need, and I'll make sure it looks like you didn't have any other choice. Just bear with me. I'll explain."

Koning was in no position to negotiate. His sidearm was gone and he was paralyzed by the barrel of the revolver. Even still, he didn't seem to know how to respond.

"You've broken the law," he said, scowling.

"Let's you and me go on into the armory and have us a chat," Maddie said. "Geert. I'm going to need those bolt cutters. When you go out there take a few looks back at the door like you're fixing to make a run for it. Then grab the cutters and come on back in."

Maddie made a spinning motion with the Colt.

"Just to make this safer for both of us, I need to get your hands behind your back. You understand?" Koning nodded and rotated toward the wall. He offered the wrists behind his back without a struggle.

Maddie pulled the phone from her pocket to ask PTang to buzz her back in. The message on the screen read, 'someone's coming'. PTang had seen Koning approach, but it had come too late.

PTang answered before the first ring ended. "Is everything okay?"

"Thanks for the heads up. You're about to meet Captain Koning on the security cameras. He's joining our team."

"I couldn't see him coming until he was ten feet from the building. The coverage is not good."

"We'll be alright. Buzz me back into the armory, please."

The door buzzed and Maddie pushed it open with her right hand. She signaled Koning through with the revolver, then held the door open until Geert returned from the truck.

Koning had to be wondering about the person on the other end of the phone and their ability to open secure doors at will. But he said nothing.

Geert offered to carry the cutters into the armory, but Maddie refused. She needed him in the hall to run cover for any other surprises. Besides that, she didn't want the cameras inside the armory recording Geert seeming to help. Maddie now had two accomplices that needed to appear reluctant for the video recorders.

Once they were inside, Maddie scanned the workbenches for anything she could use to restrain Koning. The best she could do was a roll of metal tag wire. The armorers used it to attach manila tags to the weapons. Labeling them with the serial number allowed an inventory to be run without pulling every weapon.

It proved to be more than adequate filling in for handcuffs. Maddie wrapped Koning's wrists six or seven times. She took care to ensure the wraps weren't biting into the skin, but that they were tight enough to prevent him wiggling out.

Maddie pulled a stool out from beneath one of the workbenches.

"Have a seat."

After Koning sat, Maddie had him position his feet side-by-side and wrapped the ankles. With his arms secure behind his back and legs immobilized, Koning was officially hog-tied and ready to learn more.

"You've got a pretty wife and a little daughter. I bet you think about 'em all day." Maddie stood in front of Koning with hands on hips. The captain was sitting tall, listening intently. "I'm an American. I was a Marine like you. Fifteen years. When I was deployed, my family was there in my mind every minute of every day. I couldn't wait to get back home." Maddie paused and Koning nodded.

"You and I are very similar, Captain. I have two daughters and a husband and they're the best thing in the world as far as I can tell." She paused again and waited for agreement to hit Koning's face. "Yeah, see, you know what I mean. You'd do anything for them, wouldn't you?"

Koning again nodded agreement.

Maddie squatted down in front of the man. She rubbed her forehead, massaging the skin above her left eye.

"So imagine this, Captain Koning... Imagine you went on vacation to Aruba... except, instead of going all together, your husband and oldest daughter went first. Why, you ask. Why do we not all arrive here on the island at the same time? Because you forgot a fucking passport for the baby. Imagine that for a minute." Maddie looked up from the floor. Koning's gaze was locked on her. His fear and anger had softened.

"Trust me... One kid is roses and butterflies. Having two is a battle to keep your head on straight." Maddie smiled at the man. She was connecting.

"So the husband and daughter go ahead... to the Surfside resort." Maddie said it slow. Koning looked like a boy in the midst of a damn good campfire story. His posture straightened and eyes grew wider.

"Then a group of fucking terrorists take over the hotel. Imagine that... They take it over the morning you arrive. Worst goddamn timing you can imagine, Captain. So bad, you couldn't make this shit up."

Maddie spat a piece of something off her tongue toward the floor. She stood and pulled her phone from her pocket. She typed a message into it, hit send and then bent, placing the phone on one knee and the open hand on the other.

"You seen those videos of the people they're gonna murder tonight if they don't get paid?"

Koning shook his head.

"The Americans... that dad and his daughter... They're mine."

The phone chimed. She turned it over and tapped on the photo PTang had sent. She turned it and held it up for Koning.

"Imagine if it were them, Captain. Imagine that was your wife and daughter. Your wife's head swollen and bruised. Your daughter's face blank with fear." Maddie bit her lip. "Imagine that."

54

SURFSIDE RESORT, Aruba

"WHAT THE HELL does he mean? Is he saying there's a SWAT team at the marina?" Fazul had read the emails from Adnan four times.

5:32am: *Both jets on ground. Taxiing to military hangar on west end.*

6:12am: *Something strange here. One jet pushed into hangar and doors closed. Marines exit outside jet and go to buses. No one come from hangar. Cannot see hangar entrance from outside of airport. Only from where I am on this side. Suspicious.*

6:21am: *Buses departing airport. Two trucks still being loaded with supplies from outside jet. Still nothing from hangar. No people or supplies from jet inside hangar.*

6:33am: *Trucks departing. Nothing from jet inside hangar.*

6:37am: *Hiding. 4 vans drove into the marina. SWAT team!*

"Can you call him?" Fazul asked.

"We knocked out the cell service," Anas responded.

"I know that, you fucking idiot. I meant through the computer. Call his phone through the computer."

"It's unsecure." Anas was quick with his response. "Even the email communication presents a risk."

Fazul imagined slamming the butt of his rifle into his brother's temple. "How many times do I have to ask? Can you not explain yourself? Do you think the emails compromised his position?"

Anas shrugged. He shook his head, clearly agitated by the angry tone.

"We're giving this ten more minutes, Anas. Ten. Minutes. Then someone needs to die."

"You're over reacting again, Fazul." It took every ounce of Fazul's remaining willpower to not grab his brother by the throat. "What does it matter?" Anas continued. "We need to get on with releasing the hostages. They'll make for a human shield if we let them go in a trickle throughout the day."

"You and your soft defense will get us nowhere. I'm through talking to you about this. It's my call."

"It's OUR call!" Anas yelled as he jumped up from his chair. Fazul was surprised his brother had the nerve to go eye-to-eye. "I say we send notice! We tell them we know they're hiding something in the hangar. We let them know we're watching. Even if they took Adnan. Still! We watch."

Fazul considered the idea. "The first proactive suggestion you've made. Do that now. Can you take the drone all the way to Adnan?" asked Fazul.

"We've got the range. With the antenna on top of the buildings we've got enough range to cover the whole island."

"Then get on it. See if he's there. See if these vans are still there. Post videos of it all. Show the hangar and tell the world these doors need to be opened. We want to see inside." Fazul turned and pushed his way out of the security suite and into the lobby. He hated compromising with his brother.

If Adnan did not check in and the drone found nothing, then Americans would die. The father and the daughter in the office would go first. Anas was too close to them.

"Where's Hassan?" Fazul asked one of the guards.

The soldier pointed toward the back of the lobby. "Just left."

Fazul ran out the back entrance. "Hassan!" he called.

Hassan was second in command to Fazul. He was walking the corridor along the edge of building two. He stopped and turned back.

"Yes, Fazul."

"Get me more Americans. Eight or ten. Men, women and children. Bring them to the game room."

"Is everything okay?" Hassan asked.

"No. Adnan reported suspicious activity at the airport. A military plane being hidden in a hangar. He said something about a SWAT team and we haven't heard from him since. If he doesn't check in, we're going to kill the father and the girl."

"What of the eight or ten you request then?"

"We'll line them up behind and make them watch. They'll be in the video. If they don't show us the inside of the hangar, then we'll kill the rest."

55

DUTCH MARINE BASE, Aruba

THE FIRST OF four gray buses pulled through the gate as Maddie and Geert approached. 6:37 glowed on the dash. Maddie leaned down low as it passed and could see it was filled with Dutch Marines.

"Cutting it close," Geert said. "Now we're a pair of lunatics."

A rumpled blanket was spread across the rear cab of the pickup. Koning was seated on the floor, beneath the blanket, with his back against the passenger side door. After explaining her predicament to the captain, Maddie had made a show of ordering him around at gunpoint. Koning had secured the keys to the weapons lockers.

Maddie had gone in looking for a weapon she could use to kill a few men at a distance. She left with enough firepower to start a war. She'd decided on one of each—a Glock 17 to replace the snub-nosed 38, a Canadian made AR-15 carbine, and perhaps the cream of the crop when it came to sniper rifles, an Accuracy International chambered in 338 Lapua Magnum. It was a haul that had her giddy with excitement. If she was going to do the unthinkable, what better way to go than armed to the teeth.

The footprint of the magazine room was nearly identical to the arsenal. Military establishments almost always stored weapons and ammunition separately. They were usually accessible to different soldiers and managed by different MOS's. The separation prevented hot headed privates from easily taking revenge with lethal force.

Ammunition was stored in movable lockers that matched the ones where she'd taken the weapons. Again, Koning used a digital code to open a safe containing the keys to tens of thousands of rounds of ammunition.

The Glock fired the 9x19mm Parabellum round. The carbine, 5.56x45. Both types were stored in the traditional green ammo boxes. A box of 9mm included 1000 rounds. A box of 5.56, 900. Maddie took one of each.

The ammunition for the Accuracy International was harder to find. Like the rifles, Maddie found it in the last locker, almost hidden in the corner. It was in limited supply compared to the rest. Just twenty flip top cases sat on the shelves. Each blue plastic case contained fifty rounds. Maddie took three.

Before they left, Maddie re-bound Koning's wrists. She tied them behind the captain's back in plain view of the camera, watching and recording from above. Maddie had even added a gag. She'd done it as much for the camera as to prevent him from calling out as they passed by the guard shack. Maddie sensed that the two of them had reached an unspoken agreement, but she couldn't be certain or take any chances.

Maddie smiled and waved as they drove by the gatehouse. They cleared the base without incident and navigated the streets of Savaneta back to the neighboring town of San Nicolas.

"Is this walk-in you have in mind going to be strong enough to hold him?" Maddie asked.

"There's a heavy door. Giant latch. We can prop a chair as well."

"He won't suffocate in there?"

"The cooling unit was removed. There's a hole that lets air in and out. It doesn't get very hot. The insulation keeps the temperature from going too high. I was in there on a pisser of a hot one before we opened the restaurant. I'll never forget how cool it was. Like a basement back home."

They pulled up to the critical intersection leading to Baby Beach. To the left, up the hill a bit, was the old restaurant. To the right, the new building and the big sign that would forever reassure worried tourists that they were on the right track.

Geert turned right. "Kavita's putting together some supplies for you. We'll need some for Koning there as well... Now that you've kidnapped the poor guy." He pulled into the parking lot. "I'll be back in a jiff," Geert said.

Maddie checked on her prisoner. She pulled the blanket from off his head. "You doing okay?"

Koning nodded and grunted.

The gag was overkill by then. She got out and went to the back, untied it and stuffed it in her pocket.

"Thanks. That thing was drying out my mouth."

"Geert's going to get some food and water. The place we're going to leave you is nearby."

"You really think you can get in there?" Koning asked.

"I have no idea, Captain. What I do know, is if I sat by and didn't do anything... I couldn't live with myself."

Koning nodded.

"Yeah, you get it. It's a giant suck of a situation."

Before long, Geert returned. He had a cloth bag filled with foil-wrapped Roti and another stacked with bottles of water. A sweating coke-cola sat on top. It was hard to tell from his toothpick frame but the sugary indulgence was Geert's vice.

He shifted into gear and turned a circle in the parking lot. "After I drop you off, we're taking Charlotte and the girls to a friend's house. They've plenty of space. Live mid-island. We'll hold up there until things are over."

The mention of Charlotte's name changed the feeling in Maddie's gut. A nervous anticipation had been lurking there all morning. She'd felt like a girl in the midst of an adventure she knew would get her in trouble. Hearing Charlotte's name sent that excitement into a teeter. The unanswerable questions returned. Was it better to stay back and protect one? Was the decision to go down range a suicide mission? Maybe, but the decision had been made. She wanted them all back, and she had no doubts.

"Alright, Geert. Thanks, my friend." Maddie had left a list of numbers for him and Kavita to call. Her sister would take Charlotte. She had two of her own, but she was a fine mother. Charlotte was young enough to forget. She would take well to a new family.

Maddie shook away the thought. "Unless you hear otherwise from me or PTang... come back in the morning and let Koning out."

"Got it, chief," Geert responded.

As they pulled passed the old restaurant, Maddie could see that the integrity of the structure was flagging. The eaves sagged in the center and the bright colors were worn away by the blowing sand. The backyard was littered with forgotten restaurant remnants. A broken wire fence marked the spot where Kavita kept the chickens. Health inspectors had forced her to remove them from the property.

Geert parked and they guided Koning to the cooler. A quarter inch of dust had accumulated on the floor but Geert was right, the temperature was cooler than outside. It wasn't the beach, but it wasn't the worst way to spend a day either.

Maddie unwound the wire around Koning's wrists. Geert went to the truck and brought his battery-powered radio. They set him up with a chair to sit on and a bucket for his business. Maddie took two of the foil packets and left the rest for Koning. There was more than enough roti to carry him a day. Geert sat the bag of waters on the ground and then pulled a pair of oranges from his pockets.

"Gonna bar the door, Captain," Maddie said. "I hate to do it... You've been such a good sport, but I can't let the cat out of the bag too early. You've been a big help, though. I really appreciate it." She paused. "The video will make it obvious you didn't have a choice. Geert here will back you up. He was forced into it as well." Maddie nudged him.

"That's my story and I'm sticking to it," he replied. "That's a Yank song, isn't it?"

Maddie laughed.

"Alright, then. Geert'll be back to let you out. No more than twenty-four hours." Maddie brought her posture to attention. She dropped her arms to her sides then snapped the right hand up into a crisp salute. Geert did the same.

The door locked on its own and couldn't be opened from the inside. Even still, Maddie wanted insurance. She wrapped a rusty chain around the handle and hooked it to the stanchion of a shelf around the corner.

She pat the door of the cooler twice and turned to leave.

"Now get me to the desert, you old Dutchman," Maddie said.

"Yes, lunatic. Practice you will."

Geert started the truck and turned north on Sero Colorado, following the road away from popular Baby Beach. When it hooked left back toward Savaneta, Geert picked up an unnamed road that continued north into what appeared to be increasingly arid nothingness. The intersection lacked a sign with the name of the road but there was a touristy plaque telling them that *Bachelor's Beach, Boca Grandi* and *Grapefield* Beach were all this way.

Improvised dirt roads peeled off to the right as they drove. They ran to the edge of the island and disappeared. Little-known beaches lined this windward side of the island. The sea had an opposite personality here, darker and rougher than the idyllic leeward paradise. Angry waves threatened the stony cliffs that hid the beaches chiseled from the rock below.

A brown sign announcing the *Korrectie Instituut Aruba*, caught Maddie's attention. She looked left and was again reminded of the Arubans' preference for geometric precision. The lines of the prison ran straight and at right angles to one another.

"That looks like a shithole," Maddie said.

Geert turned his attention to the side window. "They don't accept lunatics. So no worries."

A dust devil swirled in the distance, the vortex of dry sandy air sending cold chills down Maddie's back. The facility looked lonely and extremely fucking hot. She'd rather die than waste away in there on account of her bad decisions.

Before long they passed another sign announcing that they'd entered Arikok National Park. White letters on a brown background looked something like the National Park signs in the States.

A mule slept on the side of the road. It painted a compelling picture with rugged textured hills rising in the background. Almost immediately, the landscape took on a more desert-like appearance. The low-slung bunches of cacti that had dotted the landscape a few miles back, had grown into tall pin cushions. Hardy ground covering plants and clumps of aloe vera filled the space between cacti.

"There's a road just ahead that dead ends in a draw. Tourists drive it sometimes but not much else. There's a cave or something," Geert said.

Hills rose on both sides immediately after the turn. The road snaked away from the shore for a mile and then ended at a circle.

"This is good. The hill there makes for a good backstop." Maddie pointed out the front windshield. "I'll drop the drum and then we can drive back out a ways."

They both got out and went to the back of the truck. On their way back from the Marine base, they'd secured a rusty fifty-five-gallon drum from a forgotten gas station. Geert helped Maddie lift it from the bed. They stood it up and pushed it back against the fence.

As they drove away, Maddie turned in her seat. The road veered around a pile of rock that had slipped down the hill years ago. Above it, she could still make out the hilltop that loomed over the drum.

Maddie tapped Geert on the shoulder. "That should do it."

She exited the truck, went to the bed and laid the tailgate down. The weapons had been wrapped in a painter's drop cloth Geert had stored in the lock boxes running along the sides of the truck bed.

Maddie slid the blanket onto the tailgate and unwrapped its lethal contents. She picked up the black assault rifle first and ejected the magazine. Next, she uncovered the ammo boxes hidden beneath another cloth and popped the latch on the one labeled 5.56mm. Inside thin cardboard boxes sat in an orderly row. Each box contained three stripper clips, each with ten rounds.

It had been a while and her fingers had lost the muscle memory associated with loading a mag. In the minutes it took her to load all thirty rounds, Geert followed suit with the Glock. He was on the second clip before Maddie had finished her first.

"Show-off," Maddie quipped. Geert paused just long enough for a victory nod.

Next, Maddie pulled the Accuracy International from the canvas drop cloth. Its desert color had a matte finish, good enough that it would've disappeared if she set it on the ground. Accuracy International wasn't a household name among shooters in the US. The predominant reason for this was because its products were manufactured in England. There were plenty of solid US manufacturers with long range systems. Unlike most material goods, the US had a thing for *Made in America* when it came to the military and their weapons.

Internationally, the AI rifles were revered with a sort of mystical fervor. Many nations fielded their snipers with AI models. International sniper competitions were filled with AI shooters, and the weapons system were credited with the longest kills in the Afghan war—a hunting ground where open space offered ample opportunity for real world max range testing. Firing at the resort from across the salt pan would be a cakewalk. Maddie just needed to get acquainted and make sure it was threading half dollar groupings at five hundred yards.

She pinched the protective plastic off the scope. A black Schmidt and Bender appeared. Her heart skipped a beat. It was the first time she'd thought about the reticle. She shouldered the weapon.

"Whew."

"Mildot or MOA?" Geert asked.

Maddie lower the rifle. It was heavy, maybe fifteen to twenty pounds unloaded. She looked at Geert and smiled. "You're a smarter son-of-a-bitch than you let on. You damn Dutchmen are trouble." She paused a beat. "Mildot, thank God."

Maddie loaded three mags with the Lapua Magnum rounds. "I'll be back," she said turning to her left. The hill was lower on that side and it provided an unobstructed sight line past the rock slide.

"Try to keep it down. Not too loud," Geert said.

Maddie held an 'okay' sign over her head.

Rocks and gravel filled the road bed with boulders marking the hill. Several were weathered flat over the eons. Maddie scrambled up and found one shaped just enough like a tabletop to work.

She unfolded the bipod and stretched out on the bare rock. It supported the rifle and her body, except for her sneakers which hung off the edge. She rolled to her side and extracted the phone from her pocket. After launching the calculator app, she set it down on the rock near the trigger.

Using her right hand, Maddie lifted the bolt action. She slid it back, the even sound of oiled surfaces gliding past one another returning some sense of familiarity. It clunked at the back as the breach opened wide enough for the round at the top of the magazine. A hint of the slick tang wafted up, the gun oil sweet like buttered coconut.

She pushed the round home, into the chamber, but left the safety on while she made adjustments. Starting with the cheek piece, Maddie fine-tuned the rifle until it fit comfortably. Then she focused on ranging the target.

Modern snipers are blessed with the simplicity afforded by laser range finders. Maddie had found none in the lockers and Koning said designated soldiers were responsible for managing the equipment. Luckily, the mildot equation was still stuck in her head, like her childhood telephone number. Using the height or width of a target and the mildot measurement, a long-range shooter could accurately estimate the distance to target.

Maddie looked over the top of the scope. It had been a while since she'd played the range guessing game. For years, it was more a habit than conscious task. Driving in the car or from the window of a building, she'd pick a person or object in the distance to estimate. It was easiest when humans were involved. Different human characteristics such as the face, hands and head become indiscernible at specific ranges. The face can be seen at 100 meters but disappears by 200. At 400 meters, the body appears headless, and so on.

Oxidation had overwhelmed the 55-gallon-drum many years ago. The auburn flakes served as compelling camouflage in the desert landscape. With the naked eye, Maddie could see the circle where they'd turned around. The fence posts and rails where wisps, lines thinner than you get from a sharpened number two pencil. The drum was just a smudge of color variation amidst the sea of brown.

"Five hundred and fifty meters," Maddie guessed. She laid her cheek on the stock of the rifle and scanned for the drum with the wide three power magnification of the scope.

The breadth of the scopes zoom range was beyond anything Maddie had used in the past. Zoomed out, it magnified objects three times their actual size. Ridges on the side of the drum were visible and the rails of the fence were contoured. Maddie turned the adjustment to the full twenty-seven magnification. Peering through the lens again, she felt like she could reach out and scrape the rusty chips flaking from the side of the drum.

Even better was the fact that the reticle was in the first focal plane of the scope. This allowed the crosshairs and mildots to change in size with the magnification. It was modern technology. The lack of this functionality had long prevented variable power scopes from being adopted for military use. If the reticle didn't accurately resize with the magnification, then distance estimation was impossible.

After turning down the magnification, Maddie set about measuring the height of the drum. She ran its top edge through the center of one mildot and held it steady as she assessed its size.

"One point five," Maddie said out loud. She lifted her head from the optic and let the rifle rest on the rock. With her left hand, she tapped the calculation into her phone. "Height of the drum is thirty-five inches. Multiply that by the twenty-five point four constant... Then divide by the one point seven-five mildot measurement." She hit the equal key. "Five hundred and eight meters."

Maddie studied the windage and elevation dials on the scope. Both were set to their zero-stops. Assuming a one hundred meter zero and a standard elevation adjustment, Maddie clicked the elevation knob five times to compensate for the distance. Based on the rifle's reputation, she was skeptical if she needed to make any changes off the zero setting.

The Lapua Magnum round left the barrel at over nine hundred meters per second. It would remain supersonic way beyond one thousand meters. This wasn't necessarily a good thing for Maddie. Although the snap of the rifle would be muted from inside the house, the soldiers would hear the supersonic crack of the round as it tore by them on a miss or through them on a hit. Any soldiers in the area would hear the smack of torn flesh and the supersonic wave of the bullet at nearly the same time. The two sounds arriving together would tell them a bullet was the source of the destruction.

Rounds like the 7.62mm fell below supersonic speed around 600 meters. The benefit is that the bullet impacts and no sonic wave accompanies it. People near the impact are stunned by the spontaneous explosion of gore without anything to associate it with. This hesitation allows the sniper to acquire and hit, one, and sometimes two more targets before enemy combatants sort out what's happening. Maddie wouldn't have that luxury.

Even though she was unfamiliar with Accuracy International rifles, she was keenly aware of the 338 Lapua Magnum round. The Lapua was designed to penetrate body armor at distances beyond ten football fields. It had been adopted by big game hunters to hunt the big five animals in Africa. The round was a beast.

It would tear through the hot, low density air of Aruba, its trajectory remaining flat over ridiculous distances. With the wind at her back, as it would be in the house, she expected the notorious trade winds to have less effect than one might have imagined when mentioning 'sniper' and 'Aruba' in the same sentence.

Maddie lay her cheek back on the adjusted stock and sighted the helpless drum. It had been five years since she pulled a trigger. With the crosshairs resting center of mass, she drew back on the thin strip of metal married to her pointer finger.

The rifle bucked. A charge of flames and heat jetted at right angles, directed out by the muzzle break. Cupped by the valley, the report ran out and away with tremendous speed.

Maddie reacquired the target just as the metallic *dong* rung out. The drum was shrouded in a haze of auburn dust, a black dot marking the hit.

56

SURFSIDE RESORT, Aruba

ANAS HAD SOUNDED the fire alarm around 7:30 that morning. This first alarm was to direct the hostages to the website. He'd updated it with a map of the resort that showed numbers for each of the four buildings. A schedule was also posted. The evacuation was to begin at 9 A.M., and he didn't want it delayed.

The website instructions were specifically directed to hostages holding a passport from any country besides the United States or Great Britain. Anyone who could prove they were not citizens of those two countries was to be released.

Each of the four buildings had a time. The schedule showed the first would be cleared beginning at 9 o'clock. The plan was to continue in two hour increments. Building Two at 11 o'clock, Building Three at 1, and Building Four at 3 in the afternoon.

It was just minutes before nine in the morning. Teams were in motion, moving into position to begin the evacuation. Anas waited to deploy another drone to the airport. This decision was made in part because it was counter to what Fazul wanted. In addition, he waited because he wanted to focus on the evacuation, which he feared might turn into another bloodbath.

He watched from the comfort of his office as the team started at the twelfth floor of building one. The doors were opened and passports checked one at a time. There looked to be twenty or more hostages standing single file in the first hall.

Halfway through the line, a call came on the radio. "We've got two hostages who claim to have lost their passports."

"Tell them to get back in their room, or you'll shoot them," Fazul responded.

They complied.

The rest disappeared from the hall, moving out of the camera's eye as they were released to head down. Anas lost them in the stairwell but picked them up as they emerged at the base of the building. A second team of eight soldiers corralled the group until the last of the hostages emerged from the stairwell. The team that had checked the passports accompanied the last hostages out and then transitioned them to the second team. The group was then escorted to the front entrance of the resort and released. They were told to walk to the main road and turn right.

"Walk down the highway past the mall. Police are waiting there. Anyone who runs in panic will be shot." That's what they were told as they were released.

Soldiers on the roof monitored their progress down LG Smith Boulevard. Anas had them turn the webcam so he could live stream the exodus for the world to see. They'd walk to the edge of the mall, their pace quickening the further they went. Eventually they veered right, off LG Smith Boulevard and into the mall where Aruban police, tucked behind cover and safe from another rogue RPG attack, called them in off the street.

Why do I not force my opinion when I know I am right? Anas wondered. He had worried that the evacuations would take longer than planned. Just ten minutes had been allotted to clear each floor. Walking the hostages from the stairwell of Building One to LG Smith Boulevard took nearly ten minutes by itself. The soldiers then still had to hurry back to receive the next group.

Fazul had dictated that it be done one floor at a time. Multiple floors would create a hostage to solider ratio that he felt was dangerous. And so, instead, the team in the building complained of impatience while the one doing the escorting was run as if training for a marathon.

By the time they released the hostages from the ninth floor, they were already twenty minutes behind schedule.

It was nearly ten o'clock by the time a fully-charged drone was up and off to the airport. Anas stopped it briefly, hovering above the police to watch as they loaded released hostages onto buses. He'd download that video to the web for all to see.

From there, it was only seven miles to the airport. The flight took under ten minutes. Using the map on his computer, Anas directed the drone to the center of the airport. He stopped it short of the runway and initiated a pirouette to have look at the hangar. As the building panned into view, the connection with the drone was lost. The video feed went blank first, and then a second later, he lost the flight data.

The drone was preprogramed to handle this situation. It would automatically climb to two thousand feet and begin a return flight home. Anas waited for the connection to reestablish, assuming he'd recapture it once it gained altitude.

"The evacuation goes well," Fazul said as he entered the office. "Slow but orderly. They fear for their lives."

Anas was staring at the blank screen.

"Tell me you have good news," Fazul continued.

"I need more time Fazul. I'll call you when I have something."

Fazul came over to Anas's side and leaned down toward the blank screen. "Where is it?"

"I've lost contact."

"You said it could cover the island. The airport is only a short distance away."

"It made it to the airport, but then I lost it."

"Send another."

"Dammit, Fazul. Get out! I can't work with you hovering over my shoulder. It'll come back on its own."

"It better. It's been hours." Fazul straightened. Anas could feel him looming above.

"What have you been doing in here with all the time?" Fazul asked from behind.

It was yet another dagger. The handle on the office door clicked as Fazul unlocked it. Anas looked back and made eye contact with Isabelle as the door swung open. She was on the floor, playing with a deck of cards.

"Look, so cute. Like the child you never had, Anas."

Anas stood. "I've had enough, Fazul. Get out." He pushed his brother from the door.

"Thirty minutes. That's it. Show me video. Otherwise I kill the girl and her father. Then I put a gun to your head while you post it."

PART IV

CONQUER

57

REGAL PALMS NEIGHBORHOOD, **Aruba**

WITHIN MINUTES OF GEERT LEAVING, Maddie had pulled the mattress from the bed and was busy setting up a shooting position.

"We'll see you when we see you," had been Geert's words of goodbye. Maddie had shaken his hand, gripping it with both of hers. There was nothing left to say. He had evolved from a twice-a-year acquaintance to a dear friend in days. Like a comrade in arms, Maddie would never forget Geert, no matter how long she lived.

For the next several hours, Maddie alternated between watching the stream of hostages, practicing her rhythm of attack, and talking with PTang via Skype.

"They've received 85 million dollars so far," said PTang. Maddie might have felt lonely, might have questioned the lunacy of her plan, if not for PTang's voice in the room. She was almost two thousand miles away but her unquestioning company was encouraging.

"Jesus, they've started a whole new industry," Maddie replied. The terrorists were releasing hostages. The Netherlands, Germany, Sweden, Italy and Wincopia Corporation had all paid the ransom.

"If you had that many bitcoin just five years ago, it would be worth six times the amount. Five-hundred and ten million. News say that bitcoin prices jumping again now. All this ransom money good for the market."

"Wow. We live in a fucked-up world, PTang... Any news on the good ol' USA or Great Britain paying for the lives of their people?"

"Speculation that England might pay before the deadline. The US government went silent. Nothing left to say." That was unwelcome news but served as validation. Maddie just needed the damn foreigners out of the way now.

Wincopia had announced that there were nearly nineteen hundred people checked into the resort when it was taken over. Something on the order of sixty-five percent listed their flights as arriving from Great Britain and the United States. PTang ran the numbers. There were eight hundred to a thousand due to be released. That didn't account for the deaths, a toll that some speculated might run into the hundreds based on videos released by the terrorists.

"Oh, I got into his control computer," PTang added.

The comment took a pair of seconds to land. "What? How do you not tell me that?"

"You've been asking so many questions."

"Damn. My fault. Sorry about that. Next time I'll start by asking if there's anything critical you need to tell me before I get to talking."

"Okay," PTang replied. There was silence for several seconds.

"Goddamn, PTang. Are you going tell me if this is a good thing?"

"I detected a minesweeper on the system."

Maddie hated when PTang spoke in lingo she didn't understand. She'd throw something technical out there and not elaborate. Maddie didn't think it was intentional, but it drove her nuts.

"Keep going, PTang. You know I'm old, slow and don't know my way around a computer."

"It's a program. It scan computer looking for foreign software. It machine learn what make sense for you then check for anything foreign. Whoever is running it knows what they're doing."

"How'd you get around it?"

"It was a problem I've considered in the past. Different tactics have been used. The best I have seen so far was also the most simple. You mask the software. There was a folder filled with huge videos. I made the emulator look like a video and stuck it in with the others."

"Jesus. An emulator? Can you control the machine?"

"Not quite. Once I open it, the bandwidth will be noticeable. I wait for now. It send me low res screen scrapes every four seconds until I make it active."

"Where the hell did you get that?" An emulator attack was the golden egg hack. An emulator, if done right, could allow a person to take control of another system. They could lurk, just waiting and watching, or take control and completely fuck with the person on the other end.

"Remember small-time hacker that was getting into auto body shops and running duplicate charges to his accounts?"

"Uh-huh." Maddie did remember the conversation. Auto body shops didn't wield enough cash to be customers, but they'd discussed the attacks in a weekly emerging threats meeting.

"He was using an emulator. He loaded it on a thumb drive and made it look like vehicle part manuals. Once the emulator was installed, he took advantage of it for a couple of days then moved on."

"Stole something like a hundred thousand in a week," Maddie finished.

"I modify his code. Make it better. I load from your machine to internal web host and programed it to download when he connected the computers."

"You're one scary Cambodian computer geek."

"Earlier he pushed a graphic of the buildings and updated text with instructions for the hostages being released. This was very fast, though. Just enough time to have a quick look around. Later, he reconnected and set up live stream of the hostages being released. He left the connection open so other hostages could see they were making good on promises. I assume, anyway." PTang paused. "Plenty of time to load my program to its hiding spot."

"If the CIA got ahold of you, they'd lock you in a room and turn you into a full-time spook."

PTang ignored Maddie's comment. "They set up a deadline timer on outside web." She hesitated. "It's counting down to the executions set for 10 P.M. They say they leave with boat full of hostages and detonate explosives if the final two ransoms are not paid."

"What time is sunset?"

A pause.

"Quarter to seven."

"I'll have light for a good bit after that."

Maddie peered down the scope. The building facing her had a machine gun nest on either end. Both were protected with sandbags that made the target window small. Several other armed men came in and out of view as the day wore on. Two were armed with Dragunov sniper rifles. The others carried what looked to be a variant of the AK-47.

One sniper in particular, caught Maddie's attention. He had

arranged a makeshift shooting position using a shipping pallet that looked to have been sawed in half. Behind it, he sat on a chair. It allowed him to rest the weight of the rifle and gave him an angle down to the ground where he watched the released hostages through his scope. The man had fired two rounds while she watched but Maddie couldn't see the targets.

"Take some notes and pass them on to Chuckles when you call. That way at least they'll have the intel."

"Okay. Ready," PTang replied.

"I've got six or seven on the roof. Some wearing skeleton masks, others with scarfs or bandanas tied up to the nose. There's a party of six or so escorting the hostages. They watch them to the road then go back for more."

"Latest information has total numbers somewhere around forty men," PTang added. "Several were killed at the mall."

"They've got men along the perimeter, but I can't see through the vegetation." Maddie had been trying to see through the grass that lined the parking lot. In the breaks, she'd caught glimpses of masked men and glints from rifles.

"Add this up, PTang. Seven on the roof I can see. Say... seven I can't. Let's say four along the front, four along each side and four keeping an eye on the water. How many's that?"

"Thirty."

"Six running the hostages and probably more working the buildings... That about does it."

She planned to clear as many from the roof as she could. Her plan was to make an initial pass, moving left to right, and then drop to the entrance where another machine gunner protected the lobby.

It was just a matter of time now. As it passed, she became increasingly confident in her decision and plan. For once, she would put her ridiculous amount of training and experience to use for a cause that mattered. She would get to Ross and Izzy, or she'd die trying.

58

Surfside Resort, Aruba

All day, Ross had heard yelling and arguing in Anas's office. He'd listened closely enough to know that they'd lost several drones and it had something to do with the airport.

The tension had him on edge. He'd been monitoring the updates to the website. He'd watched video of the hostages being released. It was painful to witness, knowing they couldn't go with them. Plastic and paper from certain countries, separated the freed from the uncertain.

The United States still hadn't paid. It was time to run if given the chance. Deadlines came with terms. There were none listed on the webpage, but Ross knew better.

He wanted to ask Anas but he hadn't been in all day. The only sighting had come early when his brother threw open the door.

"Do you want something to eat, sweets?" Ross asked.

"I'm so bored, Papa. When are these mean people going away?"

"I don't know, sweets. We just..." The door flew open, cutting him off.

"Gather some things and come with me." Anas looked terrified. Sweat ran down his forehead, and he appeared to be hyperventilating.

"Where?"

"Away from here. Someplace safer."

"What's happening?"

"Get your things. We must go! We only have a short time."

Ross stared for a second longer, deciding whether to run. "Anas?"

"It's okay. You're just not safe here anymore. I'm taking you up to a room."

Ross grabbed the bag of food that was nearly empty and looked around the room feeling like there should be more. The iPad was lying on the mattress.

"Hurry!"

Ross reached for his daughter. "Hold my hand, Izzy."

Anas turned back to them. "Listen to me. Keep your eyes down and don't look at anyone. Do you understand?"

Ross and Izzy both nodded.

"Stay close." Anas went first.

Ross pulled Izzy in front of him and pushed her forward at the back of her shoulders. As they passed from the office where Anas had been working, Ross sensed another man watching from a chair in front of a bank of computer screens. He didn't turn to look. His eyes remained focused on Anas's back as he opened the door to the lobby.

Another man, masked and armed, turned and watched as Anas led them around the desk toward the hall. Ross realized he hadn't taken a breath.

"Hurry, Izzy," he said, encouraging her to keep up.

They turned right at the elevators and Anas took three quick steps ahead to open the door to the stairwell. He ushered them through then forced it closed and stole a glance back through the window.

Anas ran past them, taking the stairs two at a time. Ross lifted his daughter and followed as quickly as possible. At the door to the first floor, Anas again checked the window.

There was a bar blocking the door. It was slightly crooked and entirely out of place. Anas lifted handles on either side, then leaned it in the corner.

They've turned the building into a prison, Ross thought.

Seconds later, they were through the door and into the hall. Anas hurried to the first room on the right. He stopped and looked up. Ross followed his eyes up to the ceiling and a black domed security camera. He flashed a key card across the handle and the lock beeped.

Anas held the door wide and hurried them inside.

"Stay here. Only I have a key. Don't answer the door unless you hear my voice. If someone knocks and you don't hear me calling, hide in the closet or something. Okay?" The panic he wore shot through the space that separated them.

"Okay," Ross replied. Anas waited an instant more, his gaze locked on Izzy.

"No children need to die. Enough is enough. This is one Isabelle I could save." Anas turned to go.

"Thank you," Ross called after him as the door drifted closed.

59

REGAL PALMS NEIGHBORHOOD, **Aruba**

LIGHT WAS FADING FAST as Maddie peered through the scope. She tracked a black form walking along the roofline, backlit by the setting sun.

"I'm ready to roll, PTang. Gonna hang up because it's about to get real loud in here. Thanks for your help, and good luck."

"No such thing as luck," PTang replied. "I see you when I see you."

Maddie snapped her attention away from the rifle and stared at the computer. "How'd you know to say that?"

"I'm not sure what you mean, Mrs. Gunt."

Maddie shook her head. "Never mind. You're right… I'll see you when I see you." She clicked the hang-up button.

Target number one was eating some type of pie in a package. He'd been snacking the better part of the day. Maddie had the scope zoomed to three-quarters its max. She wanted a big target but also the ability to see laterally in the sight picture as she swept the roof.

The ring of the fire alarm met Maddie's ears. She'd heard it several times throughout the day.

"Class dismissed," Maddie whispered.

The jihadi in her scope had removed his mask and was studying the nutritional information on the pie package. He was sitting cross-legged, and because of the sandbags, wasn't much of a target. Cross hairs hung on the center of his face.

"I'll see you when I see you," Maddie muttered. The rifle bucked, filling the bedroom with a violent flash of light. Her ears went from hearing the subtle moans of the house, to a loud ringing.

Five-hundred and twenty meters provided just enough time to relocate the target. The dark orb that had been the man's head, erupted into a black screen of mist in the waning light.

Shifting right, Maddie zeroed in on two soldiers sitting at the roof's edge. Apparently, it was snack time for the whole crew. They looked like a pair of young co-eds, too into one another to notice the Caribbean sunset behind them. Both were looking to their right, no doubt still trying to comprehend what had happened to their comrade.

Maddie placed the reticle center of mass on the leftmost man.

"Nighty-night." A second explosion of energy consumed the room.

Muscle memory cycled the bolt. Maddie had it down to a fraction of a second. Target number two had been thrown back, leaving just his legs in view, still dangling over the edge.

Target number three met a less pleasant fate. The bullet tore away the base of his neck. The kinetic energy transfer wasn't enough to throw him back. He clutched at the void, rolled to his side and then fell from the edge of the building.

Continuing right, Maddie acquired her nemesis in arms. Only one of the snipers had hung around into the evening. He was still sitting on the chair behind his makeshift bench rest.

The Dragunov was laying on the pallet but his head was up, still searching for his mark. He hadn't made Maddie's hide.

There had been plenty of time to fortify her concealment. Maddie had pulled mattresses from both spare beds. She leaned them against the windows, left and right of her shooting hole. The mattresses muffled the sound to the point that it couldn't be heard from across the salt pan. They also cut down the size of the flash. Instead of two windows strobing with light, the visual report from her rifle was the size of a cookie sheet.

Half a second passed as Maddie waited for the bottom of her breath. The staccato, clackety-clack of a belt-fed machine gun barked the open salt pan into war.

"Just business." Maddie drew back on the trigger, sending another spinning needle of lead into the Aruban dusk. It crossed the space in a fraction of a second, tore through the pallet and dropped the sniper from view.

The machine gun fell silent as the gunner repositioned his aim. Maddie was on him with the scope before the muzzle flashes returned. Within the width of a heartbeat, bullets started chipping at the siding along the back of the house. One buzzed through the drywall at the far end of the bedroom and thudded into the back wall.

The target was hunkered down behind the sandbags. Every four or five rounds, a bright tracer streaked through the void, arching in toward Maddie's position.

She set the crosshairs on the sparking muzzle and pulled the trigger. Sand from the bag holding the rifle plumed over the attack. Maddie hesitated, searching for any sign of movement.

There was stillness.

She shifted her sights down to the lobby and was again greeted by bursts of fire. Maddie had been impressed with the care taken to protect the lobby gunner. Sandbags were piled around the base of a desk. Additional layers were stacked on top.

The flashes came in a series of three and then four. Where they were landing, Maddie hadn't a clue. Even with the fluorescence of the lobby casting light on the position, there was little in the way of a silhouette. Maddie waited and watched.

"Show yourself, motherfucker," she growled to herself.

Like a gift from the divine listener, a form appeared. The jihadi stood, seeming to pull back on the receiver handle to clear a jam. Maddie fired.

The round missed, spiderwebbing the plate glass lobby just inches left of the target. She cycled the bolt a sixth time.

No sooner had her eye picked up renewed flashes from the roofline, the window above her shattered. The bullet split open the mattress with a puff and showered her in foam padding.

She'd missed twice. The machine gun on the top right corner poured rounds into the house. The room came alive as drywall was torn from the exterior walls.

Maddie stayed focused on the lobby. A half-moon silhouette of the man's skull bobbed in time with the flashes from the desk. She lowered the crosshairs just beyond its edge and sent another .338 down range.

A veil of black spatter caught as a fuzzy blot on the glass and the weapon fell silent.

Maddie panned up quickly.

The gunner had locked her position. Tracer rounds tore in with warp speed. One sailed high, the next curved off to Maddie's right. Only a portion of his rounds were still hitting the house. The distance and dancing of the 7.62 automatic were working in Maddie's favor.

As soon as the crosshairs covered the muzzle flashes, Maddie fired her eighth round. She cycled again, waited half a breath and pumped the ninth and tenth into the sandbags in quick succession.

With one in the chamber and the magazine dry, Maddie dropped it and slammed a fresh one home. She was back on the sandbags searching the stillness when her open left eye registered movement from the lobby.

She swooped the sights down and picked up a form standing behind the gore-covered glass. Maddie zeroed him. Just as she was about to pull the trigger, the mark moved. Maddie jumped the sight picture right and fired, hoping to score another hit before the target disappeared. A second hole opened in the blotted section of the glass, but she couldn't see much else. She returned to the roofline, gave it a final scan, then gathered the rifle to leave.

60

Surfside Resort, **Aruba**

Fazul tripped over the threshold and fell into the security suite. The bullet had been so close that he'd felt the pressure wave roll across his body.

Staring at the floor between his hands, the shock quickly gave way to a burning needle prick on his neck. He lifted a hand to the spot and wiped the bloody heat away. A shard of shattered glass came down with his red hand.

"We're under attack," he said, drawing himself up to a knee. The door to Anas's office was propped open, his brother gaping from inside.

"The glass is breaking?" Fahd asked from his chair. He was sitting in front of the security displays, being as useless as before.

"Gaafar's head is all over the glass." Fazul stood. He took control of his submachine gun and turned to Fahd. "You have anything worthwhile to report?"

"Nothing, Fazul. Cameras are empty."

He hooked around the desk to his brother. "How about you? Anything?"

"The drones haven't picked up a thing," Anas said.

A call cracked in their earpieces.

"I'm on the roof." There was a pause where the soldiers breathing filled everyone's ears. "Half of Malik's face is missing. Three are dead." Malik was a machine gunner assigned to the roof of Building Three.

"Farook?" Fazul asked into the mic. The leader of the rooftop defense for Buildings Three and Four was also his best sniper.

"Shot in the chest. He's gone," came the reply from the radio.

"Dammit. What's happening?" Fazul asked out loud without activating his mic. He turned his attention back to Anas. "Why did you sound the fire alarm?"

"I didn't. I don't know why it went off."

"Not you? Then who? You control it. No?"

"I don't know, Fazul."

"Of course you don't! You're worthless." Fazul shook his finger at his brother, his blood pressure threatening to pop his carotid.

He activated his mic again. "Ismail. Tell me what you see in front of the resort."

Two beats of silence past before the soldier who'd reported the casualties responded. "It's dark. I see nothing. No one. It's quiet."

"Stay there. Let me know if you see anything." As he said it, Fazul watched Anas scroll the far computer. His brother leaned in, reading text in large red font. It didn't fit with what he remembered. The case of the letters was disorganized. "What's that?" he asked.

Anas said nothing.

Fazul moved closer to read.

JiHaDi bastards. I aM One WomaN. NO goVernMent. NO PoliCe. 40+ to 1. I See yOu. DO you sEE mE?

ARUBA, MAD GUNT IS COMING.

"What the hell is that?" Fazul asked.

"I don't know. Someone has updated the website." Anas minimized the webpage and pulled up a screen showing lines of code that was unreadable to Fazul.

Fazul shouldered the Vityaz submachine gun. He centered the barrel on the back of Anas's head.

"You're fucking worthless..." He dropped the barrel and pulled the trigger.

A single round huffed from the weapon. The bullet skimmed the font edge of the chairs arm and popped through the seat into the floor.

Anas was at the edge of his seat. He jumped, his hands flying up from the keyboard. After a frozen moment, he clutched at his leg with both hands, grabbing at the pants where his butt and leg met.

He pulled his right hand out from beneath his leg to reveal two blood-soaked fingers. Only then did he look up at Fazul, his jaw quivering.

Fazul raised the barrel, pointing it at his brother's face. "You're done. I don't need you anymore." Fazul's finger tightened on the trigger. Just a twitch more and his brother would vanish.

Fazul let the Vityaz fall on its sling. He unlocked the door to the office on his left and went in. The lights burned bright but there was no sign of the girl or her father. He spun back to the door, re-shouldering the weapon.

"Where are they?"

Anas bit his bottom lip and squinted.

Fazul sensed Fahd standing in the door adjacent. He turned the barrel on him. "Where are they?"

Fahd's eyes doubled and his mouth dropped open.

"Where did he take them?" Fazul asked, stepping closer.

"Upstairs." Fahd pointed to the ceiling with a shaking hand. "The first room on the right."

Fazul pulled the trigger. The bullet caught Fahd where the eye socket meets the bridge of the nose. It lifted him from his feet. Both hands dropped to his sides as the momentum carried him up and away. For an instant, he appeared to float at an angle to the floor. Then he dropped and bounced into stillness.

Stepping over him, Fazul opened the door and sprinted through the lobby, bent at the waist.

When he reached the safety of the elevator atrium he made a call on the radio. "Hassan. Bring a man and a breaching shot gun. Meet me by the elevators in building two. Hurry down the hall. This sniper killed our man out front. He's got a bead on the lobby."

"I'm on my way," Hassan replied.

61

US Consulate's Office, Curacao

The phone rang as Margaret Baker shook the tea diffuser above her bone china teacup. She answered it.

"Hello, Mrs. Baker. You're being patched into a secure conference call," came the young man's voice. He'd asked for her identification information as well as the security questions associated with Operation Clean Sweep.

An automated voice told her she was the seventeenth person to enter the meeting. The phone chimed.

"Margaret?" It was Ray Ladenburg, the Secretary of State.

"Yes."

"I think that's everyone," said an unknown voice with a southern drawl.

"Margaret, I passed the video and email you sent me on to operation command." Ray Ladenburg's voice was so stately that it stood out on calls among even the highest government officials.

Earlier in the evening, Margaret had received a call from

the Commander of the Royal Dutch Marines stationed on Aruba. One of their officers had been kidnapped. They had video of a woman and man. The man was a local electrician. In the video he was being ordered around at gunpoint by a woman, an American woman. She'd restrained and threatened the officer, ultimately kidnapping him. Weapons and ammunition had been stolen.

Local authorities had matched it with video of an American that fled the airport. Margaret had summarized the information and sent it to Ray's assistant, who passed it on to the aide-de-camp for Operation Clean Sweep.

"We've got something happening at the Surfside, Margaret. We've brought you in for your perspective," said Ray.

"Very well, let's proceed," commanded the voice with the thick southern accent.

Major General Douglas Graff was the commander of US Marine Corps Special Operation Command, better known as MARSOC. As a branch commander of the larger Special Operations Command, he had been chosen to lead intelligence gathering for Operation Clean Sweep.

"I'll start with some intel," said the general. "First, I can now confirm with certainty that there were at least two operatives on the island working separate from the resort. I say *were,* because we killed one early this morning, shortly after the planes landed. We spent the rest of the day zeroing in on the second. The team is setting up to take him down as we speak." General Graff cleared his throat.

"What's the hostile drone situation, General?" asked a voice Margaret didn't recognize.

"Good question. We've got a pair of Eagle Eye drone detection systems operating in the area. This morning, after the troops landed, we tracked a drone that left the resort. Prior to that, they'd all been operating on preprogramed grids around the resort perimeter. We were forced to bring down the first drone. We had Special Forces visible at the airport and used a signal disruption device to bring it down." The general cleared his throat a second time.

"We sped things up after that. And a good thing we did... about an hour later a second drone was sent down range to inspect the hangar. By then the men had cleared the area and we let it have a look around. Damn thing practically flew into the hangar. They pulled it back to the resort and nothing has left the perimeter since." There was a pause. "Other questions?"

Silence.

"Very well then. Operational overwatch, your turn."

"General Graff. Others... Just a short time ago, a fire fight broke out on the eastern side of the resort. Our drone on station registered several terrorist casualties on the roof. The engagement lasted just three minutes. We are currently seeing a clustering of hostages in the courtyard. There also has been movement to bolster the eastern defense of the building. That's it for now, sir."

"Cyber command... Go," the general ordered.

"At approximately the same time an update was published to the internal website. Font, color and mixed case letters were used to call attention. An email with the exact language has been forwarded to everyone on this call. It insinuates an attack by a woman and includes taunting language. It closes with the words, 'Aruba, Mad Gunt is coming.'"

"Good god. Sounds like it was made for TV," came the southern accent. "Master Sergeant Lee. You're next."

"Thank you, sir. I received a call from a woman. The voice was unfamiliar to me, sir. She claimed to be assisting retired Marine Staff Sergeant, Madeline Günther. We were in basic together, sir. Fought side-by-side in Iraq with 1st Battalion, 6th Marines. Maddie asked her to call me."

"Madeline Günther. There's a name I've missed hearing. I commanded 1st Battalion."

"Yes, sir."

"Excuse me," Ray Landenburg said, interrupting the conversation. "Margaret, does this name, Madeline Günther, match the name of our woman who went AWOL from the airport down there?"

"Yes, it does. We believe it is *the* Madeline Günther. She and her infant daughter were held up at the airport. She walked out when security wasn't looking."

"Madeline Günther... You all do understand who we are talking about here. Are we to think this is—" general Graff paused again, seeming to lean away from the phone to clear his throat this time. "Is this the Mad Gunt that's coming?"

"Yes, sir," Sergeant Lee shot back. "That was her call sign within the unit, sir."

"Now that's one I had not heard. Mrs. Günther apparently has a number of nicknames and acronyms following her around."

"Sir, the woman that called me is helping Sergeant Günther by hacking."

"Hacking? As in computers?"

"Yes, sir. She's apparently infiltrated the terrorist computers. She claims to have posted the text on the website, sir. Claims that Sergeant Günther provided the language."

"Okay. Did our people know about this?"

A pause.

"No, sir," came the voice from Cyber Command.

"Umm, hmm. Continue please, Sergeant."

"As you know, Sergeant Günther is a decorated sniper, sir."

"Of course, the first of her kind and one of the best ever," said the General.

"There's no doubt that Sergeant Günther is a bit of a folk hero in one-six hard. But more importantly, sir, the father and child who stand to be executed... The ones in the video. Those are her family, sir. Ross and Isabelle Günther. Her husband and eldest daughter, sir."

"Jesus. And there it is. The connection I was missing. Once a Marine, always a Marine. But why throw yourself into the grinder? Now we know." The general huffed into the phone then continued. "Is RMK taking things into her own hands?"

"Yes, sir. It appears so."

A pause.

"Can someone clarify, please? We're not familiar with the acronym." The voice, asking for clarification, was new to the call. They hadn't spoken before.

"Go ahead. You explain it, Sergeant," said General Graff.

"Yes, sir. RMK stands for *Running Man Killer*. Sergeant Günther was credited with thirty-six kills over five days in Ramadi. Almost all of those kills occurred as combatants attempted to run from one building to another."

"The combatants, as Sergeant Lee calls them," said the General. "They put a bounty on Sergeant Günther's head. They crafted the illustrious call sign on their own and vowed vengeance on account of her being a woman."

"Yes, sir," agreed Sergeant Lee.

"What else can you tell us, Sergeant?"

"Sir, the woman assured me that the Dutch captain is safe. Sergeant Günther stole the weapons and set out on her own because she feared that a spec ops mission would lead to the execution of her daughter and husband. The weapons were stolen for an infiltration of her own."

"Yes, we see that. And she's done quite well in the opening volley. Did this accomplice provide any other details?"

"She said she was monitoring the terrorist computers and was prepared to take them down if she saw any action to detonate charges or focus in on Sergeant Günther."

"Where do we think Sergeant Günther is now, ladies and gentlemen?"

A pause.

"She planned to move in after softening their defenses," said Sergeant Lee. "Best guess is, she's making her way in that direction now."

"Our one-woman shock army. On the move," said the General. "She might just have enough mustard to see it through. Over watch, do you have anything on Sergeant Günther's whereabouts?"

"No, not at this time, sir."

A pause.

"Hue, I believe you and your team have the facts from our end," the general continued.

"Yes, General Graff. I believe we have what we need." Hue Dollar was a Navy Admiral with US Special Operations Command. "We're still greenlit here. We'll pass along the intel and consider Sergeant Günther a member of our team." He paused to take a breath. "Do we have any idea what the Sergeant is wearing? With a resort full of armed combatants, it'd be good to have something to look for."

"A ghillie suit, sir."

"Come again, Sergeant Lee," Admiral Dollar responded.

"The woman told me that Sergeant Günther is wearing a ghillie suit. She told her to tell me, I'd be proud. She'd finally gotten a chance to test out the space blanket idea."

"I'm not sure we're following," General Graff said.

"Well sir, we had this idea that a space blanket could be shredded like Christmas tree tinsel. You'd paint it black of course, and then weave clumps of it into the ghillie suit. We wanted to give it a try, sir. See if it would defeat infrared."

"I see. Well, that does paint an image," said General Graff. "Sergeant Günther, our RMK, should certainly stand out in that. A decorated, ghillie-suited Marine, charging headlong into the fight. Gives me goose pimples."

“Okay,” General Graff continued. “Anything material we’re missing here?”

A pause.

General Graff cleared his throat again. “I do believe we’re officially handing you the baton, Hue.”

“Wait,” interrupted Sergeant Lee. “I’ve got one more. I’ve just received a message from the hacker. There’s a picture of an email that she believes is from an operative on the island. They appear to be emailing someone at the resort. It says, “Military forces on the move from airport. Large group. 50+ heading your way.”

62

SURFSIDE RESORT, Aruba: Room #2101

ROSS GÜNTHER HAD WORN a path between the front door and the bedroom. He'd built Izzy a bed of blankets and pillows on the floor of the closet.

When the fire alarm had gone off the last time, he'd seen the image of the iPad on the mattress—it had been left behind in the office. He ran back and forth to the door listening for footsteps. His fear was that they were being released and had no way of knowing when or if it was time to leave.

He was still trembling from the gunfire. More than once, Ross thought the building was shaking, ready to come down around them. The shooting had only lasted a couple of minutes, but it left his chest tight with stress.

"You know what, Papa?" Izzy asked. They were the first words either of them had spoken since the shooting had stopped.

Ross drew in a long breath. "What, sweets?

"I think we're going to be just fine. The mean men will get

hungry... or sleepy... and when they do... we can leave. I mean, you gotta get sleepy some time. Right?"

Ross marveled at the simplicity of the pre-adolescent mind. Watching his daughter cope with the terror of their ordeal had taught him more than a year's worth of books ever could.

"That's true, sweets– everyone does need to sleep."

"I miss Charlotte, Papa. Do you think she remembered to bring my doll?"

"I hope so, honey." Ross couldn't hold back the tears any longer. Days of stress weighed down Izzy's words.

"Papa?"

Ross lifted the blanket to his face and wiped his eyes. "Daddy's okay, sweets."

"Shuussh, Papa. We'll stay in here just a little longer... then we'll go see if they're sleeping." Izzy left her spot at the opposite side of the closet and climbed between her father's legs. She stroked Ross's shoulder. "It's gonna be okay, Papa. You'll see."

Ross didn't say any more. He didn't want Izzy to hear him get choked up over the words. He wrapped his daughter, pulling her tight to the chest.

More minutes of silence passed with just their breathing and the smell of the musty closet for company.

They both jumped at the first explosion. Ross covered Izzy's mouth with his hand and pressed his own lips together. It sounded like it was coming from their room.

Ross felt Izzy shudder from the second blast. Through the thin plaster that separated them from the living room, Ross could hear something metal skitter across the tile floor.

"You're hurting me, Daddy," Izzy said.

"Be very quiet, sweets. No more talking or noise." He whispered it into Izzy's ear. "Lay down."

They fell to their sides, spooning with Ross's back against the wall. He reached out and wedged his fingers under the door, pulling it closed. He took the pillow from under his shoulder and set it on top of them. Then he pulled the blankets up and over, hoping they'd look like dirty bedding piled on the floor.

A thumping started up. There were five or six and then another blast and another skittering of metal on tile. A wall had never felt so thin.

Two more thumps boomed. By the second, Ross knew what it was. There was a loud crash as the door to the room fell to the floor. They'd blasted and kicked their way in.

"Shush," Ross repeated, stroking Izzy's hair.

"Come out, it's time to go." Fazul's voice was seared into Ross's mind.

He hugged Izzy tighter. An emotion beyond fear overwhelmed him. Ross tracked the sound of the men through the main room to the master. There was more than one.

Seconds after the main door slammed against the wall, they opened the closet. He could hear breathing and then felt the stiff poke of a gun barrel in his side.

63

Noord Salina, Aruba

Maddie was moving too fast. You'd a thought she'd lost her virginity a third time for all the excitement. This wasn't good enough to qualify though, at least not yet.

Senior prom and the morning of her forty-seventh day in country—they were memories etched into the eternity of her mind. High school had been better—living fast and loose without a care in the world, that was the secret sauce. Your first kill was a hit of adrenaline, but an anxious one. It was like cheating on your guy—the high faded fast and no matter how hard your ass, guilt crept in—a wry questioning bastard.

She forced herself to stop and double check that she had everything. She patted the 9mm strapped to her right leg, tightened the sling holding the sniper rifle to her shoulder and pulled the straps on the backpack.

The last of her equipment rested on the bed. She picked up the carbine and drew the receiver back. The first round clicked off the top of the magazine and slid home into the chamber.

Turning to leave, she caught a glimpse of herself in the mirror. She'd used a thin, hooded sweatshirt and a pair of painter's overalls to create the ghillie suit. It wasn't her best work, but she hoped it'd be enough to get by the drone and across the salt pan.

She shouldered the carbine twice in quick succession, watching herself in the mirror. A Halloween yeti glared back. Shaggy shards of black fabric bounced like Rastafarian dreadlocks. Painted shreds of the space blankets she'd attacked with a leaf rake, drifted down slower. She looked like an armed sasquatch sent to assassinate the asinine believers that still hunted the mythical beast after decades of finding nothing.

"Time to move out, Sergeant," she said to herself, turning for the back door.

The slider was locked. Maddie flipped the latch and rumbled it open. Dry, Aruban heat caught in her mouth. She licked her chops, spit on the cement step and broke across the backyard.

Dark came slow on Aruba. With no terrain to mask the light, it felt brighter at dusk. The sun played off the roof of the sky in shades of orange and purple you didn't get back home.

She was through the back gate and squatting at the edge of the salt pan seconds later. Satellite images showed the pan filled with water, but all day she'd looked out across a dry, cracked wasteland.

Maddie checked her watch. The drones had been passing overhead every ten minutes or so. She waited for its dragonfly sound to transit above, then shot to her feet and took off across the low, open ground.

It was under a half mile to the resort, a distance that looked much farther across open space. As she ran, Maddie eyed the roofline where she'd reaped death. There was still enough light in the western sky to provide a silhouette. The problem was the bounce in her step. She was moving at double-time, sort of a half run, half walk, that sucked the detail out of everything in the distance.

Suddenly, a column of dirt shot up. The sound of an open hand slapping the ground was followed by the audible wave that lagged the supersonic bullet.

There were silencers on the Dragunov's, she remembered. In one fluid motion, Maddie dropped to a knee and laid the carbine down on the ground. She whipped the Accuracy International off her back and flipped up the lens caps on the scope.

There was no cover, not even a wiry desert bush. Quickness was her only defense. Unfortunately, the sniper rifle was long and heavy. Firing from a knee was less than ideal.

A bee buzzed by at twice the speed of sound. The crack of the second wave made Maddie flinch. The follow-up shot had been closer. It had missed by less than a foot.

Maddie pulled the trigger.

The noise from the shot spread out and away in a retreating donut that called back from behind when it reached the hill and the houses. Her target dropped, but moved too slowly. She'd missed again, but the shot had sent the shooter looking for cover.

Maddie cycled the bolt and waited. *One Mississippi, two Mississippi*, she thought.

Automatic weapons fired indiscriminately from the base of the resort, no doubt reacting to the sound of her shot.

She reached *four* and was just about to lay into the front edge of the *M*, when the shooter reappeared. Maddie pulled the trigger a second time.

"MISSISSIPPI," she finished out loud. The mark was dead before she finished the word.

Back on her feet, she leaned into the remaining distance,

sprinting for the other side. The ghillie suit danced and shook like wet fur on a dog bred for the snowy hinterlands. Halfway there, the dragonfly whirl of the drone reappeared. It moved behind her from left to right and almost faded from earshot before the sound flared and returned.

Maddie completed the one-hundred-yard dash, moving as fast as her legs could carry her. She dropped onto the berm leading up to the road, hugging the earth to block some of the heat signature from her dripping body. She was panting into the dirt.

She listened for footsteps over the dragonfly beat of the drone's rotors, sure she'd been spotted. Instincts told her to move, to bring the carbine up in front, but her mind told her to hold still. Any movement out here couldn't be mistaken for anything other than what it was.

No footsteps materialized and the drone moved on seconds later. Maddie got to a knee and scanned the hill as she caught her breath and eyeballed her next move.

The gnarled twisting trunk of a Divi Divi tree caught her attention. Its top was proportionately larger on the resort side, same as most, but its trunk had more girth than usual.

Maddie took the hill in long strides. She hit the trunk and swept the field of view. Bushes on the other side of the road broke the sightline to the base of the resort.

The Surfside building running parallel to the road stood tall above Maddie on the other side. The warmth of the day's pent-up heat radiated down.

Maddie was almost directly across from the resort entrance. With the edge of the building ahead and to the right, her plan was to hit a stairwell door in the parking garage. She could see it in her mind, clear as an Aruban sky. Ross always wanted to park the rental car under the building to shield it from the boiling sun.

She toggled the fire selector from single shot to three-round-burst. Then she surged across the road, keeping low and moving evenly with the carbine shouldered. The barrel moved from the lobby, still lit and empty, through the buildings edge and along the grasses that hid the sentries.

A voice called out from the far end of the building. Maddie didn't slow. She drifted into the grasses like a ghost and settled into a catcher's squat, listening.

Another voice, closer, grunted three words in return. This one was straight out in front. Maddie elevated into a crouch and stepped forward. Still moving like a wraith, she glided through the first row of cars.

The window in the stairwell door was the only light visible. They'd killed the fluorescents in the garage to conceal their perimeter defense. Maddie could see the tops of cars shining in dull color. Her eyes scanned from the source of the light, looking for an anomaly.

The close voice spoke again. "Perimeter, Building Three. We don't see anything."

They were words Maddie understood. English words, projected right at her, that marked the source as accurately as a stage spotlight.

Maddie stood taller and took aim. The man was just four car lengths away. With a side step, she exposed herself to clear the view to the target. She floated into the center aisle of cars, each heel settling softly and rolling to the toe as she moved with the purpose of an approaching wave.

The target had just started to speak another word when Maddie pulled the trigger. Jets of fire erupted from the muzzle in a strobing orange X. At least one of the three rounds found its mark. The smacking of flesh stood out from the cracking of glass.

Maddie knew better than to stand still. She advanced, using the cars for concealment.

She reached the hip high wall at the base of the building when the voice from the left called out again.

"Shooting! Parking lot! Building Three!" the voice yelled.

Below her, the wounded soldier struggled for breath. Maddie sat on the wall and swung her legs up and over. With her sights locked on the corner of the stairwell, she stepped back and into a lane between cars that wasn't blocked by a dying man.

Footsteps from behind captured Maddie's attention. She spun and picked up a running target whose silhouette was painted by the bright lobby entrance. The burst caught him in the chest. His torso stopped in an instant, but his legs continued to run.

Maddie was swinging back to the stairwell when the other man opened with a vengeance. The hail of full automatic fire turned the garage into a clamor of light and concussion. The first few rounds tore apart glass and sheered metal. Maddie dove for protection along the trunk of the car. She turned her head in and shielded it with the carbine. The stream of fire moved up. Rounds ricocheted off the garage ceiling, sending hunks of deformed lead zinging into the car opposite her position.

A roaring jet engine couldn't have drowned out the sound. The cacophony of death lasted a full three seconds before the AK-47's magazine ran dry.

It took a beat for the wobbling racket to run out from under the building. Maddie came to her senses, popped up and took aim. The target was frozen from the violence. Maddie pulled the trigger and stitched the three rounds from the man's sternum to his forehead.

Like a good schoolgirl, she checked right and then left before breaking for the door. A handful of steps separated her from it. She'd only taken two when a line of sparks stripped the concrete in front of her. The bullets angled off the stairwell apron and thudded dents into the door.

More shots poured in from behind. They pocked the ground and chewed pits in the concrete around the door. As she hit the latch and made for safety, Maddie felt a flick along her right calf. By the second bound up, she could feel the warmth of blood pouring down into her shoe. There was no time to stop.

She took the stairs two at a time, doubling back once on her way to the first floor. The moment she made the turn, she saw the bar blocking the door. By the time she'd reached it, her mind had figured the purpose and function. She flipped up on the latches to the left and right and threw the bar to the side. It chattered down the stairs as she looked up into the hallway.

A trail of bodies littered the floor. The horror hit her as a matter of fact. Then her vison tightened. The hall became a pinhole. The sound in her ears was blotted out by a tone. She loped forward into a haze of confusion, eyes jumping from one form to another.

Ross! Ross! The words were in her head but she wanted to call out. She needed to know they weren't there.

Tar-colored stains framed the corpses. An acidic dankness shocked Maddie from her stupor. She shook her head to clear the air. The bodies had been here a while. Decomposition hadn't taken hold yet, but they were ripening.

Still moving slowly, her eyes continued down the hall, searching for any bodies small enough to be a child. There were none. Immediately after arriving at the realization, she heard footsteps in the stairwell and checked over her shoulder.

Two apartments ahead on the right, a door was propped open by a crumpled body. She made for it. Maddie pushed it open enough to clear the body and made the mistake of checking the hall one last time.

A muzzle flashed. A sledgehammer pounded Maddie's hip.

It threw her into the doorframe like an NFL linebacker. She let out a miserable grunt as the weight of her body curled into the frame. The butt of the carbine careened off the wall and bounced to the tile in front of her. Tripped up by the body, Maddie fell forward to safety, landing hard on her knees and hands.

Bullets cracked behind her, chewing sheetrock in the hall. Using the leg that worked, she rolled herself. She made it onto her back before the realization of her dysfunction set in. Propped at a forty-five-degree angle by the back pack, she could see the right leg was a mangled phantom of itself. Any attempt to move it made her bowels flip and sent a white heat scorching along its length.

Using her left leg, Maddie inched herself away from the door. The sniper rifle, which had somehow remained hooked over her shoulder during the fall, slid in tow by her side. She felt for the pistol on the right hip. The bullet had to have just missed it. The roughness of the grip found the tips of her fingers. She yanked it from the holster and pointed it, two-handed, at the door which was mostly closed but once again resting on the body.

Each push with the leg required its own deep inhale and gritting exhale. She wanted to scream like a banshee. She wanted to writhe at the unmitigated agony that was blooming at her hip. Surging with prickles and heat, the hip and leg stood in stark contrast to the rest of her body. Between the gritted exhales, Maddie's teeth chattered with cold. She'd done what she could. She'd made another mistake. This time the cost would be greater. Not only was she going to die, but she'd failed to save her family.

Still inching and pointing, Maddie angled away from the centerline of the walkway leading to the door. Using the edge of the breakfast bar, she garnered some semblance of defense. Angling more and more with each push, she sensed that the room wasn't altogether dark. A light behind her, maybe a lamp in the living area, lit the room.

The door flew open. She could see the barrel of a gun but the man holding it remained out of sight. The door drifted back closed on the body.

Maddie inched away, again and again. It opened a second time, slower, the barrel of the gun rubbing along its length as the man used it to push the door. Maddie felt the leg of a chair touch the back of her head. She'd come as far as she could. This was her Alamo.

The soldier, still hidden by the door which wasn't fully open, hopped the body and landed two-footed in front Maddie. She barely had to adjust her aim and fired just once. The round caught the bottom of the man's chin. It flung him back into the door just as it came to rest on the other crumbled body.

64

Surfside Resort, Aruba

Fazul was prodding the man forward with the barrel of his gun, jamming it into the small of his back. Hassan had the daughter by the arm. She was screaming and flailing.

"Up against the wall," Fazul ordered. The father was bigger than him and his beard and bald head were mildly intimidating. To account for it, Fazul increased his violence. He slammed him into the wall and used the side of the gun's steel barrel to pin his face to the paint. "Put on the zip ties." Fazul shook his head and eyeballed Assad.

The boy produced a set of zip cuffs and stepped up. The man fought to separate his arms. Fazul drew back and punched him in the jaw. His fist glanced off and marked the wall.

"Accept your fate. Go out like a man." He pulled the gun down from the father's face and slung it, taking control of the father's wrists. "Put the ties on, dammit!" Fazul yelled at Assad.

"Stop hurting my Daddy!" the girl cried.

"Take the girl down," Fazul said to Hassan.

Once the father's hands were secure, Fazul spun him and pinned him to the wall with the barrel pressed hard into his sternum.

"She'll be the first child I've executed."

The man's lip quivered. His cheeks dimpled and then he shot his head forward, spitting in Fazul's face. His knee came up, and his shoulder down, knocking the barrel of Fazul's gun to the side. The father lunged, bringing the crown of his head down across Fazul's temple.

THE HEAD-BUTT KNOCKED Fazul back and buckled his knees. Hassan streaked in from the side and brought the butt of his weapon down on the father's shoulder, dropping him to a knee.

Fazul righted himself. He shouldered his rifle and wanted very badly to punish the man with a non-lethal shot, but he held back. Having a father and daughter stare into the camera and then die together, that would be the motivation America needed to move their politicians.

"Disobedient American trash!" Fazul kicked the father in the head with the heel of his boot. "I'll *enjoy* killing her. And letting you watch."

Fazul's radio cracked as he and Hassan herded the father and daughter down the stairs.

"I've got something in the open." It was Ismail calling from the top of building three.

"How many?" Fazul asked.

He wondered if his time spent killing the father and daughter might be better served managing the defense. But they'd waited too long to demonstrate that they meant what they'd said.

"One. Just one. I have him in the scope." Ismail's nerves clung to his words.

"Kill him, Ismail. Kill him," called Fazul.

Fazul continued down the steps. The crack of a bullet soared above the resort as they stepped from the door into the night. Automatic weapons started up.

They'd chosen the spot beside the pool because ambient lights on the palms made it bright enough for the webcam and everyone watching it.

Hassan had the girl in a chair in front of the camera. Behind her, a row of eight more Americans were blindfolded and gagged, their wrists and ankles bound.

"Ismail. What's happening? Did you get him?"

There was no response.

He pushed the father past Hassan toward his daughter.

"We need to do this quickly," he said, when his eyes met Hassan's.

His earpiece cracked again. "Perimeter, Building Three. We don't see anything."

Fazul activated his microphone. "Send two men out to recon the open space."

"Cop—" The transmission was cut short as gunfire erupted from the far side of the building.

Already in the view of the camera, Fazul took his mask from his pocket. He pulled it over his head before he turned to face the international audience. The skeleton's forehead was marked with the crescent moon and star of Pakistan. Fazul had painted it on himself.

"Shooting! Parking lot! Building Three!" A voice cried in his earpiece.

He turned to the father and daughter. "On your knees," he commanded. "Listen to my words and I'll kill you first." He was speaking to the father. "Or don't, and you can watch."

Fazul kicked at the back of the father's knees. "Down!"

The daughter fell from the chair and embraced her father.

Fazul moved to the side and took the razor-sharp machete from its scabbard.

More gunfire erupted from building three as he lifted it over his head and stared into the camera. “Our demands were simple. The repercussions clear. The Americans have—"

65

SURFSIDE RESORT, Aruba

ROSS CLOSED HIS EYES. An image of his children as infants rose on the back of his lids. Side by side like twins, the detail of the visual was impeccable—delicate features, fragile fingers and toes, creamy skin and faces filled with hope, with recognition and love. In the fleeting seconds, his mind brought him to the beginning of the cycle, to avoid the end that was coming.

Their deaths had been a foregone conclusion for some time. Terrorists didn't film you and keep you isolated for no reason. Ross and Izzy were the bargaining chips, and it hadn't been enough.

Fazul's words to the camera were distorted in his ears. Coping mechanisms had already taken his hand to the next reality.

A bang thundered. Ross's breath caught in his chest. A shivering cower ran up his neck. He opened his eyes.

The man behind the camera rushed to pick up his rifle from the table in front of him. He pointed it to Ross's right.

Was he alive? Ross turned his head.

There, standing with a gun at his shoulder, was Anas. A trail of white smoke spiraled up and away from the end.

"Fazul killed Fahd!" Anas yelled. "Killed him in cold blood for no reason!" His eyes flitted back and forth between the two other terrorists both staring at him wide-eyed.

"He shot me." Anas turned and pointed to a hole in his pants. "Look!" The fabric running down the leg was stained. "I did not answer correctly...so he shot me. He's been out of control since this started! He's compromised our plan! You've seen it!"

The man and young boy stared at Anas. There was quiet.

Suddenly, all three of them reached up and touched their earpieces. Seconds later, the rapid fire of a machine gun echoed out from the building behind Ross.

Izzy's hug grew tighter. Ross could feel the heat of her sobs wetting his t-shirt.

Anas reached up and touched his ear. "Defeat this man, and then we leave. We have accomplished our mission, Brothers! I have spoken with the leaders. They have agreed. Our work is done."

Anas stared at Ross for a confusing moment, and then moved closer.

"Cut their legs free!" he ordered of the men watching. "Remove the gags and blindfolds. We must move quickly. Line them up against the wall. We'll take them with us."

Anas reached for Izzy first. "It's okay," he said, calming his tone. "You're going to be okay." He slid his hands under Izzy's armpits and helped her to her feet. "Follow me."

He turned toward the lobby door then stopped and looked back. "Assad. Bring your knife. Cut him free."

Anas turned Ross's back to the boy. A moment later, Ross felt the blade slide between his wrists and then pressure on the opposite side before it popped free.

"Quickly." Anas waved them toward the door.

Ross's head swam with confusion. He hadn't fully returned to the physical realm. The final ticks of the clock had come so close, and yet now, he was back inside being hurried toward the office.

"What's happened, Anas?" Ross asked.

"What do you mean?" He didn't wait for an answer. "I did it. I took control. He's dead."

"Who's dead?"

"Fazul. I shot him. Right in the head. The problem is gone. Now I must show the world our true intentions. Now that the root of our evil is gone."

With each passing word, the implications became more apparent to Ross. It was hard to digest, but one thing was certain, the madness that was these two brothers had bought him and Izzy a new lease on life.

"Are you leaving?" Ross asked.

"Yes. You'll come with us." He stopped and got behind them, pushing them forward. "Hurry through this area."

The rush across broken glass wasn't fast enough for Ross to miss the bullet holes and blood on the windows.

Anas hooked them around the main desk and back into the office.

"What did you mean? Come with you?" Ross asked.

Anas turned to face them. He rested a hand on Izzy's shoulder. "Yes. You, Isabelle and many others are coming with us. But first, I must let the world know we're leaving."

"We can't come with you, Anas."

"You must." His expression shifted, the brow furrowing. "Just a few more days. I need you and Isabelle. The world knows your faces. They saw everything that just happened out there."

"If you take us... If you take hostages... It'll come off the wrong way. You can't just post some words to the internet and expect it to undo what's happened here. You need to cut yourself loose. Then claim that your brother, who's dead, ordered all the killing."

Anas smiled and nodded. "Yes, Ross. I agree. But I still need you, Isabelle and the others to get me there. Once that happens... You and Isabelle can go back."

Ross wasn't winning. Not now. He also wasn't leaving.

"Wait here," Anas said. The door to his office was open.

Ross led Izzy to the cube where her coloring supplies were still spread on the desk. He leaned down and kissed her head.

"This is almost over. Hang in there, sweets." Izzy picked up a stub of a crayon and stared at the paper.

Ross turned to leave.

"No, Papa. Don't leave me."

Ross stopped and reached back with a hand. "I'm here. I'm not leaving."

He stood in the entry to the cube watching Anas work the keyboard. A maddening, intermittent tone was coming from the computer on the right. He stepped closer, still reaching his arm back as if to reassure Izzy he wasn't leaving. The screen wasn't fully up on the computer emitting the tone. It was folded down enough that Ross couldn't see the source of the warning. Anas had told him that the sound indicated that the drones had picked something up. He was so caught up in thought and typing so frantically that it seemed he was deaf to the sound.

The black rifle Anas had used to kill his brother was leaning against the desk. Ross hadn't seen the body, but he knew only one shot had been fired.

Could he do it? Should he do it? He stared at it, wide-eyed, wondering if the safety was on.

"You need to go alone, Anas," he said, continuing his argument. "Please. I'm begging you. Don't take us. Isabelle has been through too much."

Anas didn't respond. His pace unwavering, he clicked the

keys so fast that it sounded like a horse carriage rolling down a gravel road.

On the left computer, Ross noticed red text in mixed case letters. Another step closer and he was able to read it.

JiHaDi bastards. I aM One WomaN. NO goVernMent. NO PoliCe. 40+ to 1. I See yOu. DO you sEE mE?

ARUBA, MAD GUNT IS COMING.

Mad Gunt. Mad Gunt. He repeated the words in his mind. When they were young, before Izzy, Maddie would send cheesy text messages using military radio words. *Whiskey Tango Foxtrot are we doing tonight?*

Apparently her call sign on the radio was *The Mad Gunt.* One text he'd always remember was the one he received when she landed back home after her first deployment. *The Mad Gunt is stateside! I'm di di mau for some home cooking.* She'd used mixed case letters. Later, he asked her why she'd done it. "Just worked up and doing something different."

One WoMan. 40+ to 1. I See yOu. DO you sEE mE?

It was taunting. The tone and the mixed case felt like Maddie's oddball tendencies. If words on a page could have an aura, the ones he was reading felt like Maddie. It was her style. It was her call sign. But what did it mean?

He had wondered what had happened to Maddie and Charlotte. The terrorists had taken over the night before they were due to arrive. He was supposed to pick them up from the airport. He'd imagined them stranded, waiting for him, calling on a phone that wouldn't connect. But then he had no idea if they'd even made it. Maybe the world had known. Surely they would have stopped flights from coming into the island. If not, where would she have gone?

He re-read the words over and over. *MAD GUNT IS COMING.* It was too much of a coincidence to not have meaning. There was no way he and Izzy were leaving.

"Why's the computer making that noise?" Ross asked.

"I'm almost done!" Anas continued to click the keyboard at a feverish pace. Ross thought about stepping into the room and lifting the screen to see for himself.

Anas raised his right hand and brought it down hard on the enter key.

"There!" he said. "Update sent. The world knows we are leaving. I've told them to call off the dogs and we'll leave the buildings intact. No way they can hit us now. It would be a PR nightmare."

He turned to the computer on the right, lifted the screen and used the trackpad on the laptop to call up a window. A couple of clicks later a video started to play.

"Looks like it picked something up... Drone number one. That's the one running back and forth across the front of the resort. Ismail saw someone out there."

As the video played, Ross saw a ripple of orange and red movement on the screen. The picture from the drone seemed to stop moving along its course. It came back and the wrinkle of color danced on the screen for an instant. It faded in and out.

"Strange," Anas said. He clicked a button and the video replayed. "There is something there... but it doesn't look like a person."

More like a ghost, Ross thought.

Anas had showed him images of people captured in the drone's video camera. This was different. There was something in the camera, but it wasn't shaped like a person. Anas toggled the view from the one that tracked heat to the actual image. He replayed the video a third time. The screen remained black except for an instant where an image took shape in the waning light.

"There," Anas said. He took the video back several frames and zoomed the view. He'd barely hit the enter key when the screens on all three computers turned blue.

"What the hell just happened?" Anas sat tall in his chair.

There was a message on the screen with a frowning emoticon at the top.

'Your PC ran into a problem that it couldn't handle, and now needs to restart. Bye-Bye!'

"What the hell..." Anas said. "No matter. It's time to go."

Starting on the left, he held down the power buttons one at a time, pressing them for several seconds before the laptops shut down and the blue screens disappeared.

He reached up and touched his ear. "Everyone report to the yacht. Start the engines. We'll take what's been loaded and leave the rest. We're pushing off in five minutes."

Ross reached for the black rifle without thinking.

Anas turned to face him. He shook his head. "No, Ross. Don't do that."

Izzy ran in from behind and grabbed Ross's leg.

"We can't go with you, Anas. Isabelle can't take any more. You've done so much for us. I can't thank you enough, but..."

Anas stood. "But I need you and Isabelle. To come out of this, I need your support. I need you to explain what's happened here."

"We can help you more if you leave us. I promise, Anas. We'll be your voice. The voice of reason. When the world is ready to come down on you, we'll be there to tell them what happened. You can call your men, have them shoot me and Isabelle, or, you can leave us to speak for you. We can be your voice to the world. You are a good man, Anas. Isabelle and I will tell them all."

Anas hung his head. "Please, Ross. I'm begging. Please bring Isabelle and come with me. You can get me out of this."

"We'll help you. But only if you leave us behind, Anas."

Anas's shoulders slumped in surrender. "It won't be the same. I've grown to care for Isabelle a great deal. We will meet again." He looked up at Ross. "May I give her a hug?"

The question baffled Ross. *A hug?*

Anas dropped to a knee and opened his arms. Izzy looked up, the grip easing around his leg. She let go and took a step forward. Anas wrapped her shoulders.

Ross stood watching, ready to bring the rifle to bear if Anas tried to make off with her.

"Thank you, Isabelle. We will forever be united in history. You are a good girl."

Ross wanted to kick him away from his daughter but let it linger. Anas let go and Izzy jumped back to his leg.

"Good luck, Anas." Ross lifted the gun back up.

Anas turned and went to his computers. He flipped each of the screens down and pulled cords from the back. With care and patience, he slid each of them into a backpack and then slung it over his shoulders. He turned to Ross, still standing with the gun.

"Goodbye, friends," he said. He turned for the door and disappeared.

66

Surfside Resort, Aruba

Despite the adrenaline, Anas missed Isabelle and Ross before he left the room. The door was like a portal from connection back to isolation. He stepped out of the office and into a wave of fear. Fear of the challenges that lay ahead. It crackled across his skin like a pocket of hot summer air.

Ross had seen his vision. He could tell them of the conversations the two men had. The fact that Anas protected them and saved so many others, was livestreamed for the world to see. Once he got to the boat he'd tell the story. It needed out sooner rather than later. Then, Ross could confirm what was posted as the truth. He would seal Anas's fate, helping him to rise above the disaster Fazul had left behind.

Brain matter on the lobby window took his mind away from all that.

"I'm on my way out. Everyone to the boat," he called over the radio.

He almost slipped on the broken glass, clutching at the

screaming wound, still open at the back of his leg. Despite the limp, he was out beneath the moon in no time.

He turned right along the sidewalk. Across the promenade, on the other side of the pool, two soldiers hurried toward the beach. The pool water was still lit from within, but it had turned a nasty shade of brown.

It was hard to believe the operation was over. Like a vacation you anticipate for months in advance, he'd imagined every minute. Events had unfolded differently, but in the end, he regained control. Fazul was gone for good. The image of the bullet catching his head would be with Anas forever, but there was no sense of loss.

The two men on the far side of the pool were sprinting now. With the wind howling at his back, Anas hobbled along, taking his time. Things felt safer without Fazul. Besides that, they were leaving. Many of their objectives had been reached. The money was probably in the bank by now, laundered through hundreds of different bitcoin accounts on its way to the coffers. He was wounded but alive, and their great crusade had been a success.

He would miss Aruba. The dry wind felt like a cleansing force, sweeping the filth and bacteria out to sea. He'd have to deal with Venezuela again for a time. Then he'd be off to Indonesia on a boat, and eventually home. Of course, he was questioning that part of the plan now. Once he broke from the group, he might consider a detour. Maybe cash in his portion of the proceeds and start a new life. International man of intrigue. The terrorist who never wanted to hurt anyone. Once people understood his motives, they'd feel differently. Once Ross and Isabelle explained the truth, his stock would rise.

Anas made his way along the hedgerow that rimmed the adult pool. As he rounded it, the *Contagious* came into view. It was almost bright out. Between the moon and the resort lights, his path to the boat felt ordained.

Out in front, his men streamed across the beach and down

the winding path that led to the dock. One jogged passed him, slapping him on the back.

His eyes were fixed on the young Assad. The boy was leading the group of hostages toward the boat. They were shuffling, single-file, beneath a light above the sidewalk. Assad was shorter than them all. Walking off to the side, down in the sand, he looked like a prepubescent boy doing a man's job.

What Anas saw next was not something his brain was capable of registering. Assad's head was there one instant and gone the next. Anas hunched from the crack that resounded above him.

Assad's headless body continued for a step or two then fell to the side. The hostages ran into one another, the straight line jumbling together like an uncoordinated inchworm.

Another shot rang out, streaking above Anas, who was still frozen with confusion. The line of hostages broke. Most darted left for the safety of the beach restaurant. A few ran right, struggling to escape through the soft sand.

Anas looked back toward the pool. He saw a flash of light. The crack that followed knocked him from his feet. Every hair on his body was sent on end.

He touched his ear. "Run! They're attacking! Everyone onboard now!"

He stood and sprinted for the boat, ignoring the pain in his leg. His shoes scratched four steps across the sand covered sidewalk, before a jolt rocketed him forward. He felt his body sail through the air as if slung from a catapult. His hands were out in front to absorb the impact but he was moving so fast they were of little consequence.

His head cracked off the cement. The crest of his forehead gave way. He felt it press in behind his eyes. A pulse of pain ran from the impact through to the opposite side of his head. It felt like an electric shock, his eyes twitching in their sockets.

The static and twitching quickly faded into a hazy recognition of the present. He was on the sidewalk, still and unmoving.

More shots pierced the air above him, traveling with incalculable speed. Footsteps passed. Voices came and went. He felt sleepy. Sound oscillated in and out of recognition.

A low guttural thunder bloomed. His eyes opened. Sand in the lines of stamped concrete ran up to greet them. There was movement in his peripheral vision. With his body unmoving, his eyes instinctively jumped to focus on the motion. Another rod of lightning rocked his head.

He squinted and waited for the worst to pass, then opened them again. Grains of sand at the tip of his nose. He turned his head, ever so slightly, to elevate his vision without having to move his eyes. Glimmers of light hovered across the water. They receded on ribbons of white roiling water.

They're leaving me, he thought. *Why am I on the ground? Why did I stop running?* His mind was functioning as a detached entity. It felt decoupled from his body, which was draped heavily on the sandy walkway.

Throbbing pain started mercifully at first. Within seconds, the spot where his head had hit the ground began to throb with each beat of his heart. The sensation of the impact left him worried that his brain might slip out if he moved. Beyond the fear of seeing his gray matter fall to the ground before he died, the sounds of the passing bullets had created a paralysis of their own.

And so, he lay there, conscious but paralyzed, not sure if by mechanical or psychological means. The moon lit the sky as it had the night they arrived. He watched his ride motor out and away from the success he'd cultivated. The silhouette of the *Contagious* took shape on the horizon as the sound of the engines became too faint to hear.

Anas was left alone, the wind sweeping above him in a steady gale. Palm fronds streamed their rustling song. Grains of sand blew up under the cuffs of his pants. He'd die here, and it wasn't all bad. He could think of worse ways to go.

Closing his eyes as if to sleep, Anas adjusted his head. He opened them again. At the center of his vision now, the moon hung bright in the clear Aruban sky. Its jejune craters pockmarking the surface reminded Anas of his own adolescent skin.

Staring captivated, his mind stopped racing. Stillness found him.

As he gazed up, he sensed movement in the sky. A line of white, like a cloud, streamed in from the left. It crossed the face of the moon then dropped like a roll of toilet paper from a table's edge. The cloud turned at a right angle and dove toward the *Contagious*.

A white light met his eyes. The intensity triggered another flash of pain through his head. When he reopened them, fiery wreckage was still falling back to the surface of the Caribbean.

67

Dr. Horacio E. Oduber Hospital, Aruba

The sixth time, Maddie thought. She was positive of it.

She'd decided to keep count after the second... or was it the third?

The wake-ups only lasted a second or two so she had to act fast and add another mark to the cell wall. She'd done the slanted one for the fifth and started a new set this time.

She knew she'd been captured and drugged. There'd been bright, blinding lights and then blackness. Time had been passing, but tracking it in the dark was impossible.

The drugs hurt her veins. It bloated them up and her body was running out of space. She had a dream where she exploded.

The wake-ups are coming more frequently, she thought. The drugs were wearing off and she needed to escape before they realized it. Her mother had been calling her to dinner for hours. She had to get home. Her mother would be worried.

Let me go! Let me go! There they were again, the tubes in her arms. She was strapped to the floor of the cell. The only thing she could reach was the wall, to scratch the lines.

It started to get dark again. *Wait! Wait! Please wait!* It went black. *It's okay, I need to get clothes. I... I can't run away naked. Next time, I'll get clothes.*

At least it was quiet. They'd turned off the speakers. The voices were gone. These son-of-a-bitches were ruthless. They'd piped in psychological warfare. When she heard their voices, her insides kept dying and her mother cried. They had recorded Ross and Izzy talking. Baby sounds. Grunts and moans and noises like first words. They recorded it and forced it into her head with a pipe. They were torturing her with it like the Manchurian Candidate.

That's right! Now she remembered. *I'm their Manchurian Candidate! But I won't kill my family. No... No... fight it! I won't kill my family!* They were using her. She had to repeat it. They were programing her like a robot to go destroy her America.

The wake-up. It's coming again. The light was back, the hoses, the straps. *Mark the wall,* she told herself. *Mark the fucking wall! You always forget!*

Movement stopped the voice in her head for an instant. She checked again. The movement was still there. *I can move. My head moves.*

"Papa! Mommy's head moved." The voice was so loud. They'd turned up the volume. They knew about the wake-ups. *Fuck!*

"Mommy! Mommy! Can you hear me?" It sounded just like her. The worst kind of torture.

"They said you might wake up today."

You're a liar, Maddie yelled in her head.

"What's the matter, sweets?"

It was him. Sometimes instead of blocking it she pretended they were there, but for real, instead of the speakers. She felt a hand in hers. They'd gone so far as to get a child's hand. She'd felt it before. Soft and small. It was too much. She wanted to kill them. She wanted the rifle back. The rifle was so loud. Hurt her ears. Still ringing.

Another wake-up was coming. She could feel it but she needed to hide behind her eyes. If they saw the color they'd know the drugs were wearing off. Then they'd give her more Manchurian medicine.

She could see shapes through her eyelashes. The lids quivered from her trying to keep them closed. *Keep your fucking head still! You dumb SOB! You moved!*

"See, Papa!"

"Honey... Maddie... Can you hear me?" They were patting her hand. She couldn't take it anymore. She opened her eyes.

Ross smiled. He covered his mouth with a hand and hugged Izzy with the other. Tears welled in his eyes. He leaned in and hugged her.

Everything she thought she knew was gone. She closed her eyes but the wake-up stayed this time.

"Mommy, you're awake!" Izzy ran around to the other side of the bed. Maddie turned her head to look. She reached a hand out and Izzy hugged it, hoses and all.

"Izzy..." Her voice was gruff, rumbling up from the center of her chest.

"Shush... Mommy. You're gonna be okay. The doctor told us."

Maddie squeezed Izzy's arm. Then she lifted her free right arm and wrapped it around Ross.

"Next time... let's come down together," she whispered in his ear. Ross laughed and cried. Their cheeks were touching. She kissed his beard.

"Good thing you brought the superhero cape," Ross said.

"Where's the Char-monster?" she asked.

"Oh. She's next door! The hospital emptied the room so we

could stay here with you. I'll get her." Ross rose. He reached out and touched her face. "Don't go anywhere."

"Let me put down this rail," Maddie said. Izzy was cradling her arm, stroking it gently. She pulled it back, pressed the button and lowered the rail. Izzy leaned in and rested her head on her mother's stomach.

"My Mommy!" she said.

She was rubbing the soft brown hair on Izzy's head when Ross returned.

"Mooommyyy," Charlotte said, pointing.

"She said her first words!" Ross's eyes were filled with tears. "When we brought her into the room and she saw you in the bed. It just came out."

Maddie lifted her arm to make room on the bed for her baby girl. Ross set her down and Charlotte leaned in, mumbling, "mooommyyy," a second time. Maddie closed her eyes and felt the energy of her children being drawn down through the blankets.

68

38,500 Feet Above the Atlantic Ocean

The Hellfire missile launched from the Predator drone killed all hands. For days after, news coverage showed pieces of the yacht being recovered.

There had been two operatives outside the resort. Both were confronted and killed.

Only one of the terrorists had survived.

Opening statements in the trial were to be held seventy-two days after his capture. Known as the international city of peace and justice, The Hague was the ideal setting for the trial.

Ross Günther was escorted by armed guards and flown via private government jet. He'd told his story countless times already.

"Anas Atwah masterminded the operation. He'd made claims that minimizing loss of life was a key to his concept, but had failed to prevent the killing and been unwilling to stop it once it started." It was to be a swift trial and Ross was the star of the show.

After it was over, he and his family were going to disappear for the summer. He was done with work as he knew it, and doctors said Maddie would need a year to fully recover. They had received an anonymous offer to use a sprawling beach house. The benevolent owner said they'd need a place to, "get away,"—a place without prying eyes. It was a beachfront home in the sleepy resort town of Emerald Isle, North Carolina. They'd be able to enjoy being a family and retreat from the onslaught of media attention.

What a long, strange trip it had been, Ross thought as he stared at the clouds below him. In the days following the end, stories of what had happened at the Surfside Resort trickled out. The last hour before the missile strike was the subject of intense focus by the media.

Maddie had regained consciousness and summoned the strength to crawl her way to the balcony. She had killed three and wounded one.

The bullet that hit Anas was stopped by the computers in his backpack. It didn't make it through but it carried adequate energy to throw him to the ground, crack his skull, and knock him unconscious.

US Special Forces swarmed the resort minutes later.

There were some international pundits who argued that charges should be brought against Maddie. She'd violated a series of laws that spanned simple misdemeanors to capital crimes of violence.

Instead of an indictment, Madeline Günther was awarded the oldest and highest honor of the Kingdom of the Netherlands. The Military William Order was bestowed, "for her excellent bravery in battle which spared the blood of the innocent and brought a swift end to this confrontation against humanity." Despite the rarity of the chivalric order, she declined the public ceremony that routinely accompanied its awarding.

Ross was again in high demand, albeit for a different reason this time. He was the only hostage that interacted with the terrorists. He was able to detail the orchestration and purpose of the attack. He'd sat in the command post and been privy to the computers that where the epicenter of the operation.

Some suggested he'd gotten too close to Anas. Ross ignored them. When asked about him, Ross limited his comments. "A troubled man whose poor decisions allowed his intelligence to be used for bad instead of good."

Charlotte and Izzy were doing well. It'd been hard to leave them. Ross had snuck out when it came time to leave for the airport.

The first question he'd been asked came from Izzy, after the last shots had been fired and the resort fell silent. "Can we go in the wazy river now, Daddy?"

ACKNOWLEDGMENTS

First, to all my beta readers... you indulged my newest pursuit by taking the time to read and provide honest, constructive feedback. Every comment propelled me along this journey. To my amazing wife, who, while reading my first manuscript (Paragon Tide), got to about the mid-way point and said, "This is actually really good!" Whether it was truth or kindness, I'll never know, but it meant the world to me. To my parents, sister, Phil (who not only read my books but then discussed them with me over hundreds of miles of the Appalachian Trail), Pete, Angel, Danielle(s), Cecelia and all the others... Thank you!

Thank you as well to the editors and cover artists that helped me along the way.

ABOUT THE AUTHOR

Thanks for reading! If you enjoyed this book, ***please*** leave an honest review on your favorite store.

And stay in touch at: tlyeager.com

Yeager is that guy who's always ascribed to the belief that "a jack of all trades is a master of none, though oftentimes it's better than a master of one." Writing was just another lark, something new and interesting, something to learn. He dabbled for a while, and then early one January he challenged himself to take the idea for *Paragon Tide* and put it to paper. Through the spring and summer the word count continued to grow, the quality of his writing improved, and for the first time he experienced the essence of the creative process. He was in the flow. By the fall, the full story had taken shape and something he set out to write for himself became something he was willing to share. The early reviews were positive, so he forged on, honing the craft and calling on professionals for help. At some point writing became a daily catharsis... release the story to paper or suffer the feeling of loss... like the day was missing something.

With the spark to write coming from Henry David Thoreau's *Walden*, it's no surprise that Yeager believes that the secret sauce of life is simply enjoying the journey... And so, with no destination in mind, he continues forging ahead to see where this new adventure takes him.

START READING

T.L. YEAGER'S
PARAGON TRILOGY

Science-Based Thrillers
set in a
Post-Apocalyptic Pandemic
Caribbean

PARAGON TIDE - CHAPTER 1

Every morning I'm greeted by the same water stain on the ceiling. It's a coffee colored cloud the size of a dinner plate that appears to have wicked down from the galley above. Before today I was convinced that it dried up long ago. This morning it looks bigger. Its wavy hazel outline is spreading like the virus. I can't help but think I should have voted my way out of here last night.

My fingers search for the edge of the blanket. The calluses in my palms hook the silky border. I pull it tight to my chin. My legs stretch, toes point, ankles crack. I roll to my side and curl into a ball, the blanket a warm cocoon.

I live in the belly of a boat, forward of the engine, in a quaint abode with a tinted shoebox-shaped window high on the wall providing a hint of natural light. The window is just a few feet above the waterline and doesn't open. My stateroom is ten feet long by eight wide with a double bed and two tiny lamps on articulating arms are attached to the wall. The floor is patterned linoleum, the color of sand. The wallpaper is hypnotizing, an alternating mirror image of a quintessential seashell in blue print on a blond background. A small, chair-less desk serves as the footboard for the bed.

The smell of the bilge always seems stronger at the dock. It's the dank heaviness of oil that forces me from the bed. I sit up into the glow of the morning sun coming through the window and finally rub the sleep from my eyes. With a grunt, I roll out of bed and follow the worn path to the bathroom. As I brush, I try to remember where I got a pink toothbrush. The paste is gritty but fresh and quickly knocks-out the morning funk.

It would have been fitting for me to leave today considering that it's my anniversary. On this day last year I got up early and quietly disappeared, leaving Maryland and my old life behind. It's hard to believe that the earth has completed a full lap around the sun since I took a taxi to Baltimore Washington International for a one-way flight south. So long calculated life. Hello new experiences, each one kicking my past further into the recesses of memory. You can't force the bad memories away. I tried that for years without success. You have to crowd them out with new, good ones. My ghosts aren't quite distant yet, but they're losing focus. Like a sepia photo purposely dropped at the ocean's edge, the waves are lapping at the discolored ink of my past.

I spit the foam from my mouth and stare into the pocket-size oval mirror that's glued to the bathroom wall. My face is deeply tanned and the skin has tightened making my jawbone more prominent. My eyes seem clearer. I know my muscles are far more toned than they were a year ago. Back home I pushed weights around in a windowless gym to stay fit. Out here the work and scuba diving is more than enough.

Back in my room I make the bed and fold a shirt that's been laying on the desk the past few days. Besides the hum of the air conditioner and the occasional clank of kitchen utensils, there's no commotion coming from the salon above. Most of the passengers are probably in bed, reluctant to get up—denial mixed with a hearty dose of hangover from drinking late into their last night. But it's strange for a Saturday morning. They're usually up early, milling about, sipping coffee and waiting on a final breakfast before leaving for the airport. Saturday is turn-around day. A relaxed but sullen group of passengers leaves in the morning and a fresh set of personalities comes aboard a few hours later. We're at the dock here on Providenciales for just over twenty-four hours each week. The rest of the time we're moored in crystalline waters off uninhabited islands in the Turks and Caicos chain. Caribbean gems strung into a tropical necklace with names like West Caicos, French Cay and West Sand Spit.

As I'm putting the shirt into one of the drawers of the dresser built into my closet, the aroma of breakfast hits me. It's rolled down the stairs and squeezed under my door. I pull on the gray board shorts I've been wearing the last few days and a black T-shirt with a map of the islands and surrounding dive sites on the back. The word *Crew* is affixed over my heart like a name tag.

On my way out of my room I clip the door frame with my shoulder, still sleepy and too eager for food. Food has become an obsession since I arrived. My high daily calorie burn leaves me in a state of perpetual hunger.

From the corridor I pad bare foot up the stairs, rubbing the sting in my shoulder on my way to the salon. Peeking around the edge of the galley I spot Madre busy in front of the stove. She senses my presence and greets me with her broad, enchanting smile.

"Good mornin' Mista Marlin. How you feelin' today?"

Madre means "mother" in Spanish, and it's a fitting nick-name. She's the kind of woman people feel they've known forever. On this boat, eating Madre's food is a pleasure second only to diving.

"Feeling great Madre. What's cooking?" I look over her

shoulder, hands resting on my woefully empty belly. Sometimes I think her food tastes better because the aroma permeates my body before I even taste it. It fills the compartments and draws guests to meals without an invitation. Madre's real name is Natori Kurvink. She's Trinidadian, her cooking a fusion of Indian, African, Asian, and Creole.

"You get your coffee, Mista Marlin, and come back in ten minutes. Cilantro eggs, pumpkin curry and buss-up-shut this mornin'." She points to what looks like Indian flat bread rising in a heavy pan. "Bring Miss Mira with you."

I eke forward, my jaw opens in preparation to speak, but no words come out. *What was your vote last night?* I want to ask it but I don't. I turn and leave.

Around the corner I pump the coffee dispenser on the counter. Through the glass doors, I see Amira spraying down the dive platform. The angle of the morning sun highlights streaks of mahogany that are usually hidden in her black hair. Water flowing from the hose shines brilliantly. The droplets escaping the stream look like flying sparks in the morning light.

Eight minutes for those photons to reach earth. More than ninety million miles traveled in eight minutes. Eight minutes for the sunlight to reach Amira and the hose and the arching drops of water. Staring transfixed, I work the plunger on the coffee thermos.

When I sailed into the Turks and Caicos the plan was a quick stop. Before I arrived I had spent two weeks sailing through the outback of the Bahamas. Providenciales is the main island in the Turks and Caicos chain. It's loaded with tourists and was the ideal place to restock my sailboat, *Walden*.

I had plotted a course south and east that ran along the north coast of the Dominican Republic and Puerto Rico. The plan was to slip around the eastern end of Puerto Rico and make a stop at her smaller sister island of Vieques. From there I'd continue east crossing into the Lesser Antilles. Following the volcanic arc of islands would gradually turn my compass heading toward South America. I thought I might spend a month at the top of the arc exploring the Virgin Islands before continuing on to points undecided.

Plans changed quickly eight Saturdays ago when I motored *Walden* into this marina. I radioed ahead to confirm they had space. Well before I entered the canal leading to the marina, I could see *Voyager* standing proud amidst the other boats. Once I cleared the canal and entered the harbor I turned to starboard, right beside *Voyager*. As I passed her stern I could see a dockhand waving to me from the bulkhead. He guided me to a slip where I tied up. On my way to the office to pay the dock fees, I saw Reuben getting off of *Voyager*. The office is only twenty yards from the bulkhead where *Voyager* docks. He beat me there but I immediately struck up a conversation once I was inside.

Reuben is the Captain of the *Turks and Caicos Voyager*. It's a purpose-built dive boat that looks more like a yacht. She's longer than most boats in the marina at just over one hundred twenty feet and her covered fly bridge tops out some thirty feet above the water. The windows on the main deck are heavily tinted and glossy black paint surrounds them from the front to the back where the dive deck opens up. From a distance, *Voyager* is sleek, like a private jet stripped of its wings and parked on the water.

Scalding-hot coffee runs down my hand. I shake it off and lick the base of my thumb as I head toward the door. The slider barely starts to rumble open when the smell of the marina hits me. Creamed corn and steamed clams. The tangy air is close but the humidity is still bearable. Here at the dock the winds are blocked by the island and the temperatures can make you feel like you're melting.

I pause and take what Amira calls 'a purposeful breath'. One morning I overheard her tell a guest that your first breath of fresh air for the day should be made with purpose. "Only so many opportunities," she'd said. It was one of those times when I'd realized the full potential of her wow factor. Comments that blow you out of the water while you're searching for the fine print.

I watch her move methodically back and forth with the hose as she makes her way down the starboard aisle of the dive deck. Each night after the last dive and first thing in the morning, we spray down the outside decks to wash away the salt that's drifted in on the breeze.

As Amira nears the stairs on the stern that lead to the swim platform, I realize I'm staring. I turn away to ease my embarrassment but her image is burned into my mind.

People fall for Amira. They fall hard. She's an enigma with enough magnetism to keep me here longer than I planned. Eccentric and organic, untroubled and full of energy, exotic and completely adorable—can you be all those things at once?

When I met Captain Reuben in the office that first time, he explained that the *Turks and Caicos Voyager* is a scuba diving live-aboard. Each Saturday she takes on passengers whose idea of a good vacation consists of scuba diving non-stop for six straight days. Sunday through Friday, passengers are able to dive up to five times a day. Working the world class reefs and sheer vertical walls that surround the islands, *Voyager* treats her passengers to one of the sport's Mecca's.

Six days of diving sounded great. "We've got room if you'd like to come along," Reuben had said. We shook hands. I filled out a rental form for the slip and put one hundred twenty dollars in the envelope to cover a week. Then I went back to *Walden* and packed a bag. Within an hour of entering the marina I had paid for the trip with my credit card and was being shown to a guest room and offered a beer.

The week exceeded my expectations. When it was over, I wanted to keep diving and I couldn't get Amira out of my mind.

"You're up early." The shout surprises me. I turn back and catch Amira smiling at me from the corner of her eye. She goes back to her work, leaning down and aiming the stream of water up under the bench seat.

Having never been a morning person, I tend to be one of the last crew members falling in for morning duties. Amira, on the other hand, is usually up before the sun.

"Listen, rest is vital to your health." I yell it over the sound of the water rushing into the metal floor.

"I thought you might snooze until all the work was done."

"Just because you deprive yourself of sleep doesn't mean we all have to." Turning back toward the sun, I soak up the warmth of the morning rays.

After another pull of coffee, I walk toward the back of the boat, following the path she's sprayed clean. *Voyager* has four levels but all the action happens here on the main deck. The door at the back of the salon separates the inside space of the main deck from this rear quarter which is open on the sides and back. Passengers begin and end each of their dives here. It's technically part of the main deck but everyone calls it the dive deck. Aisles down each side are outlined with metal benches where the passengers sit to gear up.

"Where is everyone?" I ask.

Amira releases her grip on the hose. She shrugs and shakes her head then points over my shoulder. I turn and see the dry erase board hanging on the wall. It's to the right of the door leading back inside. The passenger's last names are listed along with the times of their departing flights. The first is listed as 10:45.

"It's only seven fifteen. They've got time," says Amira. There's conviction in her tone but turning back, I can see her face telling a different story.

I drain the last of the coffee in my cup. "Madre's cooking up cilantro eggs and flat bread. It's just about ready."

Amira squeezes the handle. "I can smell it from here."

Back inside, Madre is setting up chafing dishes along the buffet at the front of the room. I wait impatiently, keeping my distance to prevent her feeling rushed.

Voyager's salon is like a great room without the high ceilings. Two dining tables on the port side lead up to the buffet counter which shares a wall with the galley. There's enough room to accommodate all the passengers for Madre's three daily meals. A flat screen TV is angled toward the wrap-around sofa which fills the starboard half of the room. At the front there's a hallway leading to the galley and forward staterooms. The right wall of the hallway separates it from split stairs that lead to the lower and upper decks. A wet bar and set of bookshelves complete the front wall.

Saturday Breakfast is usually a time to say goodbyes. The passengers congregate in the salon to reminisce about the week of diving. We exchange contact information and well wishes. "You could always stay another week," I like to tell them. The passengers try to be happy, but you can see them watching the clock with slumped shoulders. You can feel them contemplating the realities of regular life and sense their reluctance to reenter the daily grind. Who enjoys leaving the Caribbean? Bidding farewell to the blue zenith and giving up the extraordinary for the ordinary.

"Go on and help yourself," says Madre. She steps back, opening the view to the breakfast spread she's assembled.

I take a plate from the stack and slide the lid of the eggs up and out of the way. Steam rises but I turn and avoid the facial.

"Awful quiet in here this morning," I say as I scoop the eggs.

"Uh huh," says Madre. She's standing to the side looking down the counter. Like a mother who enjoys cooking for family, she seems to derive satisfaction from watching my meal-time excitement. "Cap'n Reuben left round six-thirty. He told me Bart woke him up in the middle of the night. The flu was giv'in him a hell of a time." Bart Houtman is the first mate and mechanic on the boat. He's the longest-running member of the crew and is usually up and about early with Amira. Last night, at the meeting, he was the only one not present.

Behind me I hear the door rumble open. "It smells great in here," says Amira. She takes a plate and moves down the line. I lean against the window using one hand to hold my plate and the other to scoop eggs and the orange curry with the flatbread.

"You think we made the right decision last night Madre?" Amira asks.

Around eight last night captain Reuben gathered the crew on the bridge for an emergency meeting. He started by saying that while the *Turks and Caicos Voyager* is a business, it can't operate without us. He wanted to see where our heads were. We hadn't met as a group since Jeff and Cheri Cosgrove were sent back to the island on Thursday.

"There's been a lot going on. We need to talk it over as a crew," Reuben had said. He wanted to take a vote on whether to go this week or not. "We have to make the decision tonight because if we decide not to go this week then Mitch needs to call everyone and keep them from flying down in the morning."

Last week we left the dock four hours late after waiting for a couple from Pittsburgh. Their flight arrived on time but they weren't on it. We called the two numbers we had on file trying to track them down. It wasn't until nine that night that someone got back to the captain and said they were canceling due to the flu. Then, just this past Thursday, the Cosgroves were sent back to the island because Jeff was sick. We'd heard passengers mention that the flu was getting out of hand. They talked about it being a global pandemic, but being on the boat we're cut off from the news. The lack of internet and cell service keeps us in the dark on current events. Hell, I had to ask someone which team had won the World Series this year.

At the meeting, Captain Reuben said that Mitch had called

to tell him that they were shutting down the *Bahamas Voyager*. Three of the crew were sick and half the passengers canceled. Mitch is one of the owners. He heads an investment group that owns the *Turks and Caicos Voyager* and her sister ship that operates out of Nassau. He manages the operation from Fort Lauderdale.

Madre looks up at the ceiling. "I suppose it's the right decision. I couldn't see voting not to go if we have paying customers on the way." Reuben told us that Mitch had emailed our group for this week and most responded that they were still planning to come.

For me, the decision was less about the flu and more about seizing the opportunity to leave. I had already stayed in the Turks and Caicos longer than planned. As Reuben was talking my mind was imploring me to go. I had to vote against this week's trip. The pit of my gut was playing devil's advocate. It was harping on the reason to stay. Amira was looking down and I couldn't get a read on what she was thinking. But the logic was simple. I had to get my plan back on track. If we didn't take passengers diving this week, then I'd have no reason to remain in the Turks and Caicos. Saying goodbye would be hard but I'd be free to press on with my Walden experiment.

"I'm in." Amira had blurted out.

Reuben had closed his eyes and shook his head. "I should have been clear. I wanted it to be a silent vote so no one was influenced into making a decision one way or the other."

And that was it. I buckled in an instant with a promise to myself—just one more week.

I stare at Amira as she slides a chair around to the end of the table. She sits down to eat her breakfast. "Have either of you heard any news on the Cosgroves?" she asks.

The Cosgroves are a retired couple who cruised and dove with us last week. On Wednesday, Cheri Cosgrove arrived at breakfast alone. She reported that Jeff was ill and she was shaken up because she was convinced he had 'it.' Amira is an Emergency Medical Technician. The captain and I are certified in CPR but Amira takes the lead on all things medical. She donned a mask and gloves and went up to check on Jeff. He was congested, his eyes were red and puffy, his lymph nodes were swollen and he reported back aches and general muscle pain. He had a low grade fever and elevated heart rate. After the assessment and a liberal application of germ gel, Amira reviewed the medical information in his folder. He reported a diagnosis of angina from six months before the trip. Not a life-threatening condition by any stretch, but a preexisting heart problem combined with the signs and symptoms of a nasty flu was cause for alarm. She recommended he be taken back to the island for treatment.

"Cap'n Reuben said he was goin' to check on the Cosgroves before we leave this afternoon. Said he was headed home for a bit and then to the post office to pick up a package from Mitch." Madre leans in to inspect the buffet. "I forgot the orange juice." She disappears around the corner then returns with a pitcher.

I mop up the last of the curry juice with my final chunk of flatbread. In the galley I rinse my plate and deposit it into the dishwasher.

"So is there anything left for me to do out there?" I ask Amira, crossing the salon toward the door.

"I haven't touched the upper deck or the flybridge. That's all you," she says between bites.

"I'm on it." I rumble the slider open then closed before climbing the steps two at a time. The ladder brings me up through a hole to the aft portion of the upper deck. It's open air and filled with chaise loungers in two neat rows. The passengers spend time here enjoying the Caribbean sun in between dives. There's a four person hot tub in the back corner and the housings for the self deploying life rafts are bolted to the floor on the far side of the stern railing. The front half of the upper deck includes the two largest passenger staterooms along with the Captain's quarters and the bridge.

I uncoil the hose and turn on the water, spraying down the lounge chairs one at a time. Back in Maryland there was a popular bumper sticker that said, 'A bad day fishing is better than a good day at the office.' Out here, even mundane tasks are rewarding. Since I left home I've never had that feeling where I looked forward to what's next. I don't feel hurried. The episodes of rage have disappeared as well. I think the two facts are linked. Before I left home I was always in a hurry. I was constantly on the road traveling to meet with prospective customers. I was just another angry ant marching bumper to bumper. Navigating the miserable smog and bad morning radio that polluted the super highway spaghetti junctions—that could summon the rage in an instant. It would rise up through layers of reason and hit my brain unfiltered. But that's all in my past now. It's fading away like the wake of a ship.

When I told friends that I was selling my business they were baffled. "You're crazy Marlin, you've got it made."

One year after I started the business I landed on the coveted list— *Thirty Entrepreneurs Under Thirty*. I can still see my name, middle of the magazine article. Marlin Mack – age 28, Baltimore Maryland. One year after making the list, I sold my social media app for one million two hundred fifty thousand dollars. Apparently I walked away from tens of millions.

"Keep it another year," people told me. "Establish yourself in a few more cities, and then sell."

"Worst business decision of the digital age," was the proclamation made by one magazine.

The advice and negative comments were all about money. It boggled people's minds that I could walk away from the money. The very way we think is corrupt. Like moths unaware of the damage caused by the flame, we fly toward the promise of the light, never stopping to evaluate its realities. Just spark some tinder, and we soar like kamikazes toward the pain and suffering.

The smart phone app I created ushered social media into the lucrative bar scene. Computer code that makes the cocktail peddler more money. The concept was only innovative in the capitalistic sense of the word. It was moderately entertaining for a while, but after Mr. Henniker died, it became intolerable.

It was Marie and Eugene Henniker who reached out to me when my life turned upside-down. I was thirteen years old when I met them. They were high school sweethearts, well known philanthropists, and the closest thing I ever had to a family. Mrs. Henniker died first and Mr. Henniker followed close behind. Mrs. Henniker was the penultimate mother figure. Her passion was caring for other people's children. She wasn't able to have any of her own. Mr. Henniker was a distinguished judge. Once he retired he became my personal professor on the intricacy and interworking of life. From astronomy to mechanics, philosophy to flying, he taught me everything except the law.

"Steer clear of the law. It doesn't suit you. You need to be outdoors." He'd waggle his finger every time he said it.

"The mass of men lead lives of quiet desperation." He quoted from *Walden* on a daily basis. Mr. Henniker had me reading Henry David Thoreau and Ralph Waldo Emerson before I could understand what they were saying. "Someday the light bulb will glow," he'd tell me.

After Mrs. Henniker died, Mr. Henniker promised to get his own funeral arrangements in order before he passed. "I don't want you shouldering the load." It was the only promise he failed to keep. Eugene Henniker spent the closing days of his life unconscious in a hospital bed I had brought into the house. Reading out loud from a wing backed chair, *Walden* became my Bible. I repeated passages over and over until I thought I understood them. Then I talked through them in my own words to cement the concepts. Mr. Henniker was in a liquid morphine fog and never responded, but he hung on for days. I'm convinced he was listening and waiting for the light bulb to glow.

Two days after his death, at the funeral home, the director led me solemnly to a solid bronze casket. "No doubt you'll want the best for someone as prominent as the Honorable Eugene Henniker." The words had barely left his lips when I realized the mousy director was little more than a greasy salesman. Anyone who *knew* the Honorable Eugene Henniker would have *known* that he'd want the same as everyone else. Nothing more. I had been battling episodes of rage for years at that point.

"Seriously? You fucking up sell everyone don't you?" The venom running through my veins must have been visible. The funeral director's eyes grew to saucers and he stepped back without a word.

"And if I went down the road to another funeral home it'd be the same garbage. It's just business, right?" My head was filled with blood by that point—throbbing above the ears.

The funeral director said nothing.

"What's the best seller when your shitty up-sell doesn't work? I want that one."

After the death and the up selling and *Walden*, success started to feel more like shackles than a path to freedom. Building a business was never going to elevate me from the trauma of my youth. Happiness was always going to be one step ahead. The realization quickly jaded my perspective. I started to see the world as a struggle for status, power, and the tallest pile of greenbacks. How was I any different than the greasy funeral director? I realized I was part of a vast army of automatons operating with the same set of faulty software— programming laid down over time, erasing the wisdom of youth, forcing us into a death march down the road of materialism.

Walden changed how I wanted to live my life. It offered

alternatives that I'd never considered. Could a simple life based on self-reliance with heavy doses of nature be the key to true happiness? Could work and leisure be equals? Was solitude as healthy as Thoreau suggested? Was it possible to create a life where cherishing the present moment was religion enough?

In 1845 as a twenty-seven year old man, Thoreau built a tiny cabin near Walden Pond. The sojourn lasted two years, two months and two days. I had no intention of living alone by a pond like Thoreau. My craving was for nature on a larger, grander scale. The translucent waters of the Caribbean had filled my imagination since I first stared down mesmerized from an airplane window.

I sold the business and its stressors, gave away my possessions and embarked on my own experiment to spend two years, two months and two days on a solitary adventure. One year in and here I am, rinsing lounge chairs and thinking about dead people.

Spraying my way forward up the starboard walkway toward the bow, I hear the roll of a garage door. I look over and see Cletus holding the rope, slowing the shop door as it opens. The main marina building is baby-blue. It's about twice the length of *Voyager* and runs parallel to the bulkhead where we're docked. To the left of the office door there's a garage door that's wide and tall enough to accommodate a thirty to forty foot power boat.

I lean on the railing and yell down at him. "Morning Cletus."

He lets go of the rope and steps out into the sun, shielding his eyes with a hand. "Howdy," he grumbles.

Cletus isn't much of a talker. He's from South Carolina and is the only ex-pat I've encountered who loathes his decision to move. His move was prompted by an article claiming that a dockhand in the Caribbean could make twice what they make in the states. I've heard the story twice and both times it's ended with, "More money my ass. Fuck'in island."

His name fits him perfectly: Cletus Grimm. Even though he's a pisser I look forward to seeing him each week, when he's tasked with fueling *Voyager*, topping the water tanks and pumping the sewage. The captain is adamant that Cletus's work on *Voyager* occur between the hours of eleven and one. Although the captain hasn't confirmed it I'm fairly certain it has something to do with keeping him from interacting with the passengers. Cletus makes it a point to disobey the request.

Last week he had a devilish hillbilly grin—the first time I'd ever seen him smile. When I commented on his good mood he said, "Made out all right at the bar last night is all."

Cletus walks to *Voyager*, the hand still shielding his eyes from the low sun. "Did you score again at the bar last night?" I ask.

"Ah hell. That was a one-time deal." He swats toward me with the hand. I drop the hose to the floor and walk along the railing following him toward the fuel pump near the stern.

"What's the word on the street this week Cletus?" I ask as he activates the pump.

He lays the fuel dispenser on the wood and pulls a set of keys from his belt to open the fuel door on *Voyager*. "The Redskins suck again and the fuckin' flu. That's about it." He talks with an assertiveness that makes you believe this truly is all there is to know. "I just tell people to keep their fuckin' distance man. Ought a get a fuckin' mask like all the Orientals wear. That's all they show on the news. Orientals in fuckin' masks."

I contemplate explaining that Asian is the politically correct term.

In the distance, above the marina building, I can see Captain Reuben's tan Datsun coming down the hill. A trail of dust rises above the prickly coastal scrub brush and drifts inland on the breeze. As he comes around the far end of the marina building he swerves to avoid a large pothole but under compensates and the pickup sinks and bounds, nearly bottoming out.

"That pothole is going to swallow someone's car one day," I say.

"Don't tell me. Not in my fuckin' job description man."

I back down the ladder to the main deck and step off *Voyager*. The captain pulls up alongside just past Cletus and gets out of the worn miniature pickup. "Cletus. Marlin," he says.

"Captain," Cletus replies in kind. I sense their relationship is strained.

"How's it going?" I ask the captain.

"Terrible," he says reaching back into the cab to recover his phone. "Rose at the post office says they're out of beds at the hospital. They've got people in the halls up there."

"All because of the flu?" I ask. Cletus grunts and goes back to his work.

"Seems that's the case. Rose said they've opened a ward in the elementary school up by the airport." He looks at the ground and pauses. "She says people are dying."

"I had no idea it was that bad..."

"Yeah, sounds like it spreads pretty easy too. I stopped by Bart's place. He's rougher than last night for Christ's sakes." He shakes his head and throws up his arms.

"If it spreads that easily..." I trail off.

"Yeah... How are you and Amira feeling?" he asks.

"Fine." I shrug. "Great."

"I think I might regret it but I'm gonna take a ride up to the hospital and see how Cheri and Jeff are making out. I called three times while I was out and about but nobody answered the main number."

"You want some company? I can ride along." I regret it as

soon as I say it. It's good to get away from the boat for a bit but volunteering to go to the hospital immediately feels like a bad idea.

"Your call. Climb in." I hesitate and consider backing out but can't bring myself to do it.

"Where you two headed?" asks Amira leaning out the sliding door of the salon.

Reuben has one foot on the floor of the Datsun and the other outside on the ground. "Running up to the hospital to check on the Cosgroves. Be back in a few." The keys jingle as he falls to the seat. Amira waves from the door.

Captain Reuben makes a u-turn and avoids the pothole on the way out of the marina. The Datsun bounces with each rock and rut.

"How many passengers do we have coming in today?" I ask.

"You hear they gave this thing a name?" The captain acts as if I haven't asked the question. A commercial plays on the radio, the volume low enough that it's barely audible.

"A name?" I ask.

"Yeah, they're calling it the Paragon virus. It means top or best or something along those lines. Like the top virus." He bounds up nearly bumping his head on the ceiling as we roll across the threshold out of the marina parking lot. "And eleven. Guests that is... To answer your question."

"You think they'll all show?" The boat can hold a maximum of twenty paying guests but rarely runs at capacity. Since I've been here we've never had more than seventeen and we've always been a crew of six.

"Hell. Hard to say. Hopefully not because Theo is apparently off island bringing in a boat from Bimini, so we're going to be short as hell." Theo from the marina is a jack of all trades mechanic that's filled in for Bart on occasion in the past.

"I doubt we'll get them all. Based on last week and the flu getting worse," I say.

"You know I really screwed up last week. I should have listened to Amira," says the captain. "I don't take that lightly either." Reuben hadn't followed Amira's recommendation that the Cosgroves be removed from the boat on Wednesday. No one asked my opinion, but I agreed with Amira. Flu on a boat is a very ugly situation. I can't imagine there's anything a virus exploits more than a bevy of potential hosts packed together in a small space.

"Not this week though. First sign of anything and we're shipping them in," Reuben continues.

"The scariest part was how quickly they both got worse. I mean they were a mess on Thursday," I say. By Thursday Cheri was developing symptoms and Jeff Cosgrove's condition had grown considerably more severe. Jeff's breathing was rapid and shallow. His pulse ox level was low and Amira said he was confused about time and place. They were in the stateroom on the upper deck, right behind the captain's quarters. Reuben could hear Jeff's whooping cough all through Wednesday night into Thursday morning. As soon as Amira broke out the oxygen tank for Jeff, Captain Reuben changed his mind.

After the Thursday morning dive a fishing charter run by a friend of the captain pulled up on our port side. Captain Reuben spotted them with binoculars in the distance running in deep water off the ledge. He raised them on the radio and found out they were about to head home. They agreed to ferry the Cosgroves in to shore. I think the captain felt torn about whether we should have taken them but the Cosgroves were insistent on not ruining the last full day of diving for everyone else. Cheri seemed tortured over her husband and sick about making a mess of the trip. *Screw the trip*, was all I could think.

Although no one would say it, I think everyone was happy to see them go. Bart and I ferried them via dinghy to the *TCI Hooker* and wished them luck. As we returned to *Voyager* everyone was watching them disappear north across the Caicos Bank, anxious about what they'd left behind.

The captain and I ride in silence up the main road toward town. Palms lining the highway are bent to the left from the prevailing northerly winds that sweep the island. The radio goes from commercial to talk show. The commentators sound mumbled so I turn it up.

"The religious fanatics are climbing on the apocalypse bandwagon," says a commentator. "Listen to this guy spout off."

"The day of judgment is upon us." The man's voice is stern and even, almost commanding. "This wand of death we have named the Paragon is Gods way of sweeping the damned to hell and calling his children home. It is a time of atonement, a time to ask for God's forgiveness, a time to welcome the second coming."

A second commentator laughs. "Is it me or is there something completely screwed up here. You've got Islamic extremists claiming responsibility for creating this thing. You've got other religious zealots claiming it the work of their god. Let's stop worrying about who started it and figure out how to stop it. That's what I say."

"Absolutely. We're a nutty bunch," says commentator number one. "There's nothing better for creating religious fervor than death and uncertainty."

"You got that right," says commentator number two with a chuckle. "And in other, real news, Paul Lane, the head of Health and Human Services announced the release of more grant funding today." The commentators drone on about millions in funding being poured into speeding research. They talk about university and private sector collaboration, failed clinical trials and top level firings at the CDC.

"You mind if I turn this down?" I ask. Reuben reaches down and clicks it off.

More quiet minutes pass as we cover the last of the six or

seven miles into town. "Damn. I was hoping Rose was exaggerating again," says the captain as he turns into the hospital entrance. A sea of vehicles line the drive and several are parked on the hills to the sides. The Datsun is small and barely fits through the narrow corridor.

"Fricken mess up here," says Reuben. The circle in front is blocked, preventing us from going any further. Reuben sets the Datsun to park. We shut the doors and stand in apprehensive silence. There's a landscaped circle in the center of the drive. The Turks and Caicos flag whips in the breeze above us, snapping at the modern looking hospital.

To the right of the turnstile entrance an a-frame sign lays face down like it's been blown over. I lift the corner and read, 'Isolation Protocols In Effect.'

"Don't touch a damn thing," says the captain. "Keep your hands in your pockets." I let go of the edge and stuff my hands into the top of my pocket-less board shorts.

I follow Reuben, pressing through the turnstile using my shoulder. Chills run down my arms as we enter the lobby. The air conditioning feels like its set to frigid.

The reception desk is empty. It consumes the lobby and a sign secured to the back wall says, *National Hospital – Providenciales.* I follow Reuben up to the counter. Visitor badges and marketing pamphlets litter the desktop and the floor beyond. To the left, a door is propped open. Beyond the door I make out the muted echo of footsteps and coughing.

We move toward the door, stepping over the brochures that have spilled through the open gate of the reception desk. An elevator atrium comes into view. Then we make eye contact with a weathered man. He's wearing a cream colored gown and is positioned upright in a hospital bed along the wall opposite a pair of elevator doors. His eyes are slivers amidst deep wrinkles. His wheezing is evident from across the room, like a smoker in the last days of emphysema.

Looking left we can see down the hall where the doors to patient rooms are separated by occupied beds lining the corridor. A chorus of distant coughing tunnels toward us. It's a different kind of coughing. Not like the common cold. It's more of a deep chesty rasp, the octave low like a subwoofer—you can feel it pass through you.

A nurse in full protective gear slogs up the hall. Captain Reuben cups his hands as if to yell. "Excuse me." It comes out a normal talking volume and she's turned into the closest room before he can get it out. "Damn."

The wrinkled man in the bed points at us. Or behind us. I turn around, and then the captain and I look at each other.

"The door. I think he's pointing at the door," I say, tapping the frame of the door beside me. The man lowers the hand to his thigh. "Hello," I say, stepping toward him and smiling. His expression remains fixed. He raises the hand and points at the door again, wheezing as he does.

"Let's go," says Reuben. He pats me on the shoulder and heads for the room where the nurse disappeared. I reluctantly follow; feeling chills from the old man's stare.

We make it to the door and establish eye contact with the nurse. "Excuse me, we're looking for Cheri and Jeff Cosgrove," Reuben says.

"No visitors allowed. You don't want to be here. We're under isolation protocol... You'll be exposed." She turns to a choking patient. There are two beds in a room that only looks suitable for one. The choking man's bed is separated by only a few feet from another holding the still form of a thin, uncovered woman. Her clothes are soaked in sweat.

"Listen, I'm a local. These folks were passengers on my boat and came down sick on my watch. You mind if I drop by for just a minute to check on them. I tried to call." The nurse takes a spit tray from the coughing patient and dumps a red slime into the sink at the side of the room. Chills run down my neck and the smell of the place hits me. *Mucus and blood,* I think.

The man in the bed is stuck in a rhythm of three coughs, then a wheezing inhale. "Here you go sweetie." The nurse tucks the pink spittoon back along the man's side. "Cosgrove is two rooms down. Opposite side." Her tone has an air of surrender. We turn to walk away. "Wait," says the nurse. "You really don't want to be here. It's a nice thought but stay out of the room. The wife is delirious and the husband is gone. She won't let us take him."

I stare at my feet as if walking a path along a steep cliff. On either side of me I can sense patients in the beds along the corridor. They're staring. They've got to be staring. But I can't look up. I watch one foot fall in front of the next. *He's gone? What did she mean by that?*

The smell grows heavier as we walk. I pull the collar of my shirt up over my nose to keep the nausea at bay. I don't look up until we make it to the second door on the left. "Cheri?" The captain frames it as a question. He raises a hand up over his mouth and nose.

Jeff is gray in the bed. His head is turned to the side away from Cheri who is sitting in a chair by his side. Jeff's mouth is hanging open. The white top sheet is pulled up to his chin and it's spread flat like he was tucked into a perfectly made bed. The lower half of the sheet, toward the foot of the bed, is stained in an oval with rings of brown deepening in color toward the center.

Cheri lifts her head from her husband's side and strains to make us out. Her eyes are a ring of irritation and red tinged snot is dried in a line from her nose down along her cheek toward the ear.

"Jesus, he really is gone," I say.

Made in the USA
Middletown, DE
26 April 2020

92012563R00243